WICKED BLUES

I0687691

WICKED BLUES Deszion Nasir

Also By Deszion Nasir

Published by Bluefoot Publishing

WICKED BLUES

Deszion Amani Nasir

Bluefoot Publishing

Hampton, VA 23663

Bluefoot Publishing
Copyright 2013 by Deszion Nasir

To order this book wholesale contact Bluefoot Publshing: deszionnasir@yahoo.com

ISBN-13-978-0615779928
ISBN-10-0615779921

First Printing March 2013
10 9 8 7 6 5 4 3 2 1
Printed in USA

DEDICATION

This book is dedicated to slaves.

To every person still trapped in slavery, be it mental, physical, chemical, spiritual, or a combination of the four.

This book is dedicated to former and partial slaves who may be free from one but remain trapped from memories. Don't remain bound.

This book is dedicated to those who are slaves to ignorance and prejudice, specifically about abuse and mental disorders. Educate yourselves. You never know who cries at night and pretends to laugh at your jokes.

WICKED BLUES

PROLOGUE
ST. MARTIN PARRISH, LOUISIANNA

A 16-yr. old girl ran through the muddy swamp water, clutching something in her arms. Fearfully, she glanced behind her, making sure her pirogue was still tied to the tree she'd hidden it behind. Her heart raced. It was still there. She didn't have much time before she was found. But if by some small chance she escaped, she'd need her pirogue. It bobbed against the swamp plants, almost seeming to be waving goodbye to her. She shivered, turned in the cold water and tramped through the marsh to drier land, her legs more tired than they'd ever been, her arms growing heavier by the second. She heard a dog barking across the swamps, and knew they were gaining on her. She ran for what seemed like hours, but was actually around 10 minutes, until a dim light shone through the night and gave her hope. She stumbled up to the raggedy door and pounded on it with one hand, clutching her other around what she had hidden inside her shabby coat.

A minute later, the door swung open and a middle aged woman with silver hair that made her look older despite the lack of wrinkles on her face was gazing down at her. Her face held no emotion or surprised to find a terrified girl shivering at her door.

"Please, Madame Touroux," the girl gasped. "Please help me. They gon' kill me."

"Who, child?"

"Monsieur Landry. "

Madame Touroux looked down at the bundle in the girl's arms as it squirmed. She sighed and stepped back inside her house. The girl rushed inside gratefully. As Madame closed the door, the girl's hood fell away some and a heavy lock of silky, raven-colored hair fell into her ice-blue eyes. Madame sighed to herself.

7

"The pretty ones always cause all the trouble for me," she told the girl, picking her up by the arm and setting her down on an old settee. "Lemme see what the fuss about, child."

The girl slowly handed the bundle to Madame, who moved the rags used as a blanket from around it and looked down into the ice-blue eyes of a baby boy.

"This here a beautiful one," Madame commented, smiling. She looked at the young girl closely. "You been in this kinda trouble before, ain't you?'

The girl lowered her eyes. "He took the last one... sent him off to some place, some island I never heard of. But I was to keep this one. He told me I could keep him and he'd let me leave..."

Madame sat back and sighed. Monsieur Landry was known for dabbling in between the creamy thighs of black Creole girls, much to the distress of his wife and the rest of New Orleans. A mayor mingling with black girls wasn't good for their image. According to the girl's tearful story, the mayor had returned to be with her, only she'd refused him because she was still hurt from him giving away her last baby, and he'd forced himself on her. He'd gotten her pregnant again, and was going to let the girl keep the baby and send her away, but his wife found out, so he'd made up a lie about the girl seducing him and getting him drunk. The punishment was to be the death of her and her baby, so she'd fled to Madame, hoping the Cajun healer could do something to protect her child.

"What about you, child?" Madame asked.

She shook her head tearfully. "I have to let them find me. They'll stop looking for the baby if they find me... I'll... tell them the baby fell in the swamp. They gon kill me eventually anyway. But this baby... he special. He cain't die like this."

Madame looked down at the silent baby. He seemed either oblivious or comfortable inside the chaos surrounding

8

him.   Something in his beautiful eyes scared her for a moment.

"Has he cried since you ran?"

The girl shook her head in confusion. "No, ma'am. He don't never cry. Not ever. Not even when he came out of me."

"That be a bad sign, child.   This child born out of evil. He got a bad cloud hangin over him when trouble don't bother him none. Might not be a good idea to let him reach that cloud and bring down his storms…"

"No! Please… it ain't none a his fault… please… I lost one baby, I cain't let another be killed because of another person."

"This chile be *cursed*, girl. He'll never bring nobody nothing but pain. And his children… if they be born with these demon eyes, they be cursed, too. Cursed with beauty that will destroy the lives of all they love and who love them."

The girl was shaking, looking so beautifully small and terrified. "Is there something you can do??? Please…"

Madame sighed. "Sometimes… sometimes the curse can be broken by one of them who be born different."

The girl looked confused.

"Them *eyes*, child. Them eyes is the heart of the curse. One gotta be born of him or you that don't have them blue eyes to break the curse. That mean the evil done ran its course. The one *without* the blue eyes can end it."

The sound of dogs in the distance grew louder. The girl looked at the door, then Madame in fear.

Madame finally sighed. "Come kiss your baby, girl. Come kiss him with all the love you gonna be able to give him. I do this for you. My sister goin to Virginia in 2 days. She gon' take this child to a home there. He be safe."

The girl wiped water from her eyes and came over to the baby. She raked her waist-length hair back and kissed the baby on his soft cheek. Then she hugged Madame and ran to the back door. She gave Madame one last look and fled into the night, her ebony hair vanishing behind her.

Madame closed the door and sat down on the settee. Only minutes passed before she heard barking, shouting, screaming, then gunshots. Then silence.

"It be done," Madame said, sadly, glancing down at the baby. She lifted a ragged shoelace tied around the baby's neck with an old leather strip attached. In scratched handwriting she read his name. "Gemini. It be done wit yo ma, but you only getting' started…"

18 YEARS LATER...

Hampton, Virginia- Campus of Hampton University

TEASHA

Teashauna Jones, better known as Teasha-or me-, smiled, my bright green eyes betraying my tiredness and handed the man in front of me $6.17. "Here's your change, sir," I told him. I shivered in disgust as his fingers curled purposefully around mine as he took his money from me. He kept staring for a few seconds which prompted me to say "Is there something else you wanted?"

His beady eyes peered down my slightly unbuttoned shirt to the tops of my 32C breasts, which seemed even larger attached to my tiny 5'2" body. Then he looked at my name tag. "Teasha," he read in his smoked-way-too-many-cigarettes-voice. "You got a man?"

I sighed. "Would you like to try one of our desserts?" I asked robotically.

"Them yo real eyes?" the guy went on, ignoring my words. "What kinda weave is that? I ain't never seen no black girl with hair that color red befo-" And this fool actually reached out to touch my red-orange hair hanging down in tired strands from under my Burger King visor. I grabbed his tray of food off the counter and swung it with as much force as I had in my little arms and slapped him in the face with it, food flying all over customers and the counter. The man, caught by surprise, staggered back and tripped over the line divider, landing on his back and looking like an idiot. Which he was.

I got on my tiptoes and glared down at him. "Thank you for visiting Hampton University Burger King, *asshole*," I snapped. The other customers laughed and snickered, and I turned to see the other workers staring at me. I sighed. I was the manager, and losing my temper wasn't something I'd planned on doing in front of my workers, but today had just

11

been a rough day. "I'm on break," I announced, walking away from the counter and outside into the crisp fall air.

I leaned on the side of the building and closed my eyes. What was I doing here? I moved here from Columbus, Ohio when my parents were killed years ago. I used to go to school at Hampton University, but lost my track scholarship when I tore a ligament. I had to get a job here to pay for school, but couldn't make ends meet with a part-time job. I eventually had to drop out and work full-time. I was a manager now, so the pay was better, but I'd have to save another semester or to so I'd have a good cushion before going back to school. I had no family and no real friends here because I'd only hung out with the track team. When I dropped out of school, they dropped out on me. The only reason I didn't just go back to Columbus was because there wasn't anything there for me. Both my parents were only children. It was just me against the world. Right now the world was winning...

As I leaned back against the cool bricks, I heard a heavy car pull up into a parking space. I didn't pay it any attention until I got a whiff of cologne that took a choke hold on my senses and shook my poor, tired eyes open. When my green eyes adjusted to the light I saw two guys around my age talking and laughing. One was about 5'9", milk chocolate brown with a razor-sharp cut, a clean shaven face and a smile that said he liked to laugh a lot. The other guy was huge. He had to be over 6'6", and he was built like a football player. His features were unlike any I'd seen before. He had a strange light caramel complexion and a large mass of wavy black hair blowing in the wind around his head. The main thing I noticed were his eyes: they were an icy shade of blue I'd never witnessed on anyone's face, black, white or otherwise. His blue eyes immediately caught my green ones and his boy, who was telling a joke or something, noticed that his friend wasn't responding and turned to him. He saw him staring, followed his gaze, looked at me, then looked back at his boy, grinning. He smiled and told the tall male he'd go

12

scoop the food and walked into the restaurant, grinning to himself.

I straightened up and wished I'd taken this stupid visor off as the guy closed his car door and walked over to me. His cologne got stronger and I felt myself sweating the closer he got to me. I crossed my arms, praying I didn't have any pit stains.

"I'm not gonna bite you," the guy grinned, showing off a mouth full of toothpaste commercial teeth. He'd mistaken my body language, but I'd rather him thinking that then thinking I was musty.

"So you say," I responded. He stepped close to me, closer than most people stood to other people they didn't know. He looked around. "It feels good out here today. Maybe I should stand with you, huh?" he asked, taking it upon himself to lean against the wall to my right.

"If you want," I responded, shrugging like it made no difference to me.

"If I want," he repeated, shaking his head to himself. "There's a lot of shit I want right now," he added, glancing around, seeming to drift off in a thought for a moment.

"Like what?" I asked. He seemed to remember I was there then and turned back to me, all smiles again.

"The man 'posed to ask the woman that," he said, an accent I couldn't identify becoming more pronounced.

"Okay… so… how about you tell me something you want and I tell you something I want," I proposed.

He nodded like he was in serious thought. "Ok. Ladies first."

"Well, I wanna know where you're from with that accent," I asked, smiling.

He laughed. "The lady who raised me is from Louisiana. The accent is Creole."

"The lady who raised you? Your mother didn't raise you?" I asked, instantly regretting my nosiness when I saw a dark look pass over his face.

13

"I never knew my old lady or my dad. I don't know nothing about myself other than what I remember. Nobody does. I don't even know what race I am, tell you the truth." He shrugged like he'd told the story 100 times before.

"Oh, I'm sorry…"

"Don't be. I got over that a long time ago, ma." He turned to me. "So now it's my turn."

"Okay," I smiled, grateful he was changing the subject.

"I wanna know if you're scared of roller coasters, for one," he asked.

"Roller coasters? No, never." I laughed. I was a fanatic.

"Okay, okay… so you gonna let me take you to college weekend at Kings Dominion Saturday?" he pushed, his smile widening.

"What? I don't even *know* you to be traveling out of town with you," I said, waving a hand at him. "You could be crazy."

He nodded. "True. But it ain't like we'd be alone. And we'd be being videotaped the whole ride, so, you know… I couldn't attack you or nothing."

"Videotaped? What kind of freaky shit are *you* into?" I demanded, stepping away from him.

He laughed again. "You don't know who I am, do you?" he asked. I opened my mouth to say something smart when a group of females screeched and rushed up to us. They pretty much shoved me to the side and started demanding autographs and shout-outs. Standing where I was now, I could get a better view of the guy's truck. One the side was his face and the banner for the biggest radio station in the area: 103 Jamz. The man I'd been kicking it with was the infamous DJ Gemini the Wicked, a phenomenal radio personality that seemed to explode onto the airwaves in the last year. I felt like an asshole. And a slow one at that.

Gemini made quick work of the groupies and came back to me as his boy came outside. Seeing us still talking,

14

he said that he'd run over to one of his girl's apartments around the corner and come back in a few. Gemini nodded and his boy trotted off, leaving us alone again.

"I'm sorry I didn't recognize you-" I started, embarrassed, but Gemini waved me off.

"Naw, that's my ego's fault." he said. "I just hope you ain't gonna let that little scene keep you from coming with me Saturday," he went on.

"How many girls did you invite?" I asked, now suspicious of his intentions. Rumor had it Gemini had chicks breaking their necks to get with him. Not only was he fine and locally famous, he was paid. I'd heard he'd made a few good investments that had paid off well and now he was on his way to becoming a big player at Clear Channel Communications. What was he bothering with me for? I wasn't on his level and he was out of my league.

"A lot. But I only invited *you* to go with me *personally*." he stressed.

"But... why?" I couldn't help asking.

Gemini laughed. "Well for one, you're working. I couldn't do what you do in there," he motioned toward the BK. "And even though you look tired, sweaty and pissed off, I can still see how gorgeous you are under there," he added, lifting my visor off my head. My hair fell down my shoulders and lifted in the breeze, probably sending the scent of onion rings over to him. "Why do I need another reason?"

I couldn't help smiling. I still thought he was full of shit, but before I could tell him so his phone started ringing. He sighed and answered it, telling me to hold up a minute. He said "What?" gruffly, and a few seconds later he whirled around behind him. Just as he did, a black on black Explorer was tearing into the parking lot. Gemini shoved me roughly behind the Express Mail drop box just as the shots started. My head hit the concrete and the world started spinning. By the time the smoke cleared, I had ringing in my ears from the sounds of shots, screaming, broken glass and the screeching of tires. I shook my head and climbed to my feet. I was a

15

little dizzy, but my now sore head cleared in a few seconds and that's when I saw Gemini stretched out on the ground, his phone still in his hand as blood stained the sidewalk he was lying on. The screams in my ears were now my own.

12 HOURS AGO...

Louisville glanced at his watch again and sighed. It was just like that yellow nigga to make him wait when Louisville was supposed to be doing HIM a favor. He glanced around the alley, suddenly slightly nervous. You wouldn't think he needed to be. He was called Louisville because everybody in the 7 Cities who walked the streets knew he carried a Louisville Slugger in place of a gun. He'd been shot 15 times and lived, but every nigga that'd shot him had been beat to death by his bat, even if he'd had to track them for days. There was only one person he knew whose nose for sniffing bitch-niggas out was keener than his. And his ass was late.

While he was busy being pissed, he never saw the man he was waiting on coming up to him. He never heard him, either. At 6'8", you'd think the man would make at least a little noise, but the only one who made a noise was Louisville when he turned and found himself staring up into a pair of cold blue eyes that sent a chill through him every time he saw them.

The blue-eyed man didn't flinch, just grinned as he lit up a black. "You look like you seen a ghost, my man..." he said in a creepy deep voice Louisville hated.

"Almost," Louisville snapped, recovering quickly. "You got me out here with rats and shit... you *know* I hate rats, man... what took you so damn long?"

The man blew a smoke ring in the air. "Did you have something to tell me or didn't you? You know my time is already in the negative,"

"Look," Louisville started. "This thing you got going with the 804 Boyz... it's goin bad, man."

The blue-eyed giant had an affiliation with the 804 Boyz, an organization out of Richmond, Va. He got a job at a popular radio station and used the open spots in his show to play coded songs that had different meanings to send messages to the group. The songs changed weekly or more

17

often as needed. The man was paid twenty grand a week to keep the 804 Boyz's business contacts in line and in order. This way there were no cell phones to trace, no landlines to bug. Things had worked out so good in the last year the DJ, known as Gemini The Wicked, had gotten several jobs hosting parties and DJing events, which added to his ability to reach more people on more occasions for the 804 Boyz. Things had turned sour when Gemini had demanded 100 grand a week from the 804 Boyz or 30% of their weekly profits. While it was true Gemini had made it possible for them to make money like never before, they didn't like the idea of him trying to take such a huge chunk of their profits. They'd responded back with an offer of 15% or 50 grand. Gemini's response was to change up songs without letting the group know and threw the set into chaos. Three leaders and several runners were killed in four days due to the dysfunction and now they were out for Gemini's head. They'd originally just seen him as a cocky-ass DJ who was getting too far ahead of himself. Louisville, however, having gone to school with Gemini for only a small amount of time, knew just how dangerous the young man could be. He'd watched Gemini snap the necks of grown men with his bare hands since he was 14. By the time he was 21, the age he was now, Gemini's body count had long ago surpassed his age or point of remembrance. Gemini killed for no other reason than someone might have crossed in front of him walking down the street. He had no conscious, no remorse and definitely no apologies for anything he did. He was just crazy, touched, demented, whatever you wanted to call it… but the nigga was The Grim Reaper. Louisville figured by giving Gemini a heads-up he could avoid the bloodshed that was surely coming to the 7 Cities in the near future.

Gemini shrugged. "Them cats always crying, man. I don't give a fuck about that shit, nigga."

"Well, maybe you should. I was up in Richtown a few days ago and them niggas talking 'bout they want your head, G."

18

"Oh yeah?" Gemini asked casually, taking one more hit from his black and flicking it onto the damp pavement, the sweet smell lingering in the air. It was as if they were talking about the weather.

"Yeah. I heard Patron and them niggas offering like, 50 grand for you, man."

Gemini stared for a second. "50 grand?" he repeated flatly, insulted.

"50 grand," Louisville confirmed, nodding.

Gemini looked deep in thought for a minute, scratched his neat beard, then walked over to a couple of stacked boxes and picked up a huge sledgehammer leaning against a pile of wooden crates Louisville hadn't noticed until now.

"Yo, G," Louisville grew unnerved quickly. "What the fuck is that for?"

"We been boys for how many years now?" Gemini asked, letting the head of the sledgehammer hit the wet ground and clutching the end of the handle, his face thoughtful.

"Shit... almost a dime now," Louisville said, his eyes on the weapon.

Gemini nodded. "Yeah, that sounds right... In all those years... we never bullshitted each other."

"Naw, never."

"So that made we wonder about what you just told me... you said you heard that them 804 bitches was coming for my head, right?"

"That's my heavenly *word*, G," Louisville swore.

"How many days ago?"

"Like... 3..."

"So..." Gemini laughed to himself like he was listening to someone tell a joke in his head-"*you* heard some sore loser niggaz was tryna kill me and it took you *3 DAYS* to holla at me about it...that what you tellin me?"

Louisville started to panic. "C'mon, G. I was at my mom's house. "You know she sick-"

"You think I give a fuck about your moms?!" Gemini yelled, the streetlight making his blue eyes a weird shade of purple. "If you heard a muthafucka planning on comin for *my* head you shoulda been on the phone with me *3 days ago* if you weren't gonna handle that shit yourself... *unless* you figured you'd take a crack at them lil table scraps they giving out for knocking me off..." Gemini took a step toward Louisville, who backed up until his back hit a slimy brick wall.

"Gemini, c'mon, man, you know that ain't how we roll, man... DAMN!"

"I know that's not how *I* roll... I *also* know that you got in contact with Hoss and Pick and his bitches to get at me for half the money. Right before I took *them* niggas' heads off with this here sledgehammer-" he swung it up in the air once for dramatic effect, then let it hit the rain soaked ground with a loud *clang!-* "I asked them boys what-or *who*-gave them the balls to come at me on some night-night shit cuz *they* don't got the heart to come at me on their own." Gemini watched as Louisville's eyes widened fearfully. "Guess whose name popped up? And guess who's in my face 2 days later?"

"G, let me explain-" Louisville stammered, right before Gemini raised the sledgehammer again. It cut through the air with a large WHOOSH! and the cracking sound that came from the sledgehammer connecting with Louisville's head echoed up and down the alley. Louisville flew up in the air and landed on an overflowing pile of garbage cans with a groan. By the time he managed to get one eye open he wished he'd kept it closed. His last memory was of Gemini's wild hair plastered to his face by the rain, his maniacal eyes wild and glowing in the dim light and he brought the blood mixed with rain-covered hammer down on Louisville's face, closing his eyes forever.

His coat covered in rain, blood and bone matter, Gemini wiped the sledgehammer on what was left of Louisville and walked back to his car parked around the corner, the next step to head to the house where Louisville's wife and newborn lived. Gemini never left a stone unturned, and never left anyone to claim the bodies of the recipients of his horrible temper.

TRE

I strolled away from Gemini and another one of his weekend projects and decided to go see one of my shorties that stayed in the fancy apartments behind Hampton University. I had been avoiding her for the last few days because every time we went somewhere she threw a tantrum. Figured if I left her on stuck for a few days and kept my wallet and my attention to myself she'd straighten herself out.

I was just crossing into the parking lot when a car beeped angrily as it was almost sideswiped. I turned and saw an Expedition coming at me. I stepped out of the street and onto the curb as the truck drove past me. I watched it pull into a space 2 buildings away from where I was going and shut off. The driver door opened and a pair of long golden legs slid out of the truck. My plans got rearranged the second I saw the body attached to those legs. The girl driving the truck was tall, thick and curvy, with her golden hair was blowing all around her face. She was trying to move it and grab her stuff out of the car at the same time, but the wind wasn't making it easy. I saw what looked like mail fly out of the car and I kicked into gear. I ran the paper down for her and walked it back to her. She was busy pulling her hair back in a ponytail, but she was smiling at me. As I got close to her, I saw the golden brown shade of her eyes flashing.

"Thanks, I wasn't about to chase that across the lot in these shoes," she laughed, a Caribbean accent light like the breeze.

"It's cool," I said, trying not to look up and down at her body. She seemed to be able to tell and grinned wider.

"Do you live out here?" she asked, her eyes bright.

"Me? Naw… my friend stays out here. I drove over to BK with my boy, but he busy tryna holla at this girl so I figured I'd pop over here right quick," I said, shrugging like it was no big deal. "You live over here?" I asked.

"Just moved in last week…" she nodded.

22

"Okay, okay..." I nodded. "Nice apartments," I added.

She shrugged. "I guess so..." she added, still smiling at me.

"So... you a student at HU?" I asked.

She laughed. "Listen, I have to go pee really bad, honestly, so..."

I laughed.

"-I'ma have to cut this short... but... if you were to swing by here... maybe Friday night... we could finish this conversation." she said, looking me directly in the eye.

A girl who didn't bullshit. She won't from around here, obviously.

"That's cool. We can do that... I guess I should tell you my name, huh?" I asked, feeling stupid. But I was caught off guard by the heat radiating off this girl.

"You don't have to... I could just call you 'Cutie,'" she grinned, running her fingers across one of my dimples.

"See, if you do that, then what would I call *you*?" I asked, stepping into her space more. Once a chick touches a guy's face, the rules change.

"You can call me by my name: 'Rio.'" she told me, not backing away from me. Normally I haul ass from chicks with skeezer tendencies cuz they nothin but a big-ass hassle, but Rio wasn't coming off like that. What she was coming off as was a female who knew her power over men and liked measuring that power. I could dig it. I made sure I looked into her eyes to let her know I was focused on her, even though faint whispers were sounding inside my head telling me to leave this girl alone for some reason.

"Rio..." I repeated. "Where you from with a name like that?"

"It's Portuguese. My father's from Brazil," she explained.

"Oh yeah? That's cool... everyone calls me-," I stared, but she shook her head and cut me off.

"I'll like 'Cutie' better," she insisted.

23

WICKED BLUES Deszion Nasir

I grinned. "So, where can I pick you up at?" I asked, my other chick long forgotten.

Rio looked around. "Right here. Be right here at 8:00," she said.

I opened my mouth to answer when I saw a familiar dark truck tearing up the street. It only took me a second before I recognized it. I whipped out my cell and dialed Gemini. I took off running, leaving Rio standing there mid-conversation.

"What?" Gemini demanded on the 2nd ring.

"Yo, them niggas from up top bending the corner, man, get low!" I yelled, snatching my .40 cal from my waist. The 1st gun shots rang out a few seconds later. I heard screaming as I rounded the corner running top speed, gun already up and ready to go. I saw Gemini hit the ground and I fired at the truck. The driver swerved and side-swiped another car. I kept firing and hit the driver. The car crashed into a car parked illegally by the exit. The driver got out, holding his arm as the passenger got out, screaming in a phone. Another car appeared out of nowhere, and by the time I ran out of bullets, the driver and passenger's bodies were being slung in the back seat as the car sped off without closing the door. I memorized the plates on the car and ran over to Gemini as the girl he'd been talking to laid on the ground near him, shocked and screaming.

People were running and screaming and trying to get out of the way. I ran over to Gemini and turned him over. I saw blood all over his face, but from my short examination, it looked like the bullet had grazed his eyelid and another had gone into his arm maybe. I won't no doctor, but other than a nasty scar, he'd probably be fine. But since I *wasn't* a doctor, I called 911 as everyone came running out of the Burger King and the other buildings in the little strip mall. They weren't asking if he was okay, of course. All they wanted to know was if "that was the real Gemini the Wicked from the radio."

As soon as I hung up with the dispatcher my phone was ringing again. I looked at the number that showed up on my phone and sighed.

"Tre? What the *hell*?" came the high-pitched voice of Jari, the chick I'd originally gone to see when I'd ran into Rio.

"Jari, my bad, ma, I meant to call you-"

"But you *didn't*-" she cut in.

I held my tongue and took a deep breath. "I *couldn't* call you because Gemini just got shot."

"Whatever. Nigga it's *always* some bullshit with you."

"Jari, if you'd get out the fuckin *mirror* for two seconds and paid attention, you'd know he was just gunned down at the BK around the corner from your *muthafuckin* house. Didn't you hear the shots and the screaming?"

Silence. "That was Gemini?"

"We still out here. I'm waiting on the ambulance and shit right now."

Jari hung up. Two minutes later I saw a tall female with about a foot and a half of thick black hair with light brown streaks in it and dark brown skin running around the corner. As pissed off as she kept me, I was glad to see her. She looked around, shocked at the blood and shells all over the floor.

She looked up at the girl, whose name tag read "Teasha," still frozen but standing, blood on her shirt, and the first thing she asked was "Who is she?"

"Some girl Gemini was talking to when he got shot," I said, as the wailing sirens grew louder in the distance and finally tore around the corner.

As the paramedics ran over to Gemini, they asked Teasha what happened. She recounted what had gone down, seeming to come back to life as they loaded him in the ambulance. She tried to hop in the back with him, but one of the paramedics stopped her. She looked him dead in the eye and told him "I'm going with him. If you wanna argue about it, get me arrested and we can do this downtown." The medic glared at her a second then nodded, letting her squeeze past him and into the back of the ambulance. Seconds later they were gone.

I figured I didn't need to be there when Hampton PD showed up, so I grabbed Jari's arm and we jumped in the truck and zoomed off after the ambulance, leaving the questions and spectators staring after us, wondering what the hell had just happened.

WICKED BLUES Deszion Nasir

GEMINI

When you realize you're not dead-after you *think* you are, of course- the first thing that lets you know you're not is pain. Forget all that shit about white lights, some dead loved one or a voice from heaven talking to you. All that shit is a fuckin lie. Shit, all that could be a dream. A hallucination. *Pain* is the number one way you can tell you're still alive. Why? You cain't hurt if you dead. And I *know* I ain't dead cuz I'm hurting like a *muthafucka* right now.

The morphine, or whatever they gave me at the hospital must have worn off, because a sharp pain was ripping through my chest and my face. I tried to open my eyes but I could only get one open. With my one good eye I saw a bright-ass light on the ceiling that made me groan out in protest. My noise caused someone to jump, and I went on the defense instantly. When your ass gets shot at, a nigga tends to get a lil paranoid when he learns other muthafuckas are near him.

I tried again to open my right eye, but it was taped shut or something. A messy head of long red hair came into my line of vision. I was tryna figure out where the hell I knew that orange-red hair from when a tearful little brown face came into my sight and my memory came rushing back.

"Hey," I got out, sounding like I had been eating sand.

"Hey," she tried to smile.

"What you doin here?" I asked.

She kind of laughed. "You never told me what time you were gonna pick me up to go to that amusement park you promised to take me too."

I laughed. It hurt, but I laughed.

"I don't remember promising you nothin,"

"You just got shot, your memory's a little fucked up," Teasha reasoned.

I smirked, then looked around the room. "What happened to my eye?" I asked, turning my one good blue one back on Teasha.

Her smile faded some. "A bullet sliced your eyelid. You ain't really have no damage to your eye, but you gonna have a nasty scar there."

All I heard was that I didn't have any eye damage. The rest of that shit was superficial.

"Anything else wrong with me?" I asked her, my mind already cranking back up.

Teasha shook her head. "Superficial wounds."

"Bet. I'm out." I sat up and started snatching all those little monitor patches off of me when Teasha put a hand on my arm.

"You cain't get out of here right now. The lobby and the outside of the hospital is crammed with fans waiting to see if you were gonna be ok. The best thing for you to do is maybe call the radio station and wave or something out the window so people can see you're alright and then they'll go on about they business. You can slip out later tonight maybe, if you're hell bent on leaving..." she suggested.

I looked over at her and stared for a minute.

"What?" she asked. "I mean, it seems like you wanna get out of here, but, you know... I just don't think it's a good idea right now. Not tryna tell you what to do, I was just tryna help."

"Naw, naw, it's cool... you just... that sounded like something *I'd* say, that's all," I told her. She beamed. "Guess I should keep you around for awhile."

She laughed, then went out and got a nurse and called Tre for me. He'd been down in the cafeteria with the girl he'd been playing around with lately, Jari, getting something to eat, but before he got off the phone with Teasha he came bursting into the room with a tall chocolate thing. I saw Teasha suddenly try to straighten herself up, but acted like I didn't.

28

Jari saw it too. She smirked, then she turned to me and narrowed her eyes. "Ain't you the guy from the radio?" she asked bluntly.

"Jari," Tre said, sighing.

"What? I was just asking…" she said defensively.

"Yeah, it's me," I said, amused by the way she was talking to Tre. He always was a sucker for women.

"How come you never told me your boy Gemini was the one from the radio?" she demanded, turning her dark eyes on Tre.

"You never asked," Tre shrugged, giving her the eye.

"I had to ask?"

"How many other Geminis do you know?" Teasha laughed, not missing the look of interest Jari slipped me when I confirmed who I was.

Jari glared at Teasha for a minute before responding. "I think I know *you,* though. Didn't you used to be in my physics class? I heard you dropped out." she stated loudly. "What did you drop out to do?" she asked, looking at Teasha's uniform with obvious resentment. I saw Teasha's jaw tighten and smiled. Teasha was about to say something back but 2 nurses rushed into the room to take my vitals and a minute later a doctor rushed into the room. While they were looking me over a police officer came into the room and told Teasha he wanted her to come answer some questions downtown. She glanced at me, then at Jari, obviously not wanting to leave me and her in the same building. I grinned at her and reached out and put her tiny hand in my huge one. "I'm good, ma. And thanks for staying here with me." I pulled her down to me and kissed her to ease the tension I saw in her face. I told her to write her number down so I could call her later. She did and finally left with the cop, looking like a little runaway. Another officer came over to Tre and said he wanted a statement from him as well since he fired on the shooters. Tre's gun was licensed, but we all knew how the HPD worked. They'd take him down to see if he was on any hot lists, ask him some bullshit questions and

29

then be pissed they'd have to let him go. He looked at Jari, who waved him off. "I'll call my sister to pick me up," she waved him off. Tre looked from me to her, then nodded. He left when Jari walked over to the phone to call her sister. Once she made the call, the nurses had left. She glanced around at the empty room, then sat down in the chair beside my bed.

"So, who shot you?" she asked flatly.

"Someone I pissed off," I grinned.

"Obviously," she rolled her eyes.

"How long you and my cousin been going out?" I asked her, changing the subject. Nosey females were a powerful man's downfall.

"Oh, it ain't even like that. We hang out, but you know… we not official or anything," she said, adding that last part in purposefully, I thought.

"Oh, yeah? He made it sound more serious." I told her.

Jari rolled her eyes. "He's just sprung. He does his thing and I do mines," she assured me, sliding her chair closer to my bed.

I looked her up and down, feeling a grin slide around my face. Sometimes females were so obvious it made my stomach hurt. I sat up in the bed and leaned toward her. "What exactly is your *thing*?"

Her phone rang. She had a lightning quick conversation-you know how females do when they don't want us to know what they talking about- and stood up. She grabbed the same piece of paper Teasha had written her number on and scribbled her cell number down under it. "Call me and we can talk about what my 'thing' is," she whispered in my ear while she slid the paper into my right hand. She straightened up, raked her hair back, and left the room, taking the scent of her sweet perfume and betrayal with her.

WICKED BLUES Deszion Nasir

JARI

I was feeling pretty good about my day until I got home and saw my mom's car parked next to my sister's. I slammed Curtis' door while he was asking if we were still going out tonight and walked away. Why did I say I was getting picked up by my sister? Because nobody needed to know all my fucking business. And nobody certainly needed to know I couldn't stand my sister. I didn't feel like explaining the long story to anyone so I called one of my old reliable uglies who I knew would do whatever I said just to be seen with me in his car for a few minutes. I'd get a ride home and he'd get to drive through his hood real slow like he could pull a bitch like me. Whatever. As long as I got where the fuck I needed to go. My mother wasn't normally home this time of day and I was planning how to pull a disappearing act like David Blaine when my mother stuck her head out of the front door of our apartment and screamed down "Jari, get your fast ass in this house!"

I swallowed back a smart-ass response and trudged up the stairs. Me and my mother have never gotten along for two reasons: 1-we were both bitches, and 2-*that* bitch thought my sister was better than me. It wasn't a secret, so don't roll your eyes or shake your head. My mother had *always* treated us different. I didn't get any special treatment even though I was the baby. My sister was the perfect daughter and my mother never stopped taking credit for it even though she didn't raise her, especially when she got a good job and traveled all over the world as an international translator. My moms was so busy kissing and licking my sister's ass-who was everything my mother wanted to be-that she never paid two shits worth of attention to anything I said or did unless I was in trouble. She never came to my school award ceremonies, none of my mother-daughter lunches, plays, honor roll events and she missed my graduation from high school because my sister's job had transferred overseas and my mom refused to leave her at the airport alone when her

32

plane to Europe was delayed. I ended up having to spend two hours wandering the mall because she wouldn't answer her phone and I'd left my keys and purse at home in my rush to get to my girl's car. We'd carpooled to the ceremony and the girl had a family dinner to go to, so I played it off and told her I was going shopping to celebrate. I left my graduation cap and gown in the mall's bathroom; glad I had on a cute outfit under it. I'd barely graduated anyway. My mother certainly didn't give a fuck about my education and the only reason I did was because even back then I kinda knew I wouldn't get much farther in life. Not with all the shit I'd already gone through by then...

I snapped out of my thoughts of a happier time and place and trudged up the stairs to my apartment. My mother looked me up and down like I owed her money and stood back away from me like I stank as I walked into the house. My sister was in the kitchen making a sandwich, shaking her head. She already knew I wasn't gonna let my mother keep talking slick out of her mouth to me for long. She was right.

"You screamed?" I asked sarcastically, tossing my coat on the couch on top of the track hair she was gluing-poorly-into her hair. My mother was about as bald-headed as she could be from overuse of tracks and braids as she tried to make the rest of the world think me and my sister got our naturally long hair from her. Whatever.

"Where did your nasty-ass run off to this time?" she demanded, hands on her rippled hips.

"I was with Tre." I said simply, walking past her and my sister and grabbing a glass to get some water from the sink.

My mother came over and sniffed me. "Well, you don't *smell* like you been out fuckin... I'm not checking your breath," she muttered.

I slammed my glass down on the counter so hard it broke at the same time my sister yelled "Mom! *Come* on now, that wasn't even called for!"

WICKED BLUES Deszion Nasir

"Don't stand up for that girl. You're never here, you don't see how many of these dirty muthafuckas come through here for that girl or hear how many of them call here. You can *damn* near hear them beating they dicks through the phone," my mother shook her head at me. "That Tremeil the worst one, carrying her out and buying her all this fancy shit like she some kinda *saddity* hoe. *That's* why her nose stuck up in the air all the damn time."

"You know *what*?" I flipped. I snatched away from my sister, who tried to grab my arm, and stepped nose-to-nose with my mother, as the only thing I'd gotten from her was my height. "You're such a jealous-ass, *miserable* bitch, you know that?"

"*I'm* a bitch?!" my mother yelled.

"No, I said a 'jealous-ass *miserable* bitch.' Maybe I need to add 'deaf as all hell' to the end of that. Tremeil's boy got shot around the corner and if you'd put that *bottle* down for three seconds you'd know that's what all the cops and news trucks were out here for. I was tryna be there for him... but *you* wouldn't know *shit* about that kind of thing..."

"Bitch, *please*. Youz a hoe just like your damn daddy... may he burn in hell..."

White sparks flashed in front of my eyes and the next thing I know, I was on top of my mother, snatching out her real *and* fake hair at the same time. She was screaming and squealing, trying to fight back, but I'd caught her off guard and she was laid on her back, trying to block my blows and strike back at the same time. Unfortunately for her, due to my rage she couldn't do neither and it was my sister who pulled me off of my mother. I was taller than my sister, but she was built like a porn star and she had a good 15-20 pounds on me. While she was trying to calm me down my mother got up, ran to my room and started grabbing my clothes, perfume and shoes and throwing them out the door and over the balcony onto the parking lot pavement. I snatched away from my sister and tackled my mom again, but she got away cuz my sister grabbed me again, yelling for us to stop. She couldn't

34

hold me and our mother at the same time, though, and within a couple of minutes all of my clothes, underwear, shoes and most of my jewelry and accessories were laying on the pavement, wet up by the puddles from the night's rain and being ran over by surprised residents driving through the parking lot. Before I knew it I was being shoved out of the door, despite my sister pleading with my mother to stop it, just stop it. I ended up on the outside of the door, clutching a huge handful of my mother's thin hair in torn clothes, tears on my face and trying to control the pain ripping through my chest as I gasped the crisp air. My breasts were exposed due to my shirt and bra being ripped to hell, so I hurriedly held the shirt up over myself and looked around, feeling sick as I saw all my neighbors staring at me. I hated the pity in their eyes. Nobody offered to help me, though. That was cool. I was used to taking care of myself. I heard my mother and sister still arguing, but fuck them. Fuck the both of them.

TREMEIL

I picked up my remote and turned down the stereo, wiping sweat from my eyes as my ears strained to hear. Yeah, my phone was ringing. I was working out in one of my spare bedrooms and over the music I'd thought I'd heard ringing. I hopped up and jogged to the living room and snatched the phone up.

"Hello,"

"Hey, Cutie."

It took me a second to catch the voice, then I smiled. It was Rio, the sexy-ass Brazilian chick I'd met the other day.

"What's good?" I asked, grinning.

"That's what I'm tryna figure out."

I frowned. "Why? You cain't make it Friday or something?"

"No... actually I was calling because I wanted to see you tonight."

"Is that right?" I asked, grinning to myself. Rio was an upfront female, and I loved that shit.

"Yeah, that's right. Why wait till Friday, you know? I'm not doing nothing *tonight*. Are you busy?"

"Naw, naw, tonight is cool... you have anything in mind that you wanted to do?"

"Just see you," Rio answered. I could hear her smiling through the phone.

"Okay, I'll surprise you, then. So... how you wanna do this? You still want me to meet you in the parking lot?"

"God, no. There is *so* much drama over here... people are acting all crazy in the parking lot... you wouldn't believe what I saw today... No, I can just meet you somewhere and we can go from there."

I thought for a minute. "Hmm... aight, check it: you be at Cheddar's restaurant on Jefferson Ave. out Denbigh at 9:00 tonight. Then we can swing over to this spot I know in Virginia Beach near the Oceanfront and go listen to some reggae and work off the shit we just ate."

Rio laughed. "Aight, I know where that is…"

I was about to say something else when someone banged on my door. "Hold up, let me answer the door-"

"No, you go ahead, I got some stuff to do anyways-"

"Naw, hold on, I just got you on the phone," I protested. Rio laughed as I grabbed the knob and swung my door open.

At the sight of Jari standing on my doorstep looking like she'd been jumped into a gang, I hung up on Rio mid-laugh.

"What the *fuck*?" I demanded. As long as I'd known Jari I'd *never* seen her look nothing less than on point. The chick standing in front of me looked like Jari as far as features went, but her face was scratched, her hair was looking like she just rolled out of bed, and her clothes were torn. I looked behind her at her raggedy car and saw clothes strewn all over her back seat like a suitcase had exploded in her backseat.

"Can I just come in, please?" Jari asked, her voice tight but sounding like she was about to burst out crying. I was no good at shit like that so I stepped to the side and let her in.

I didn't say anything, just watched her walk around my apartment, looking at everything like she'd never been there before. After a few strange minutes, she opens her mouth and "Can I stay here for a few days?" falls out.

My stomach dropped and I almost screamed out "*HELLLL* NAW..." but her eyes calmed me down. I still had shit to do tonight, though, so…

"What happened, Jari?" I asked instead.

"Me and my mother got into a fight," Jari said flatly. She was still walking around, not sitting down.

"You and your moms what? Where was your sister? What was ya'll fighting about?"

"Being out with you," Jari spat. "She started calling me all kinds of hoes and saying she hoped my daddy was burning in hell and whatever… my sister was tryna break it up, but in the end, my mom threw all my shit downstairs in the street and in puddles and shit."

My mind flipped back to what Rio was just telling me about the crazy shit going down at her apartment building and sighed. I'd never met Jari's sister, but if she was anything like her mother and sister, the whole situation must have been channel 13 news crazy. What was I supposed to say to her? Damn... I felt bad for the girl, but *that* shit was in the way. Me and Jari wasn't that serious-I'd tried to be, but she kept talking shit about us staying casual, so I let it go. She did her and I did me. How was I supposed to keep that shit smooth when she was staying up in my spot? And I knew her. There was no way in *hell* I'd be able to carry shit the way I been carrying it with her here. I broke out of deep thought and looked over at Jari. She'd already kicked her shoes off and was walking to my linen closet. "Well, since you seem to be having such a hard time making a decision, can I at least take a shower and put some Neosporin on the scratches? I'll go to a motel or something until I can figure this shit out."

I fought my first instinct to call and make a reservation for her and sighed again. Jari was a pain in the ass, but when she wasn't being a bitch she was actually pretty sweet and always boosting a nigga's ego. She always looked good when we went out and she knew how to keep everyone's attention on us. She was a custom-made baller's wife, and it had been my plan to make that official as soon as I got rid of some of the bones in my closet and get the money I knew it'd take to keep a woman like her. But shit had been so crazy lately...

I worked in security, and I'd been discharged from the Marines for a shoulder I'd fucked up in a training accident overseas, so when Gemini first came at me with his offer to just have his back and shit, I jumped. A wounded veteran as young as me didn't have a whole lot of options and my GI bill for school had me jumping through so many hoops I'd said fuck it. At the time Gemini's offer seemed like the best option...

The sound of the water running and the scent of the Bath and Body Works shower gel Jari kept over my spot brought me back to reality again. I walked back to the bathroom and I saw Jari standing in front of my bathroom mirror, using a washcloth to clean off all the blood and scratches I couldn't see under her clothes. I checked her eyes in the mirror. They were full of water, but she wasn't crying. She looked more angry than anything. I almost went in there, but I ended up backing away and letting her deal with her pain her own way. I went in the living room and picked up my watch. It was only around 2 p.m.

When Jari finally came out of the shower, I'd run to the little store on the corner where I saw a lot of college students shopping and bought her a couple of outfits.

She walked into the living room drying her hair and body off with a couple of towels. She saw the clothes on the couch and stopped. "Are those for me?" she demanded.

"Shit, they ain't for *me*," I laughed. She threw the towel down and snatched the clothes up. She was dressed in like, a minute. She went in the bathroom, grabbed one of my brushes, wet it and put her hair back in a slick ponytail. She still looked a little beaten up, but she looked more like herself than she did when she first got to my townhouse.

I took her out to eat to this little Mexican restaurant she always liked to go to in Norfolk. She finally started smiling again and I relaxed. If I was gonna suck shit up and have Jari staying in my house for a few days, I damn sure wasn't gonna have her being a bitch the whole time and make *my* life all kinds of hell.

I was watching her eat like she was starving and that soft spot in me I had for her reared its head. She finally sensed me looking at her and paused. "What? Why you lookin' at me like that?"

I was silent a tick before I answered her. "Why you won't let me take care of you on the regular, Jari?"

Jari paused in her chewing a second, then broke our gaze. "I don't need a *nigga* to take care of me. I'm good."

39

"I understand that... but do you see a *nigga* at this table?" I demanded, leaning forward on my elbows and peering into her eyes. I reached out and took her free hand in one of mine.

Jari pulled her hand out of mine. "I'm good," she repeated.

Stinging from her rejection, I sat back. "So... you just content to use me like a fuckin trick, huh? You just trick off my fuckin paper when you *need* shit?"

"Tre, that's fucked up," Jari snapped, dropping her fork and glaring at me from across the table.

"You gatdamn right it's fucked up," I said loudly. A few tables glanced over at us and I lowered my voice. "Ain't too many niggas like me left, Jari. And silly-minded young bitches like yourself is the reason for it. Being a good dude ain't shit no more. Ya'll want a nigga to treat you like you ain't shit before you think we give a shit."

"That's bullshit, nigga."

"Is it? Look at your fuckin face if you think I'm wrong. I bet you money your pops did that same shit to your mother that she did to you; talking shit, putting his hands on her, fucking her over... and she doing the same shit to you. Now you doin that kid shit to me. You hate her cuz you just like her."

Something in Jari's eyes flashed and she grabbed her glass to throw it at me. I intercepted her arm mid-throw and she ended up spilling it on the table instead of on me. "Oh, you wanna be on some gorilla shit?" I said. I grabbed her arm and snatched her up with one hand. With the other I grabbed my wallet and tossed a fifty on the table.

"Get off me," Jari snapped, but I drug her out of the restaurant into the lobby, where she snatched away from me. "Nigga, don't you *ever* put your fuckin-"

I stepped up to her so fast she backed into the payphone, causing the change in it to rattle fearfully as her back hit it. "I done already told you, Jari. I ain't no *fuckin* nigga. I'm a *grown-ass* man, and that's the *only* reason I didn't break your ass up just now." I put my index finger on her forehead and pushed her head back. "I'm a patient muthafucka but I'm *not* no bitch. Never *been* one, won't never *be* one. You keep talking to me like you crazy and the last person who gives a fuck about if you live or die is gonna walk the *fuck* out of here and leave your ungrateful ass right where the fuck you seem to wanna be-by your *gatdamn* self."

Jari stared in my eyes, I guess tryna figure out if I was serious. When she saw smoke damn near coming out of my eyes, she backed down, sighed and apologized, pushing her bangs out of her eyes. I nodded finally, feeling my rage simmering down, and hugged her to me, not letting her go until her tense body relaxed and she hugged me tight. I bent down and kissed her on top of her head and handed her coat to her.

We had climbed back on my motorcycle and were heading back home when I saw the dark car following me. Being a Marine, you learn real quick how to watch your back and tell when someone is behind you. And someone was on my ass, no question. If I had been by my myself I could have handled that shit easily, but Jari was behind me, holding onto me real tight and going on about something I wasn't listening to. I'd told her a million times I couldn't hear shit she was saying when we were rolling, but she never stopped talking anyway. I just let her go usually and figured whatever she was running off at the mouth about would be something I wouldn't have to listen to when we got wherever we were going.

My mind kicked into gear instantaneously, and I got over three lanes without signaling. Jari screeched something in protest, but I ignored her and glanced behind me and through her wind-whipped hair. The car swerved behind me, cutting off another car. The other driver honked, the car sounding as pissed off as the driver. Jari turned to see what was going on and that's when we both saw the car following us roll down the window. I knew what time it was. Without warning, I drove off the road and across the highway to the

41

median, bouncing over the grass and dips in the middle of the highway and spinning around until I was heading in the opposite direction, going back the way we came. The car tried to follow but lost control and crashed into another car.

"What the *fuck*?!" Jari screamed, confused as hell. She kept talking but I ignored her and got off on the next exit. When we finally stopped at a red light Jari punched me in the shoulder. "What the hell was all that about?!" she demanded.

I lifted the mask on my helmet and put on my smile. "You know you like that crazy shit, Jari, stop trippin'," I laughed, like I'd planned the whole thing.

She studied me for a moment, then grinned at me. "You almost killed them people behind us," she laughed.

I smirked and pulled the mask back down as the light changed to green. "Yeah," I told her. "Almost."

We got back to me house and as soon as we got inside, Jari went straight for my cabinet where I kept all my liquor bottles. My one flaw. Well, my second one. Jari was my first flaw, and liquor was the second one.

"I need a drink," Jari announced, cracking open a bottle of vodka and taking it to the head. I shook my head and walked into my room, trying to wrap my head around the shit that had just gone down. There won't no way in hell them niggaz accidently rolled up on me on the damn highway. They had to have been following me. They probably knew where I lived, too. That made me wonder: If they knew where I lived, why hadn't they just come for me here? With that thought rolling around in my head, I went to my closet and shoved all my clothes out of the way and stared down at my safe, something I didn't think I'd have to look at ever again. I stared at it for a long time, dark memories swirling through my cluttered mind before I spun the combination, pulled the door open, and pulled out 3 of the 7 guns I had in there. I made sure they were loaded and put one in my bathroom, one under my pillows and was on my way to put another one in the living room when Jari burst into the room, holding a half-empty bottle of vodka in her hand. Her eyes dropped to the gun in my hand, then lifted back up to my eyes. She stepped closer to me and leaned in close to me. "You need a drink more than I do," she told me, her liquor breath hot on my neck. She'd already been drinking at the restaurant, so the liquor didn't need a lot of help pushing her over the edge.

"Jari," I pushed her off of me, but she stepped right back to me, wrapped her arms around my neck and kissed me on the side of my neck. I didn't need this shit, not right now, when so much other shit was going on, but you know how that shit goes. She kept fucking with me, rubbing on my dick and shit, and when I wasn't paying attention she slipped the gun out of my hand and clanked it on my dresser. She held the bottle up to my lips and tipped it up until the clear liquid was sliding down my throat, leaving a familiar burning sensation behind. I looked down at Jari and saw her eyes already dipping low in response to the vodka. She tipped the bottle to my mouth again, longer this time. As soon as I'd gulped the drink down she pushed me back on the bed and climbed on top of me, dropping the nearly empty bottle on my hardwood floor. As I listened to the clear liquid spill on the shiny floor, I pulled her down on me and snatched her new shirt over her head while she was trying to wiggle out of her tight pants. Impatient, I rolled her off of me and snatched the rest of her clothes off. I had all mines off in less than a minute and she tackled me, both of us falling onto the floor, the vodka sliding over our bodies and mingling with the sweat. Sex with Jari was always bold, always rough and always left at least one of us with some bruises. Despite the situation, I was still planning on sliding out to see Rio so I couldn't let Jari scratch me all up. I flipped her on her stomach, grabbed her by the hair and when she hiked her ass in the air I plowed into her like I was mad at her. She screamed out for me to do it harder and I did until sweat was dropping off of my body and sliding down her arched back and mixing in with the sweat coming from her scalp. She tightened her pussy around me like a new leather glove and

43

sucked me back in hard, released her grip, and sucked me back in again. She knew that type of muscle control was one of the reasons she had me open like she did. It felt like I was fucking and getting head at the same time and I had to grab the bed with my other hand for support so my legs wouldn't give out and make me fall on her. The louder she got, the tighter I gripped her hair. I felt some strands snapping, but I couldn't stop or slow down, the slick, warm sensation of her pussy, the smell of her pussy, the sounds she was making, all of that stimulation had me fucking her so hard my balls hitting her ass sounded like I was slapping the shit out of her. Jari, in the middle of the escapade, reached over and up to my nightstand, rumbled in the drawer, and pulled a little tube out, handing it to me.

"Ma, you ain't gotta do that. We already talked about this," I told her. Her response was to reach behind her and throw the tube at me.

"It ain't about you. Fuck me how I like it, baby... fuck me, Tre," she panted. She laid on her stomach and pulled me out of her. She pulled her knees high and began fingering herself with two, then three fingers. "Hurry, baby," she told me. I stared at her a minute, then unscrewed the tube, squirted some on my fingers, parted her ass cheeks, then spread the gel on her ass hole. I slowly slid my middle finger in and Jari moaned so sweet. When Jari was drunk, she always wanted to get fucked this way. I pulled her closer to the edge of the bed, still sliding my finger in and out of her ass then slid in two. "Baby, stop playing," she groaned. I took my dick and placed it against Jari's ass hole. Her breathing deepened in anticipation. As I slid my fingers out, I placed the head in and she exhaled. "Do it, Tre. Do it..." she kept saying. I slid in further and she started fingering herself faster. I pulled out to the tip, put some more gel on the tip of my dick, then slid back in, going in a little more each time until I was all the way in. The lobster-grip sensation sent a shock through me as I tried to hold my nut in. I started pumping in and out slowly, then picked the pace up as Jari

44

was frozen in place in a mix of pain and pleasure as she moaned louder and more frantically. I reached one hand under her, and replaced her fingers with my own, cupping her pussy and damn near burning my hand off from the heat coming from it. I felt the flames shoot out and I knew she was coming. I picked up my pace in both holes and Jari screamed as she deposited her warm, sweet juices in my cupped hand, the liquid overflowing and spilling out of my hand, down her legs and onto my sheets. The girl was like faucet. Jari came like 3 times and was telling me she couldn't take anymore, but I knew better and I kept giving it to her until I felt that heat rising up my legs and concentrating into one ball of fire. I squeezed Jari's hips and knew if she was lighter she'd be looking like a Lifetime movie with all the bruises in the morning. I tried to hold back longer but it'd been a minute since I'd had some so I lost that fight. I came so hard I thought I'd blow a hole in Jari's stomach and fell beside her, not wanting to crush her body under my weight, breathing heavy. When my vision came back, I looked over at Jari. She wasn't moving. I got up, cleaned myself off, and was bringing a washcloth back to give to her when I heard her snoring, the liquor finally putting her in a temporary coma. I sighed, shook my head, tossed the washcloth in the hamper and turned on the shower. Looking at the clock I saw I still had time to meet Rio...

45

RIO

I flipped down the mirror on my sun visor and waited for the light to pop on before looking at myself again. My hazel eyes ran over my curly, bushy hairdo, wondering if Cutie was gonna recognize me with different hair. I decided I looked fine and flipped the visor up and got out of the car. This was the first date I'd been on in forever because I was always working, so I was backed up in a whole lot of different ways and I was determined to scratch a lot of itches tonight.

I felt all the eyes on me as I walked into Cheddar's in my fitted Dior dress. I knew what the men were thinking, and I had a pretty good idea what the women were thinking: Where'd she get a Dior dress that size?

I was 5'9 and a size 14, but all that 14 was in the bottom half of my body. I loved the size I was and so did every man I'd ever dated. I learned long ago to stop worrying about shit other females thought and said, especially since I wasn't trying to date any females. The more I didn't sweat that shit the more they paid attention and hated on me, but the whole thing was funny to me now.

As I followed the hostess to a table in the back by a window, I kept my laugh in as all the men I passed stared. Some of them tried to play it off, some of them didn't. I sat down and ordered a cosmopolitan. While I sipped on it, I wondered if he would think I was moving too fast. I hadn't dated a guy from Virginia in years...

Before I could sit there and think the date into disaster, Cutie walked into the restaurant. Like the last time I'd seen him, he looked sexy as hell and I could smell his cologne before he got to the table. As soon as his eyes hit me I smiled and crossed my legs, already feeling a leak coming on.

"Hey," he said, sliding into the booth in front of me.

"You're late," I told him, grinning back and downing the rest of my drink.

46

"Yeah, a lil' bit. My fault. It ain't a habit," he added, waving the waitress over and ordering me another drink and a Sprite for himself.

"Oh, you don't drink?" I asked.

"Not tonight," he shook his head and leaned back.

I smiled. "Aw, you tryna make sure all your attention is on me?" I asked, half-joking.

"Of course," he said.

We ordered our food and Cutie leaned forward on the table. "Aight, tell me about Rio," he said after I'd taken a couple of sips. "Let's start off that way."

I shrugged. "I was born in Brazil, my parents split up and one of them left me and came back here. My other parent was killed when I was younger and I ended up back over here until I found my other DNA donor. I graduated from high school and been on the go ever since. No kids, no man, no drama cuz I'm not usually around long enough to cause none or be involved in any. I just live life everyday and don't think about yesterday or tomorrow. Yesterday is over and tomorrow might not be here so..." I trailed off.

Cutie sat back, taking in everything I'd just said. "So, you don't have no plans for your future?"

"For what? Everyone I know who spent forever trying to plan for the future was disappointed as hell when something that won't on their list happened. The way I live my life means I'm never disappointed and everything good that happens to me is a surprise, and everything bad that happens'll be over in less than 24 hours."

Cutie was just staring at me. "What? I sound crazy?" I asked, laughing.

He shook his head. "Sounds lonely."

My smile dropped. He saw it and quickly added "But that's what I'm here for, right?"

I smiled again. "Maybe. We'll see."

He just grinned, showing off a set of dimples. The rest of dinner was spent talking about lighter subjects until the waitress told us they were about to close up. Cutie looked at

47

his watch. "Damn, we been here a minute." He pulled out his wallet and tossed three $20s on the table as we got up to leave. We got to the parking lot and stood beside my car.

"So," he said, looking around and then at his watch again. "Tomorrow'll be here in a few hours… we should find something else to do before then and you don't care no more about today,"

I laughed and looked around. "What else is there to do around here, other than go to a club?" I asked. "I don't really feel like dancing tonight."

"Nothin', for real," he said, scratching his head. "We can go shoot pool," he said suddenly. "I know a spot."

"Cool. Pool. Let's go shoot some pool."

I was tipsy, so we left my car at Cheddar's and Cutie handed me his other helmet and we zoomed off to a spot a few miles away. When we got there, the vibration from the bike had me kind of horny, so I made it a point to watch how I walked. I only had on a thong, so if I started dripping again I couldn't hide it for long. It wasn't just the liquor, though. Something about this man had a sexual hold on me like a voodoo spell.

All eyes in the dim hall were on us as Cutie greeted the occupants he knew and nodded at the ones he didn't. We got a table in the back corner and picked our sticks out. Cutie watched me take my time selecting one. "You do that like you done it a few times," he commented, grinning at me.

"A time or twenty," I smiled at him.

"Let me find out you a fucking pool hustler," he laughed, grabbing a pool rack off a nail on the wall next to the table.

"Oh, you gonna find out more than that," I teased him, taking the rack from him and putting the balls inside of it. As I placed the balls on the table, I could feel Cutie and the other men's eyes on me. Knowing I had their attention, I bent over in front of them, knowing my short dress was giving them all a nice shot of my ass cheeks. A couple of men whistled and a moment later I felt Tre behind me, the slightly bulging crotch of his jeans pressed up against my ass.

"You tryna get some shit popping off in here?" he whispered.

I slowly ground my ass on him. "Don't feel like I'm trying. Feels like I'm doing it," I told him, lifting the rack off the balls and smiling wickedly at Cutie.

"Aight, keep playin," he warned me. "We just got here and you got me about to act up in here."

"What, you scared?" I challenged him.

"Scared of what?" he asked, raising an eyebrow.

"Scared somebody might see us enjoying ourselves. That's what we're supposed to be doing, right? Enjoying each other?"

Cutie laughed in his deep, throaty voice. "That's how you do, huh? You an exhibitionist?"

"Everyday, all day." I loved sex, and I loved doing it where everyone could see me. Just a freaky thing about me. The lifestyle I had chosen to live had opened my eyes to a lot of new things. If I was living everyday for everyday, it didn't make sense to be so inhibited when it came to sex.

"*I* think you bullshittin. But I'm not the cat you need to prove shit to. I'm just diggin being around you," Cutie tried to reassure me.

"Oh, I *know* you not bitchin up on me, are you?" I demanded, having fun with him.

"No bitches over here, sexy," he shook his head at me, looking me up and down hungrily.

I slid away from him and walked over to break the table in. It just so happened that end of the table that I'd decided was going to be the shooting end of the table was pretty much in the dark. It was in an unlighted corner. I locked eyes with my sexy, chocolate companion as I picked up the cue chalk, rubbed the tip of it over my stick slowly, then suggestively blew the chalk dust off of the tip. Cutie licked his bottom lip, scratched his chin, then followed me into the dark corner. I bent over to break, and he pushed up

49

on me, his warm hands sliding over my ass and under the rim of my dress. When I didn't stop him and he felt the thong I was wearing, he slid his fingers under my ass and rubbed them over my clit. Electricity erupted from the waist up and I held in a moan. I bent over further to take my shot and Cutie slipped a finger inside my already wet box, curling his long finger up inside me and touching a spot that made me shiver and miss my shot.

I looked up and around the pool hall until I spotted a sign that read "Restrooms."

"C'mon," I told him, taking his hand in mine and tugging him.

"You want me to take you in the bathroom?" he asked me.

I took the finger he'd slid in me and licked my essence off of it. "No, I want you to *fuck* me in the bathroom," I corrected him, looking in his eyes to make sure he knew I wasn't playing.

Cutie grinned, then glanced around. Nobody was paying us any particular attention anymore. People were either drunk, or drunk and heavily involved in their game. Cutie led me through a sliding door that separated the bathroom from the front area before I grabbed his neck and pulled him to me, kissing him and sucking his tongue in my mouth hungrily. He tried to pull me in the men's room, but I resisted and tugged him to the women's room. When he paused, I leaned over to him and bit his ear, saying "There ain't no other women in this building,"

The light went off in his head and he pushed us through the door. We backed in, kissing and tasting, as Cutie shrugged out of his jacket. He spread it on the counter and picked me up. He sat me on his coat as I tugged my dress up and over my head, dropping it beside me. I wrapped my legs around him and used them to pull him to me while he damn near snatched his pants down.

"That's what mamma likes, let me have that," I told him, reaching down and wrapping my hands around his

50

swollen dick. I bent down, slid my fingers inside myself, and used those juices to slick his dick up before sliding it in my waiting mouth. Cutie immediately grabbed onto the soap dispenser and groaned loudly.

"Shh," I giggled before I deep-throated him. He held my hair up so he could watch me make him vanish and reappear smoothly, wrapping my tongue around his dick and sucking every time I slid him out of my mouth.

"Gatdayum, girl," Cutie rasped, looking down at me, sweating. I responded by taking him out of my mouth with a *pop* and grabbing his balls with my tongue. I sucked one into my mouth, then the other as his grip on me tightened. I would have kept going but he soon pulled out of my mouth, sat me up straight, grabbed me under my thighs and yanked me to the edge of the counter. He kissed me aggressively and slid himself inside me with no hands. I shuddered and he gripped me by the ass and he ground his way inside my eager pussy. At first I leaned back, placing both my hands on the sink to give him a better angle, but he soon picked me up off the counter and I found myself being bounced up and down, me moaning and Cutie grunting his lust out. I felt myself cumming quickly. He must have felt it too, because he put me down, turned me against the wall and pressed himself back into me, sucking on my neck and moving in and out of me until I shuddered and slid down to the floor, unable to stand up during my orgasm. He followed me and then I was on my hands and knees, Cutie pounding my guts out until he gasped like he was drowning and I felt his penis jerk inside me roughly. His sweat dripped on my back, and he wiped it off with the edge of his shirt when he got his composure together and stood up. He pulled me to my feet and leaned against the counter, getting himself together.

"Shit," he muttered, looking at me and grinning. "*Damn* you crazy girl."

I laughed and used damp paper towels to clean myself up. I tossed them in the trash and wiggled back into my dress.

"You know they heard our asses out there, right?" Cutie grinned, meaning the other patrons of the pool hall.

"So?" I asked, shrugging and fluffing my hair back in place. "Let's just go out the window," I suggested, nodding toward the window to his right.

"The window?"

"Why not? Let 'em think we killed each other in here," I laughed, moving past him and sliding the window up. I stuck my head out and saw no one around. The pool hall was situated in between a closed check cashing place, so no one would know we were gone for awhile.

"Damn, Rio... so where we headed next?"

"Home. I have an early morning."

"Dayum, girl. Just like that, huh?" Cutie asked, shaking his head at me.

I slid out of my cum-stained thong and tossed it in the trash. "C'mon, Cutie, let's be for real about this shit: You a sexy-ass muthafucka and I wanted to fuck you from the moment I saw you in the parking lot. If I'm lucky I'll get to do it again a few more times. I stay on the road for work so there's no point in trying to start a relationship when I know I won't be here in a few weeks. But I'm not a hoe. You're the only man I plan to be with while I'm in town, but I keep shit honest with me. Now, I don't *think* you got a problem with that, but if you *do* let me know, cuz I don't want no miscommunication later on."

"That won't my intention, Rio. But if that's what *you're* cool with... it's cool with me." Cutie said after a long thoughtful moment.

"Just enjoy me while I'm here," I told him, wrapping my arms around his neck and kissing him again, smiling. He relaxed, then shook his head as I climbed out of the window. He bent his long frame up and followed me. We ran like two kids across the parking lot and jumped on his bike and zoomed off.

52

WICKED BLUES Deszion Nasir

JARI

The blasting from Tre's stereo alarm woke me the next morning, pounding unwanted music into my head and forcing my hangover to wake me up. I tried to jump out of bed, got my feet tangled in the sheets and fell out of the bed, ending up on the floor, staring under Tre's bed at a pair of dirty drawers and an empty bag of Cheetos.

I groaned and yelled out for Tre to cut the fuckin radio off, but nobody answered. I climbed up to the bed and glanced around the room. I didn't see Tre's keys or his jacket and realized he must've gone to work already. I sighed and got up to walk over to the stereo, since Tre never knew where the remote to the stereo was. Right before I was about to turn it off, the song playing went off and the DJ came on the air, giving a shout out and sending a speedy recovery to Gemini the Wicked, who was still recovering from an "injury."

I listened for a second, then I cut off the radio and looked around the room closer. I went to his closet and riffled through, and realized all of his work uniforms were still hanging up. I knew how many he had because he was extremely organized-military trained thinking- and I picked his uniforms up from the cleaners when I was around. He hadn't gone to work. If Tre hadn't gone to work… that meant he hadn't been home yet… so where the fuck was he?

I went to the living room, snatched up his house phone, and called his job. "Hi, may I please speak to Tremeil Whitmore... Oh, he's not there? Is he working later... he called in this morning... okay... no, no message..." I slammed the phone down, pissed off. I *know* this nigga wasn't out fucking around when I was going through shit…

Wrapped up in my leftover anger and adding it to my new fury, I went to Tre's answer machine and started scrolling through numbers. I didn't come across any unfamiliar numbers, but one in particular got my attention anyway. I snatched the phone back up and dialed the number carefully before common sense made me change my mind.

54

The phone rang 3 times before it was picked up.

"Yeah," a sleepy voice said.

"You were supposed to call me back so we could talk about what my 'thing' was," I said into the phone.

There was dead silence on the other end for a minute, and then Gemini responded. "Come see me."

"Now?" I asked.

"*Right* now," he told me.

"Okay," I said simply.

He hung up.

Excited, pissed off and nervous all at the same time, I got in the shower and scrubbed myself awake. I threw on some of the new clothes Tre'd bought me, made sure I looked as good going as I did coming, went in Tre's drawer and got some money out and was on the way to the hospital in under an hour.

When I got to Gemini's room, the bathroom door was open and he was wrapping a towel around his body. My eyes ran over all the muscles and I forgot the slick-ass comment I'd practiced in my head on the way over here.

Gemini stared at me a second, then went over to where he had a t-shirt and a pair of sweat pants laid out on a chair. "You gonna close the door or you just planning on letting all the heat out?" he asked.

Realizing I was just standing there looking stupid, I quickly came into the room and pushed the door closed. When I turned back around, Gemini was getting dressed like I wasn't even standing there. When he finished, he climbed back on the bed, his feet hanging off of the end when he stretched out.

"Those don't look like hospital clothes to me," I said, figuring I needed to say something instead of standing there and looking stupid.

"They don't got no gowns I can fit," Gemini said, shrugging. "I'm going home in a day anyway, so whatever,"

I nodded, feeling stupid.

Gemini nodded at the chair beside his bed. "Sit down," he told me, pulling his wild hair back and wrapping a rubber band around it. I did like he said, feeling those blue eyes on me, and sat my purse down on the nightstand next to his bed.

"Where's Tre?" he asked pointedly.

"I don't know... not at work," I said, my pissitivity creeping into my voice.

Gemini grinned. "So you decided to come here to hang out until he showed up?" he asked disbelievingly.

Feeling stupid, I stood up. "You know what? Never mind. This was a bad idea anyway..."

"Sit down," Gemini told me, reaching out and grabbing my arm. His huge hand made my arm look like he was holding a stick as he sat me back down in the chair. "Look, *I* don't give a fuck what he's doing. I don't give a fuck what *you* do after you leave here. If you came here on some get back shit, it's whatever," he told me, pulling me and the chair closer to the bed, making a loud scraping sound on the floor.

"It's that simple?" I asked.

Gemini sucked through his teeth. "C'mon, man. I seen how you looked at me when you came in here. You seen me looking back at you. We can bullshit around and drag this out *or* we can do what you want to do right now. I don't give a *fuck* what you wanna do about Tre, that's between you and *that* man," he told me, pulling me to him.

"You not worried about your girl at all, huh?" I asked, grinning.

"You ain't worried about her neither," he laughed, laying a kiss on me that made me shiver. "Fuck them. Just roll with this shit," he instructed me, kissing me again. I got lost in it for a minute until I heard a doctor walking past the door and I jumped.

"We can't do this right here," I told him, nodding at the door.

Gemini looked around the room for a moment, then grabbed my pocketbook in one hand and my arm in the other and drug us in the bathroom, closing and locking the door behind us. He turned the shower on, tossed my purse over in the corner and crushed my lips against his. I blocked Tre out of my mind and let Gemini peel my clothes off of me. He tossed those in the corner on top of my purse and stripped out of his own clothes. He pushed me against the wall and licked up and down my neck as we stood under next to the hot water, which sprinkled our bodies with heated drops. He squeezed my breasts and ran his hands all over my body, making me exhale softly. Someone knocked on the door to the room next to Gemini's and I jumped.

"I cain't do this here," I protested, breaking away from him. Gemini's eyes flashed for a moment, then he let me go and walked out of the bathroom. He massaged his injured arm for a minute, then used the other to snatch up his pants and pulled something out of his pocket. He came back into the bathroom and closed the door.

"Hit some of this," he told me, holding a baggie up. My heart skipped, then started racing as I stared at the white powder in a baggie.

"Is that… cocaine?" I demanded. "You brought that shit in a hospital?!"

Gemini sucked through his teeth. "We not in prison, girl," he said, opening the tiny bag up. He dumped some on the back of his hand and snorted it up quickly, closing his eyes briefly. He dumped some more on his hand and held it out to me. I hesitated and he frowned at me disapprovingly. "What, you scared? Come on, Jari… you know you ain't finna get fucked up behind this lil bit of shit here,"

I actually *didn't* know because I'd never done it, but I didn't like the way Gemini was looking at me, and I did need to loosen up some. That's the reason I came over here, right? I wiped the scared look off of my face and looked in Gemini's face. He brought his hand to my face, and I sniffed all the powder up quickly the way I'd seen him do it. I sneezed and

57

WICKED BLUES Deszion Nasir

he laughed at me as I backed away from him, bumping into the door.

"Shit!" I exclaimed. Blue stepped to me and gently tilted my head up while I tried to steady myself. It didn't take but a few moments for a warm sensation to settle over me. I blinked in relief, then felt Gemini's lips on my shoulder. He picked me back up and brought his mouth to my nipple. I moaned at the sexual pleasure I got from that simple gesture and dug my nails into him, hungry for more. It wasn't long before I felt him trying to slide his dick in me, but I cried out. There was no way he was gonna get that in me without ripping me open.

"Shh, I got you," he whispered, reaching for the sink and scooping some more cocaine in his pinky nail and sticking it in my nose. I hesitated. "C'mon, baby," he coaxed. I moved my hair back and snorted the powder into my nose. Before it had taken effect he had another scoop under my nostrils. I didn't fight him this time, and accepted the dose as he gripped my ass cheek and pulled at it roughly. When his fingernail was sniffed clean, he grabbed my other cheek and lifted me up, bringing me down on his dick. It hurt like a *muthafucka*, but somewhere in my head the pain wasn't logging in and making me tell him to stop. Soon I was moaning and bobbing, and my eyes rolled in the back of my head. After another scoop of cocaine, my body was so over-sensitive it felt like the sexual sensors in my body were being magnified. Blue had to put his hand over my mouth and turn the shower on full blast to keep the noise down. All I wanted him to do was pound my pussy harder and harder, and as I said that out loud he obliged, grunting out his own pleasure. Before I knew it he had me face down in the shower on my hands and knees, the hot water bouncing off his back and onto mine as he hammered in and out of me so hard I was scooting across the hard shower floor. I looked down and saw blood mixing with the water from where my knees were being torn up on the gritty shower floor, but as much as I wanted to tell him to stop I couldn't. The only thing important to me right now was that he kept his dick inside me, the orgasms I was repeatedly experiencing back-to-back transporting me to another time and place where I couldn't focus on anything else. I think I was trying to pass out when I felt Gemini's breathing speed up as he wrestled with his nut. He snatched out of my pussy and I gasped like he'd cut off my life support. He yanked me around and shoved his huge dick in my mouth and before I knew what was happening, warm cum was shooting down my throat, filling my mouth and spilling down the sides of my face. I almost choked because I wasn't prepared, but I held it together until he pulled himself out of my mouth and I collapsed on the floor like a rag doll, disoriented as hell while his cum was sliding out the side of my mouth and rinsing down the shower drain. I bumped my head and as I closed my eyes passing out I faintly remember seeing Gemini stand up, glance down at me, and step over me to take a shower.

I woke up sometime later. I was redressed and propped up in the big easy chair on the side of Gemini's bed. I felt crazy and not in total control of myself as I struggled to turn over.

When I did, I froze at the sight next to me. Teasha was curled up on the end of Gemini's bed while he sat on the other end and fed her what looked like cheddar broccoli soup from Jason's Deli.

My movement got Teasha's attention and she turned to me and smiled. "You feeling better?" she asked.

I must've been looking at her like she was an alien because she glanced at Gemini.

"I told her about you slipping when you came up here awhile ago. Sorry, but Tre never showed up, ma. I apologize for him having you meet him all the way out here and leaving you stranded. Don't look embarrassed. I already told her you was tryna shower right quick before he got here since you'd been running around all day. She snuck your clothes down to the dryer and everything. Yo, Teasha even helped me get you off the floor, cleaned you up, dressed you *and* she got you in

59

the chair while I called Tre again, but nobody answered his phone. He's probably doing his rounds or some shit like that," Gemini shrugged, looking totally normal.

Either I was crazy or Gemini was one *hell* of a fuckin liar. Slivers of my memory came and went, replaying the kisses, coke and sex he and I had just gone through, but the room showed no traces of any of that.

"Baby girl wanted to call a nurse, but I know you ain't tryna be stuck up in here no more that I am," Gemini laughed. "I figured you just needed to rest right quick."

"I still think she should get a CAT scan or something," Teasha protested quietly. "She could have a concussion or something."

"No, no... I'm fine," I blurted, finally coming to life. I threw the hospital blanket off of me and tried to stand, but the sexual beating Gemini'd put on my ass paired with the workout I'd gotten from Tre last night had my legs weak as hell. They wobbled and I crashed back down in the chair. Teasha moved like she wanted to help me, but Gemini grabbed her arm. "She's okay, baby. She just got up too fast, right?"

I glanced in his icy eyes and nodded. "I'm good. Just give me a minute."

Teasha looked me up and down intently for a minute, then shrugged and turned back to Gemini, holding up a thick sandwich for him to bite as he grinned at her. Their laughter made me want to throw up and I forced myself to stand. I was sturdier this time and didn't stumble. I glanced around the room for my purse. "Bathroom," Gemini mumbled, his mouth full, knowing what I was looking for. I walked slowly and carefully in the bathroom and saw my purse neatly sitting on top of the sink. I opened it to get my keys out and noticed something sitting at the top. It was something wrapped up in a paper towel. I glanced over my shoulder, but Teasha was in her own world, laughing at Gemini, her back to me. I opened the paper up and found another baggie of cocaine and a piece of paper with "Come see me tomorrow morning," scribbled

60

WICKED BLUES Deszion Nasir

on it. I looked back out the bathroom at Teasha and Gemini. Teasha was shaking her drink, eating ice out of it. Gemini was glancing in my direction. He nodded at me, and after a moment I nodded back. I don't know why, but I wanted to see him again. I zipped my bag up and left the two of them in their world as I walked out of the hospital and back into mine.

GEMINI

Jari was peeking in my hospital room at exactly 8 a.m. the next morning. I grinned to myself at her eagerness and waved her inside.

"Am I too early?" she asked. Her hair was pulled back in a ponytail, and she had on a sundress that was easy to get on and off.

"Naw, I told them I ain't want no breakfast, and I know my doctor ain't coming in before noon, since I'm not being discharged till like, one or two this afternoon... so come on in and close that door," I told her, licking my lips at her body that was still visible under her dress. She came inside, dropped her purse on a chair, and climbed into my bed and straddled me, sliding her hands under my sheets. Her warm hands slid up my bare chest, then down and over my dick and she smiled.

"Already nekked and waiting, huh?" she whispered. I grinned and pulled her dress up, sliding my hands around and up her thighs.

"I won't tryna waste time." I gripped her naked ass and smirked. "Guess you won't tryna waste none, neither, huh?"

"Never that," she told me, bending down and kissing my chest, biting my right nipple.

I laid my head back on my pillow as she slid down my body under the sheets. Right before she took me in her mouth she looked up at me. "Oh, you got anymore of that stuff?" she asked casually.

"I gave you some already," I reminded her.

"Shit, I thought that was a gift," she laughed. "I did that when I was in the tub last night."

I raised an eyebrow at her, but just grinned to myself, leaned over and pulled another baggie out of my jeans. I handed it to her and she took it, opened the bag and poured some on my chest. She grabbed a dollar out of her purse, bent it up, scooped some of the powder up and snorted it. She threw her head back, and soon a smile settled on her face. She did that one more time and dropped what was left in the baggie on the chair her purse was sitting on. Her eyes glazed over and she scooted back down and went to work waxing my dick.

This shit was working out for me perfectly. I hadn't fucked Teasha yet cuz she still thought I was a decent nigga. This arrangement let me still seem like the good guy and I'd still get some good pussy when I felt like it. Jari was obviously willing to fuck her way up the ladder, and I'd let her do it, even though it wouldn't get her where she was tryna go. Let that be Tre's problem.

After I bust once in Jari's mouth, I pulled her up and sat her on my still semi-hard dick. I grabbed her by the hips and banged the living shit out that pussy as my dick swole back up. Jari was so high I knew if I was hurting her she'd never say nothing about it. She'd feel it later, but right now she was my own personal sex toy. I fucked Jari in every position I could squeeze in under an hour before I finally let the second nut loose. I ain't wanna fuck her dress up and make her look suspect, so I rammed into her pussy like I was mining for diamonds and made sure nothing leaked out when I came. Was I scared she'd get pregnant? Fuck naw. That's *her* pussy, *her* uterus. Ain't that what females are always screaming? "This *my* shit, nigga!" and all that assorted bullshit. If she got pregnant what would I give a shit for? Nigga please…

I had let off two good nuts, let Jari catch a nap, and had her out the door and on about her business by the time my doctor came to discharge me. By then I'd showered, got dressed and was eating the little bullshit lunch they'd brought me from downstairs.

"Glad to see you eating," the doctor chirped, nodding his head in approval. He removed the bandage from my eye, cleaned the scar, and told me how to care for it. He pulled his little clipboard out and was signing me my discharge papers when Tre walked into the room, a big-ass grin on his face.

63

Once he doctor handed me my pain prescriptions and discharge papers, he left.

"What you smiling so hard about?" I demanded, grinning.

Tre just smiled harder.

"Aw, it's a bitch, ain't it? Who is it, nigga?" I knew it won't Jari. For one, she'd been here. Secondly, she'd come over here cuz she ain't know where Tre was.

"Man… don't even worry about it… but I *can* just say Shorty changed the game for a nigga. All she wanna do is *fuck*, yo. No strings, none of that. She ain't even asked a nigga his name yet."

"What the fuck do she call you, then?" I demanded, laughing.

"'Cutie'."

I smirked and shook my head. "I met a girl or two like that in my life," I mused, recalling memories.

"Naw you don't know this one," Tre assured me. "She international and shit," he joked.

I just smiled and swung my legs over the side of the bed. "Get me the fuck outta here, yo," I told him, standing up. 5 minutes later we were in a borrowed car and pulling out of the hospital parking lot. I pulled the bandage off the top of my eyelid before we'd even pulled off. Tre refused to buy a car, so he had "borrowed" this one to scoop me up. Tre got ready to take a left after the light, but I told him to take a right, which would lead to the highway.

"Where you goin?" Tre demanded.

"*We* bout to ride out Richmond and fuck these punk-ass 804 niggas up, that's where *we* bout to go," I told him, putting an emphasis on 'we.'

"Now, nigga? You fresh out the bed, man," Tre protested.

"So then you know them niggas not expecting the shit. You got them thangs in the trunk like I told you?"

"Yeah, nigga. You told me we was about to sell them, though. Lyin muthafucka."

64

"We *are* gonna sell em. We just running a test run on 'em first."

Tre shook my head as he turned onto the exit to take us on I64 W to Richmond. "You gonna sell them niggas dirty guns?"

"The cats tryna buy this shit ain't gangstas, Tre. They some punk-ass kids tryna spend they pack money on some heat so they can *look* like real gangstas. They asses'll be dead in a week," I swore.

Another hustle I'd started doing was selling high-powered weapons to stupid-ass wannabe hustlers who were willing to pay *way* too much for shit that'd make them look like gangstas to their even dumber friends. I called them 'cracker jack gangstas' cuz they wanted the shiny prize so bad they never paid attention to what was really going on within the box. About a year ago, one of the kids who'd bought some work off me tried to step to me. I took his assault rifle out of his hands and blew his nuts off. *Just* his nuts. He begged me not to shoot his dick off so I made him hold it up while I shot his balls off. He wouldn't stop screaming so I put another one in his skull. I kept my money, my work, took *his* money and the other guns he had laying around his dirty apartment. I ain't wanna carry the guns around since one of em was dirty now, anyways, so I drove a couple of blocks until I saw some assholes standing on a corner shooting dice and tryna battle rap. I could tell off top they were some suckas, and when I saw the large bills they were tossing around in the dice game, I figured they were some low-level corner boys tryna show off. Didn't take nothing to get 'em to buy used, dirty guns for 3x what a skilled killer would pay. All I had to do was hype 'em up. They bought everything I had and put me onto some other young-ass boys. I knew they were inexperienced cuz they conducted all their business on cell phones. Fucking idiots. I would do shit like go to Wal-mart, spend $150-350 on regular shit and sell it for a couple grand, using that money to buy grown-man shit. In a few weeks, the word had spread-cuz you know niggaz ran they

65

mouth more than females-and I made enough to start buying better shit for bigger clients. I got a connect that ran through Richmond. He lived in North Carolina, and about a month later I drove down there and blew his face off of his neck. I took all his shit, all his drugs, and killed all the lil niggaz he had working for him in his house. I told the one I'd let live to get the word out that this was my shit now and we could either eat together or they could sleep together. I served bigger servings at the table when it was time to eat, so nobody gave me no problems. I was soon in a position to do more work for fewer clients. I only dealt with a select few cats, but they were big spenders and bought their guns and drugs in bulk. This was how I'd come under the radar of the 804 Boyz. The nigga whose spot I'd snatched was their competition. He'd never been a threat to them for real, but when my shit started moving, they looked into it and found out who I was. Even though I only had one or two niggas who worked with me, they'd heard enough about me to come at me respectfully. In hindsight, they saved a lot of lives that day, and we made the arrangement we had now...but I was tired of being a middle man and I decided it was time for me to stop bullshitting and run everything. I was smarter and stronger than all them cats, so what was I wasting my time going through them for? They was in the way as far as I was concerned. And now that they'd tried to *kill* my ass, they'd violated. Fuck a gradual takeover. I was coming for them bitches right now.

I knew Tre'd roll with me no matter what I did cuz we was like brothers. He was tryna come up himself, and he was just the type of nigga that knew how to think on his feet and attack without having to be given an order. I know he was pissed about how I was handling shit right now, but I'd never been wrong before, so he rolled with it.

I knew exactly where to find the niggas that put that stupid-ass idea in Louisville's head to have me clipped. Patron, the nigga who'd put the money on me, owned a barber shop out off Broad Street in downtown Richmond. It was a front business, but it was where Patron ran his money through the counter machines in the back. Right before we got into town, about an hour away from Hampton, we pulled over and pulled two gym bags out of the trunk. Between the tinted windows of the out-of-state vehicle, me and Tre put our shit together and rode on into town. It was about 3 in the afternoon and I knew Richmond PD was in the middle of changing shifts and getting ready to patrol rush hour, so there wouldn't be too much shit from them if shit got that serious. Which it probably would. I had something hot for their asses, too, but a saved bullet is a saved headache.

Tre tore down a side street toward the barbershop. The sound of screeching tires caused all the people smoking and shooting dice outside to look up in alarm, but only one or two got out of the way before I was cutting niggas down, a glock in each hand. Tre had one hand on the wheel and one out the window, firing into the shop. Without stopping, he drove over the curb and straight into the shop, which had a whole front made of glass. The muthafuckas inside didn't have time to do shit, not expecting a car to drive straight through the building. Tre was knocking down every nigga in his sight. I jumped out of the car, ignoring the fact I was probably ripping my stitches open, and started blasting cats out of their shell-toed Addidas. Whoever reached a gun died with it in his hand. I kicked over a barber chair as I saw Patron's bitch ass hauling ass toward the back. Tre ran around the back while I stayed on that nigga's ass. I heard more gunfire, screams and bodies dropping by the time I got to the stash room. Blood-covered money was scattered all over the room, some of it still fluttering in the air. Tre'd shot 4 cats who were holding 9mms, and I capped the other 3 who'd been trying to get to the closet where I saw more weapons stashed. I also laid down two chicks who'd been counting the money. I dropped my gun, walked up to Patron and punched his ass dead in the center of his face. I heard a loud crack and he fell back, clutching his face and rolling on the scattered money in pain.

WICKED BLUES Deszion Nasir

"Nigga, you thought shit was that fuckin simple?" I yelled, kicking him in the face with my size 15's and watching a handful of teeth fly out of his mouth. "Tried to get at me in my *own* yard?? You ain't know who you was *dealin* with, muthafucka?!" I yelled, my voice shaking the room. I kicked Patron in the face again and ended up with a shoe covered in blood. Patron was laid out after that, unconscious. I picked that bitch nigga up, slung him over my shoulder, reached in his pocket for his keys to his new truck, and me and Tre' strolled out of the wrecked shop. His crew, if any of them present had been left alive, were nowhere to be found as we strolled across the street to his truck, threw him in the back and screeched off. We hopped back on the highway and drove back south to Portsmouth.

Patron was the top dog in the 804 Boyz. I wasn't the type of nigga to fuck around with the pawns. Take the king out, and the pawns would follow whoever was on top. Charger was 2nd in command to Patron. We drove straight to the stash house out Jefferson Park where I knew he'd be this time of day. The hood was jumping, probably because news of our attack on Patron was spreading by phone. When niggas saw the truck coming, they started firing at us, but I knew the truck was bullet-proof. We screeched to a stop in front of Charger, who was standing up in his yard, surrounded by 804 Boyz, their guns drawn. Waiting. I climbed in the back, grabbed Patron's now semi-conscious body and kicked the door open. Seeing their leader still alive but fucked up caused Charger to put his hand up, motioning for the 804 Boyz to hold their fire. Tre got out of the truck, a gun in each hand and made sure no one tried to roll up on us from behind.

"You see this bitch-ass nigga here?" I shouted. "*This* nigga hired some bitches to murder my ass, yo. He won't man enough to do the shit himself; he had to put 50 grand on my head. I'd *never* pay no '*nother* muthafucka to body a nigga *I* wanted dead. That takes the soldiers away from what the fuck they 'posed to be doing: holding shit down and making sure shit run smooth. Now, a nigga like myself? If *I*

68

was tryna off a nigga-" I put my gun to the side of Patron's head and pulled the trigger. The onlookers screamed as the leader of the notorious 804 Boyz's brain was used as graffiti all over me and the people closest to me. I dropped Patron's body on the street and turned to Charger. "Now, I'm *usually* a reasonable type of muthafucka. I ain't come down here to fuck ya'll shit up. I was just making a social call to let ya'll meet the new HNIC and see if anyone had an issue with it. If not, *cool*. Shit keeps rolling. I'll run shit a lil different, of course, cuz I know how to make sure everyone at the table eats. I ain't tryna strong arm nobody... just doing some editing in management. Of course, if there's a muthafucka who don't agree with the change in management, never let it be said I won't a nigga who listened to the troops." I stopped and looked around, not bothering to wipe any of Patron's blood off of my face.

Everyone looked at Charger. He was deep in thought for a minute, but never took his Newport out of his mouth. "Other than my life, what a nigga gonna benefit from this shit?" he asked.

"A bigger cut than you already getting. 30% bigger. All ya'll gotta do is tighten ya'll shit up and you can make a shitload more paper than what you been getting. It ain't ya'llz fault though. Sloppy leaders leave sloppy pockets behind, my nigga. Patron was only in charge cuz the top nigga over him, that nigga Niko, got them football numbers upstate. Bigger leader, bigger pockets. And you can best *believe* I don't got *no* problems laying down disrespectful niggas like this bitch here *personally* if they don't seem to agree with our new team." I added, kicking Patron's body and making sure to throw in "our" to pull him in. I could easily just off that nigga Charger and pull some more cats in, but I was an impatient dude and the time I wasted schooling a new team could be spent making more money. Of course, Charger'd take it as a sign of loyalty. Whatever's clever.

Charger ran his hands over the stubble on his chin, looked down at Patron, and nodded finally. "You got that, baby."

"Cool. You got the number. Get at me tomorrow for details and shit. You got till then to get all the other niggas up on this new shit."

Charger nodded. Tre used his foot to roll Patron's body from in front of the truck. "Happy Birthday, muthafuckaz," he called out."A new movement was born today." We climbed back in the truck and pulled off, now the top niggaz in the 804 Boyz' crew.

TEASHA

I didn't see Gemini the day he came home. I had to work overtime that day because a lot of employees had been using the shooting and media attention as an excuse to call into work for all kinds of reasons: "I'm on disability, cain't let myself get filmed working."

"My kids saw the news and now they scared to let me come in until the situation dies down." I told that girl her kids'd be more scared of their lights being cut off if I fired her ass. Gemini called me every day, several times a day to the point he was calling more than the newspapers. He told me he'd been running in and out of town for meetings with some new investors who were willing to help him open his own business after seeing his story on the news, so of course I had to let him get his hustle on. He sent flowers, candy-grams, and lunch to my job and gifts to my apartment every day, and as of now we hadn't even been on a date, much less had sex yet. Being a real woman was finally paying off and all the girls from school who used to come by and talk shit were either ignoring me or trying to get close to me, looking for their 15 minutes of fame.

All the gifts were nice, but I'd never been the kind of female who was in it for the money, so today, when I got a break, I walked out to my car and called Gemini. He answered right away.

"Hey, baby," he greeted me, but sounded like he was busy.

"Hey... just checking in to make sure you're good," I told him, smiling.

"Like you always do. You know I'm diggin that about you," he told me. "What's goin on, though? You never call me this time of day. Something wrong?"

"Well... no... kind of..."

"Come on, T. I cain't fix it if you don't put a repair order in..."

"I just want to see you, that's all. I mean, all the gifts and whatnot are sweet, but I really just wanna spend some time with you, you know."

Gemini was silent on his end for a minute. "Aight, listen. I'm a come to your spot tonight. We can swing by Mama Rosa's out Phoebus and get some dinner and drinks and then go hang out somewhere. That sound good? I'll pick up Jari and Tre, too and we can all shoot the shit."

"Okay, that sounds perfect," I agreed, bubbling over. I was kind of hoping me and Gemini'd be alone, but having his friends around might make him more willing to open up to me, or at least let me see more of the real Gemini and not the radio personality so I was cool with it. We hung up and I sailed through the rest of my shift in a helluva better mood.

After work I had to burn rubber over to Norfolk to get my hair hooked. My copper hair was looking dry and limp due to me working so many hours and squeezing in running a few miles on the mornings I didn't have to open the shop. By the time Salita finished deep conditioning, blowing my hair out with a brush and glossing it up, my hair was bouncy, shiny, and had its natural deeper red color back. I even dipped in my savings and bought a new blue dress that matched Gemini's eyes and a pair of stilettos. The dress was only held together in the front by a clasp made of stones, and showed off the curves on my little frame. I was going all out because this was the first time Gemini'd see me with my hair done and looking like a woman and not a sweaty teenager. On a side note, I was also making sure I looked over the top because Jari was coming. I'd seen the way she was looking at Gemini even if nobody else had. I was looking a hot mess the last time she'd seen me and I'd be dammed if she was gonna outshine me again. Bitches like her made a lot of trouble for women like me so I might as well nip that shit early. Ladies, you know we often dress more for other women anyway. Men will try to get at us no matter if we have on a dress or sweatpants.

By the time Gemini's Lexus pulled up outside my small townhouse out Queen's Terrace, I was doing a bad job of calming my nerves. The neighbors were peeking outside to see who was driving that kind of car. In this neighborhood, it was either a dope boy or a pimp. I peeked out of the upstairs window when I heard a car door slam. I saw Gemini straightening his sweater and slacks and looking around him. His wild hair had been braided in a funky pattern and the ends reached down to his shoulder blades.

It didn't take long for someone to recognize him, and soon people were coming outside to see him, but he politely shook his head and headed for my door, leaving people standing around and whispering to themselves. I understood it, cuz I never had guys come to my house to get me. I was real cautious about letting cats know where I lived, and they weren't used to seeing nobody come to my door. For a second I was afraid this had all been a joke, but Gemini's heavy knocking on the door brought me to reality quickly as I made my was downstairs, being careful not to fall down in my 6 inch heels.

When I swung the front door open, Gemini was smiling down at me. He took a step back and looked me over, and his smiled widened. "Damn," he commented, obviously surprised and pleased by what he saw. "Is a nigga at the right house?"

I laughed and blushed, rolling my eyes to play it off. "Silly." I stepped back to let him in, and caught glimpse of Tre and Jari looking our way in the car. Tre looked as surprised as Gemini had, but of course Jari was frowning. Good. I flashed her a smile and closed the door.

"I'm ready, I just gotta get my coat," I told him, heading for my downstairs closet while he looked around the small living room.

"Take your time," he called, bending his long frame down on the couch. I thought he'd snatch me up and we'd be out, but Gemini was obviously in no hurry. I wasn't sure if that was good or bad yet.

73

I took my coat out of my closet and glanced once more in the mirror next to it before going back out to the living room. Gemini had his long arm outstretched along the back of the couch and his left ankle on his right knee. He smiled up at me. "You know what, I gotta apologize to you."

"Why?"

"I been so busy, Teasha. You been *real* patient with a nigga... and then... to see that you're as beautiful on the outside as you are on the inside?" He shook his head. "I mean, don't misunderstand a man. I obviously thought you were, you know, attractive, because I stepped to you at your job, but I ain't know you was hiding all *that* under a Burger King uniform..." he shook his head again and I laughed.

"You ready to go, silly?"

Gemini licked his lips. "C'mere for a minute," he said, sitting up straighter.

Thrown off, I glanced out the front window at his car. "What about them?"

He waved them off. "They alright. They just accessories to our night," he smirked, then reached his hand out to me. I was nervous, but I took it and he pulled me down in his huge lap.

"What're you doing, Gemini?" I giggled to cover my nerves.

"Tryna get this out the way now so you can relax when we leave," he said pointedly, taking my chin in his huge hand and bringing our lips together. Now, I hadn't been on anything *close* to a date in months, so my body was backed up like you wouldn't believe. I don't know if it was the kiss or my sexual drought that caused my hormones' switch to instantly turn on, but it did. Gemini slid his hands from my face, to my neck, shoulders and then down to my breasts. I wrapped my arms around his neck and tangled my fingers in the braids hanging down his back. He squeezed my breasts through my thin dress, then slid his hands under the material, taking my nipple in his thick fingers and gently squeezing it. I moaned, and, encouraged by my response, Gemini bent his

74

head and ran his tongue across it before taking the whole nipple in his mouth and sucking on it, biting it gently. I moaned louder and grabbed his ear with my teeth, swirling my tongue around the outside and inside rim. I felt him shudder and his dick started rising under me. He lifted his head to my neck and slid my dress down off my shoulders while he sucked on my neck. He took one of my hands and slid it down his body and onto the crotch of his pants so I could feel the huge lump building there. It sent me into a panic and I pulled back from him. "Wait, wait," I moaned, putting a hand on his chest.

"Shit, I'm sorry," he apologized, breathing hard. "I ain't mean to do that. I ain't come in here for that; don't think that I did, okay?"

"No, it's cool,"

"Naw, it's not. I mean, I meant to kiss you and get it out the way, like I said. I was planning on doin that before I got here, but I ain't expect you to look this fine and a nigga kinda got beside hisself," Gemini laughed, pulling my dress back together.

"You weren't the only one," I pointed out, trying to make him feel better.

"I noticed," he smirked, giving me a devilish smile. He scooted me to the side and stood up. "Barely touched a nigga and got my dick all hard and shit," he complained playfully, trying to rearrange himself in his pants. I laughed and tried not to stare. "Tre gonna clown the shit out of me," he went on, but he was still smiling.

"Don't worry, I got you," I told him as he picked my coat up and helped me slip it on. I flipped my hair over the collar of my coat and reapplied my gloss in the small mirror by the door.

"Oh, you do?" he asked, looking amused.

"Yeah. Just keep your arms around me when we go outside. I'll be walking in front of you, right? Once you get me in the car, just walk around the back instead of the front and no one in the car will see... alla that," I waved a finger at the tent in his pants. He laughed, but did like I said. We'd been in the house for awhile so the crowd had broken up except for a few people a building or so over who had been enjoying the Indian summer weather before Gemini'd pulled up.

As we walked to the car, Gemini's arms around me, I could see that Jari was clearly pissed. To her left, though, Tre glanced at me again, then did a double-take-again, his eyebrow raised. He recovered by the time Jari looked at him, but I saw it anyway.

"What's good, T?" Tre asked, greeting me after Gemini closed my door and was walking behind the car.

"Hey, Tre," I said, offering him a bright smile. Tre seemed cool as hell as far as I was concerned. Made me wonder how guys like him ended up with girls like Jari, who waited until Gemini was pulling off before quipping "Damn, Gemini, I didn't know you even knew where this spot was. Lemme find out you hangin out in the 'hood like a corner boy," she laughed.

I cut my eyes at Jari in the rearview. She was talking to Gemini but she was *definitely* looking at me. Tre looked at her disapprovingly and Gemini reached over and grabbed my hand, as if telling me to ignore her. I glanced at him and calmed down, his blue eyes looking at me peacefully. "How would you know where I be and where I don't?" Gemini asked her, giving her a cold glance. It was actually almost a threatening kinda look he tossed her in the mirror, and I made a mental bookmark of the look to process later.

The whole ride to the restaurant, Gemini kept glancing at me and smiling, even though he was talking to everyone in the car.

Mama Rosa's was small and cozy on the inside. Gemini had us seated at a table in the back of the building behind a privacy screen so Gemini wouldn't be recognized and able to eat in peace. As soon as we ordered our drinks, Jari got fidgety and excused herself to go to the bathroom, rubbing her eyes and saying her contacts were being irritated by the candle smoke at the table.

Tre stood up to pull her chair out for her, and when she was out of earshot, he leaned forward. "So, ya'll was in the house a *minute* before ya'll came out," he said, grinning a smile of an innocent college boy. "Got sidetracked?" he teased.

"A little bit," Gemini admitted, laughing. His arm was over my shoulder and he pulled me to him and kissed me on my forehead, which was turning as red as my hair along with the rest of my face. Tre's playful smile made it worse, as he seemed to get a kick out of teasing me.

A minute later, my leg vibrated when Gemini's phone went off. He sighed, clearly irritated, took his arm from around me, and pulled it out. He glanced at the number, frowned, and excused himself as he answered.

"What, nigga... So... Do I gotta do this right now, Charger? I'm out with my fam, man..." He listened for a few seconds, pissitivity all over his face. He told Charger to hold on and looked at me apologetically. "My bad, T. I gotta take this. I won't be but a minute, I promise."

I nodded, and he got up and headed for the front door, speaking heatedly as he walked outside, leaving me and Tre at the table and customers and staff tripping over each other to get out of his way.

"Sooo," Tre said, leaning forward on his elbows. "Since we all friends now, tell me how you got my nigga acting all gracious and polite and shit," he grinned.

"You mean he ain't always like that?" I asked, half-joking.

"*Shiiit*," Tre laughed. I laughed with him, and then he said "Naw, I'm just playing. He's cool. He ain't usually the most *polite* cat when it comes to females, but I cain't lie, he on his grown-man shit tonight." he explained, nodding. He took a sip of ice water and shook his head. "Cain't blame him, though. You look..." he trailed off and drank more water. "Lemme stop before you have a nigga saying shit that'll get him in trouble," he laughed again.

I returned the laugh, flattered. Tre was actually pretty easy to talk to and in a minute or so we'd forgotten about where our dates were.

GEMINI

As soon as I stepped outside, I hung my phone up and walked to my car. I opened a special compartment I had installed on the driver side and grabbed something inside, smoothly sticking it in my pocket. I locked my car back up and slipped back into the retaraunt unnoticed. Before I went into the bar area I slipped over to my left behind some secluded doors and opened the women's bathroom door. Jari was perched on the little sink, her legs crossed, waiting for me.

"That's some bold shit you doin, calling my phone in the middle of dinner and shit," I told her, shaking my head and locking the door behind me.

"You know how I do," she grinned, looking at me anxiously.

"Yeah, I do," I agreed, unzipping my pants. I pulled a gram out my pocket and tossed it on the sink beside her. She was already pulling her hair up in a clip she'd pulled out of her purse. I watched her carefully as she dumped the powder on the counter and pulled her driver's license out and made two lines. She bent down and one of the lines dissapeared. Jari threw her head back and sighed. While she went to work on the other line, I took my dick out and massaged it, eyeing her ass up in the air as she snorted. Before she was done I had pulled her skirt up, slid her panties to the side and was sliding the head inside her hot pussy. She moaned softly and I watched her eyes slide closed as I gripped her waist and pumped in and out of her quickly, trying to hurry up and let off the nut that Teasha had built up in me a little while ago. I picked my pace up and soon I was pounding Jari's pussy out as she gripped the sink. I pulled my pants up slightly to cut down on the slapping sound. I glanced at my watch and kicked it into high gear.

"Damn, baby, slow down, my shit still sore as hell from yesterday," Jari whispered.

79

"Shut that shit up," I hissed. She moaned and I put my hand over her mouth and rammed into her pussy like I was never gonna get it again, ignoring her efforts to slow me down until I'd exploded inside her. When I pulled out and took my hand off her mouth, her legs were shaking and there was some blood on my dick, but I didn't give a fuck. I could do whatever I wanted to Jari's pussy as long as I hit her up with some coke. She was convinced she just loved the way I fucked her, which was probably true, too, but I knew what the fuck I was doing: Everytime I fucked her I gave her some powder, so whenever I got her high she associated that with fucking me, which made it easy as hell to get her whenever and however I wanted. I had a high sex drive and she was hooked on my little bags of inspiration. She didn't know it yet, but I had plans for her.

Satisfied, I yanked out of her and quickly cleaned myself up as Jari stayed bent over the sink, breathing heavily. Her eyes were low and she was sweating a little. "Yo, get your shit together and hurry up and come back out here," I told her, buckling my pants up.

Jari nodded and tried to stand up. "We still going out Thursday night?" I'd told her I'd take her somewhere. My mind spun through my mental calendar. Teasha was working the night shift.

"No question," I assured, her, nodding. "Hurry up," I said, slapping her on the ass and slipping out of the bathroom and back out the front door. In actuality, I hadn't been gone 10 minutes, so when I came back to the table, phone in my hand, my fake pissed-off expression on my face, nobody paid much attention. Teasha and Tre were laughing at something and I slipped back beside Teasha, making sure she saw me turning my phone off. "No more interruptions," I told her, kissing her. She smiled up at me and fed me a piece of bread from the basket that had arrived when I was gone.

Tre glanced around and tried to see to the other end of the restaurant. "Did you see Jari?" he asked me, frowning slightly, concerned.

80

"Naw," I said simply, then turned my attention back to Teasha. The waitress returned with our drinks and took all our orders. Tre ordered for Jari, but was still looking all concerned. Just as he stood up to go check on her she appeared, all smiles, her attitude from earlier gone.

"You okay?" I heard Tre ask her, staring at her red eyes and slightly strange behavior.

"Yeah, babe. The stupid contact fell out and I couldn't find it for nothing. When I finally got it I had to clean it, you know... the red in my eyes is from all the rubbing. You know how it is when something gets on your contact, right?" she turned and asked Teasha.

"Actually, I don't. I don't wear contacts, but I've heard people say that," Teasha told her a little tensely, but still polite.

"Your eyes are really that color? Hmm... didn't know that. Are you half white or something?" Jari went on, still smiling to mask the bitchiness.

"No, I look like my mother. She has the same color hair. She told me when I was little most of her family has red hair. I got my eyes from my dad."

Jari shrugged. "You never know. Mama's baby, Daddy's maybe," she laughed. Teasha threw down her fork and tried to stand up, but I expertly slid my arms around her and held her tight. "Tre, maybe Jari needs some fresh air," I suggested, giving him the "Check that bitch" look. He nodded, stood up and grabbed Jari by the arm and pulled her to her feet.

"Ow, *Tre*," Jari snapped, but followed behind him and out of the restaurant.

Teasha whirled on me, anger dancing around her green eyes. "*What* is her fucking problem?"

"You," I told her, smiling.

"*Me*? I never did *shit* to her."

"Except look like you do tonight," I pointed out. "You know how females be when they get all intimidated and shit,"

"Are you *serious*?" Teasha demanded.

"Dead-ass," I nodded. Teasha's scowl turned to a smirk and she shook her head. "No disrespect, but *that* bitch needs help."

I grinned and pulled Teasha to me and kissed her soft lips. "She'll get it, one way or the other."

WICKED BLUES Deszion Nasir

TRE

I drug Jari outside and backed her against the wall of the restaurant. "What the *fuck* is wrong with you, Jari?" I snapped, pissed off and embarrassed. She'd been extra bitchy lately and it was wearing on a nigga's nerves.

"What's *your* problem, nigga?" Jari laughed, snatching away from me and stumbling. I frowned and grabbed her by the arm again, pulling her to me and studying her face closely.

"Are you fucking *high*?!" I demanded, recognizing that look.

"Fuck you, Tremeil," Jari tried to pull away from me. I didn't let her go and snatched her back and made her face me.

"What the *fuck* was you doin in the bathroom?" I growled.

"What the *fuck* was you doing when you wasn't at work Tuesday?" she snapped back, now peering into my eyes. "And before you *lie*, I called down to your job so I already know you called out, muthafucka. You won't home the night before, neither. You fucked me and then went out? Nigga please..."

I sighed.

"Yeah, that's what the fuck I *thought*, nigga. It's cool, we not *official*, nigga; I know that. I know I fucked your little plans up when I moved in, but you never said shit. You coulda been a fuckin man and just said what the fuck was on your mind, nigga. Yeah, I lied about the contact lens shit, but nigga *you* lied, too. So don't be out here preaching to a bitch about what the fuck *I* do. You blowing my fuckin high,"

I took in what she said and lowered my voice. "Aight, you got that, Jari. But remember: we ain't official cuz *you* ain't want that. *Your* words, not mine." I pointed out. "So if me steppin out with another chick fucks with you, *say* that shit. Don't keep it in then put whatever bullshit you on

83

in your body. Where'd *you* get some fuckin drugs any damn way?"

Jari rolled her eyes and sighed, looking away from me.

"Okay, cool. Don't tell me. But know this, ma: seeing you like this? Fucks with a nigga hard. There ain't no light at the end of this tunnel. You gonna let me take care of you so we can both stop this bullshit?" I demanded, turning her face up to mine. Jari kept her game face on, but I saw tears leaking out of the corner of her eyes. I sighed and hugged her to me. She wrapped her arms around me and squeezed me tight.

"Can we just go home, please?" she sniffled.

"Yeah." I reached down, took her pocketbook from her and dug around in it until I found a loose single folded at a suspect angle. I held it up and saw white residue on it. I shook my head, pulled out my lighter, and lit the dollar bill and tossed it in the outdoor ashtray. My arm still around her, I reached into my back pocket and pulled out my phone. I called Gemini.

"Yeah," he answered.

"Ay, man. Jari ain't feeling too sharp. I'm just gonna take her home, man."

"You sure? Want me to run you home?" Gemini asked.

"Naw, I'ma call a cab. Ya'll enjoy ya'll selves and I'll get at you sometime tomorrow."

"Aight, bruh."

Gemini hung up and I called a Yellow Cab. Jari laid on me with her eyes closed all the way back to my house. I told her to go take a hot shower and she nodded, her eyes going in and out of focus. While she was in there, I went through all her shit and found a few other empty packs. I didn't know how long she'd been on whatever the fuck she was on, but judging by the evidence, she'd either been going at it awhile under my nose or she was recent and doing it real big. She was probably in between a recreational user and on her way to an addict, I figured, judging by the way she couldn't sit still at Mama Rosa's for 5 minutes. I was gonna find out who had her on this shit, and when I did, that nigga was *done*.

When Jari came out of the shower she was exhausted. She climbed in the bed where I was stretched out, looking for a football game to watch. She got under the covers naked and crawled into my lap and closed her eyes. I kissed the top of her head, shook mine and sighed. She was knocked out in under 10 minutes. I settled back and was watching the end of a Pittsburg Steelers game when my phone rang. I leaned over and picked it up off my nightstand, eyes still on the game.

"What's goin' on?"

"Ay, we gotta make a move," came Gemini's voice over the line.

"Make a move where?"

"Charger hit me up, man. Them cats out Hopewell ain't feelin the new management decision and told us to go 'suck on a rotten dick,' some faggot shit like that."

I sighed to myself. I wasn't in the mood for no more ride-or-die shit, but I knew that came with this new territory Gemini'd slung us into.

I didn't have no trouble getting away from Jari. Her ass was knocked out. I threw on a vest under my battle gear, and slipped on my holster that held my twins. I had a few other weapons on me besides my guns, and more shit would go on under my coat. I walked out of the door and over a few blocks until I ran up on a new Thunderbird. I pulled my jack out and had the door open and the car started in under 10 seconds, and was pulling off by 15.

I picked Gemini up and we hit the highway. Hopewell was about an hour and some change away, 50 minutes by the way I was driving. It was around 2 a.m., and Gemini said the cats bucking on us was about to be on their way to the stash house with their take for the day. Charger was doing his job, it seemed, but I told Gemini to keep his ears low in case Charger was on some bitch-type behavior.

WICKED BLUES Deszion Nasir

Hopewell was a city that the news loved to show when it talked about urban crime, since the city's violent crime rate was a lot higher than in the rest of not just Virginia, but the whole country. That won't surprising, since the average age of the residents was only 35. I hated coming out here, cuz it reminded me of when I was overseas. Niggas out here would cut your head off to get your chain.

I pushed all that shit to the back of my head as I followed Gemini's directions through a run-down neighborhood. We parked a block over and went up the street to an abandoned house. Blue was carrying a gym bag and we pulled the boards off a window and we climbed in. We went upstairs and found a room that had a good clear view of the stash house. The junkies were hanging around outside, but I didn't see anyone coming out or going in as I peered through the crosshairs on top of the assault rifle I'd set up. Gemini told me to be patient, and about 20 minutes later, I see the door open and a tall guy flanked in all black, a cigarette lighting the night up in his mouth, came out of the house, clutching a large book bag. He slung it over his shoulder and I saw the handle of a gun in his waist. I motioned to Blue, who peered down at the guy.

"Yeah, that's that, nigga," he confirmed, crouching behind the riffle. As if he could feel the murder in the wind, the guy stopped for a minute, then looked around the dark street, a frown on his face. He waited a few seconds, then pulled his gun out, spooked. He took his straight out of his mouth and tossed it in the gutter, looking behind him. He finally calmed and started walking toward a car parked one house over when his phone rang. He stopped and answered it. While he was distracted, I got downstairs and kept low to the ground, using the bushes and other cars as a cover till I was on the far left of the house. Behind the bush next to the house, I could see inside the stash house. I got a visual of the people inside, then took a pen light and flashed it once up at the window where Gemini was posted. Less than a second later a single shot cut through the thick night air, nearly unheard due to the silencer screwed on the end of Gemini's gun and the cat holding the bag dropped, a hole through his heart. His phone slid away and into a drain sewer, and his gun fell a few feet away. Seeing a body drop, the crack heads scattered; hearing the commotion outside, the guys in the house rushed for the door. I raised my arm, screwed my own the silencer on my burner, and fired into the house through the window. I dropped two cats before the other niggas knew what happened cuz they were busy rushing for the front door. When I saw them whirl around to see the niggas I dropped, I hit the ground and crawled towards the back of the house right before they started firing out the window, yelling and cursing. Gemini fired two more shots through the now open door, dropping another cat.

I ran to the back of the house and fired through the kitchen window and hit two more of em in the back. They fell and the 4 niggaz left were shook, thinking they were surrounded when there were really only two of us. They wasted a lot of ammo firing in all the wrong directions. I knew by the time they figured out Gemini's position he'd be gone, and I was proven right when less than a minute later bullets came from the right side of the house. The cats were panicking because they didn't know where we were or how many of us were outside. They were yelling and arguing with each other loudly, and while they did that, they made a stupid ass mistake and ran into the living room, where I could see inside the house from the left and Gemini could see from the right. We both fired at the same time and hit all they asses. Once they all were down, Gemini stormed up to the house and kicked the screen door in while I remained in my same position in case another muthafucka was hiding somewhere in the house.

Gemini yelled for the 3 men left alive to stand the fuck up and they did so, moaning and groaning, still not really understanding what was going on.

"Suck a rotten dick?" he yelled to the 3 men. "Who told me to suck a rotten dick?"

Nobody answered.

"Oh, okay. Shit's like that? Aight then. *You* suck a rotten dick, muthafucka, "Gemini pointed his gun at one of the men. "Pull that other nigga's dick out and *suck* it, faggot-ass nigga."

"Man just *shoot* me," the man yelled loudly. I obliged and put a bullet through the back of his head from my position outside. It exited through the front of his head and sank into the wall right above the head of another one of the men. Both of them ducked in terror, one screaming like Ned Flanders from *The Simpsons.*

Gemini turned the gun on the other two. "Next?" he called out. The two men stared at each other, horrified, then at their boy, whose brains were scattered across the dull hardwood floor. "Hurry up, muthafucka. I ain't gonna tell your bitch-ass crew what I seen, I just want ya'll to know who you fuckin with." He leaned over and put the barrel of his gun to one man's head. "Now suck that rotten dick, *nucca.*"

Trembling, the man reached over and unzipped the other man's jeans, who was shaking so bad in pain and anger tears were coming out of his eyes. But he was helpless as he was forced to watch his boy put his limp dick in his mouth.

"I ain't say *kiss* it, muthafucka. I said *suck* it," Gemini yelled, jamming the gun in the degraded man's ear. He obeyed the order and Gemini burst out laughing. "Punk-ass niggas," he said finally, lifting the rifle higher and pulling the trigger and shooting both men in the heart. "*Man,* when your boys find you like this it's gon be some *shit,*" he said to the two dead men, shaking his head at the sight of them dead in that position. I came into the house and we grabbed another bag of money in a corner to go with the one I got of the cat on the street before we disappeared the same way we'd come. By the morning the 7 remaining 804 Boyz from Hopewell had evacuated the city back to Richmond and Gemini never had another problem out of them.

One the way back to Hampton, I was driving and Gemini was counting the money in the two bags. "A few

88

funky-ass grand," he spat finally, splitting the money up. "We shoulda waited till he got to the stash house and copped the work, too. Damn…"

"Naw, you did right, yo. There woulda been more heads at the house. Besides, man. We was just tryna make a point," I reminded him. He nodded as my phone rang. It was now almost five in the morning. I thought it was Jari but Rio's number was showing up. I wanted to just hit ignore and let that shit go, remembering what I'd been through with Jari, but I went against my better judgment and took the call.

"Hey, Cutie," Rio sang. As soon as I heard her voice I knew I was gonna have a problem cutting her off.

"Sup, mami?" I responded. Gemini raised an eyebrow at me, but didn't say nothing. "You up early as hell, ain't you?"

"I haven't been to sleep yet," she revealed, laughing.

"Oh yeah? Why not?"

"Every time I close my eyes I imagine you bending me over and feeding my pussy that good dick," she purred into the phone, making my dick rise instantly.

I sighed. "Wish I could help, ma. I ain't in a position to get to you right now."

"I'm off today. I'll be here all day. I'm goin out tonight, but that's like, after 7 or 8 I'm thinking."

"Ma… my girl's at home…"

Gemini punched me in the shoulder but I ignored him.

"That's where she's supposed to be, right? Look, Cutie. I already told you I'm not tryna break up your happy home or whatever. I just wanna fuck you for a few hours and send you back home, that's all… Don't you want some more of this good shit?" she asked me.

Shit.

"I'll hit you up later," I told her finally.

"Just meet me at the Courtyard Marriott at 4 this afternoon," Rio suggested instead.

"You got that."

"Cool. Bye Cutie."

I closed my phone silently. I felt Gemini looking at me. "Shut up, nigga," I said finally.

He burst out laughing, and I grinned.

RIO

When Cutie finally knocked on my hotel room door, I was more than ready for him. Cutie was a beast in the bed and he was quickly becoming my new addiction. He was also becoming a problem. I was getting feelings for him. I usually dealt with a guy one or two times as needed, but I also was usually traveling from place to place on business. Business had been stagnant and crazy lately, so I was being forced to stay put for longer than usual while this one deal was being set up. That meant I had more free time to fuck around and get infected with feelings that I didn't want, or need, to have.

I stood up, glanced in the mirror at myself. I had on a delicate lace/silk combination bra and thong set, complete with matching thigh highs and needle-point stilettos that I nearly broke an ankle in. I had Birds of Paradise flowers strewn all about the room, and soft R&B music playing in the background. Large, scented candles had the whole room smelling like carrot cake, Cutie's favorite dessert. Men were more attracted to food smells than flower-scented smells, so the combination of the candles, plus the butterscotch smell of the shower gel and lotion I had on would make his mouth water. As soon as I swung the door open, his nostrils flared out and his eyes ran over my graciously proportioned body.

"Hey," he greeted me, grinning and running his tongue over his sexy-ass lips. His face was clean-shaven, as usual, making him look like a built teenager.

"I missed you," I responded, pulling him to me and kissing him softly. He slid his warm hands around me and pulled me to him firmly, running his hands over the curves I know he loved. I backed into the room and he let the door close, reaching behind him and locking it. I pushed his coat off his shoulders and took his motorcycle helmet from him, sitting it on the counter next to a bucket of ice.

"I missed you, too," he told me as I sat him down on the edge of the bed. His eyes were locked on my every move

91

as I strolled across the room to dim the lights and let the candles do all he work. He kicked his boots off as I took two wine glasses and filled them with the chilled, expensive wine and handed him a glass. He gulped his as I straddled him. He watched me sip mine slowly, then I reached behind him to sit my glass on the nightstand.

"Looks nice in here, real nice," he commented, glancing around the room.

"I did it all for you," I smiled down at him, pressing my 36 DD's against his chest as I wrapped my arms around his neck. I felt his hands sliding around my back and gripping my ass as he pulled me tighter against him. I looked down in his eyes and paused.

"What?" he asked.

"I was gonna say you look tired,-"

"I am-"

"But I just noticed something... your eyes... are you wearing contact lenses?"

"Naw," he grinned, knowing what I was about to say.

"Your eyes are... like a forest green. I've never seen eyes that color... especially not on a dark-skinned man."

"Most people don't notice," he shrugged.

"Because they're so dark... I only caught it cuz of the candles... they're beautiful," I commented, mesmerized by the uniqueness of the shade of green in his eyes.

"So are you," he added, leaning over and kissing my collar bone. I threw my head back as his juicy lips explored my body, and slowly got him out of his heavy T-shirt and jeans to reveal his dark skin. I laid him down, then went over to where I had a pot on the stove at the mini kitchenette. In the pot was a bottle of chocolate syrup I'd warmed before he'd gotten there. I took the bottle out and waved it at him.

"Aw, shit," he said, lights dancing in his eyes. I climbed on the bed, pushed him down, and let him reach up and take my bra off. As he tossed it to the side I opened the bottle and slowly poured the warm syrup over my body, letting it slide down over my breasts, neck, stomach and eventually puddle where my long legs separated. Cutie sat up and began licking all over my body like he was starving, making me shudder and cry out passionately and he expertly cleaned me off. I felt myself growing wet and trickling onto his mid-section. He felt it, too, reached down, ran his fingers over it, slipped two inside me, then lick his fingers. He stuck them inside me again, then held his fingers up to me and let me suck on his fingers. Seeing me do that made his dick pop up and I climbed off of him. I went to the mini fridge and pulled out some chocolate ice cream. I scooped some out, put a big spoonful in my mouth, walked over to him and pulled his erect penis out. I bent down and slid it in my mouth with the ice cream.

"SHIT!" he yelled out, grabbing me by the head. Once all the ice cream melted, I heated his dick up with my mouth, then cooled it down with the ice cream again. I had his ass going crazy after I did that a few times. He grew overwhelmed and finally he sat up, tossed me on my back and grabbed the bottle of still-warm syrup. He put the tip inside me and squeezed the syrup inside my body while I squirmed. He tossed the bottle on the floor, put my legs over his shoulders, then stuck his tongue deep inside me, sucking the chocolate out. This night was supposed to be about him, but he had me screaming, moaning, slapping at his head and cumming harder than I had in a long time as he alternated between licking, sucking and finger-fucking me. He finally came up for air and I pushed him down, squatted over him and slid him into me. His head fell back against the pillow and I started to bounce on him slowly. I made him hold his hands up and took his hands in my own so I could balance as I rocked him harder and harder until we were both yelling out with every bounce. I could feel his growing inside me and he was squeezing his eyes shut, wrestling with himself. Finally he yelled out "Get up get up!" I stood and as soon as I did, his cum shot out and he let out an animalistic battle cry. I fell down next to him and we tried to catch our breath in a sticky heap, quiet for a few minutes. He eventually grabbed some

WICKED BLUES Deszion Nasir

tissue off the nightstand and tried to wipe himself off and dropped the tissues next to my wallet, which I had on the nightstand from when I ordered the wine earlier. He pulled me to him and I laid my head on his chest as he kissed the side of my face and shook his head.

"You fucking a nigga's head up, he admitted, sighing.

"Yeah, I'm feeling a little extra over here, too," I admitted. I wasn't going to say anything, but since he opened the subject up, you know…

"Damn," he muttered. "It ain't just the sex, neither. I mean, the sex is… I cain't even explain *that* shit… but how I be vibing with you is mad crazy, Rio."

"I feel it too… but we wouldn't be good together," I told him.

"Why not?" he asked, turning and looking down in my eyes, frowning.

"Well… for one… you got bad habits," I joked, not wanting to get to deep and fuck the mood up. "How you just gonna leave that *nasty* tissue right there?" I demanded.

He laughed, then reached over and picked up the soiled tissue. As he pitched it into the trash, he knocked over my wallet. "Damn." He leaned over to pick it up off the floor and it fell open. He glanced at the picture I had in the front and froze. If I didn't know better, I'd say he went pale. "Who is this?" he demanded, face locked on the picture.

I glanced at the pic. "Oh, that's just my sister-"

"Jari," he finished, his face screwed up.

Startled, I sat back and looked him over carefully. "What's your real name?" I demanded, a cold reality swirling around me.

His face was grim. "Tremeil."

"*Shit*!! " I screamed, jumping up out of the bed. "Oh my fuckin-Tremeil? As in 'Tre' my *sister's boyfriend* Tremeil?!!"

"*Dammit*," Tre yelled, tossing my wallet across the room. "You Jari's sister…? Aw *hell* naw."

Suddenly, where and how we met finally fell into place. He'd been coming to see my sister when we met.

"Fuck... ya'll don't look nothing alike..."

"We have different fathers," I managed to say. "My father is from Brazil."

"Yo, your sister is staying at my house right *now*, yo," he revealed, pacing the floor.

"That's where she went? Oh, God..."

"She know I was with you the other day. I mean, she don't know it was *you*, specifically, but she knows I was out with a female. When was the last time you spoke to her?"

"Not since she left. We've never been close... I'm never home usually..."

"Aight, aight... calm down. She don't know about us. This shit is still under control."

"Control?! I've been *fucking* my sister's man!" I screeched.

"That ain't your fault. You ain't know," Tre pointed out.

"Well, *now* I do," I said, grabbing for my bag that had my regular clothes in it.

"Hold up, *hold up*... I'm saying..." Tre reached out and grabbed my arm. "I mean, this situation *is* fucked up, but I still meant that shit I told you, Rio. I'm feeling you, ma. How I feel is how the fuck I *feel*. I cain't just *ignore* that shit."

I sighed and collapsed on my butt on the bed. "You don't understand," As I was processing the new info, something flashed across my mind like a bolt of lightning. "Wait, wait... Jari said your boy was shot recently. What was his name?" I asked, dreading his answer.

"Gemini."

The name struck me across the face like I'd been slapped. I recovered quickly and started putting my clothes on.

"Hold up, hold up. What's wrong? You know that nigga?"

"I *work* for that nigga." I spat.

"I thought you had a big fancy job with an international company and shit."

"I do. Gemini has contacts all over the world. How well do you *really* know your boy?" I demanded.

Now it was Tre's turn to have the slapped look. He just sat there as I finished putting my clothes on and snatched all my stuff up, threw it in the bag, and threw my coat on.

"Wait," Tre said, coming out of his catatonic state. "Don't you think we need to talk about this shit?" He got up and tried to hug me to him.

"No," I told him firmly, using all my mental strength to push away from his warm arms. "We don't have *shit* to talk about. Take your ass home, Tre. Don't *call* me no more, and *don't* answer if I call you... *please*." I looked one more time into his shocked yet torn face before I tore the hotel room's door open and fled. As soon as I heard the hotel door slam I felt warm tears slide down my cheeks.

I drove across town to a strip club out by the water. I parked my car in the front and got out, slamming the door. The bouncer was about to protest until he got a good look at me.

"Oh, shit, hey, Rio," he greeted me, but the look on my face made him shrink back. I strolled past him and the men getting searched at the door and stormed inside. I paused for a second as my eyes adjusted to the dim light, then I walked past the various poles, stages and tables as the smell of weed and pussy assaulted my nose. I went to the stairs and stormed up to the private office in the back of the building. A big nigga was standing guard outside the door and tried to block me, but I snatched my gun out of my waist and slapped him across the face with it. He grabbed his face in shock and fell to his knees, clutching at his now broken nose. I raised my muscular leg up and kicked the door to the office open, the smell of sex floating in my nose as a greeting. One of the girls, who was giving the man in a plush desk chair a massage, jumped up, surprised. She was naked except for a

96

pair of Payless shoe store heels. Another girl was busy grinding away on the man's dick with her eyes closed- probably high on E- and didn't know what was happening until I grabbed her by her weave and tossed her over the neat desk, scattering files and knocking over an open bottle of Bacardi.

"*Bitch,*" she snapped. She climbed to her feet, dizzy and clutching her head.

I snatched the hammer back on my gun and had it pointed at her point-blank range before she could focus on who'd attacked her. "Say *what*, now?" I growled, eyes begging her to give me a reason to shoot her ass.

Recognizing my gun 1st and me second she stuttered "I-I…"

"You *what*, bitch? Repeat yourself, hoe." I snarled, my Portuguese accent so much more pronounced when I was angry.

"I'm sorry, I'm sorry-" She left her clothes and ran out of the room behind the 1st girl, tripping down the stairs and over the injured security guard.

Pants down around his ankles, Gemini sighed and sat back. His pissed off dick matched his pissed-off expression.

"My *sister*, muthafucka? You put me on my sister's nigga? Your *best* friend, nigga?" I yelled.

Gemini stood, pulling his pants up at a casual pace. "Would you have taken the job if you knew?"

"*Fuck* no." I snapped.

"Well, there you go. Chill out. A job is a job, Rio. You know that."

"But that's your *boy*, though."

"What do I always tell your ass, Rio? You never have no friends in this business. All I did was give you a picture like normal. You didn't even ask the nigga's name. You never do."

"You a fucked up cat," I shook my head, feeling like I was scolding a clever child.

"Man, come on with that. I'm *helping* him. That crazy-ass sister of yours got his mind fucked up right now and I got big things happening. I need him focused. Everybody know a nigga focus gets fucked up when he ain't getting no pussy." Gemini said smoothly, but I knew him. Nothing he did was that damn simple.

"Yeah, and you wanna have something on him in case he starts trippin," I added.

He laughed. "And I got something on you, too, now, don't I?"

I narrowed my eyes. "Nigga, *please*. You'd have to kill me. You'd never resort to no blackmail bullshit with me. And we both know you won't kill me. You need me. You can say you don't, but you know you do. We run shit *together*, nigga. Don't forget that shit. Just because I'm a silent partner, don't *get* it fucked up. Your money don't move unless *I* tell it where to go. And we both know the only thing you love more than yourself is money," I spat.

Gemini sat on the edge of his desk and smirked at me. "You so fuckin *sexy* when you on your gangsta shit. When you gonna stop playin and give a nigga some pussy?"

Exasperated, I fell into the other chair in the office and covered my face with my hands in exasperation. "The Tuesday after never, nigga."

"Aw, come on, Rio. You got that nigga Tre damn near singing. You should have *seen* his ass when we was out Hopewell and Richmond. That nigga was *on* it," Gemini said proudly.

"I will *never* let you get within licking distance of this here," I snapped, running my hand over my love box.

"What about sniffing distance?" Gemini asked, getting up, coming over and placing an arm on either side of my chair.

"Fuck you, Gemini,"

"I'm trying to, *Rio*."

I pushed him away from me. "I'm not doing this no more." I declared.

98

"Why? You and your sister ain't even close."

"That ain't the point, nigga."

"What *is* the point, then?" Gemini demanded, squinting at me. "You diggin that nigga?"

I crossed my arms and glared at him.

Gemini broke out in a huge smile and burst out laughing. "Aw, *shit… this* shit is fuckin hilarious."

"No, it's not," I snapped, irritated my emotions were funny to him.

"*Shiit*, it is too me," he laughed. He leaned down in my face and grew serious. "I already told you what I got going on. If you back out now, you gonna cause a domino effect and fuck our money up. And we both know the *only* person who loves money more than me is *you*," he added. He stared in my eyes for a second, then brought his finger up to the top of my shirt, ran his finger along the collar and pulled it toward him slightly, looking down at my breasts. I smacked his hand away and he stood up, shaking his head. "Ran my bitches out of here, left my dick hard and won't even give me no pussy. And you think *I'm* the fucked up individual," he said over his shoulder as he opened the door to the office and walked out, leaving me alone with my conflicting thoughts.

JARI

Banging on the door woke me up the next morning, making me curl up in the fetal position as I covered my ears with my hands. I opened my eyes slightly and the light in Tre's bedroom made me slap my hands over my eyes, making me wish for more hands. Gemini had come over last night while Tre was working the night shift, and after a few hours of smoking, drinking and fucking, I was exhausted with a hangover. I had seen Gemini nearly every day for awhile now. We didn't always have sex, but he usually had a little package for me and I always had some head for him. He told me when I was high I gave head like a vet. Being around him gave me the rush I didn't get from Tre, who was busy working a new job during the day. When he was off, he took me shopping, to dinner at restaurants I'd never been to... he spent quality time with me, knowing I didn't like being home alone, but saying he needed more hours so he could keep me living the way I deserved to live. He was so exhausted from work most times he came home like a zombie and passed out, so we didn't have sex as much as we used to, but it was cool with me cuz Gemini usually left me sore and drained. I sucked it up, though, figuring I was getting the best of both worlds.

The only sore spot was Teasha. I know that was Gemini's girlfriend and I didn't have a right to be jealous, but it was like every time he made plans to hang out with me, Teasha was calling and calling. And he just had to answer *every* single call. Once I got so pissed I asked him why the hell he even came over here, and he just smiled and goes "You know we have a fuckin ball together, don't stress that other shit." And that ended the conversation.

The banging on the door continued and I remembered the landlord was supposed to come over and check a leaky pipe in the kitchen some day this week, so I sighed and got up, not bothering to put on a robe or brush my hair.

100

"I'm coming, dammit!" I screamed as the banging continued seconds later. I snatched the door open with an attitude and froze as I looked up into Gemini's grinning face. I'd never seen Gemini come over here before noon, so I was thrown off... and embarrassed by my appearance.

"Sup, Jari?" he asked, looking down at me with a grim smile on his face.

"Nothing... I was in the bed, actually," I told him, yawning for good measure.

"That's cool. We can head back there," he laughed.

"Damn, Gemini, is sex all you think about?"

"*Hell, yeah.* That and money. You *know* I gotta stack my paper when I ain't fuckin," he laughed.

I shook my head. "For real? I'm sooo tired, Gemini. I cain't even do it today."

"What you mean you 'can't?'" Gemini asked, frowning. "What do you gotta do except lay there?" he demanded.

"Oh, real romantic," I snapped, rolling my eyes and walking away from the door.

"What the fuck you mean, romantic?" Gemini asked, coming in, closing the door and putting on the dead bolt. "Baby, ain't no romance here. We *fuck.* And we fuck *a lot.* It's good and shit, but keep it real. It is what it is. And all *you* need to do is get *nekked* and hold them legs open fo' me," he added, coming up to me and wrapping his arms around me. I tried to resist, but his lip on my neck were making my exhausted body respond. "Hey," he said suddenly, reaching in his pocket. "I brought you something."

"I still got some. I had to hide it, though... Tre's trippin," I rolled my eyes.

"Naw, naw. Something different. It's a better high than what you had. Shit hits you hard as fuck, man... keeps you there longer."

My mouth started to water involuntarily. Coke kept my mind off all the bullshit in my life. I wasn't no junkie or nothin... cuz I only did it a few times a day. I didn't have to have it, but it felt good as hell when I did. I figured controlling it was easy. I usually only used before I had sex. I didn't understand how these crack-heads lost control.

And then I scrunched my face up when Gemini pulled a needle out of his pocket.

"Nigga *what*?" I demanded, pulling away from him.

"Aw, come on, Jari. Stop being a fucking clown. This is the same kinda shit… you just get a rush faster cuz it's already liquid."

"Nigga, please." I backed away from him, but my mouth was still wet.

"Just try it before you start bitchin," Gemini complained, shaking his head. "If you don't like it, you ain't gotta do it again. It's a lot less in here than sniffing all that powder and you still be feelin right," Gemini went on, walking over to the counter and pulling out some supplies. I watched him prepare the needle with a weird sense of guilt and excitement. I never deemed myself perfect, but I also never thought I'd be shooting drugs. He was right, though. I couldn't keep hiding grams of cocaine around the house with Tre searching my shit all the time. If anything, I could just get nice this one time and Gemini could take the needle with him, leaving nothing for Tre to find with his square ass. I was just a recreational user. I was in total control.

Gemini tapping the needle got my attention and I turned to see him coming at me, holding the needle up.

"Don't put that shit in my arm… he'll see that," I said quickly.

"I *got* this," Gemini assured me. He bent down, picked my foot up, and examined it. He rubbed his finger over the big vein across the top and glanced at me. "Ready for this good shit?" he asked, smiling at me.

I nodded, my heart beating loudly. I flinched when he stuck the needle in, but it was over in seconds.

I looked down at my foot, wiggling my toes. I couldn't even see where he'd stuck me. I looked up at him questioningly, then I was suddenly nauseous, but that passed

WICKED BLUES Deszion Nasir

after a few seconds. Then, all of a sudden, I felt an overwhelming sensation take a choke hold over me. I'd never felt so... happy. I felt warm all over, like I needed to be touched or held because I might wiggle apart.

"Oh, shit," I moaned.

"See? I told you that shit had get you right," Gemini said triumphantly. I looked Gemini in the face and felt butterflies in my stomach when he touched me.

"Oh, shit," I moaned again, dropping my head back against the couch. I was drifting above my body, and it seemed like I was looking down at myself. I wasn't totally focusing, but I heard Gemini on the phone with someone. I couldn't turn to him because my body suddenly felt sooo heavy I couldn't move my head, but the rest of me felt fidgety. I think I heard him step outside, but a second later he was back, moving my hair off my face gently. I smiled at him, trying to focus through dizziness. I felt his lips on my neck and shoulders and moaned as the sexual excitement in me sparked instantly.

I felt myself being picked up and laid on the floor gently. I reached up and rubbed my breasts through my clothes, one hand drifting down and inside my pajama bottoms to my dampening pussy. I slid an anxious finger inside myself and closed my eyes as Gemini stripped my clothes off my body. I was sexually aroused but sooo drowsy. I heard him unzipping his pants, and moments later Gemini was inching his way inside me. I was aware of increased sexual energy and pleasure, but I was still nearly oblivious, feeling like my body was being molded like clay. Gemini didn't seem to mind and started to fuck me harder, holding my legs up as I couldn't do it on my own. After a little while of him punishing my pussy, he picked me up, sat on the couch on and kept me on top of him, moving my hips up and down, back and forth.

"I can't ride," I muttered.

"It's cool," he rasped, not even making an attempt to slow down. He pulled me down against his chest as he leaned back, and started fingering my ass hole. I gasped out, but then he got a little rougher.

"Gemini, chill with that," I protested painfully. "Get some KY or something."

"Yeah, I got some," he said, pausing momentarily. I felt him reach over and grab something, then I felt a heavy weight on either side of me on the couch. I know I was high, but I was still thrown when I felt an extra pair of hands rubbing on me, sliding from my back, to my breasts, then ass cheeks.

"Who is that?" I wanted to ask, but couldn't get it out. I was unable to turn around since my head was fucked up, but I was feeling so damn good I didn't give a shit.

"That's just my boy, baby. Don't sweat that shit. Just go with it," Gemini assured me, still rocking me on his dick with his head back, eyes closed.

I wanted to protest, but I couldn't. A second later I felt the warming sensation from the KY jelly on my ass, and then another dick was trying to force its way inside my asshole. I made a weak attempt to stir, but Gemini was easily holding me down firmly as the unnamed man shoved himself roughly into my ass and started grunting and panting. He started pounding my ass out, and Gemini was bucking into my pussy roughly, neither man making any attempt to be gentle. I was actually in a lot of pain, but I was too fucked up to do anything about it. Besides, the way I was feeling right now? Gemini could do whatever he wanted to me as long as he could make me feel like this. Gemini was holding me tighter as the two men fucked me harshly and slapped, bit and squeezed me repeatedly as my mind continued to ride its new wave.

The other man finally came and yelled out as he released his semen inside my hole. As he pulled out, Gemini started slamming me up and down on his dick until I had tears in my glassy eyes. He came with a force that a sent pain up through my abdomen, but all I could do was lay there, panting and moaning, not sure if it was from pain or pleasure.

WICKED BLUES Deszion Nasir

Gemini rolled me off of him and I slid on my back to the cool carpet, chest heaving. Through my blurred vision, I saw the unidentifiable man buckling his pants and speaking in a low voice to Gemini. I saw him hand Gemini something as my eyes slid closed. I couldn't see it, but it smelled like money.

A while later, I woke up, still naked on the floor. I felt like shit and my whole body was aching like I'd been in a title match. I was THAT exhausted. My memory was fuzzy and trying to reboot memories, but it wouldn't let me.

My movement brought Gemini out of the kitchen, where he was drinking a Pepsi and talking on the phone. Seeing I was awake, he ended the call and sat down at the kitchen table, watching me. He didn't offer to help me up, instead choosing to sit back and watch me struggle to get to my feet.

"What did you give me?" I whispered, no longer believing it was cocaine.

"Just a lil bit of heroin. It ain't shit."

"Heroin?! Gemini are you fucking crazy? How could you do that to me? That's the hardest drug to get off of when you get addicted!" I cried hoarsely.

"You ain't addicted," he laughed. "You had it one time. You was getting hooked on that *powder* though, weren't you?" he asked, lighting a cigarette, his eyes studying me.

"Nigga, *you* buggin'," I waved him off, my hand dropping heavily in my lap

"Oh am I?" he laughed and sat forward in his chair. "You know how many grams you was using a day? Damn near 4 grams, Jari. I'm tryna help you out, love." He stared at me, amused for a minute, then stood up. "Well, let me get my shit and go."

"What? What time is it? How long I been sleep?"

Gemini glanced at his watch. "A couple of hours."

"What?" I said again, shocked. "I gotta get to the bank. I can't drive…"

Gemini finished his Pepsi. "Well, hurry up, I'll run you round there right quick."

I climbed to my feet, slowly, and went through the process of putting some clothes on. I didn't feel guilty about what had happened. Not yet. I mean, come on. Everybody's experimented with something, be it drugs, sexuality or a different hairstyle. The way I looked at it, Gemini was opening my eyes to so many things I hadn't experienced before. The main thing was that I was still in control. That's the thought I'd kept in my head as me and Gemini headed for the door. I was a zombie on my feet and sore from all the rough sex I'd been involved in lately, and all I wanted to do was go to the bank, come back, curl up and pass out in front of Tre's huge TV.

Right as I pulled the door open, I heard a click. As I turned my head toward the sound, I felt Gemini's body slam into mine and I was on the ground, dazed and scared as the patio doors exploded, glass and bullets swirling around the apartment like a tornado had dropped in the room. I was paralyzed on the floor, but I quickly realized half the bullets flying had come from Gemini's gun. He jumped to his feet, used one foot to roll me behind a wall, and snatched a second gun from his waist all simultaneously. His retaliation must have been too much for the shooter because he retreated. That didn't deter Gemini as he took off top speed behind the assailant, going through the broken patio doors and jumping the fence in one leap. I heard an explosion of gunshots, then screams... and they weren't coming from Gemini. The shots ceased, and all was left was screaming that made my soul shiver. The screaming went from pain to pleading, then silence after one more shot. Seconds later Gemini jumped over the fence again, his clothes stained in blood.

"What the fuck just happened?" I demanded, trembling from head to toe.

Instead of answering, Gemini snatched me up, grabbed his cell phone and made a call, telling someone to "Come and snatch these bodies up before the cops get here."

WICKED BLUES Deszion Nasir

He barked out the order and hung up as we got to the parking lot. "Did you all Tre?" I asked.

"Can you shut the fuck up for two seconds?" Gemini yelled, causing me to jump and wince at the same time as his grip on my arm tightened. He was acting like the shooting was my fault or something.

We walked to his truck and he pulled is keys out. Right before he stuck the key in, he froze as if he heard a voice whispering in his ear. I wanted to ask what the problem was, but I took one look at the look on his face and decided now wasn't a good time for anymore questions. Gemini looked around and saw a kid, about 9 or so, bouncing a basketball off to the side of one of the apartment buildings.

"Hey, Ricky!" Gemini called out. The little boy looked up and broke out in a smile as he came rushing over, nearly tripping over himself.

"Hey, Gemini!" he said, out of breath. "I got that CD you gave my mom for me. Thanks, man!"

"No problem, youngin. I got a few more for you, too-" He broke off. "Aw, damn. I left em upstairs at Tre's spot. Hey, I'm in a hurry, can you start the truck up for me while I run back upstairs and get em? I might not be back around this way for a minute and you know Tre gon' forget to get em to you." He tossed the little boy his keys and he caught them in awe, as if they were made of gold.

"Sure!" he exclaimed, a huge grin dancing around his little face.

"Don't drive nowhere, now," Gemini scolded jokingly.

"Naw, never! I promise!" Ricky exclaimed.

Before I could ask Gemini what CD he was talking about-I hadn't seen him bring none over, he gripped my arm again and backed away from the car quickly, acting like we were walking back to Tre's building. But as soon as we were a few hundred feet away, he stopped, studying Ricky intently. I watched Ricky fumble with a couple of keys, then he finally got the truck door open. It took him a couple of efforts to

107

climb up in the driver's seat, but when he did, I watched as he slid the large key in the ignition, excitement on his little face. He took a deep breath and turned the key, and instantly, I went deaf as a huge explosion took me off of my feet and once again, my head was being slammed against the ground. A rush of heat seemed to fly over me, followed by smoke, then a rush of wind. After a few moments, I felt someone pulling me away from the madness. I looked up, expecting to see Gemini, but it was one of Tre's neighbors.

"Are you okay?" he kept yelling, shaking me as my hearing went in and out.

I finally nodded, looking around. Shock covered my face as I saw Gemini standing off to the side, not a speck of dust on him. Where the hell had he gone that damn quick?

Then realization set in as I realized what he'd done. He'd figured his car was rigged after the shooting... and he used that poor kid... little Ricky... Ricky's happy face was burned into my brain, destined to remain there for many sleepless nights. I glanced over at Gemini. Sensing me staring at him, he paused in the phone call he was making and turned a cold look on me that nearly made me collapse. I looked away from his icy stare, suddenly afraid.

Minutes later police are on the scene behind the fire department. Gemini makes it his business to wander back over to where I am right before the officers come over to question me. He takes over the questioning immediately. I catch the hint and act as if I'm too shook up to answer questions.

Ricky's mother comes outside and begins screaming when she'd told what happened. She looks around, sees Gemini, and breaks away from a cop and runs at him full force, attacking him and calling him all kinds of names and screaming "What the fuck did you do?!" over and over until she has to be restrained. Gemini has a mask of sorrow over his face like he's hurt, but only I saw the flicker of anger in his eyes as he watched the woman being restrained and finally sedated by the emergency technicians.

About 2 minutes later Tre zooms up on his bike, jumping off almost before it stops. He snatches his helmet off and runs over to me, grabbing me in his arms. Finally, I relax and let myself cry as his strong hold melts my shock away and transforms it into sorrow.

"What the fuck happened?" he demanded loudly, looking at the large knot forming on my head where I hit the sidewalk. A cop breaks it down to him, and his gaze turns to Gemini, who gives him the same story he gave the cops about how he came over to get some paperwork from Tre's house and offering to run me to the bank, seeing as I wasn't feeling well enough to drive. We came out to the car and the explosion occurred.

Tre looked from Gemini to me, searching in my eyes, asking silently if that's what happened. I nodded quickly, avoiding looking at Gemini. I didn't have to, as I could feel his eyes burning a hole in my back.

When the police and fire department left us alone for a moment, Gemini came closer to us and told Tre about the shooting in more detail. They gave each other a knowing glance and Tre's face went from shocked confusion to grim understanding. They had an unspoken conversation for a minute, then Tre turned to me.

"Listen… I'm gonna have to make some moves, Jari. I know you don't want to hear this, but you gonna have to go back home for now."

"No," I moaned.

"Baby, you have to. You can't stay here," he waved behind him at all the wreckage. "Whoever shot at ya'll knows where I live. You gotta go where it's safe." he added firmly, his tone letting me know the decision was non-negotiable.

"That's probably a good idea," Gemini nodded. Tre whirled on him with a fury that even raised Gemini's eyebrow.

"And until this shit gets straight, *you* stay the fuck away from my house, too," Tre snapped, taking a heated step in Gemini's direction.

"Nigga, they shot *YOUR* shit up. " Gemini pointed out.

"Yeah, but for some reason they ain't do it until *you* was in it," Tre snapped back. "Until this shit gets straightened out and we clap these niggas, don't even bother yourself coming through here, yo."

Gemini's jaw clenched, but he kept his tone even. "You upset right now, and you got a reason to be, so I'm assuming that's why you acting like that," he stated, giving both of us a long stare before walking off.

We're out there nearly another hour before Tre takes me to what's left his apartment to get my stuff. He shakes his head at the wreckage to his normally spotless house and tells me not to move. He gets all of my things he can and calls a cab, as I'm too shaky to get on back of his bike. As we climb into the Yellow Cab, it finally hits me that I have to go back to a place that's the mental equivalent of where I'm leaving now. I could really use another hit.

RIO

I'm sitting back on the couch, stunned as I listen to Tre tell me what happened. First, when Tre shows up at my mother's door with Jari, I'm thinking he told her what went on with the two of us. I'm nervous, happy to see Tre and sad about how we left everything all at the same time. When Tre tells me the real reason for the visit, that there was an explosion and shooting with Gemini present at his house, my expression changes. I already have an idea of what the fuck's going on but I keep my mouth closed and try to comfort my sister, who looks like she's been traumatized. I promise Tre I'll take care of her and not to worry about mom. I walk Jari back to her room and leave her to settle down and walk back to the door to get her stuff for her.

"Rio," Tre whispers, reaching out to grab my hand. I look back at him coldly, wanting to pull away, but not quite being able to. "I really wanna talk to you. I know shit is crazy right now… but I think can trust you… I need to talk to you about something important. Please, baby," he added, squeezing my hand gently. My emotions are battling each other and I eventually break his gaze, feeling like I'm snatching his life support. I turn away and carry my things back to my sister's room, hearing him leave and close the door a few seconds later.

I put my game face back on and walk into Jari's room, where she's laying across her bed, balled up under the coves.

"You wanna talk about it?" I asked her softly, sitting on her bed beside her.

Jari shocks the hell out of me and suddenly shoves me off her bed and onto the floor. "Bitch, *please*. You didn't wanna talk when Momma was throwing my shit outside. If you had of stood up for me like a sister *supposed* to, I wouldn't have been over Tre's fucking house and caught up in this bullshit in the *first* fucking place."

111

I stood up, unbelieving. "Hold the fuck on… are you saying this shit is *MY* fault??"

"You *muthafuckin* right. Don't come in here acting all sympathetic, bitch. You wasn't worrying about me when I ain't have nowhere to stay, so fuck you *and* your muthafuckin fake-ass concern. I shouldn't even be mad. All fake-ass bitches know how to be is a *fake-ass* bitch." Jari spat.

"You don't think I wanted to talk to you? You *never* turn your phone on, Jari. I leave you messages, you *never* called back. I figured you was trying to keep to yourself. And you weren't in the fuckin street, you were with Tre."

Jari sucked her teeth. "Fuck that nigga,"

"What?"

"All he do is work. I'm stuck up in that fucking house *all* day without shit to do. I *told* his ass to buy a car so I can get rid of my piece of shit cuz it keeps breaking down. He said he would, but do you see one yet? *Fuck* naw. He be on all that 'Baby let me take care of you' bullshit, but that nigga ain't nothin but a fuckin trick. You gotta pay to play and that nigga got an outstanding balance. So *fuck* him. I'ma get me another muthafucka who knows how to follow orders, bitch-ass nigga…" Jari snatched up some clothes and stormed into her bathroom to shower, leaving me speechless. I couldn't believe she was taking all her shit about the explosion out on me. I was genuinely concerned about her ass, and I know deep down, Tre was too. For her to just toss my concern and his feelings aside like we were nothing pissed me off to no end. She didn't even know the hard decisions I had made for her recently, including cutting off the first man I'd had feelings for in years. Tre won't perfect, but he was a good nigga and he could take care of her. I know one thing: I understood why he'd fuck around on her. Who wants to be around an ungrateful bitch like that?

Fuming, I waited until I heard the shower come on before I pulled out my phone and dialed a number. I walked into the living room and outside on the balcony before the call was picked up.

WICKED BLUES   Deszion Nasir

"Hello?"

I took a deep breath. "Hey, Tre... you still wanna talk?"

--RETALIATION--

Charger slammed the door closed to his new Benz, admiring how the sun made it sparkle like a Christmas tree. The car was the first thing he'd purchased since Gemini'd taken the reigns of the 804 Boyz. True to his word, they'd been loaded up with work that kept him away from his newborn and girl for days at a time, but the benefits were pouring in. The bittersweet part was that Charger couldn't stand Gemini. He'd already had plans to off Patron himself and assume leadership, as Patron had always been an asshole in Charger's eyes. But before he could get his plan together Gemini'd swooped in like a fucking negro cowboy and fucked shit up for him. Charger was heated about how everything had gone down, but knew he couldn't just go head up with Gemini without a rock-solid plan. Everyone knew Gemini wasn't the easiest nigga to touch, so strategic planning had to go into everything. Distracted by his treacherous thoughts, Charger walked up onto his porch didn't notice anyone behind him until he felt something loop round his neck and immediately begin choking him.

"What-" he gasped, grabbing at what felt like a leather belt around his neck.

"Sucka-ass nigga," Gemini's voice hissed in his ear from above him. Charger was snatched around and saw Gemini hanging from the roof of the porch, his hands wrapped around the other end of the belt. "I thought we had a *fucking* understanding. You must've lost yo *muthafuckin* mind tryna kill me, nigga."

Charger managed to shake his head, unable to fight because he was trying to breathe. Gemini had tightened the belt around his neck quickly and Charger knew he'd be dead in under a minute.

"I didn't-not me..." he rasped, feeling lightheaded.

"Of course not *you*, nigga. You ain't got the muthafuckin heart to shoot at me. But your stupid-ass

114

flunkies do. I know them niggaz'll do anything for a fucking bag of Dro."

"No!" Charger shook his head violently. "I swear for *God*, G, I ain't have *shit* to do with that. I don't even know what the fuck you *talking* bout, son."

"Don't swear to God, swear to *me*, nigga. I got waaay less patience," Gemini hissed in the dying man's ear.

"I *swear* to you, G-" Charger gasped, starting to black out, his struggling becoming rapidly weaker.

Gemini thought for a second, then let the belt go and Charger fell on the cold concrete slap like a corpse, gasping. He jumped off the roof and stood up over Charger, glaring down at him.

"If it *won't* you, it was one of your boys. You find out who the *fuck* tried to off me and get at me... or I'll be back nigga. You posed to be watching over them niggaz... you either a part of it, or you slippin." Gemini bent down and snatched Charger's dropped keys. "You owe me a ride, muthafucka." He turned and stormed off, hopping in Charger's car and screeching off, leaving the original owner furious, fearful and grateful at the same time.

JARI

The next day I was walking toward the Chinese food spot around the corner when I heard a car honking at me. I ignored it, used to men-and women-trying to get my attention. Besides, I was too wrapped up in my thoughts lately. Rio had stopped trying to speak to me, which was cool. I wasn't with her little fake shit. Our whole life she'd put on this bullshit front like she felt bad for me for the way our mom treated me. My father was just a run-of-the-mill nigga who jumped ship after my mom had me because he was tired of my mom's drama and ho-ish ways. Rio's dad, mom met when she was on a cruise with her girlfriends 6 months after she had me. She left me with my dad to go to an exotic destination and ended up fucking around on my dad with a local cat. He was married, but my mom got him twisted and seduced him, thinking she'd get in his pocket that way and maybe trick off on a rich guy from another country. That's the way it went at first. Rio's dad was steady sending money to America and coming to see her for the first two years. My dad, who'd always had his suspicions about Rio because she looked so different from us, followed her one night and whooped our mom's ass at the hotel he caught them at. *Rio's* dad, who had *no* idea what was going on, was hurt and left for home. He refused to speak to my mom or have anything to do with Rio until she was old enough to come see him on her own, at 10. She did, and her father showered her with everything she'd missed over the years. She never came back to America until recently. My dad was long gone by then and my mother forever blamed him for messing up her meal ticket with Rio's father, and never stopped taking it out on me. Rio could talk all that shit about how she never looked at me no different, but I know it was all a front. She had everyone else fooled with her bullshit, but not me...

"Yo, Jari!"

I swung out of my dark mood and turned to see Gemini grinning at me. He was driving a new car and it was full of young males who were all hanging out of the window.

I stopped walking, rolling my eyes at Gemini.

"Come on, love, you know I ain't mean for all that shit to go down... I been trying to get at you for a few days, but you ain't been answering your phone... Come hang out with ya boy for awhile," he suggested, licking his lips.

I put my hands on my hips. Even though I don' remember much, the last time I hung out with Gemini had left me in a compromising position. I might have gotten a good blast, but that wasn't enough. I mean, I'm no hoe or nothing, but time is money. I just figured I was blessed with special talents, so I should make money off of them and not end up like all these other broke-down bitches in this neighborhood.

Reading my hesitation, Gemini rolled down the window and held up a knot of money. "C'mon, now... you know your boy gonna take care of you, now. My niggas are just in town for a couple of days and was tryna hang out with a cool-ass female. You know ain't nobody cooler than you," he laughed.

I grinned, sucking up his attention like I always did, totally forgetting about him basically murdering a child recently. Gemini smiled wider and reached over and opened the passenger-side door.

I hopped in and we hit the highway, zooming out to Virginia Beach. It was cool hanging out with all guys cuz they all were competing for my attention and doing stupid shit to impress me, keeping me laughing all day while Gemini kept his arm draped around my shoulder. We ate dinner at an outdoor Italian restaurant, Gemini being funny and feeding me while the other guys made small talk. After a couple glasses of wine I was feeling kinda tipsy and told Gemini.

"Yeah, me too," he agreed, rubbing his eyes. "Fuck it. Let's just get a room on the water and relax,"

"Oh, I'm feelin that idea," I agreed, happy to finally be spending some one-on-one time with him.

Of course, I was wrong, again. When we got to the hotel, I leaned over and whispered, "Where are your boys gonna stay?"

Gemini just laughed like I was a little kid that had told a knock-knock joke. "I drove, ma. Quit playin. They're cool." I closed my mouth, but apprehension had started to creep up on me and whisper in my ear like a chilled wind in November.

As we got in the elevator, his boys seemed to be getting more and more anxious and I thought they were all staring at me funny. I asked Gemini what the fuck was up he just told me they were just anxious to get to the room and blaze up. "Don't worry," he whispered, leaning close to my ear. "I got something special for you for putting up with us all day."

"Other than my money?" I hissed back, not about to be played.

"*Better* than the money..." he said, looking me in the eye.

My heart started racing in anticipation as we all got off the elevator. The suite was huge and beautiful, overlooking Virginia Beach's oceanfront. While his boys instantly whipped out bags of weed and Dutch Masters, Gemini took me out to the patio and handed me a glass of champagne.

"Thank you," I told him, accepting it. I glanced at it and thought I saw some extra fizz in the bottom, but when I blinked it was gone. I gulped the champagne thirstily, and Gemini refilled my glass. He set the bottle down on a table on the patio and slid an arm around me.

"This is nice," I commented, feeling extra good from the champagne. "I wish we could do this all the time."

"Well, maybe not all the time, but we can do it more often," Gemini said, sitting his glass down. He slid the patio doors to and put his arm back around me. "What would you think of getting paid 3 grand a day to hang out with cats like them in there?"

WICKED BLUES Deszion Nasir

I choked on my bubbly and looked at Gemini to see if he was laughing. He wasn't.

"Are you serious?"

"Dead ass, baby. You ain't doing nothin but laying up under Tre waiting for him to make moves. You're fine as hell and your smart... and you're sexy as fuck. You could get paid out the ass just to be yourself... then if Tre starts showing his ass, you got your own shit, you know?"

"He'd flip."

"What the fuck would you tell him for?" Gemini laughed. "Do he tell you what he do when he ain't home?" he asked pointedly, no doubt meaning the night Tre decided not to come home. He still hadn't really disclosed where he'd been...

"No," I said flatly.

"Okay then. You gotta look out for *you*, ma," Gemini pointed out.

The idea was appealing, but I had to make sure Gemini wasn't getting the wrong idea. "I ain't no hoe, Gemini. I'm not tryna fuck for paper."

"Jari. You'd be an escort. Not a hoe. You wouldn't have to do *shit* you ain't wanna do. I mean, if you *feelin* the nigga, that's on you. *I'd* make him pay out the ass for that, but it's an option, not a job requirement. Most of these niggas could never get a chick as bad as you, but they got they head so far up they ass they'd pay thousands just to perpetrate in front of other niggas." Gemini explained. "Do you know how my business jumped off? Making money off cats tryna show-off for other niggas like females. There ain't no future in frontin, but there's *damn* sure a lot of money in it for niggas like you and me,"

What he was saying made sense, and the thought of having power over men and being paid to just dress up and make a dude look good had me excited... excited and kind of horny, actually. Must be the champagne...

"So what's good, you wit it?" Gemini asked me, drinking the rest of his drink.

"Sounds cool. What do I have to do?"

"Nothin. Let me worry about the technical shit... hey, got a present for you," he said, pulling out a needle. My heart started racing and my pussy started throbbing. That's how bad I wanted what he had in his hand. He must've seen my reaction in my eyes because he smiled. He squatted down, took off my sandal and a few moments later my body was engulfed in that familiar warm sensation. I threw my head back and my eyes slid closed, but mixed with the high I was experiencing was an overwhelming need to be touched. I reached out and ran my hands over Gemini's chest, squeezing his nipples. He leaned down and kissed me, then picked me up and carried me back inside the hotel room and over to the bedroom, where he laid me on the bed. I squirmed, unable to keep my hands from drifting over my breasts, down my stomach to my pussy, which was already soaking wet.

"Damn, Gemini. I need some dick, *right* now," I told him, my eyes out of focus.

"I got you ma... that's all taken care of," he promised, his voice faint. I heard buckles and zipping noises as I lay there with my eyes closed, unable to really open them.

"Hurry, *damn* I need that," I moaned. Finally, I felt hands on me, lips on me, sliding over my breasts and fingers inserted in my pussy. I cried out passionately, eager for the fingers to be replaced by Gemini's dick. The fingers were pulled out and a rock-hard dick eased inside of me... but it wasn't Gemini's. I tried to open my heavy lids and saw one of Gemini's boys over me, naked from the waist down as he started stroking in and out of me, moaning about how juicy my pussy was. I wanted to protest, but his dick felt so good to me I ended up dropping my head on the pillow and moaning myself. I got a slight glimpse of the dark room and saw shadows gathered around the bed, beating their dicks like they were waiting their turn. Masturbating phantoms. As I slid further out of reality, I felt myself being turned and twisted. I never knew which dick was inside of my pussy or which one was forcing itself into my already sore ass hole,

120

but I couldn't stop it. I was so overcome with sexual energy I allowed every man in the room to fuck me however he wanted, wherever he wanted, and I got drunk on their cum as the shot their loads in my mouth, on my breasts and all over my body. I just kept screaming for more and more, as it seemed my sexual appetite and my pussy couldn't be satisfied. No orgasm was enough to bring my body down. At one point my head was lifted and powder was shoved up my nose, which I readily snorted, all my inhibitions out the window. I remember being held up and bounced on dicks, slapped on the ass until it was tender, and fucked in my ass until I felt something warm and sticky on the sheets. I finally passed out while one guy was fucking me doggy style. While I was on my way out, he never slowed down…

Hours later I awoke, feeling like I'd been in a car accident. I was so fucked up it took me forever to even roll over. When my eyes focused I could see the men leaving, shaking their heads and wearing shit-eating grins as they handed Gemini large wads of money. When the door closed I looked down at myself and saw my thighs and body, sticky, covered in the semen of many men, and sheets bloody where my ass hole had been ripped open. Gemini heard me and came to the room, staring at me like I was a science experiment, puffing on a cigar.

I coughed when I tried to speak and spit out some thick saliva and semen. I tried to speak again, my throat dry, and rasped "What was in my drink?"

"Just some E. It helps you be more in the mood."

I shook my head, not liking the situation I was in… again. Could I really be mad, though? I couldn't say I wasn't willing. Was it the E that had me like that or did the E simply erase my views that what I'd done was taboo? Then Gemini broke off what looked like barely a third of the money in his hand and tossed the money on the bed. I reached and grabbed it in my trembling hands. My anger subsided when I counted over 4g's. Seeing my reaction to the money, Gemini grinned and straightened up. He walked into the bathroom, turned on

WICKED BLUES Deszion Nasir

the shower, came in and handed me a plush towel. He walked over to the nightstand and started fixing another dose of heroin up.

"What's that for?" I asked, trying to sit up, fronting like I cared, as long as it was for me. He looked at me like I was crazy. "Your next appointment," he said. "Go ahead and get in the shower. Them niggas'll be here in 2 hours."

GEMINI

A week or two later, I was putting some figures together at my desk and smiling. The 804 Boyz's business was paying off. They were taking to the new leadership like soldiers. I know there was some initial resentment, but once them niggas realized how freely the money was flowing, they fell in line. My other investment was paying off pretty well, too. From the first time I'd banged Jari out at the hospital, I knew a snatch like that could make me a lot of money. I had other chicks that worked for me, but niggas won't gonna pay but so much for stripper pussy, no matter how good it was. Jari was a new face and she had gold between her legs. Tre'd already told me about how she got when she got drunk... so I figured I'd put liquor and drugs together and experiment. My hypothesis? Get her high and she'd turned into a Super freak. Cats at the higher end of the game would pay out their ass for a chance to be with a bitch that had no limits. They could do whatever they wanted to her, and they'd drop crazy money for a no-holds-barred bitch like that. Women always think they controlling their men by not giving in to freaky shit. Do what you want, love. Yeah, you right, it's your body. But Jari's body belongs to *me*. And what you don't wanna do with yours, *your* nigga'll pay me your shoe money to do to *her*. Think he won't? Bitch please.

So I tossed Jari a few thousand, even though I made nearly 10 when they wanted the works in combination with a group orgy. If they wanted to tape it, it'd cost more. Now, of course that could only go down when Jari was too faded to notice-and she usually was. She was the most cooperative when she was high, and I kept her full of good shit so she'd be as "agreeable" as I needed her to be. Had to watch it, though... once she switched over to junkie, her stock would fall low. Cats would still pay to fuck a freak, but I couldn't charge as much if she was a fucking crack head. They could get that on the corner. Jari wasn't there yet, but she wanted a fix so bad she was ready to work whenever I called her. She

123

was still deluding herself thinking she was still in control, but we all know the real deal. I pulled her strings with this heroin. She was my puppet and she'd do what the fuck I wanted. If a nigga wanted to fuck her till she bled-and he had enough money, I didn't wanna hear her bitching and crying. She knew what the fucking deal was. Over a few days, I could pay her a smaller and smaller cut by increasing her fixes a little. I didn't have to pay for the heroin, thanks to my new dealings with the 804 Boyz, so basically *everything* was profit for me. I already had a few girls doing what Jari was doing, but they were washed up, fucked out and fucked through. One girl had overdosed and had a heart attack while a dude had her tied up to a table. He was banging her so hard he didn't know she was dead until he untied her and she fell on the floor. I reassured him she was just passed out so I wouldn't have to give him his ends back, and got someone to dump her body in wood chipper I kept in the back of one of the construction properties I was part-owner of. I had to get some new bitches, and Jari was the first of my new batch. I'd started using heroin on her as an experiment. So far, it was working out cuz when she was high she had no morals (irony), and that meant more money. For straight fucking, I charged a grand a head. More than two niggas was 3 a head and included anal. If a muthafucka wanted to get his gorilla shit on and hit her, spank her, bite her, tie her up or some shit like that? 7 stacks a piece. I had to give her a little extra for that shit and a day off-not a *night*- in between, especially since she'd probably end up with some bruises. So far I'd had her leased out to over 25 niggas, so that was a *minimum* of 25 grand a week, made just on her. And that was a slow week. The old heads said it best: the only thing more powerful than money was pussy. And I controlled both.

I kept Tre so busy he barely paid her any attention. Rio'd said she wasn't fucking with him anymore, but I knew she still fucked with the nigga. I guess she was tryna hide it from me so I couldn't gloat about it, but I didn't give a shit. She was doing what I wanted her to do anyway. I met Rio years ago when she came to my club. I could smell the hustle in her as soon as she opened the door. I found out she was real knowledgeable in money markets and multilingual. I made a business connection with her when she came to and soon she was washing all my dirty money as well as making me a shitload of legit money. When she said my money didn't move without her, she was right to a certain extent. Some of my... *transactions* had to be handled personally, and Rio was the one who did that. She made sure the money was right, the product, be it drugs or iron, was what I ordered and she wouldn't hesitated to put a bullet in any nigga who tried to insult her intelligence. Rio was a woman who didn't play with her money by no stretch of the imagination. Her father was caked up and she'd refused to live a lifestyle of anything less than what he'd had her accustomed to living. It was soon common knowledge not to fuck with Rio Souza, and, hence, not to fuck with me. Cuz if Rio couldn't handle shit and it got back to my ears? Shiiit... let's just say I wasn't as patient as Rio. Was I worried about her finding about the shit I had her sister doing? Not for real. Rio talked big shit, but at the end of the day, she knew I had too much shit on her. She was worth more to me alive than dead anyways. The shit I had going with the 804 Boyz was just the tip of the iceberg. Their reach stretched all the way from Washington D.C. down to Miami. With my leadership, my plan was to take that shit all the way to the big money: New York. But a VA nigga couldn't just roll up in New York and I knew that. When I made my move, muthafuckas wouldn't have no choice *but* to deal with me. I'd try to offer them food at *my* table first and avoid drama that wouldn't make me no money, but if they wasn't having it, I had to have enough power to run their asses over. See, my plan was to control the street niggas *and* the white collar niggas, and Rio was helping me move closer to that goal. I knew the streets, but Rio knew the white collars and their world. I needed her brain and she needed my power.

As far as Teasha went, she was wifey. The way she held a nigga down from day one wasn't shit a nigga like me could overlook. Despite all my dirt, I had a public image, and having a wifey was good for that image. To the naked eye, Teasha perfect for that role: She was gorgeous and she'd stand out in a crowd when we appeared at public events; despite where I met her, she was educated and well spoken so she wouldn't scare the white people, and she catered to my ass like I was a king, so I ain't have no problems treating her like a queen. She was full of smiles and love whenever I seen her and she never-not one time-brought me any form of drama.

So, to reward her for that, tonight I was taking her out to an upscale reggae club in Virginia Beach to celebrate her birthday. I'd rented the whole club and had taken her to get a dress designed especially for the event so no other chick'd be wearing her outfit. Ya'll know how broads were with that bullshit. I never minded spending a shitload of money on her because 1) she never asked me for a dime and 2) even though I did fucked up shit-most she never knew about- when I was around her, she brought me the only peace I usually had in my life.

When I pulled up to her apartment, she opened the door before I even had a chance to knock. I was so shocked I was stuck on pause for a minute as I stared at the woman in front of me. The woman standing in Teasha's doorway had long, shiny, fire-red hair that hung in a sheet down the sides of her face with china bags hovering over her bright green eyes, the contrasting colors making them kinda glow. The dress she had on was snow-white, made her deep tanned skin glow like she'd just come off of a beach and clung to her little body for dear life, taking her small body proportions and pimping them out. She had on 6 inch heels that made her look like a chick straight off the red carpet. A white cashmere throw was draped over her bare shoulders, which had a jeweled fire flame accenting it. She parted her blood-red lips and smiled at my shocked face.

126

"Oh, I guess you like my outfit, right?" she teased, turning around so I could see how her dress dipped low in the back, revealing her bronze skin down to the curve in her waist, where the dress's material suddenly took a firm hold of her ass and choked it all the way down to the top of her thighs, where it ended and allowed her toned legs to escape.

"*Dayum*," was all I could stutter, which caused a flash of relief in her eyes as she beamed up at me.

Teasha laughed, and reached up to kiss me. I bent down and she pressed her soft lips against my cheek. "Thanks for taking me out,"

"Shiit... the way you lookin? Thanks for letting me," I joked as she closed and locked her door.

"Where are Jari and Tre?" she asked, looking behind me and peering inside my empty car.

"They gonna meet us there... You can make that girl jealous later," I grinned at her. She paused, then a guilty smile popped out.

"Stop frontin, girl. I know Jari gets on your nerves. She get on *everyone's* nerves," I admitted.

"Well, why do Tre keep dealing with her?" Teasha demanded.

I shrugged. "You'd have to ask him... but not tonight," I added, opening the door for her.

All the way to the club she was fidgeting, so I reached over and pulled a blunt out of the compartment by my seat. "You wanna calm down a lil bit?" I asked her. She looked at my hand like it was full of monkey shit.

"I don't smoke." she said pointedly, her tone telling me there won't no point in saying anything else about it.

"Cool wit me," I smiled, putting it away. Another boost for my image, I figured.

When we pulled up to the front of the club, I stopped in front of the club for V.I.P. parking and the cat parking the cars opened Teasha's door for her. I watched, grinning, as all the small money people were trying to see inside the car. As Teasha stood up, cameras flashed and everyone tried to figure

127

out who she was. She looked like money and everyone knew it. When I came around the side of the car and she laced her little arm with mine, the chatter picked up. This was the first public event I'd been to since my shooting, and the story was all over the 7 cities about the little red-head who'd been to the hospital everyday while I was in there. Teasha'd been interviewed by the radio station and local news, so she was official, now. Her 15 minutes of fame had her mind reeling, I could tell, but I just used that humbleness to persuade her to tell the press what I wanted them to hear, further tightening my grip in the area. Whether or not you loved *me*, everyone loved *Teasha*, and that meant more power for me.

We were ushered into the club without security even bothering with the V.I.P. list. Before I could say anything, we were taken to a private section to the left of the stage where Buju Banton was going to perform. I put my hand on the small of Teasha's back to let her go up the steps ahead of me. As I did, some random-pussy chick crossed the roped-off section and threw her arms around me like she didn't see Teasha, or at least didn't give a fuck.

"Gemini!" she screamed, jumping up to kiss me on the face. "Oh, my God, I haven't seen you in *forever*! I changed my number and forgot to tell you and shit, so I figured that's why you never called me-" Before she could finish screaming her sentence, Teasha's child-sized hand powered by grown woman fuel met the girl's face with an open-handed slap that sent her black, shiny weave flying out around her head like a halo as her head spun around. Her body followed her head and crashed down the two stairs she'd managed to clear before Teasha'd smacked the cowboy shit out of her. The crowd roared out in laughter as the girl fell back awkwardly, landing in a heap, her legs flying open, exposing her non-manicured pussy-which everyone could see because she didn't have any drawers on. I raised an eyebrow and looked at Teasha in time to see the flame of madness simmer down in her eyes until they returned to their normal green color.

WICKED BLUES Deszion Nasir

"You finished?" I asked her, grinning as security pulled the dazed girl to her feet and led her away.

"For now," she commented, raking her fingers through her hair to re-tame it. She turned and followed the bouncer to our table.

I sat down across from her and smiled. She waited for the waitress to pour us two glasses of champagne before she looked at me like "What?"

"Let me find out you're possessive." I joked.

"I'm not possessive. I'm territorial," she corrected me, picking her glass up.

"Explain the difference," I told her, watching her lips surround a corner of the glass and her tongue penetrate the gold liquid.

"Possessive people are paranoid that someone'll take what they have; territorial people are simply protecting what's theirs."

I grinned. "You think I need protecting?"

"Everyone needs protecting from *something*," Teasha said pointedly, sipping her drink again.

"So... you gonna protect me from *all* the broads that are tryna get at me?" I went on, amused.

"*That* wasn't about protection. *That* was about respect. She disrespected my position, so I touched her. But to answer your question, I'd protect you from whatever danger I could see, male, female or other, because you'd do the same for me." she finished, looking into my eyes.

I didn't know about all *that*, but it was nice to hear her say shit like that. I just smiled at her, licked my lips and leaned close to her. "Happy birthday," I told her, before leaning in and pressing my lips against hers. Her lips were hot but the champagne had cooled her tongue, sending a chill through me that made my dick rise slightly. She slid her small hands behind my head and pulled me closer to her.

"I see you couldn't wait for us," a voice spoke up. I pulled away from Teasha and saw Tre and Jari standing at our table, Tre grinning widely. Jari had a sleeveless pants suit on

129

that showed off her figure and big breasts, and her hair flowed in a mass of curls behind her, held back on either side by two clips sparkling with diamonds. She had a smile plastered on her face, but when her eyes swept over Teasha looking like a princess, I saw a look of surprise, then jealousy zip through them momentarily.

Teasha caught it, too, and smiled widely. "Hey, guys, thanks for coming," she told them both, first hugging Jari-who was thrown by her gesture and froze-then Tre, who hugged her back and sniffed her like a dog. "Damn, you smell good." Teasha laughed, slapped Tre lightly on the arm and scooted next to me at the curved table to make room for them.

"Sit down," I said to Jari, but she looked at the spot next to Teasha like it was contaminated with Ebola. Tre cleaned up the awkward moment and slid in the seat first. Jari sat on the end, and by the way Teasha was joking around with Tre, I could tell she was wondering if she'd made a wise choice.

For the next hour or so, we all drank and ate and relaxed, the drinks loosening everyone up. Jari stopped looking sour and started whispering in Tre's ear, and me and Teasha spoke to the crowds of people that kept coming to the table, wishing her a happy birthday every time the DJ made a Happy Birthday shout out to her.

"Do you know all them people?" Jari asked finally, unable to help herself.

"No… you probably know more people in this whole place than I know in Virginia," Teasha admitted easily, stirring the drink a waitress had just placed in front of her.

Jari snorted. "Most likely."

Teasha looked Jari in the eye as she picked up my lighter and lit the Newport I was putting in my mouth. "I wonder why *none* of them decided you were worth speaking to, though," she said innocently. I choked as I was inhaling, my laugh loud. Tre shook his head and Jari narrowed her eyes.

"I guess they're all too busy looking at Gemini's newest circus freak, *bitch*," she snapped, snaking her neck.

Smoothly and calmly, Teasha lifted her glass of vodka and cranberry juice and tossed it in Jari's lap. Jari screamed and jumped up, banging her knee on the table. Enraged, she reached over and grabbed a handful of Teasha's hair, but by the time Tre reached for Jari to untangle her fingers from Teasha's fire-engine-colored hair , he had to jump back to avoid the steak knife in Teasha's hand as she took a swipe at Jari. He toppled over to the right out of his seat and Jari let Teasha's hair go and fell backwards, tripping on her high heels and toppling down the V.I.P. stairs screaming.

I snatched the knife out of Teasha's hand and slammed it on the table. "Handle that," I snapped at Tre, who was already climbing down the stairs to help Jari up. I looked at Teasha, shaking my head. She was hailing a frightened waitress over to our table. "I need another drink," she told her calmly, and the girl teleported away to fill Teasha's order. Teasha straightened her dress and flipped her hair over her shoulders, raking it back, expressionless, while I stared at her.

"It's *my* birthday," she shrugged, waving my look off.

"You can't be wildin' like that, baby," I shook my head at her. "That shit ain't ladylike."

"*That* bitch ain't no lady," she hissed back heatedly. "I'm sick of that skank and her shitty-ass attitude. I know she *wants* you, but she's not gonna *get* you, so she's flipping on me. If you and Tre ain't gonna check her ass, I *will*,"

I studied Teasha's face for a minute. "My bad, love. You right. I *shoulda* said something before now, but I ain't think that kiddie shit bothered you, baby."

"I mean, she do that dumb shit *every* time I see her. Are you *fucking* her already or something?" Teasha ranted on, turning her heated green gaze at me and narrowing her eyes to slits, her head tilting slightly to the side. I knew *that* look well. That's the universal woman look for "Nigga-I-wish-you-*WOULD*-answer-that-question-wrong." Now was not the time for the truth. Probably never would be fucking with me…

"Teasha. Jari's a hoe. I could never deal with no female with her bad habits. Tre's stuck thinking her can make a hoe a housewife, but you know how that shit is gonna go down at the end of the day. I deal with her on the strength of my *nigga*, but if she gonna keep affecting you like this, I'll have to cut her ass off."

"What about Tre?"

"Hey, that man gotta come to terms with that nonsense in his own time. He don't gotta bring her around *us*, though. They not married or nothing."

Teasha grinned. "You acting like you in *love* or something, talking about cutting your boy off." she half-joked, her eyes searching mines.

"I 'on know about *love*…" I said, sitting back. It's whatever with that shit she was yapping about now; I was just glad she was off her killer shit for the moment.

"Why not?"

I shrugged with a thoughtful look on my face, knowing I had to answer this question carefully or I could kiss some birthday pussy goodbye. "I've never *been* in love, so how would I know?" I said truthfully.

Teasha tilted her head to the side again, something I noticed she did when she was deep in thought, studying me. "When you're in love, you'll know," she assured me. She leaned in toward me again and kissed me, her hands on either side of my face.

I felt bad for her. Niggas like me never fell in love. Love was a weakness I couldn't afford to have. But whatever me and Teasha had-be it love or not-was close enough for me. For now.

JARI

I snatched away from Tre's grip as I stormed into the women's bathroom to get myself together. He followed right behind me.

"*Damn*, nigga," a girl protested as he hit her with the door.

"Walk or crawl, bitch," he snapped. She opened her mouth to say something, but the look in his eyes unnerved her quickly. She looked down at his balled fist, then at my disheveled appearance, sniffed like he stank, said "C'mon, girl," to her bathroom buddy and the two of them hurried out of the bathroom.

"What the *fuck* is up with you, J?" Tre yelled.

"Don't scream at me, nigga," I hollered, rolling my neck and shoving him against the door. He pushed me back.

"Jari, don't fuckin *play* with me, right now," Tre boomed, balling his other hand into a tight fist. "What the fuck is up with all the jealousy bullshit? You tryna get at that muthafucka right in my *face*? Is that what the fuck this is?!"

"*No*," I yelled back, wiping traitor tears from my eyes.

"Then what the *fuck* is wrong with you?" he demanded, taking a step toward me as I ripped a paper towel from the dispenser and wiped my leaky eyes.

I took a staggered breath. "I'm pregnant, Tre."

The bombshell took all the fire out of his eyes rapidly.

"What?"

"Pregnant, knocked up, *embrazada*, nigga," I snapped, tossing a soaked paper towel in the trash and snatching another one to stop the tears from flowing. "Damn, I can't stop crying all the fucking time…"

"Pregnant… you gonna have a baby?"

"That's what usually happens at the end," I sniffed sarcastically. I'd found out yesterday when I threw up all day and night. At first I'd thought I'd just gotten a bug, but the

133

little bit of common sense I had left told me to run to Dollar General on the corner and snatch a test or three up. All had either turned pink, showed two lines or shown a positive sign. As I sat on the toilet, horrified, I counted backwards. I couldn't have been pregnant by any of the cats Gemini'd put me onto... it had only been a couple of weeks... there were only two other options... and one was sitting at the table with the bitch who'd just tried to stab me.

"*Fuck,*" Tre yelled, grabbing me in a bear hug. His anger was gone and replaced by joy. "Oh, shit... that's why you been in such a shitty mood... damn, I'm sorry, baby! Damn!" he kept saying over and over. I let him drag me out of the bathroom, past the girls waiting impatiently outside, through the crowd and back to our table. Security stepped in front of us, but seeing the excited look on Tre's face, Gemini held up his hand and the two bouncers backed away.

"Yo... we apologize, man. She couldn't help herself... hormones and shit... she pregnant, man," Tre boasted, excited. I locked my eyes on Gemini's face for his reaction. He raised a brow then grinned.

"What the fuck *you* gon' do with a seed, nigga?" he asked, laughing. Teasha shoved him out of the way and hugged me, like we hadn't just been in a fight.

"Oh, my God, a *baby*? You gotta let me throw you a shower. We have to go shopping... I'm sorry about earlier, girl, I totally feel your stress..." Teasha was just going non-stop and the people who'd just witnessed our fight were staring at us like we were crazy.

"No more drinks for you," Tre said, taking my champagne glass out of my hand. "I'll go get you some juice-" He hopped up from the table and moved purposefully toward the bar.

"Wait! I need another drink, too-!" Teasha hopped up and rushed off after him, talking about what colors to buy and shit.

Me and Gemini stared at each other. "Don't you have anything to say?" I demanded.

134

WICKED BLUES Deszion Nasir

"Congratulations?" Gemini shrugged.

"That's it?"

"How far along are you?"

"About a month, probably a little more I'm thinking," I said pointedly, looking him in the eye.

He nodded. "You still got a few months of work left in you, then. Shit, niggas love pregnant pussy… you can get like, *double* paper for that shit."

Stricken, I glanced around, making sure no one was listening, then leaned forward. "I can't keep doin that shit, Gemini."

"Why? It ain't like you give a fuck about that kid, Jari, quit playing."

"That's not the point. Tre does."

"Look, he don't gotta know no more than he do now. *You* need to stack your paper before that bastard pops out."

"What if it's yours?" I whispered harshly.

"Then you most *definitely* need to stack your paper," he laughed, rubbing out his cigarette butt in an ashtray.

"Oh, so, you don't care if it's yours?"

"What the fuck would *I* care for?"

"It'd be *yours*, nigga." I hissed. What the fuck was this?

"*Please.* I give less of a fuck than *you* do about that shit." He waved his hand dismissively at me.

"What about Tre?"

"Bitch, that's *your* nigga," Gemini laughed. "That nigga ain't gonna do shit to *me*. He might whoop *your* ass, though."

"I'm not working no more. No more escort shit," I said defiantly, sitting back and looking around to make sure no one was paying us any particular attention.

Now Gemini leaned forward. "If you don't work, you don't get your fix."

"I'm stopping that, too" I declared, to which he laughed.

"Jari, save the dumb shit for Tre. You don't wanna stop no more than I want you too."

"I *am*," I insisted. Gemini nodded, staring me in the eye, then reached in his pocket, pulled out a small package wrapped up in a paper towel and slid it across the table to me.

"Then I guess you don't want this, huh?" he asked, grinning wickedly.

I stared down at the paper towel and my forehead broke out in a sweat instantly.

"Go ahead and take it before your man gets back," Gemini insisted, leaning back in his seat.

With trembling hands I reached out and touched the paper, feeling something long and slim underneath it. "You just keep this shit in your pocket?" I demanded. He simply grinned, and I imagined it was the same smile the Devil gave people before they shook hands with him. I swallowed as I clutched it. "I'm gonna go throw it in the trash," I told him, shaking and hoping no one else could see it.

"Okay," Gemini shrugged, taking a swig of his drink, his ice blue eyes still on me, burning holes into my soul.

I broke our gaze and stood up, shoving the napkin in my purse. I was starting away from the table to the bathroom when Gemini reached out and grabbed my hand.

I turned back to him. "Be at the spot first thing in the morning. You gotta full day," he said, his cold eyes burning into mine. I snatched my arm away and hurried for the bathroom. I heard Tre's voice asking "Where she going?" from somewhere behind me, to which Gemini replied: "She had to pee again. You know how pregnant chicks are." I blocked his voice out and damn near burst into the bathroom, quickly locking myself in a stall, glad no one else was in there. The other partiers were busy screaming as the headliner made his way to the stage. I dropped the spoon and the metal sound echoed loud in my ears as it bounced into the other stall. It would've made more sense to just walk into the other stall and retrieve it, but the way my mind was functioning-or malfunctioning- the most direct route to my

136

salvation was by folding my long body onto the dirty floor of the club and grabbing for the spoon frantically. When my hands clutched the cold metal my heart jumped. As the heavy bass line filled the building, I frantically prepared the heroin like Gemini'd showed me, found a vein and tried to stop my hands from trembling as I slid the needle in, too desperate for a fix to notice the sting of the needle. Moments later I was warm and slid down onto the toilet as I leaned my head on the stall wall, welcoming the warm sensation. It flooded my senses and removed all the fear of being pregnant and not knowing who the father was. I drop of saliva fell from my lip onto my arm but I was feeling too good to wipe it away. I was too busy gliding and convincing myself that I wasn't a junkie. I was simply freeing myself. Some people fucked, some gambled, some spent money. I only did heroin. Nobody got hurt and I only did it a few times a day. I was fine. I could stop whenever I wanted... I'd make some excuse up to tell Tre about me being stuck behind the crowd when the show started. With me being pregnant, I knew he wouldn't question me or be checking in my purse tonight.

I dropped the paper towel and something went *clink!* on the bathroom floor. I forced my eyes to focus and picked it up. It was another needle and some more heroin. I struggled to glance at the trash can where women disposed of used tampons and started to shove the bundle in there, but I stopped halfway. Someone might come in here after me and see it. I placed the bundle in my purse, telling myself I'd throw it away later...

Maybe.

TEASHA'S STORY

It was after 3 in the morning when we finally left the club and I was somewhere in the middle of tipsy and drunk, leaning back in the passenger seat of Gemini's car as he sped along the highway. It'd taken us forever to get out of there because everyone wanted to talk to Gemini, get his attention and get a close-up glance of me. Some of the common bitches were relentless, trying to slip him numbers behind my back or right in my face. Gemini refused everyone, never once taking his arms from around me, even telling one chick "Did you see how she laid that other bitch out earlier? You want some of that? Fuck outta here,"

I felt like I was Cinderella tonight, and it had been the best birthday party I'd ever had. Actually, it's been the only birthday party I'd ever had. As Gemini's car cut through the thick night, I let my mind drift back to the last time I'd tried to have a birthday party…

I was 12 years old, and I was still living with my parents in Columbus. My daddy had promised me a birthday party this year, but as usual, he wasn't in bed when I ran into my parents' room that morning. My little feet stopped short as I saw the back of a man that wasn't my father sweating as he grunted and made the headboard my father paid for slam against the wall, adding new cracks to the old cracks. I remember seeing the sweat drip down that man's back and soak into the dingy white sheets as my mother's foot popped into view. I knew it was her foot because I saw the scar from when she'd stepped on a glass bottle in a drunken run to the bathroom. I was transfixed to the spot as the man seemed to be pounding in and out of my mother like he was running a race. After a few minutes he yelled out, shivered, and collapsed on top of her. Less than a minute later my mother was tapping him on the shoulder roughly, asking for her money. He was either ignoring her or sleep, but my mom wasn't liking either option and began hitting the man, cursing, yelling and demanding her money. As silent as a shadow, my father appeared behind me, a gun in one hand, a smoking blunt in his other hand. Horrified, I waited to see what my father was going to do to the man, and I trembled in the corner of the hallway. My dad narrowed his green eyes, pushed past me, walked up to the man, raised the gun and brought it down against the back of the man's head. He yelped out and scrambled to get out of the bed, succeeding in falling to the floor, tangled in the cum-stained sheets. My dad wasn't tall, but he was intimidating and his body was small, compact and muscular like a shark from stints in prison. The man was shaking as he looked up into my dad's bright eyes. "Give up the fuckin scratch, chump," my dad growled, putting his blunt in his mouth and cocking his gun. The man hurriedly stuck a shaking hand in his pocket and pulled out a wallet. He handed my father a fistful of wrinkled money. My dad snatched it, and while he was counting it, the man grabbed his clothes, his bleeding head and ran out of the room, damn near knocking me over on his way out of our small house. When I looked back at my parents, my mother was still stretched out on the bed. My dad was stuffing the money in his back pocket and tapping my mom on the leg. "Wanda," he said over and over. "Wanda... get your drunk ass up and fix me something to eat, now. "

"Okay, Cliff, okay..." my mom slurred. She sat up, her once long, curly red hair now a huge, poofy mess flattened on one side of her head. She slid off the edge of the bed until her size 4 feet touched the ground. My mom was barely 5 feet tall and her pussy was apparently just as wide. This morning wasn't any different than most mornings I'd seen since I was old enough to remember. My dad was counting money with his boy and/or bagging up, and my mom was on her back. Neither of them paid me any attention. I used to wonder why they didn't just give me up until a couple of years ago when it hit me: they *never* paid me no attention, I never caused them any trouble, so I guess I wasn't in their way enough to make them want to get rid of

139

me. Besides, I kept the house clean. Well, as clean as a 12-year-old girl could, anyways. My mom never did anything but drink, fuck and go into nods. My father walked back past me, like normal, went back in the extra bedroom, closed the door and soon I heard the money machine spinning again. I sighed, went back to my room and dug through my clothes to put on some clothes that smelled halfway clean and almost fit. After the drama, I didn't have time to eat anything- not like there was anything in the kitchen to eat or drink but moldy bread and Colt 45s anyway- and left to walk to school, clutching my books and notebooks close to me to block out the light rain, as I didn't have a coat or book bag to protect me or my stuff from the elements. And like you already know, I lived in Columbus, so it was cold outside. The only way I stayed warm was to run to school. I know it made me look straight crazy, but I wasn't thinking about how I looked, only about getting inside a semi-warm building. Besides, over the last couple of years I'd developed strong leg muscles and could make it to school in under 10 minutes.

As usual, I ignored everyone staring at me and walked straight to my locker. I know my clothes ain't fit right, my hair was a weird color, and everything I had on was played out, but there wasn't nothing I could do about it. My father had already told me to be cool and not bring no shit to the house, and after 12 years under my dad's heavy hand I knew that meant suck the shit up people threw at me and move on. For some reason, though, it seemed like more people than usual were staring at me. I was thinking maybe my period had come on early again and had stained my clothes. It was irregular because I was so small but no one ever gave me money to keep sanitary supplies on hand for emergencies, so unless my mother's cycle was on and I could steal hers, I'd have to change into the spare pair of old panties I kept pinned inside my pants and use toilet paper as a pad until I could get to the nurse's office. I ducked into the nearest bathroom. A quick survey told me I hadn't come on my period, and I didn't look any stranger than usual, so I was

140

stumped about all the extra attention. I made sure my $.50 butterfly bow was showing over my long ponytail-the only thing I was proud of was my long hair- and went back into the hallway. I had just spun the combination on my locker when suddenly my head slammed into the locker next to mine. Stunned, I shook my head to clear it and jerked around. A girl a few years older than me named Sharell was glaring down me, hands on her hips. "What the hell is wrong with you?" I demanded, grabbing my head.

"Your nasty-ass *momma* is what's wrong with me," Sharell said loudly. Everyone in the hallway turned and looked at us. I swallowed, knowing this wasn't going to go down easy. "My momma *caught* something from her boyfriend and *he* said he got it from ya dirty-pussy momma. And don't even *waste* yo time denying it. Everybody in Columbus know yo momma a *hoe*, Teashauna. My momma boyfriend ain't the only nigga yo momma done burnt."

"Fuck you Sharell. Even if that *is* true, what is you in *my* face for?" I demanded.

"Cuz ya trick-ass momma *also* stole the man wallet, which was *my* momma money, so now the shit done got real muthafuckin *personal*," Sharell said, shoving me into the locker again. I shoved her back, hard. I don't think she expected me to be that strong, being I was so small, but I took after my father as far as power went, and Sharell wind-milled her arms backward and fell into the crowd that was now surrounding us. They caught her and tossed her back in my direction, eager for a fight. I took advantage of her stumbling and swung, catching her in the chin. She went down on her left side, grunting. Seeing their girl stretched out, 2 of Sharell's girls came at me. I glanced around, snatched Sharell's dropped book bag up and swung it over my head. It snapped out of my hand and went with one of the girls on her journey to the tile and up the hall as the heavy bag connected with her left temple. I tried to get away but the crowd wouldn't let me, as the last girl was reaching for me. I looked around me and saw a desk that a teacher had in the hall for

WICKED BLUES Deszion Nasir

students who were acting up. I reached, grabbed at it, grunted, and lifted the whole desk up and swung it around. I hit another student before connecting with my target. Both of them were on the ground, unconscious and bleeding as the screaming crowd fell silent at the sight of blood all over the floor. Cold fear gripped me as I realized what I'd done and I dropped the desk with a loud *clang!* Sharell, still on the ground, screamed "That's okay, *bitch*, my daddy on the way to yo house *right now* to fuck yo shit up! Crazy *bitch*!" Her revelation coupled with the sight of teachers fighting to break through the crowd sent me running into an empty classroom. I slammed the door closed, then, with a burst of pure adrenaline, pushed the teacher's desk in front of the door just as teachers started banging on it. I ran to the window, tried to open it, but it was the kind that only rolled open a few inches. I grabbed the teacher's chair and threw it through the glass. As soon as the chair cleared I was climbing out of the window. I cut myself, but I was too scared to pay attention to it as I jumped out of the bushes and ran home, leaving tears and drops of bloods behind me as I ran.

I made it home in half my usual time, soaked and out of breath in the now pouring rain. I burst in the house and interrupted my daddy and his boys wrapping plastic around bricks of cocaine. My daddy was so surprised his blunt fell out of his mouth and onto the roll of plastic wrap.

"Teasha what the fuck is wrong with you?" he demanded, jumping up to save the plastic from melting while the other men stared at my breasts, the only things growing on my small body, transparent under the wet shirt I had on. I had on ripped underwear so a new bra had been out of the question when my breasts began growing prematurely over a year ago. I used to steal my mother's underwear, but all she had were thongs and they looked like they weren't cleaned properly and her bras were too big for me, so when I couldn't steal underwear from the Chinese store, I just went without. Luckily, I didn't grow much other than in my chest area, so I washed the two pairs of panties I had out every night in the

WICKED BLUES Deszion Nasir

sink when I took a bath until they ripped. I was able to sew up the pair I had on now, but the other pair was unsalvageable.

"Sharell... daddy..." I panted, trying to get the story out and catch my breath at the same time.

"Who the fuck is Sharell?" my daddy demanded, becoming more pissed off by the second.

I took a deep breath and tried again. "Girl at school... said momma took her daddy's money... her daddy's on her way here right now... I think I killed-" I was cut off as my daddy jumped up and ran back to his bedroom. His boys started snatching up the work they were wrapping and putting everything away. I followed my daddy and saw him snatch another man I'd never seen off my mother. The man, who was more than half drunk, fell to the floor, cursing with a rock-hard dick and yelling he wasn't paying because he didn't cum. My dad's response was to kick him in his naked ass with his steel-toed boot and tell him to get out before he blew his asshole out through his dick. The man sobered up just enough to grab his clothes and run out of the house naked while Daddy's workers laughed at him.

My father turned his anger toward my mother. "Wanda, you robbing niggas?" he yelled.

"What?"

"I'ma ask you one more time before I throw you the ass whooping that nigga was about to catch," Daddy snarled through clenched teeth. "A couple days ago. You pocket some chump's wallet after ya'll done ya'll business?"

I could see my mother struggling to clear her mind long enough to remember what happened two days ago. My dad decided to help her out by hitting her in the head with a clock sitting on the nightstand. She screamed and cowered into a tight ball, her memory flowing back rapidly as she screamed out she was sorry.

"Sorry? Bitch, you got that nigga on his way over here about some fuckin *change*? While I'm *working*? Where's the fuckin money? *I* didn't see no extra money come in here

2 days ago. What you do with it? Shoot it up your fucking arm? You took my money and sent it up your arm again, Wanda?" my Daddy screamed, kicking my mother in the side. She screamed and I ran into my room. I snatched open my drawer and grabbed the money I'd been saving up for a pair of shoes that fit and a matching coat and ran back in my parents' room.

"Look, Daddy, look. Here, I got this for you," I told him, tugging on his shirt, making sure I wasn't raising my voice or showing my panic or fear. I'd learned very early that panic and fear brought out the worst in my father, and I'd avoided many beatings by acting like nothing he did scared me or seemed wrong, even though most of it left me shivering inside. A few years before my hair was even falling out, but I'd since learned to control my emotions most of the time and mastered blending into my world so I could survive.

My father stopped kicking my mother and turned and looked at me like I was crazy until he saw the bills in my hand. He stared at them, then snatched them from me. "Where'd you get this?" he asked, counting it quickly. "It's like, $200 and some change here…"

"Doin' other kids' homework. I was gonna get me a coat and some shoes, but you know, it's gonna be spring soon; flip flops are like a dollar at the dollar store," I said, like it was no big deal. My dad was already shoving the money in the pocket of his brand new jeans. Then he did something I'd never seen him do in my whole life: He smiled at me. I'll never forget how I felt at that moment. My mother was laying on the floor, crying softly, her alcohol-tinged blood dripping onto the threadbare carpet. The house was falling apart, my father had on brand-new everything and my hard earned money in his pocket, but seeing him smile made me forget all of that.

"Aight," my daddy said simply, then turned and walked out of the room. I ran over and tried to help my mother off of the floor, but she surprised me by shoving me off of her.

144

"You got some more money?" she hissed, wiping her blood mouth with the back of her dirty hand.

"What? No, I gave him all of it. I just wanted to get him off of you."

"You so damn stupid. *Never* give a nigga shit he don't ask for. *Especially* your damn daddy. *You* just brought a shitload of trouble on yourself," she predicted.

"But he smiled at me," I protested.

"I bet he *did*," my mother smirked at me, pushing me away from her as she stood up and stumbled toward the bathroom. She glanced at me one more time, shaking her head and mumbling "Stupid-ass bitch," before slamming the door.

Stuck in a confusing adult world, I went in my room, took off my wet clothes and put on a half-clean t-shirt. My intention was to wait for my mother to come out of the bathroom so I could take a hot shower and warm my chilled body, but either she was taking forever or I was just mentally and physically exhausted, because when I snapped awake later, it was pitch black outside. What woke me up was the sound of my door clicking closed. Nobody ever paid me enough attention to come in my room so whenever someone did, it got my attention whether I was awake or not.

As I sat up and rubbed my eyes, I could make out my dad's form. "Hey, daddy," I mumbled, grinning a sleepy grin at him.

"Hey, T," he told me, standing at the edge of the bed and looking down at me. "Hey, I need to talk to you."

"About what? Did that girl's dad come over here?"

"Don't worry about that nigga. He won't be bothering nobody around here. Neither will his daughter," he said in a voice that chilled me. I swallowed and waited for him to finish what he came to say.

"Look… if you cain't tell… your momma got a problem, T. She's a junkie. And she cain't do what daddy need her to do no more. But you know that, though. You been cooking and cleaning in here for a couple of years now, right?"

I nodded, wondering where the conversation was going. Momma being a sorry-ass housewife wasn't new information to anyone who'd met her for longer than 8 seconds.

"So... I came to talk to you about you picking up your momma's responsibilities, T," Daddy said, sitting on the edge of the bed. It sagged heavily under his weight and I had to keep my body from sliding into him. My bed wasn't really a bed. It was an old cot I'd found in the trash in front of a house where the family'd been thrown out. I was tired of sleeping on the cold floor with the roaches who wanted the whole floor for themselves so I'd drug the whole thing 5 blocks home in the middle of December last year, then stolen someone's sheets from a Laundromat on the other side of town a few days later. No one in my house ever noticed or said a thing.

"What else do you need me to do?" I asked. I already cleaned up the best I could.

"Well...you know your momma used to be pretty, T. Almost as pretty as you are now, right? A lot of men around here pay daddy a *lot* of money to play with your momma's 'pretty', T... you understand what I'm telling you?" he asked, looking me in the eye.

I went into a panic. "Daddy... you want me to... let them men touch on me and stuff?"

"They gonna wanna do more than touch you, T," he admitted with no shame. "But it ain't really no bad thing, for real. All your friends do that shit with these ignorant niggas out there for free and they get pregnant and get STD's and shit... and they don't got they daddies lookin' out for them. Shit, how many of your friends even *got* they daddies at home?"

"None," I admitted, my confusion and fear working overtime.

"*Exactly*. You think I'ma let something happen to you? That right there-" he pointed between my legs-"is the most powerful shit in the world if you learn how to use it, T. I'm not gonna let you end up like your momma, you hear me?"

I nodded.

"Good. Good," he said, standing up. He looked around the room, then down at me. He reached down and pulled my covers back, peering at my t-shirt. "That's cool for now. I'll take you shopping when the sun come up instead of going to school. You need some new stuff anyway. See? This shit already working out, ain't it?" My daddy smiled again and opened my door and walked out.

I was terrified and scared at the same time. Everything in me said this wasn't what was supposed to be happening, but look at the world I'd grown up in. To me, I was simply being initiated into adulthood, my destiny. My daddy was just looking out for me. Well, that's what I told myself, but when my door opened again and I saw one of the guys who'd been wrapping up my daddy's bricks earlier breaking his neck to see inside my room, I panicked all over again, backing up against the wall on top of my cot and clutching the thin blanket.

My daddy stepped into the room, counting what looked like several $20 bills. "Look nigga, be easy. That's my kid, yo."

"I will, I will," the sweaty man said, nodding and licking his lips at me. My daddy looked at me. "You alright, T. Just relax or it'll hurt, okay?" He waved the money in the air. "Remember, we goin shopping in the morning," he promised before pulling my door closed. The man already had his shirt off and was unbuckling his belt.

"Damn, I'm the first, huh?" he said, grinning like he'd won something. He had to be in his mid-twenties. He came over to my bed pulled my covers off the bed. He stared at me a second before sliding his hands up my legs and under my t-shirt. He leaned over and kissed my neck, sliding me

147

down on the bed as I squeezed my eyes closed. He slid his fingers inside of me, ripping my hymen and inflicting pain on my tiny body. I tried to pretend I was my mother and just laid there like I'd seen her do, just waiting for it to be over, but I wasn't that good at pretending. Maybe it was because I wasn't drunk or high, or maybe it was just because deep down, I knew a 20-something-year old man had no business lying on top of me, spreading my legs apart, and grunting as he struggled to force himself inside my vagina. It hurt and I felt my body tearing in protest as if my virginity was screaming in panic and trying to hold onto me. The man leaned on his arms and began moving in and out of me, slowly at first but he picked up his pace quickly. I heard the cot banging against the thin walls and with every hit I felt some of my fear turn to anger. How could my daddy sit there and listen to a man do this to me? Was he going to come try me out next? Fuck *that*. Better yet, fuck *this*…

As the man grunted and pounded away, I stretched my thin arm under my pillow and under my limp mattress until my fingers ran across cold metal. I kept a steak knife under my mattress ever since our house got broken into a few months ago. Daddy shot the crack heads who were trying to get the dope he kept in the freezer, but I was so frightened I'd wet my bed, and ever since I'd kept the knife there.

The man was hammering away now, moaning about how tight my pussy was, his eyes closed in pleasure. When my knife sank into his side they popped open in pain and he jerked, trying to sit up. I snatched my knife out and slammed it into his chest. He yelled out and slapped my face, but I kept my hand on the knife, even though I was momentarily blinded by pain. I pulled it out and plunged it into his neck as my father ran in the room. Seeing me laying there, blood squirting out of his boy's neck and all over my face froze him for a second, before he ran over to me, screaming "What the *fuck* are you doing?!"

In my insane state, I was convinced he was about to attack me like I'd seen him do to my mother so many times, so I yanked the knife out of the man's neck, turned the blade on my father and took a swipe at his neck, my eyes the eyes of someone neither of us knew. The knife glimmered in the moonlight, and for a second I remembered thinking how beautiful it looked right before it opened up my father's neck and his eyes bugged out. The jagged feeling in my arm as my smooth slicing motion parted my father's skin woke me from my madness and I screamed as he grabbed his neck and fell to the floor, gasping and bleeding all over his boy's discarded pants and skid-marked underwear. He thrashed around for a minute as I sat up on my bed, on my knees, panting heavily, until he stopped moving.

There were tears streaming down my face I never felt and I gingerly climbed out of the other side of the bed. I tried to stand but fell, the shock of being fucked so roughly, so young, making my legs numb for a minute. I laid on the floor, staring into the lifeless eyes of my father, until I could get up and I ran to the still closed bathroom.

"Momma!" I called frantically, banging on the door. She didn't answer, so I took the knife, still clutched in my hand, pried off the cheap front of the knob, and pressed the inner button to unlock the door. As I swung to door open, I froze as I saw my mother laying on the floor, a glazed look on her non-blinking eyes, a needle hanging out of her arm.

I immediately turned and threw up in the toilet. After my stomach emptied itself, my mind started functioning somewhat normally and reality started waving at me. I had to get the hell out of here. I ran back in my room and went through the pockets of my father and the man on the floor. I came up with around $800 altogether. My father had rented my brand-new pussy out for a mere $200, the same amount of money I'd slaved for months and given him to stop beating my mother. The rest of the money was in the other man's pockets. Now, more determined and upset than before, I ran in my mother's room, grabbed some newer clothes and shoes and her ID. We looked enough alike, I figured, for me to pass as her. We were both around 5 feet tall. People would just figure my green eyes were contacts. I had the sense to grab a large purse of hers, run to the freezer and toss in 3 bricks of cocaine before running out of the back door never looking back.

I ran to where I knew my daddy dropped work off at, looking for his cousin, Indo. I found him posted up in front of his "house," which was really an abandoned building he claimed as his own and sold his drugs out of.

"What the fuck you doing out here, T?" he asked, obviously shocked to see me out here at this time of night.

"I need a ride to the bus station," I begged, trying to hold the tears in. Indo narrowed his eyes at me and flicked his Newport onto the damp sidewalk.

"Where's yo daddy?"

"Indo, please… just take me to the bus station…"

"Man…" Indo shook his head and took a big gulp of Old English in a bag. He knew something was seriously wrong and he obviously didn't want to be around when it all hit the fan.

"Look, I got this…" I unzipped my mom's fake Gucci tote and started to pull out a brick. Indo's eyes flew open big as saucers, he spit out the mouthful of beer in his mouth all over his shoes and he hurriedly shoved the brick back inside the bag, looking around to make sure no one saw a little girl waving around bricks of coke. He grabbed me by the arm and drug me to his old Civic. Once we got inside, he took a deep breath and lit another cigarette.

"Where you gonna go, T?" he asked quietly.

"Wherever the next bus is going. Just help me, please. I won't never tell no one I spoke to you, I swear."

Indo sighed. "That bad, huh?"

"Worse." I insisted, crying again.

"How long you think it's gonna be before your daddy come after you for these bricks?" he asked, shaking his head at me.

Tears falling harder, I made sure I looked Indo in his eye. "A real, *real* long time."

150

WICKED BLUES Deszion Nasir

"Aw, *shit*... Shit... aight, aight... stop crying and shit... look, gimmie the bricks and I'll help you."

So Indo drove me to the Greyhound station and bought me a one-way ticket to Virginia, the next bus out. All I had was $800 in a fake designer bag when I stepped off that bus in Hampton, Va. Hampton wasn't like Columbus at all, and I got picked up for stealing food the next day. I didn't have any ID on me, I'd never been to the dentist and I wouldn't give anyone my real name so I ended up in foster homes until I graduated from Phoebus High School. Despite my situation, I managed to get decent grades, but my claim to fame was my speed. I had to wear two training bras to hold down my breasts, but I was a streak on the track, a skill I'd picked up from those years of running to and from school when I was younger. That's how I'd gotten the scholarship to Hampton University...

The car jerking to a stop jerked me out of my memories as Gemini pulled up in front of my house. I looked up at the dark windows and the cold neighborhood and sighed.

"What's wrong?" Gemini asked, seeing the disturbed look on my face.

"Can I stay at your place tonight?" I asked him, looking into his eyes searchingly.

Gemini studied my face closely. "Are you sure you ready for that?"

I knew what he meant. We hadn't had sex yet, but I really just didn't want to be alone in that depressing little building. Even if it was only for a few hours, I wanted to stop being so guarded and wanted to feel needed and wanted and pampered. I knew Gemini would give that to me, and if he could give me back some of what I'd lost as a child-sincere affection-he deserved what he'd been patiently waiting on.

WICKED BLUES Deszion Nasir

"Just take your time with me," I told him. "I've been through a lot of things and trust me... this is a huge step for me, okay? I'm serious, Gemini,"

Gemini reached over and ran his fingers through my hair, pulled me to him and I curled up next to his huge body. "Don't do nothing you not comfortable with, okay? Not with me or no other muthafucka."

I nodded, and Gemini turned around. Minutes later we were back on the highway and on our way to Yorktown. Gemini's house was large and secluded, not at all like I'd expected. I was looking for fancy cars, basketball courts and whatever, but his house had two huge weeping willows in front, with a large hammock hanging between them, next to a small lake. The house itself was a wide two-story, made from stone with light-blue trim. It looked like a doctor or something lived there. As soon as we pulled up, a beautiful Great Pyrenees and a huge Siberian Husky peered over the railing of the large porch, complete with a swing, and bounded down toward us, eager for our attention.

"They ain't gonna bite you... this is Juno and Parrish," Gemini told me, petting the dogs, figuring I was frozen because the dogs were huge. I wasn't. I was frozen because I'd never been *near* a house like this, much less known someone black who owned one. I played it off and scratched Juno's –the Husky-ears, who would follow me and become my baby from that day forward. If I came over and spoke to Parrish first, she'd get jealous and whine until Parrish snapped at him. She had a temper.

When we walked inside, Gemini's phone was ringing, so he told me to look around and he went off to answer it. I wandered around with Juno in tow and marveled at how huge the house seemed on the inside. The house seemed so open and the whole back of the house was made of glass. I could stand in the foyer and see the kitchen, dining room, living room, pool room, the huge fish tank in the middle of the room that went up through the 2nd floor and had Nurse sharks swimming in it. The only rooms hidden were

WICKED BLUES Deszion Nasir

an office, gym and a full bathroom with a sauna on the first floor. A winding staircase led to 2 more bedrooms upstairs, a huge master suite with its own Jacuzzi and separate shower, balcony, library, and living room. There were bathrooms and smaller balconies in both bedrooms, and a smaller weight room on the end of the hall, as well as a small theater, which was where the shark tank concluded. There was art in every room, no TV in the guest bedrooms, only expensive stereo systems with a wall of all genres of music. The TV in the master bedroom wasn't visible from the bed either. You had to go to the living room in another part of the suite, but the theater had a wall-to wall screen.

I in the kitchen getting a glass of ginger ale for my agitated stomach-too many drinks-when Gemini found me. "Your house is beautiful," I told him, sipping and shaking my head.

"You sound shocked," he grinned, showing off his deep dimples.

"You just don't look like you live in a house like this," I admitted.

"Lemme guess. You was looking for a pit bull, game system and a Public Enemy poster, right?" he asked. I laughed, ginger ale spilling out of my mouth. Gemini shook his head and grabbed a paper towel. As he wiped my mouth he said "You cain't tell I got better taste than most niggas? I brought *you* here, didn't I?"

I blushed and smiled as he stared into my eyes. Gemini dropped the paper towel in the trash and took my hand. "Come with me."

Gemini led me up to the second floor and he gave me huge, fluffy bath sheet and let me take a long hot shower. Then we got in the sauna so I could sweat the alcohol out of my pores. I was ready to drop at that point, and I was hoping that he wasn't gonna be too disappointed about not getting any that night. I passed out, still wrapped up in the towel and draped across Gemini's King sized bed that I seemed to sink into.

153

I woke in the middle of the night to warm sensations floating over my body. I didn't know what they were, but they were like electric blankets sliding over different parts of my skin. When I opened my eyes, at first I didn't realize where I was or where the heat was coming from. I realized that the warm sensation was coming from two hands and when I turned over, the stars made the eyes of the hands' owner sparkle a midnight blue and that's when everything came rushing back. Without saying a word, I turned and slid my arms around Gemini's neck and pulled him down to me. He kissed around my mouth, sliding those hot hands all over my body before he penetrated my mouth with his tongue, which was long as all hell, I might add. He smelled like sandalwood. The scent of him, the heat coming from him and the care he seemed to be taking with me had me drunk with passion as a wrestled him on his back. I didn't share myself with anyone often at all because of my childhood issues and when I did, it was usually an aggressively passionate experience. I asked him to be gentle so he wouldn't try to dominate the situation and let me get out everything I had pent up. Gemini seemed to sense what I needed and while I dug my fingers in his thick, wild hair, he massaged my lower back while I ran my tongue around his ear, down his neck and over his muscular chest, biting his nipples while he moaned and squeezed me. He skin tasted so smooth and silky, like he went to extra measures to take care of his body past a good shower and lotion application.

As I moved down his body, I soon came head-to-head with the monstrosity he called a dick. For a moment I was stumped.

"What's wrong?" he asked, breathing hard.

"Baby... there's no way I can suck that," I said, scared I'd broken the magic.

Gemini just laughed quietly, and then I realized he'd probably heard that before. "Just get it wet, love. I love how your lips taste just the way they are," he told me. I bent down and ran my tongue around it from the head to under his balls

154

slowly while he moaned, rubbing my head until I tasted his pre cum leaking out of the huge head. Gemini finally pulled me back up and laid me on the huge pillows gently, staring down at me.

"You ready to take this to a real serious level, Teashauna?" Gemini asked me, brushing my hair back with one hand, playing with my dripping love with the other.

"Are you?" I asked him. "Don't say it just to get some pussy. The last nigga who did that was real sorry later..." I warned him, in all seriousness.

"You think I'd do all this for pussy? If I just wanted pussy I'd get it from a chick good for only that. There's only one of you, and that's what I want," Gemini told me, trying to ease the head in, but no matter how much I wanted him, it wasn't happening that easy. It took a couple of creative positions and Gemini relaxing me a little more with kisses to my breasts and neck before I was able to relax enough to allow him to slide himself inside my small frame.

"Gatdayum," he swore, gripping me as he tried to slide out and my tightness held onto him in protest. All I could do was hold him and moan as he fell into a slow and sensual rhythm as I rolled with the pain and pleasure of Gemini's lovemaking. The strokes stayed slow, but intensified in strength, and I wrapped my legs around him best I could as we rose and fell with his determined movements. Soon my back wasn't even touching the bed and my hair was sweeping the pillows and Gemini grunted out, pushing me away from him and then pulling me back to him, all while I clung to him and threw my hips at him. My hips were narrow, but my ass was round, and Gemini was digging his huge paws into my cheeks as his sounds grew louder. He eventually stood up and as he bounced me on him that way my moans turned to excited shrieks as the sexual energy pounded through me. I was glad Gemini lived on a nice sized piece of land, because the two of us were loud as all hell. Gemini staggered over to the balcony, threw the door open,

155

and staggered to the edge. At first I was scared and clung to him, thinking he'd snapped.

"Do you trust me, baby?" he panted, looking me in the eye.

Chest heaving, I finally nodded. Gemini turned me over, bent me over the edge of the balcony, grabbed my hands, held them firmly behind me, and started pounding into me while I hung over the edge of the balcony, ass naked, breasts bouncing over the railing as I screamed my appreciation with every stroke he gave me. As my eyes rolled into the back of my head, I felt my whole body convulsing. Gemini gripped me tighter. "Let it go, baby. Let it go all over this big dick. I wanna see you glaze this dick up," Gemini commanded, yanking me back into him harder. I was getting lightheaded and my orgasm was unlike any I'd ever had. When I finally came, I felt like I was having a seizure. I felt Gemini's dick jerk around inside me at the same time and I think he yelled out like he'd been shot, but I was never sure because after I came I fainted.

I woke up to love birds singing in a cage in the corner of the room. I tried to turn over but realized I couldn't because Gemini's huge arm and leg were draped over me. Feeling me stir, he opened his eyes sleepily and kissed me on the forehead. "Where you goin? You gotta pee? You hungry?"

I giggled. "No and no. I gotta go to work, though."

Gemini made a *pfft!* sound and retightened his grip on me, closing his eyes again. "Man, fuck that job."

"Oh, what? I'm supposed to up and quit now?" I laughed.

Gemini re-opened his eyes. "Did you mean what you said last night about what we talked about? Taking shit to another level?"

"Of course I did."

"Well, so did I. Quit that job, yo. I mean that shit."

"What? Gemini, I'm not *even* the kinda chick that lives off niggas like that. I got rent to pay and I need to earn it."

Gemini let me go, got up, opened a drawer, pulled out a stack of hundreds and tossed it on the bed at me. "There's the rest of the money for your lease. Pay it off. You earned it by being a real-ass female with me, Teasha. Let me be a real-ass nigga, baby. That shit is *nothing* to me. Let me be that nigga," he repeated.

I stared down at the pile of money. "You want to pay my rent for me?"

"No, Teasha. I wanna pay your lease off. I want you to move in here with me."

"Move in *here*?!" I looked around the beautiful room, taking in how much more breathtaking it was in the sunlight. Whoever had built it had designed it to make the most of the sunlight, which it was, making everything, including Gemini's eyes, sparkle.

"It's too big for just me and my babies," Gemini said, opening the door to the bedroom as the dogs scratched on the door. Juno immediately jumped on me, drooling all over me and the sheets.

"Well, if it was too big, what you buy it for?" I asked, laughing.

Gemini shrugged, grinning. "Guess I was waiting on you."

I blushed again and sighed. Gemini took that as my yes and jumped back on the bed with me. He pushed a heartbroken Juno out of the way and climbed on top of me, making me forget-or at least push to the side-all the whispers in my head telling me this was a bad idea.

GEMINI'S STORY

Yeah, yeah, niggas. I know ya'll like, "What the fuck?!" No, a nigga not getting soft. I don't expect ya'll to understand how shit works when you lead a life like I do, so sit down, stop flipping pages and pay attention.

Now, you already know the dark side of what I do. But remember how I met ol' girl? I was in the DJ truck? Yeah, forgot about that, right? A nigga *do* got legit business. And with legit business, I *gotta* have a legit reputation. Teashauna is perfect icing on the cake for the lifestyle my fans love to see me living. She held my ass *down* from the second she met me, she's a good girl, she ain't no hoe, she ain't out messing with a bunch of irregular-ass niggas, none of that. She's loyal, she's fine, she's a beast in the bed, and she smart as hell. And she got just enough hood in her to be accepted by the street side of my fans, who'd flip on me if I got up with some stuck up bitch. No, a nigga like me gotta have a grown-ass woman by his side, and even though she only 5'2", a grown ass woman is what I got. I gotta be able to trust her, even if she shouldn't trust me. The last female I trusted fucked me over so bad I never recovered…

I was 14 years old and living out in Jefferson Park in Portsmouth with my aunt. We had just moved there from Norfolk. From before there, Newport News and from before there, Virginia Beach. I kept getting in trouble at school for violent fights and we kept having to move. I wasn't *trying* to keep fucking up, but it was like the more I tried to ignore stupid shit, the more it came looking for me. I've always had a temper, and I'd let it build up until it exploded and I ended up breaking a neck or rib or giving someone a concussion or whatever. I kept getting expelled so we kept having to move from city to city. My aunt was getting sicker and more tired with each move, and now she just sat around and waited for the sun to rise and set.

158

I had slipped out before school and was walking around my new neighborhood, trying to sell the rest of the weed I'd kept from when I lived out Norfolk. I hadn't found a connect in Hampton yet and my cash was running low, so I'd dipped into my personal stash and was selling that so I could go buy some more from my boy in Virginia Beach. I didn't know how I was gonna get a ride over there, but I'd figure something out. What I *did* know is that I'd have to buy a lot of work from him, but I could make a killing up here cuz he got his weed from a cat in Miami, who got his from overseas, and the weed I'd sampled out here was some local shit anyone could get. I was about my business at 14, because I already knew my aunt Loretta Knight wasn't giving me money for nothing a young man like myself needed. She thought all I needed was drawers and socks and I was good, so I'd taken it upon myself to get my own finance plan.

I had just made $20 off this one guy when these 3 guys rolled up on me. No one had tried me out here yet cuz I was tall, but I looked skinny under my baggy clothes. Of course, I wasn't as big as I was now, but I wasn't as small as they thought. They figured they could run up on me cuz I was new and no one had no beef with me yet, but obviously that was about to change.

"Look at this lanky muthafucka *here*," one of them laughed, elbowing the other one.

I sighed and stuck my hands in my pockets, uninterested in a fight. Fights didn't make me no money unless my victims had money, and these were obviously some broke cats.

"Look, nigga, I know you *new* and all, but you ain't just gonna roll up in here and be getting our money, yo."

"*My* money, *bitch*," I snapped.

His boys looked at each other and the head pussy raised his eyebrow. "Oh, okay, I see *this* nigga tryna get his shit-" he got cut off when my fist cut through the wind and knocked him off his feet and he slid face first across the rough street. He didn't feel it cuz he was snoring. One of his

159

flunkies immediately takes off running so fast he was kicking himself in the ass, and the one left jumps at me. He clipped me in the face but the stinging is nothing compared to the pain that nigga felt when I grabbed the offending arm and brought my elbow down on it, snapping his wrist. When he grabbed his wrist, I punched him in the jaw and he fell to the ground, groaning and moaning in pain. I kicked him over on his back, raised my foot up and stomped on his knee until I heard it snap and saw it pop out at an unnatural angle. I bent down and grabbed him by the collar which was soaked with tears of pain. "When that bitch-ass boy of yours wakes up, tell him he was the lucky one," I commanded. The kid was in too much pain to answer. I let him go, and proceeded to go thru the pockets of him and the snoozer on the ground. They ain't have shit but $35 between them, so I could only catch a cab to Mc Donald's to eat while the commotion died down.

By the time I got home it was well after midnight. My aunt was sitting at the kitchen table, reading one of her books and burning something "cleansing," which meant she'd already heard what'd happened.

"Come here, you devil child," she said in a tired voice, not looking at me.

I sighed and went to her.

"They was messing with me first-"

"That don't matter none, boy. You know that. You take everything too far. You mess that boy leg up for life. He won't never walk straight no more. When you hit the other boy he hit his head on that broken slab out dere. He crack his skull open." she reported mechanically, like she was reading a report on the news.

I sighed.

"I know you feel you in the right. The devil be like that."

"Why you always call me that?" I demanded. "You always calling me 'devil child' then be all mad when I do stuff."

WICKED BLUES Deszion Nasir

"I be mad cuz my prayers don't never be answered. I call you the devil child cuz that's who you be."

"You don't know nothing about who I am," I snapped.

"Oh, I know more 'bout you than *you* do, boy," my aunt shook her head. "You the child of a curse. Your momma was cursed with a beauty that made evil men fall in love with her. She couldn't get away from it and it destroyed her. Right fo' it did, course, she had you. You a mix of that beauty and all that evil she had swimming around in her from them evil mens."

"Fuck you!" I screamed, jumping up. This was the only thing I'd ever heard about my mother and I wasn't about to sit here and listen to my aunt talk about her like this. "She your sister! How you gonna talk about her like that?"

"Boy, that chile won't no sister of *mine*. She left you with my *real* sister and *she* give you to me cuz she didn't want no demon baby. Back then… when I was younger… I was more optimistic about the world… I thought I could *love* the evil out of you… I cain't bear no children of my own… but I was wrong… she told me I couldn't stop it but I thought I could… now look at you… all big and evil, cursing me and deforming people… I was sooo wrong… I'm not moving no mo, boy… you done drained the life out of me… you got to take the evil swirling around in you and leave from here. It's too big to be contained in this house. I cain't hold it back no more and I won't let it kill me… you got to leave from here…" She waved at me like she was dismissing me.

Standing there, listening to all that, sent my mind someplace I'd never been.

"So… she left me? My momma just… ain't want me? And now… *you* don't want me neither?" I asked for clarification.

"You don't understand boy, you too young. You *cain't* be loved. That's yo curse, boy. You *cain't* love no one, so you cain't *be* loved. All you can do is destroy," my

161

aunt turned away, drained from the speech and sounding tired.

I remember I saw spots dancing in front of my eyes as I stood there, processing my only link to the world telling me I was a product of Satan. I walked up behind her and wrapped my arms around her and hugged her. "Please, Auntie. I don't got nowhere to go. If I go back out there, them people gonna kill me. Don't nobody love me in this world but you. Don't make me leave. I'll die out there."

I felt my aunt soften, then harden again. "I told you. You cain't *be* loved. Trying to love you done cost me my *whole* life. I want to live my last few years in peace..."

Something in me hardened, too. Something hardened, died and broke all at the same time. Something that never repaired, never healed, never sparked another flame in my heart when I internalized what she was telling me. It was time to accept what I was supposed to be and become what everyone had been trying to tell me that I was all along. A monster. "Well, then, if you cain't give me another chance, I *damn* sure ain't gonna give you another year." I tightened my grip around her neck and squeezed until she stopped fighting and slumped to the side. It didn't take much cuz she was already weak. As the last breath left her body, so did my compassion for other people. I vowed my aunt would be the last person who shitted on me. I threw my clothes in my book bag and walked out of the small house. I caught the Express Ride bus to the Pentran Bus station in Hampton and just started walking. Eventually, I ran into a corner store called W&W on the corner of Pembroke and LaSalle Ave. and darted inside to get something to drink. As I paid the Asian guy at the high counter for my Nestea, I saw a small crowd of teenage boys standing in front of the store by the railroad tracks smoking. My nerves were so shot I was ready to scrap for a straight. I picked up my change off the counter for my drink and headed over to them.

"Hey, can I get a cigarette?" I asked the group. All of them got quiet and looked at me like I was crazy.

"Nigga who is you?" one of them asked, looking me up and down.

"Just wanted a straight, man," I said, trying to calm my nerves before I snapped. They noticed my disposition and another one was like "Yo, look at this cat. He look like a serial killer. You a serial killer, *boy*?" Most of them laughed, and I felt myself on the verge of choking one of them when a dark-skinned kid with a low fade was like, "Chill, ya'll. He look like he just had a fucked up day. Shit, we all done had them," he reached in his pocket and handed me a Newport.

"Thanks, man," I said, taking it with shaking fingers. I barely got it lit without dropping it.

"You okay?" the dark kid asked me, looking concerned.

"Yeah," I lied.

"What's your name?" he asked.

" His *name* 'Crazy-ass-muthafucka,'" the joker answered.

I snapped, grabbed him by the collar and slammed him against the side of the building. His head hit the building so hard his teeth rattled, then I threw him on the tracks, his back hitting the metal rail. He yelled out and his boys tried to advance on me, but the dark kid held his arms out to hold them back.

"Cool out," he commanded, talking to them but his eyes on me.

"Youngblood, come talk to me, man," he said to me.

I looked into his eyes, saw no fear, yet felt no threat, and nodded, trying to calm my breathing down. He nodded back, then slowly stepped away from the group and toward me.

"You always tryna save a nigga, yo," another kid yelled as the others helped the joker off the tracks, now limping.

"I saved *your* ass, too, so shut the *fuck* up," the kid yelled back, then turned to me, shaking his head. "Yo, you gotta excuse them, man. They ignorant as hell."

"It's cool," I said in a raspy voice.

"I think it is. Not because you forgive that dumb shit, but because something worse done happened to you recently," the kid said perceptively.

"How old are you?" I demanded.

He laughed. "16."

"That's it?"

"Yeah… just been through a lot… what's your name?"

"Gemini."

"I'm Tremeil. Everyone call me Tre, though."

"Okay."

"Look, I seen that look on your face in the mirror before. You don't gotta talk about it, but I recognize it. Where you running from?"

"Portsmouth."

"Was it another nigga or a Saltine that you done?"

"Saltine?"

"A cracker, man."

"Oh… a nigga…"

"Anyone see you?"

"Naw."

Tre nodded. "You probably good, then." We crossed the street and over into a concrete complex that read "Lincoln Park." "Look," Tre said, "It ain't much, but you can crash at my spot until you get your head together. I ain't no faggot or nothing, but you in a whole different world out here, Youngblood. You cain't be walking around here with your head fucked up like that. You need to get some sleep, shower and get your head right so you can make a move. Wandering around out the Park like you are'll get yo ass laid out before the sun come up so… you can get right, you know, then be on your way, aight? My mom ain't never there. If she is, she ain't gonna give a fuck no way. She only come home when her and her nigga fight, and they only fight when his money short," Tre said pointedly. "The 1st just passed, so I can pretty damn well guarantee she won't be around for a couple of weeks. Cool?"

I didn't have no options. A day turned into a week, and a week turned into 2 years. Me and Tre ended up being best friends, as far as best friends could go with a nigga like me. I never went back to school, so I hung around with the old heads all day while Tre finished high school. I got another weed and a dope connection and got rolling again. Like Tre said, when his mother came home, she barely glanced at me. She only asked me my name once I'd been there 6 months. When I told her I handed her 3 months worth of rent money. She flipped through it, stuffed it in her bra and went on out the door.

When Tre turned 18 he joined the Marines. We had a party at a strip club called Majik City in downtown Newport News. When the owner saw how much we were spending when I went down to reserve the club, he never even asked for ID. While Tre and the others were busy getting lap dances and throwing enough money in the air to have the dancers tripping from lack of vision, I was busy watching the mechanics of how the club worked. Being used to being around old heads now, I ended up hanging out with the owner every couple of days. He eventually told me how the money broke down and how much he pulled in a week, a month, etc. I told him he'd probably make a lot more money if he fixed a few things up, hired a few more attractive girls and threw more parties.

"Shit like that takes a lot more money than I'm bringin, in, son. A *lot* more money. I'd need an investor, a partner," the owner explained.

"I could get you one," I told him. He peered at me, narrowing his eyes through the stank-ass smoke of garbage weed.

"How old are you kid?" he asked me for the 100th time. He was always asking me how old I was, but I never told him.

"Money has an age limit?" I asked him instead.

WICKED BLUES Deszion Nasir

"How much money?" he asked me, leaning over and lowering his voice, obviously no longer concerned with my birthday.

I lowered mine. "How much you need?"

The next night, I caught the bus out to the club, walked up to where the owner was sitting at the bar arguing with the bartender and dropped 3 grand on the bar in front of the owner. The bartender's red lips popped open in shock and she dropped a glass. The sound of the glass shattering caused her to snap to and she quickly bent down to clean up the mess. The noise rocked the owner out of his shocked coma as well. He stopped staring at the pile of money, picked it up and motioned for me to follow him back to his office. "How much you want, kid?" he asked after counting the rubber-banded knots.

"Half."

"*Half?* Get the fuck outta here…"

"Man, I just gave you a $3000 investment. I got that all *day*. Now… I been out there grinding, tryna figure out where to put my hard earned blood and tears so I ain't gotta be on them corners like I been my whole life. I *got* the money, I *got* the brains. All I need is the venue. If you wanna get paid, and making this kinda scratch a *night*, I want half. If you wanna go back to making this a week *before* you pay anybody…gimmie my shit and I'm gone." I said, looking him in the eye.

The owner narrowed his eyes at me, but I could smell a hungry nigga a mile away, and I could smell a hungry, *greedy* nigga from 5 miles away.

By the time Tre had finished basic training I had Majik City jumping. It was slam-packed every night: I'd upped the caliber of the dancers, hired a kid from out the park as the house DJ-he was cheaper and he was better than the one the owner had in there-and better liquor had initially cost more, but we could charge more for drinks and the customers got drunk faster, which meant they'd spend more money, which they did. And that meant I'd make a lot more money-which I did.

Tre got stationed in Afghanistan and we threw him a going away party. There was weed, liquor, ass and singles on every available inch of space in the club. That night, after the owner and me, now 18, were in the back office counting the money, the door opened and the security came inside.

"What?" I demanded, irritated. I didn't like niggas running up on me when I was counting money and they knew that. That's why the fuck I'd hired them to stand *outside* the door in the first fuckin place.

"We just tryna get paid, man," one apologized.

"The fuck is wrong wit ya'll? You know you get paid *after* we finish in here. Get the fuck out," I commanded, waving them away. They didn't move and I stopped counting again. "Are you niggaz *tryna* get fired?"

"Actually, they not the ones getting fired,"

I looked up at the owner, who'd been the one who'd spoken. He had a gun in his hand, pointing it at me. I froze, both my hands full of hundred dollar bills. "Are you crazy, Marvin?"

Marvin grinned. "Hey, kid. You were a great investor. But you've gotten way more than your initial investment back now... so I think it's time I went back to my original business plan..."

I looked over at the two guards. "And the two of you just gonna let this shit go down like this, right?"

"We just tryna get paid, G," the same one repeated.

I nodded, then sighed.

Marvin grinned. "After I pop this fool, toss him in the bin. Trash day is tomorrow morning. Then you come back and get your money and a lil something extra. Deal?"

While they were busy nodding, I shot my hand out, snatched the gun from Marvin, flipped it around and shot him in the chest before he knew what had happened. He let out one single gasp of air and fell out of his chair, money fluttering in the air. The guards were frozen. I tossed the gun calmly on the desk.

"Now that *I* popped *this* fool, toss *him* in the bin. Trash day is tomorrow morning. Then you come back and get your money and a lil something extra. *Deal?*"

The two moved instantly to grab Marvin off the money he was staining up. I didn't reach for the gun or even look at them as they carried off the last nigga I decided to trust. I just continued counting my money and no one ever had enough courage to ask me what happened after I told them the next day Marvin retired. The only thing that mattered in this world was this paper... and this paper here is what helped make me a god...

I felt Teshaunna's hand squeezing mine and I realized that we were pulling up to the waterfront in Norfolk. I'd been so trapped in my memories that I'd driven all the way through the Hampton Roads Bridge Tunnel to Waterside where the Sprit of Norfolk was docked and hadn't even realized it. I looked at her shocked face and smiled. I hadn't told her where we were going, but I knew from previous conversations she'd never been on a boat before. I was hosting a party sponsored by 103 Jamz on this ship tonight and figured she'd have fun. I had some other business to conduct, but she didn't need to know anything about that. I was multitasking tonight. I had big plans for my personal and business life, and I planned to get them both jumping off before the sun came up.

As soon as we started boarding the large ship, the lights started flashing and people were shouting. I know, you're like, okay, nigga, you a DJ, what's the big deal? The big deal was that I didn't just DJ. 103 Jamz was a powerhouse in the area and the only all-black radio station other that the college stations. I've hosted comedy shows at Hampton Coliseum and clubs, hosted damn near every concert that came through the 7 cities, judged talent shows, done spots on the news; I'd even been in calendars for the sexiest radio personalities on the East Coast. I'd been in Jet and done a small interview in Essence last year, so yeah, I had a lot going on. There was more to me that what you can read about on these few pages. And I'd done it all myself. I'd made it all happen without anyone there to show me the way, guide me or dust me off when I fell. And when you fall alone, you fall hard. So I'd learned: either stop falling or make sure there was enough money around you to keep you safe when you did fall. I don't know how shit had work out for you, but it was working out for me.

As soon as I check in with the people paying me to host the Weekend Getaway Jam, a reporter from *The Voice* comes over and wants to interview Teasha.

"Me?" she asks, looking shocked. "For what?"

"We've been following your story since you two met at Burger King and we think it'd be uplifting for people to get your side of the story, you know, get to know the woman behind the man," the reporter said, grinning at us.

"I didn't know I was that important," I laughed, thinking this was the perfect thing to distract Teasha while I handled my other business.

"I wouldn't know what to say to no reporter," she looked at me when she realized I wanted her to do it.

I leaned down and kissed her on her smooth forehead. "The truth," I said simply, catching the reporter grinning out the corner of my eye. I straightened up. "I'll leave so she can relax. I gotta go do sound check and some other technical stuff anyway so I'll be back in say... 30?"

"30's great," the reporter blurted.

"Cool." I kissed Teasha one more time and slipped away. I headed for the back of the boat by the service entrance. I passed by the workers loading food on and off the boat and stood along the edge of the dock with some of the workers who were taking smoke breaks. I pulled out a Newport and fished around in my $800 leather trench coat for a lighter.

"Damn," I muttered.

One of the guys watched me grow irritated and tossed me his lighter. "Good lookin out," I nodded at him.

He nodded back. "Hey, you Gemini the Wicked, right?"

"Yeah, today I am," I responded, shaking my head. The other guys standing around with us outside laughed.

"You don't sound all that excited. This supposed to be the biggest party of the year, man."

"Man, please. I wasn't invited. I'm working, just like you. I don't get to drink, eat, chill, relax... none a that. I'm already tired, but I gotta sit up till 3 a.m. and pretend I'm *not* tired, act all perky and shit, take my girl home, get maybe, one hour sleep and then get up and be at the opening of a damn car dealership." I shook my head. "Dead-man walking."

While the other blue-collar workers were shaking their heads were shaking with me, we had to move out of the way as another truck pulled up to the edge of the dock and started loading big boxes onto the boat.

"Hold up, hold up," the one who'd given me the lighter stood up. He snatched up a clipboard and glanced on it. "I don't see ya'll on this list."

One of the men carrying the heavy boxes started ranting in a different language and waving a piece of paper around. The first guy snatched the paper and glanced at it. After looking through a few things on a clip board, he nodded and wrote something on the irate foreigner's order form. The man snatched it back and continued on inside the boat.

I shook my head, glanced at my watch and stubbed my cigarette out on the ground by my feet. "Gotta get moving, my man. Ya'll be easy," I called to the other guys. They waved and I followed the last man inside, knocking over the clipboard the cat with the lighter had set on the railing. Cursing, I picked it up, dropped it again, then picked it up and set it back where I'd found it before going inside, draping my coat over an arm. I took a right and went out the kitchen and to a dark hallway, back to where to the

170

WICKED BLUES Deszion Nasir

mechanical room was. When I got there, I looked around and made sure no one had followed me. Then I slipped inside and waited. About 10 minutes later, a man with a custom suit and watch that had diamonds on it that lit up the dark room walked into the room, looking around like he was disgusted. His gaze landed on me and he hurried over to me.

"Let's hurry up and get this over with so I can get the hell out of here," he grumbled, his British accent strong. He was black as midnight, but he was a Black Brit, only over here on business.

"If you'd been on time you'd already be gone, on your way back to London to get your bean and toast breakfast," I snapped.

"The bloody traffic was horrible," he complained.

Uninterested in his bitch-ass whining, I handed him the sheet of paper I'd stolen from Lighter Dude's clipboard when I'd purposefully knocked it over and handed it to Black Brit. He scanned it and shook his head. "How'd you get your hands on 50 grenade launchers, bloke?"

"How I got them ain't what you should be concerned about. They're in the stock room in the boxes packaged to look like frozen cheesecakes. The boat pulls off in like 30 minutes."

Black Brit nodded. He pulled out a walkie talkie, and ordered his men to move. I knew his men were now moving into the freezer, dressed as waiters and workers, unpacking boxes in the freezers and discreetly hiding 2 launchers apiece on them. Within minutes they'd be off the chaotic boat, as there was way too much going on to pay sufficient attention to what was happening.

As soon as one of Black Brit's boys radioed back that all 50 launchers were there, he handed me his coat, which was identical to mine, except it was much heavier. $300,000 was carefully sewn inside the lining of the coat. The launchers were untraceable and made from a private manufacturer. Black Brit was going to resell them to some international customers. Too much face work for me.

171

WICKED BLUES Deszion Nasir

"I still believe that's a rather expensive overcoat," Black Brit said, hinting at an old argument we'd had when we'd first made this deal.

"Look, we been through this already. No way to trace these, the cat that builds these is totally off the radar. He does quality work and he don't just work for everybody, man."

Someone said something in a foreign tongue to Black Brit in his walkie talkie and he smiled. "I suppose you're right. The order has been transferred, so our business had been conducted."

There was silence for a minute.

"So why ain't you leaving, then?" I asked grimly, glancing at my watch and sighing.

"I think our business relationship has outlived its usefulness,"

I shook my head. This shit was getting old. The problem with the business was that no matter who I was dealing with, eventually I was always gonna end up being a threat to niggas. Marvin, the nigga who owned the strip club from years ago, was only the first muthafucka who'd tried to pull this shit on me. I was about to reach for my Glock with the silencer and blow his head off when I heard a door swing open behind me.

"Gemini?"

Fuck.

Teasha walked back into the room and froze when she saw the two of us with guns pulled on each other.

"What are you doing back here?" I asked to buy some time.

She swallowed nervously, her eyes on Black Brit. "The reporter only needed half the time. I asked around for you and one of the staff told me you went outside to smoke. Then one of *those* guys said he saw you go this way, so I just followed the voices..." she trailed off. "What... what the hell's happening back here, Gemini?"

"Bad deal," I said simply.

"This doesn't have to end in a mess," Black Brit said. "Just... you just go back out there and start your show like everything is normal or someone else'll come looking for you. This lovely bird will walk me off the boat and that'll be the end of it."

"Nigga, please, you don't run *shit* around *here*," I pulled the hammer on my gun back, but Teasha surprised me by holding a hand up.

"Go ahead, baby," she said calmly. Her eyes still hadn't left the other man's face.

"What?"

"Go back up top. Do what he says. I'll see you in a few minutes. He's right. People are starting to look for you. I'm good," she assured me. She finally glanced at me, and something in her eyes sent a cold wave through my body. She smiled at me, then turned back to the punk-ass chump in front of me.

"If you even get her heart rate up, I'll snatch yours out your chest," I threatened.

"Fuck you, wanker,"

"Naw, bitch, fuck *wit* me," I growled, but Teasha held her hand out, pushed me back.

"I'll see you in a few minutes," she said.

Fists clenched, I turned and walked out of the mechanical room. I wasn't so much mad about leaving Teasha behind, I was pissed about not being in control of the situation. I'd been spreading myself thin lately, and refused to admit this may have been a bad idea. I went upstairs and greeted people and got the party started as the boat pulled off. As the minutes ticked on, my heart started beating harder as I kept scanning the crowd, looking for Teasha's green, liquid-looking dress and her bright red hair to appear, but she never appeared. After 30 minutes, I couldn't take it anymore and put on a pre-programmed mix I saved for my break and painstakingly made my way through the crowd like I was going to the bathroom, and slipped back towards the mechanical room. The closer I got, I could've sworn I heard

173

something humming. I walked a little faster and by the time I was in front of the door, I pressed my ear against the door and was convinced I heard a loud humming noise. I tried to turn the knob but it was locked. I fished around in my pocket for one of the knives I kept on me and quickly got the common lock open. I eased the door open and peered inside, already scared I'd find my little good-luck girl in the midst of her demise. What I saw froze me in my tracks and made me drop my knife.

Directly in front of me were Teasha's 6 inch emerald green pumps I'd just bought her. A few feet away, lying across some pipes was her dress.

Then I saw the blood.

It was all over the floor.

A few feet away, standing over the body of Black Brit, was Teasha, her hair up in a rubber band, in her panties and bra, with a small electric saw in her hand. Next to her was a large black plastic bag. As I watched, she bent down and used the saw to cut off his thigh from knee to hip, then toss it in the bag like she was cutting up firewood.

"What the fuck?!"

She looked up at me through a pair of safety goggles. Then she bent down and went to work on the other leg. "Gimmie like, 15 more minutes, baby."

"Teasha, what the hell did you do?"

"I handled the situation," Teasha said firmly. "I knew he wasn't gonna let me go, so when he went to call someone on that stupid walkie talkie, I pretended to fall and twist my ankle. He was like 'Get up, take that shoe off and walk.' Cool. I grabbed the stiletto, bust his stupid ass in the eye with the heel, then when he fell he hit his head on that pipe and his ass was done," she said, pointing to a huge metal pipe hissing and emitting steam. I could see a blood stain where he must've hit his head when he'd fallen. "You should have told me what was going on. I could have helped you, you know."

WICKED BLUES Deszion Nasir

I just stared at her. The whole time she was talking she was just sawing away; sawing and bagging.

"Why are you cutting the nigga up?" I demanded.

"You think I should just leave his ass lying here?" she asked, not stopping.

Almost amused, I watched her decapitate Black Brit, dump his head and torso in another bag, then tie them together. Then she proceeded to go about, still wearing her underwear and rubber gloves left over by the crew, and clean all the blood. "I told you, I got this. You go back out there. When we get far enough out on the water, I'll drag these bags by the kitchen and the staff will dump these bags with the rest of the trash. By the time we get out there, there'll be enough bags to cover this... we'll talk about all this later."

"Teasha..."

Teasha finally stood up and looked up at me. "I told you before. I'm territorial. Now go. We'll talk."

Won't shit for me to do but go back upstairs.

About 30-45 minutes later, Teasha was back, looking like she'd just stepped off the cover of a high fashion magazine. She smiled for all the pictures and accepted all the hugs and fake kisses being tossed her way. I watched from my position on stage, seeing her in a new light. My girl wasn't a gangster, but she was a lioness, and she'd literally kill for what was hers. I'd underestimated her, and at this point, I wasn't sure if it was a good or bad thing, but one thing I was sure of was that chicks like her weren't grown in very many gardens anymore.

With that thought in my mind, I decided it'd be in my best interest to have Teasha 100% in my pocket. I couldn't afford to piss off a female capable of the shit I'd just seen her tiny ass do without blinking until I figured her out.

¾ of the way through the cruise, after everyone was feeling good off of the expensive champagne, I got on the microphone and turned the music down some.

"Can I interrupt ya'll for a minute?" I said loudly. It took a minute for the chatter to die down, and I waited until I had everyone's attention, including Teasha's who was perched in on a barstool near the stage, sipping on a deep-pink tinted drink. She looked at me curiously.

"Is everyone having a good time?" I asked.

The half-drunk crowd roared their response, and I laughed and waited for them to calm down.

"This event was held to acknowledge love, and I want to take some time out to acknowledge someone who's shown me more love in a few months than I've been shown in my whole damn life." I turned to Teasha and she blushed as everyone cheered. "C'mon up here, baby."

Stunned, Teasha got p and the crowd parted so she could make her way up to me. Once she was beside me, I took her hand.

"I know we've only existed to each other a short time, but we've already had some life-and-death drama, haven't we?" I asked her, smiling down at her. She smiled softly and nodded. "And every time I turn around, there you are again... and again... you know what that tells me?" I asked her. She shook her head.

"That you not tryna hear that 'till death do us part bullshit,'" I said, and the crowd laughed. The laughs turned to gasps as I got down on one knee in front of Teasha. "We've already done 'through sickness and health.' We've done 'till death do us part.' You've shown me everything I needed to see and I never asked you to see it. You've given me everything you have and I never knew I needed it. I know you've already given me so much but... I just need you to give me one more thing, ma..." I reached inside my suit pocket and pulled out a small jeweled box. I opened it and even the crowd could see how the 3kt. princess cut diamond ring sparkled under the dim, romantic lights of the ship. "I need you to give me your hand so I can put this engagement ring on it."

Hushed whispers, excited chatter and shushing quickly filled the room as people anxiously waited for Teasha to close her mouth and answer me. I was originally going to do this in private, but this would make a bigger impact.

"You gonna give it to me?" I asked after a long minute, my blue eyes laughing.

Teasha's mouth closed, then opened, then closed again. She wiped a tear away, then she handed me her trembling hand and I slid the ring on her ring finger. The crowd exploded in applause and cameras began flashing instantly.

The rest of the night turned into our engagement party. The passengers all made it a point to come by and congratulate us. When we finally had a second alone, we slipped off to the outside of the dancehall to the quiet, calm edge of the boat, where I put my arm around her and she shook her head.

"We're rushing," she said fearfully.

"Naw... I don't think so. I just don't see the point in bullshitting, T. I been alone a long time for a fuckin reason. I'm almost where I wanna be, and everybody knows being on top ain't shit alone. I'd never find another woman like you in a lifetime, girl. We can get to know each other as much as you want on the way."

Teasha sighed. "About earlier, though... is that gonna be a part of our lives? I grew up in that kind of drama, Gemini."

"That was rare. I'm dong big things right now, and every now and then there's gonna be muthafuckas who gonna try to overstep. He was trying to rip me off and I wasn't having it. I held up my end of the deal and he was tryna take my product *and* the money. When he don't come back, that shit'll be squashed."

Teasha took a rugged breath. "Was it drugs, Gemini?"

"No, baby. No drugs. I don't sell drugs." That wasn't a lie. That was Charger's job.

I felt Teasha's body exhale, releasing a breath she had trapped as she'd waited for my answer. She stared at the dark

177

water for a minute. "You really wanna marry me?" she asked.

"I asked you, didn't I?"

"You don't understand. I don't come from *nothing*. I don't mean *shit* to anybody in this world but you, Gemini."

I turned her to me, bent down and kissed her on her heart-shaped lips. "That just mean I ain't gotta share you, then."

RIO'S STORY

I turned down my television and sat up, my heart skipping over it's normal pattern of beats. When I heard the knock again, I forced myself to calm down and stood up. I looked around at the hotel suite I'd rented at the Williamsburg Marriott and and walked over to the door I pulled the door open and stared into Tre's dark green eyes.

"Hey," I said softly.

"Hey," he said, a troubled look in his eyes.

I mentally narrowed my eyes at him. That wasn't the hug I was expecting. Hmm.

Tre cleared his throat-always a bad fucking sign-and looked behind him for a minute before he swung his eyes back toward me. "Can I come in?"

I silently backed away from the door and he walked past me, bringing the scent of Cool Water in the room with him.

"How've you been?" he asked lamely.

"What did you wanna see me for, Tremeil?"

"*You* called *me*."

"Um, *yeah*... cuz you said you wanted to talk, remember?" I reminded him, crossing my arms. I had accepted the fact that I'd acquired some unprofessional feelings for Tre and was still struggling on what to do with them. It was hard enough for me to even invite him over here. Now that I had he was acting all suspect and shit and it was starting to piss me off.

"Yeah, I did..." Tre walked past me and sat on the King-sized bed by the balcony doors, which were open, allowing the crisp breeze to whisk in and make the room smell like freshly folded laundry.

"So what is it, Tre? The last time I seen you, you were all like 'I still got feelings for you' and whatever, now you in here looking like you about to drop a bunch of bullshit in my lap."

179

He sighed. "Your sister's pregnant, Rio."

I stared at him, my arms dropping from their pissed off position. "She's... she's what?"

"She's pregnant. I just found out."

"Shit," I flopped down on the bed next to Tre. "How far along?"

"Couple months, maybe."

There was a long silence.

"So that's what you came to tell me? She pregnant so you can't fuck wit me no more? You could've done that over the phone, Tre. I didn't have to rent this expensive ass room for you to come out here to tell me you cain't fuck with me no more," I snapped.

"I didn't come out here to tell you that, though," he spoke up loudly, cutting off my tirade.

"What you come out here for, then?"

"Cuz I don't know *what* the fuck I wanna do, Rio. Fuck... I'm tryna be wit Jari... and my kid... she got issues and shit, but if I break up with her right now, man... you know her... she gonna get rid of the baby... I ain't got no choice, man... right now I gotta keep shit real calm around her till she have this baby... after she drop that load... different story..."

"I've heard this story before," I said, getting up. "Nigga says 'let's go on pause till she have the baby, then I'ma take my kid and be out' then it changes to 'I cain't leave her right now, it wouldn't be right,' then it turns into 'she ain't gonna let me have the baby' or 'the baby needs both of us' so save me the drama Tre. I *been* here before. I *met* you before. I keep falling in love with you over and over again. This shit ends the same way everytime and I'm fuckin tired. I'm *tired*, Tre." I walked over to the balcony and pushed the doors open. "Let's just spare each other the drama later and you just go back to her and handle your business."

"You just said you love me, though," Tre interrupted me, standing up.

WICKED BLUES Deszion Nasir

Cursing myself inwardly, I shrugged. "It don't make a fucking *difference*, 'dough. You having a kid with my *sister*, yo. I *cain't* be with you, even if ya'll break up later."

"But I love you too, Rio-"

I balled my fists up and punched Tre in the chest. "Don't say that shit! *Fuck* you, Tre, don't *say* no shit like that! Nigga, don't *come* in here, tell me you knocked up my *sister* and tell me you love me in the same conversation! *Fuck* you!" I screamed, tears in my eyes as I soved him against a wall. "You don't even *know* me, dude!"

"You think this shit is easy for me either? I got love for Jari, but I know what the fuck it is with her. It's always been like it is. We was just being stupid and now a kid is gonna have to pay for the dumb ass mistake his parents made. You know I was feeling you before I knew you was Jari sister."

I flopped down on the bed, frustrated, and leaned forward, putting my hands in my blond hair. "This is all this nigga's fault," I muttered, black hate moving in my heart for Gemini.

"What?" Tre asked.

"Nothing," I said louder. "Tre, this is a brick wall. This isn't repairable."

"Rio, don't do this to me right now, baby."

I closed my eyes and shook my head at him. I couldn't let him talk me into the madness. None of this would be good for me. I lived my life strictly for everyday. This situation would force me into future plans and commitments and garaunteed bullshit and I'd vowed I'd never end up in this situation again.

The last time I'd made plans for my future was when I'd stepped out of my father's Rolls Royce in Brazil and looked up at his mansion. I'd never seen anything like the 3-story castle-like house or anything close to the sparkling pool behind it, just barely visible behind all the fruit trees. My mouth dropped open and my father hugged me to him. Right then and there, I made plans never to leave here.

When my father had come to get me from America it'd been a horrible night. I'd been asleep in the bed with Jari. As usual, she was kicking me in the back in her sleep, but when the banging on the thin front door woke her up, her foot shot out and hit me in the back so hard I tumbled onto the floor, tangled in our blanket. We both sat up, listening instead of arguing. We heard our mom, her boyfriend, and another man arguing. We looked at each other, then scrambled to the door of our tiny room. We peeked out and saw a tall, irish cream-colored man with a funny accent going off on our mother. She was trying to shove him out of the door, but he wasn't moving.

"I wanna see her, Teresea!" he was yelling. "I send you money and whatever you want, but I have to track you down to see her? Where is she? You have her living like this? What're you doing with all the fucking money I been sending you?"

Me and Jari glanced at each other. We didn't know who the hell he'd been sending *our* momma money for, but won't nobody at *this* address getting it but her. Me and Jari were already sharing clothes and socks and we wore different sizes.

Mom's boyfriend stepped up to the man. "Nigga, if you don't get yo' light-bright ass out my house-"

The light-skinned man pulled his fist back, punched the boyfriend one time and we could hear the crack as his nose broke. He screamed like a bitch and fell to the ground, moaning and groaning.

"Let me see her!" the man yelled.

"You *can't* see her!" Momma screeched back finally, swaying back and forth.

"Why not?"

"Cuz she don't know about you," our mom snapped.

This made the man paused, and a shocked look covered his face before a wave of anger replaced it. "What the hell do you mean she don't know? You never told her about me?"

182

Mom sucked through her teeth, but the man shoved her out of the way as his eyes landed on our two pairs or eyes peeking at them. He froze for a second, then he started for us. Mom grabbed for his arm, but he shrugged her off of him and she tripped over her boyfriend's foot. She grabbed for the man's foot but missed.

Me and Jari backed into the room, frightened, as the man slowly pushed the door of the room open. When he flipped the light switch on to the lamp with no shade, he got a full view of the two of us huddled in the bed, clutching each other. We'd never hugged before. No one hugged in our dysfunctional house, but instinctively, we were doing it now. Confusion bloomed over both of our faces. The angry man's face had changed to one of love and wonder. He was staring at me with that new face. He came over to where I was and squatted down next to me.

"Hey, Rio. Do you remember me?" he asked.

I shook my head no at him, although his eyes reminded me of someone.

He took a deep breath. "It's me, baby... your Daddy."

Might as well have slapped me across the face with a sock full of rocks.

"My... my what?'

"I'm your Daddy, Rio. I came to take you to visit me. Do you wanna come to my house? It's big and pretty and I have these beautiful trees you can pick fruit right off of..."

I glanced behind me at my mother's drunken, angry face and nodded. I realize now how sad that was. I didn't know this man from a can of paint and I was willing to go off with him to get away from my mother.

He smiled, held his hand out, and I took it, letting him pull me up. Then I realized his eyes were familiar because they looked just like mine. They were the same bronze-gold color as the ones I always saw staring back at me sadly in the cracked mirror in the bathroom.

WICKED BLUES Deszion Nasir

"Do I need to pack?" I looked around my room.

"Naw. You don't need nothing in here."

He started to lead me away when I heard a voice behind me- "I wanna go, too-"

I turned to see Jari, looking frightened, standing in the middle of the room, shaking.

The man looked at her, then he softened. "If your mom-"

"She ain't goin *no*-muthafuckin-where," Momma interrupted loudly, rolling her neck, her eyes red. "Her black ass ain't yours, don't worry about her. Comin' in here like you Superman or some shit..." she lit a cigarrette with shaking fingers and shook her head.

My Daddy shook his head at her, then tightened his hand around me and led me out to a sleek black limo. I never bothered to tell my mother good bye.

We'd driven straight to an airport and gotten on a plane. When I'd woke up from a mentally exhaused sleep on the plane, my father'd explained to me that he'd been trying to see me for years, but he could never find me. My mother kept giving him bad addresses and whenever he came to America, she'd always made an excuse about why she couldn't bring me to see him. She'd brought me when I was younger, but when I'd gotten old enough to remember him, the bullshit had started. I think she kept me from him so I wouldn't do like I'm doing now-leaving-and she wouldn't lose here free ride in my Daddy's pocket. I didn't know what he did, but I know my Mom never went to work. Me and Jari never had shit, but my mother had everything she and her man of the moment wanted. I think deep down she knew I wasn't gonna come back. What child would voluntarily come back to the abusive lifestyle my mother was living? My father gave me any girl's fantasy: a dream life in an exotic land. No one lived in the mansion with us but the maid, the cook and my father's body guards. Even my tutors came to the house. My father taught me Portugese, Spanish and

French, saying a woman could never learn too much and to never let a man make me think otherwise.

It took a few years for me to realize my father was a huge druglord who was responsible for moving huge shipments of cocaine and heroin from different countries to other parts of the world, mainly the United States. I was his only child and his only vice. How did I find out? He sat me down on my 14th birthday and told me like we talking about a television show. He explained that it was his job to sell things that people could die using, but they chose to kill themselves. Everyone always had a choice. People's choices were what allowed us to live the way we did, but there were a lot of people-namely the FBI-who were jealous that other people gave us money by choice. For my 14th birthday I got a 9mm. By the time I was 15 I could use a whole arsenal of weapons. My father told me that one day people would come for him and when he wasn't here anymore I'd have to have a plan for my future and a way to defend myself. Since I was good at math, he and my tutor had been focusing all my learning primarily on investments, money market accounts and how that world worked. "All that other shit in school is for motherfuckers too stupid to learn about what you're learning," he'd always told me. I did whatever my Daddy wanted and it came easy to me. I forgot all about being hungry, being scared and being frightened about life.

One night, right before I was going to turn 16, they finally came for him. I heard them kicking in the door and heard the shouting and shooting. Isabella, our housekeeper, began screaming in Portuguese, then she fell silent. I heard my father shouting and firing. He wasn't gonna be easy to take down, no matter how many had come for him.

We'd rehearsed this before, so even though I was scared to death and crying, I jumped out of the bed and rolled under the queen-sized marshmallow to the spot where the carpet came up and I snatched up the floor and pulled out my 9mm and spare clips. I also grabbed a slim metal package sealed with a combination only me and daddy knew about

185

and ran to my walk-in closet. I'd just thrown the door open when men rushed into my room with black and yellow FBI jackets on.

As soon as they entered the room, guns drawn, I pointed at their heads and fired. I dropped two of them on the first two shots and the other three fell back. Ther returned the fire and I jumped behind my closet door, which my father had bullet-proofed. When they paused, I took a breath and started firing again. I dropped the metal case and snatched out another clip as I counted down the bullets like my father'd taught me. I reloaded quickly and ducked as they fired on me again, but I grabbed the bar at the top of closet, looped my feet around it, and held myself up and fired over the top of the door, catching them off guard. I heard 3 more bodies drop.

There was more shouting and gunshots going on in the house but no more in my room, so I dropped to the floor. I peered around my door and saw all the men laid out, blood staining my beautiful carpet. I picked up my metal case and spun the combination on the mini safe quickly. When it popped open, I heard my father scream and I dropped the container as all the shooting stopped. Tears welled up in my eyes, but I refused to let them fall as I bent down and scooped up the three passkey cards that'd fallen to the ground. I pulled my closet door closed with me inside of it, then moved all of my clothes to the side quickly as I heard more feet coming up the stairs. I passed the first card over a red electronic light blinking against the wall of my closet. Nothing. Trying not to panic, I passed the 2nd, and the red light silently blinked green. A door popped open and I slipped through it in my pajamas and bare feet, sliding it closed behind me as I heard men storming my room, screaming in radios. I ran as fast and silently as I could through the walls of the house until I reached the basement. I used the second passkey to get into a sub-basement that led deeper under the house into a narrow room. At the end of the room I pressed my finger to the fingerprint scanner. It beeped and it hissed open as I slid in the last room. Inside the room was a safe. Hands trembling, I used the final passkey to open the safe. Inside that safe were three large suitcases. One was pink leather, one was black, and one was dark brown. I grabbed the pink and dark brown leather ones, swallowing my tears back as I stared at the black one I'd have to leave behind. That was supposed to be my Daddy's suitcase. I opened it and ran my hands over his clothes lovingly, touching things he'd touched. I took his cologne and stuffed it in my own bag. I changed into jeans and a shirt, threw on some sneakers and zipped the pink bag up. I reached in my father's bag and fished around until I found a set of keys, then lugged my luggage over to the small door at the back of the room. The way the escape tunnel was built, the door would lead to an area on another property away from my father's house. He owned that house too, but no one knew that. I would climb out of here, get in the car parked in the back of the house, next to the shed that was blocking the end of he escape tunnel from anyone's view, and drive to the airport. My passport and all my personal info were already in my suitcase. There was around 10 million in the other suitcase. Right as I get ready to pull off, I hear FBI agents still shouting in the distance. Fury rages over me and I dig in my bag for a t-shirt. I twist it up, stuff it in the gas tank and press in the cigarette lighter inside the car. When it pops out, I carry the gasoline-tainted shirt over to the door of the escape tunnel, light it and toss it inside, slamming the door closed.

When the final safe containing the suitcases was popped open, the escape tunnel was rigged to start releasing natural gas in case we were followed. If anyone actually made it back to where the final stop was, they'd probably die before they figured out how to get outside…

I didn't turn around or look in the rearview when I heard the explosion a block later.

As I rode the private plane my father kept on standby plane back to America, I wondered what kind of future I ws going to have now. All those preparations me and my father had made, they'd kept me alive, but what good were they gonna do me now?

I got off the plane at Newport News International Airport and got into the first Yellow Cab I found, my heart pounding. I kept waiting for someone to stop me, or arrest me, but no one did. I hadn't been here in years and everything looked different. When I was last in Virginia I was a little girl who was kept in the house most of the time, so I didn't really know where anything was. As the cab driver turned left onto Jefferson Blvd., he asked where I was headed.

"Just keep driving, I told him," trying to get my thoughts together. He peered at me in the rearview, but didn't say anything. I just stared out of the window for over 25 minutes while he fought traffic. By the time the cars lightened up, we were heading into downtown Newport News and the more dangerous side of town.

"Wait… I need to go to a hotel…" I said, realizing we were getting close to a dangerous area.

"Around here?" the cabbie asked, clearly irritated.

"Take me to Hampton," I commanded.

"Look, kid, it's late and you got me driving all over the damn city." He pulled over and crossed his arms. "Eitherer you show me some cash or you get out here."

I glanced around at some of the older, closed down stores and the people walking around looking suspect. "You'd put me out right here?"

"Show me something pretty," he demanded.

Pissed off, I bent down and unzipped my bag. I snatched out a stack of $50s and tossed them in his lap. "Pretty enough for your ass?" I snapped.

"Gorgeous," he said, grinning and pulling a gun out. He turned it on me and put the car in drive. "Get out."

I stared at him like he'd lost his mind. "Are you crazy?"

WICKED BLUES Deszion Nasir

He raised an eyebrow and looked from me to the gun and back to me again. "Bitch, are *you*? Get out and leave the suitcase. *Now*!"

"Okay, okay!" I said, my hands shaking. I reached over and unbuckled my seatbelt. I kept my scared eyes trained on him so he didn't see me slip the long, sharp, hard plastic knife I kept on me when I traveled out of my coat sleeve. You couldn't carry metal weapons on a plane, but nobody ever caught me with the plastic one. I reached over, opened the door with one hand and when I raised the other hand like I was using it to help me slide out, I quickly swiped at the cabbie's neck. The knife made contact and he jerked in surprise. He fired the gun and blew out the back window of his car. I jumped back in the car and grabbed the arm with the gun in it. I wrestled it from him as he grabbed for his neck, but he took his foot off the brake and the car started rolling again. The car rolled onto the lot next to where we were-a used car lot-and crashed into the chained off gate, bursting through the gate and crunching a Hyundai Accent to pieces on one side before it came to a stop. I banged my head on the open car door, but had managed not to fall out of the car. The cabbie was moaning and groaning, but I fixed that for him. I snatched my knife out of the side of his neck and lodged it through his vocal cords with a grunt. While he struggled with that, I snatched my two bags and jumped out of the car. The few people who'd seen us looked high or suspect enough to mind their own business, but snitches came in all shapes and sizes so I cut through the car lot and ended up in the back parking lot of a strip club with a big sign over it that read "Majik City." I frantically looked around, saw girls walkng into the back door gaurded by a fat guy with a too-small shirt on. I looked down at myself. I was tall for my age, about 5'8", and I had on the same clothes I'd left Brazil in. I ducked behind a huge truck, ripped off my bloody shirt, kicked off my sneakers and slipped on a pair of heels, glad my bra was lacy and black. I dug in my pocket and found my lip gloss, put it on in the truck's side mirror, and stuffed my

WICKED BLUES Deszion Nasir

other gear back in the bag. I raked my waist-length hair back to make it look a little wilder, then stood up and strutted over to the door and sraight up to the bouncer. He did a double-take when he saw me.

"Damn, baby… another new girl?"

"You tell me. You seen me before?" I asked sexily. At least I hoped I sounded sexy.

"Shiit… I'd remember you and that sexy-ass accent. What's your name, love?"

"Carnival," I told him, making something up instantly.

"Okay, okay… you gonna let a nigga get a ride?"

"Find me later and we can talk about it," I whispered in his ear.

He grinned a grin a mile wide and stepped to the side. I tried not to throw up and walked inside the bar.

Having never been in a strip club I was floored by what I was seeing. Women getting slapped on the ass, getting champagne poured down their bodies by men, shooting beer out of their pussies, bringing men on stage and basically letting the men lick their pussies for big bills in the middle of crowds… I could even see some women giving men lap dances, but men discreetly were pulling their dicks out and I could see women rubbing wet pussies on the heads of strangers dicks all in the name of some money. I'm pretty sure crazier shit was going on on the second floor where men wearing more expensive gear were being led by the more attractive dancers. Those stairs were being gaurded by two no-nonsense gaurds.

I had been there all of two minutes when a man rolled up behind me and grabbed my ass. "*Damn* baby, you not leavin, are you? I got $300 if you just let me *touch* it," he said to me. I shoved him off of me before I remembered I was supposed to be a stripper. He just laughed and slung his arm over another female.

WICKED BLUES Deszion Nasir

Shaking at this point, I drug my bags over to the corner of the bar, where I could sit them in a corner and survey the club.

"Can I help you?" the bartender asked me, sauntering over to me, looking me up and down curiously.

I drew a blank for a second, then ordered what my father always drank. "Jack on Ice," I told her. She raised an eyebrow at me. "With a splash of Coke." She stared a moment, then went off and filled my drink without asking for my ID. When she sat it down in front of me, I thanked her and she gave me another crazy look. I sipped the drink and tried not to make a face. I was gathering my nerves and looking around me when I saw the bartender talking to a tall man at the other end of the bar. His hair was in swirled cornrows and he had a nice build, but he didn't look that much older than me. I felt my stomach flip flop as he glanced my way, then he sat his cigar down in an ashtray and nodded at the waitress. He gulped the rest of his drink and stood up. He had to be way over 6 feet tall and the closer he got to me, I noticed he had the iciest blue eyes I'd ever seen in my life. He sat down next to me calmly and leaned on the bar.

"So… who're you running from?" he asked in a smooth voice.

"Excuse me?" I asked him, instantly defensinve.

The man grinned and remained calm. He picked up the drink I was barely sipping on and sniffed it. He sat it down and smirked. "You a dancer in here, huh?"

"Yup."

"Just started, huh? I come here a lot…" he explained.

"Yeah, just got hired this morning."

"You don't seem like the type. What made you wanna strip?"

"Hey, I gotta do what I gotta do, right? It's just me out here, you know? I gotta take care of me."

"Yeah, that's true. Shit be happening to muthafuckas everyday out Bad News. Like, this cat was *just* tellin me how this nigga was just tryna rob this chick in his cab, right?

Broad fucked his shit up. Cab crashed into a car lot. Right across the lot and shit… damn shame…" he shook his head and took a gulp of my drink while my throat tightened.

"I don't know nothing about that," I said firmly, taking my drink back and downing it like I drank everyday. I didn't cough, but the strong drink made tears pop out of my eyes. The man just grinned.

"Yeah… I own this club… and I don't know nothin about hiring no sexy ass girl that speaks Portugese, neither," he told me, picking up on my accent swiftly. Being immersed in my father's culture for so many years had caused me to pick up an accent that would stick with me the rest of my life.

Shaking, I looked at him fearfully.

He smiled like we were old friends and stood up, still holding onto my drink. "Get your bags and follow me, ma."

Caught and not knowing what else to do, I grabbed my luggage and followed the tall man past the two gaurds and up to the second floor. To my left I heard a lot of grunts, moans, change jingling and cursing down a dimly lit hallway. The tall man turned left and I sighed inwardly, relieved. We went up another shot flight of steps and into a suprisingly tastefully decorated office and he closed the door behind me.

The first thing he did was walk over to a small closet, pull out a dress shirt and toss it to me.

"Thank you," I muttered. He watched me button it up before he sat down behind his desk. I sat down in the huge chair in front of him, sinking into the leather and feeling tiny.

"Why're you hiding in my damn club?" he aked me, point blank.

I hesitated. "I don't know if I can trust you," I told him.

"You can't. You can't trust nobody. But you *can* confide in me. I don't got nothing to gain by turning you in *or* letting you go, so I'm neutral." He shrugged. "Maybe I can help, maybe I can't. But my people just called me and told me someone fucked up that punk-ass nigga Charlie that's always tryna stick up his customers. Then you walk in here

192

WICKED BLUES Deszion Nasir

like that. Out the gate I can tell you ain't from here and you a fuckin hustla, just like me. So that makes me wanna at *least* pay attention to what you have to say."

So I ended up spilling everything to him, my tired 16 yr. old mind relieved to get rid of some of the pressure that had built up. I told him everything except how much money I had in my suitcase.

He didn't ask. He was focused on something else. He sat forward on his desk and stared into my eyes. "Your daddy was Antonio Souza?"

I nodded. "You knew him?"

"I knew *of* him," he corrected me. "I heard about you, too. I heard you speak a lot of languages and you know a lot about international business and money markets."

"That's pretty much all I know…" I told him.

He nodded, then slid his desk open and started flipping through files. "Look… I gotta deal for you… if you come work for me… I'll make sure that mess outside gets cleaned up and nobody finds out anything. Everything that happened at your father's house in Brazil can stay in Brazil," he promised.

I frowned, my anger and pride rising. "Work for *you*? Nigga, I'll never be a whore," I snapped.

He laughed. "First, my name ain't 'Nigga.' It's Gemini. Second, I wouldn't never make you no dancer. Not that you ain't pretty enough. You're actually almost *too* pretty, for real. But what I mean is that your biggest asset in my eyes is your brain. I want to expand into the big money markets… and I need someone who knows how to work that. I need to make connections overseas. I have contacts, but I need someone for them to deal with who's charming, attractive without being intimidating… someone who speaks their language," Gemini said, peering at me so hard I could see the dollar signs dancing in front of his eyes.

So that's how it went down. I agreed to help Gemini get his hands in the pockets of overseas billionaires and he made all my troubles dissapear. In a strange way, he

193

reminded me of my father, and I felt safe again... except my dad never teased me about getting some pussy. I never gave Gemini any, but it turned into a running joke between the two of us. I thought about it over the years, but I saw what happened to the numerous girls Gemini ran up in. The became his slaves. They all ended up either hooked on the dick or some drug and their lives belonged to him either way. I'd never let a man have control over me like that, I vowed. Which is why I'm so pissed of at my self right now, waiting on this nigga Tre to tell me what he's gonna do. I shouldn't give a fuck. In all my 23 years I'd never given a fuck about what a nigga thought. For what? I've killed more people than most people knew. Most of the time when I first started traveling, niggas treated me like that chump-nigga Charlie did, and most of them ended up a lot worse off than he did. Most ended up dying from loss of blood from a severed body part. There was just something about seperating a man's limb from his body, usually something we all overlook, like both middle toes and middle fingers, and just sitting there and drinking Coronas until he bleeds to death. That's when I have time. Other times I'll chop off something bigger, like an arm, a nose, or semi-decapitate a head and laugh as people actually try to hold their heads on their shoulders before they collapse on the ground.

I eventually found my mother and Jari, because I needed somewhere to use as a residence when I wasn't on a run, even if I was never there. My mother shocked the hell out of me and hugged me like she missed me, but I found out quickly what that was about.

"Hey, baby, you look good... all grown up and pretty, just like your daddy... he was a pretty man," she said to me, sitting down across from on the old beat-up couch. Jari, who'd grown into a beauty herself, was leaning against a doorway, glaring at me.

Mom dumped the ashes of her cigarette into an empty Pepsi can and looked me over. "See you been eating well...

it looks good on you, though... most women cain't wear weight well..."

I shifted uncomfortably. I had put on some weight by now, a lot of it muscle, and although I'd only received positive comments from men, women were always being haters, so anytime a woman mentioned it, it irked me. But her remark was quickly forgotten with her next statement.

"I heard about your daddy," she said, looking me in the eye like she was searching for something.

"That was long time ago," I said simply.

"Yes it was... He had a beautiful house... still remember it... wonder what happened to it..." Momma sat back and stared at me through a smoke ring.

"A fire."

"Tragic. Terrible thing... tell me, though... you think that fire burned up all that money he had hidden around there?" she asked, rubbing out her cancer stick and lighting a new one up, never breaking eye contact with me.

"What do *you* think?" I asked her, irritated.

She raised an eyebrow. "Well, for *one*...I think you a little too sassy. I also think your father was too smart too let all that money burn up by accident. I heard he had a couple million hidden away. Maybe more..."

"Maybe... maybe less... nobody would know except someone who lived in the house," I said pointedly.

Momma narrowed her eyes at me, then covered it with a fake smile. "I also heard when they put the fire out, they found a safe... but it was empty..." she added, her smile turning threatning.

I uncrossed my legs and leaned forward slowly, resting my elbows on my knees and staring her dead in the pupils. "Let me tell you what *I* heard, Momma. I heard when they found my father's body, he'd killed 15 FBI agents. He was killed outside in his back yard. A shitload of agents were found dead in an *upstairs* bedroom. Those men died *after* my father. How you think he pulled that off?" I asked, faking confusion, tilting my head to the side.

195

My mother paused mid-puff, her eyes changing from a tigress to a cornered monkey. Her hands shook slightly as she sat her cigarette in the ash tray and looked away from me.

I smiled and stood up. "I'll see you later, Momma."

On my way out, I reached in my bag and handed Jari as stack of hundreds. She glared at it, then took it like it was fake. "Don't let her drink it up," I said in a low voice. Jari didn't answer or look at me as I left...

Word got out about me as I traveled more and more around the globe, because after a few months, when niggas got word Gemini was sending Rio Souza to handle the money end of business, shit started tightening up. Niggas stopped coming out of their mouths disrespectfully, the money was neater, and after I cut off one man's lips for calling me Gemini's bitch, niggas barely spoke to me above whatever was absolutely nessasary. I had money, power and respect and was determined to hold onto it. The only thing that had me fucked up was this nigga here... I'd been very closed with my heart, never opening it up this much to anyone. I fucked when I was horny, yeah, but in that respect I'd always carried it like a man. I never equated sex with emotions. Everytime I got close to love I ended up in the same fucking situation. Another bitch popped up he forgot to tell me about. There was always another bitch or some *drama* with another bitch. This was the first time in 3 years I'd felt anything for a man and I didn't like the lack of control I had over the situation. I had no friends, mother, sister or anyone else to talk about any of these feelings with, so I was running totally off these new emotions, which I knew was dangerous. But I couldn't do anything about it.

While   was bouncing back and forth between memories, Tre'd slid next to me until our legs touched. I could feel the heat from his thigh coming off of him. He reached over to me slowly and slid his hands up my back. The simple act of him touching me made my back arch and I sighed, a tear rolling down my face. I didn't want to feel shit for his ass, I swear I didn't... but I did.

"Rio, come on, baby. I know shit is real fucked up right now... but don't walk out on me in the middle of this shit. Everybody in my fuckin life walked out on me when shit got tight. I'm not no bad nigga, I just keep getting myself in real fucked up situations. If one more person walks out on me... just... look... I know you gotta be goin through shit working for Gemini. I ain't asked you what you do cuz it ain't my business... but working for him and having the mom and sister that you got... you cain't say you don't need some peace in your life, too. Skip all the other shit about babies and futures and shit. Do like you said before: live today for today. And today we need each other. Let's just be here for each other today and worry about tomorrow after the sun come up."

Well, shit. What was I supposed to say when he was using my own words against me? I was still thinking, but he took my lack of protest as an agreement and put his hand on my leg and turned me to him, placing my legs on either side of him. He peered into my eyes. "Say something, Rio."

"Say what?"

"All you gotta say is that you don't feel shit for me. Say if I leave-right now-you not gonna be fucked up and I'm gone. Gone like I won't *never* here," Tre swore, holding onto my hands.

I opened my mouth to tell him just that, but I surprised myself when a salty tear fell from my face into my mouth. It startled me that one tear had apparently turned into many, and I only got out "I... can't-"

Tre instantly jumped toward me and crushed his mouth on mine. When he sealed our lips together, he slid both his arms around me tight, creating a heated ring around my body I couldn't break free from. I wanted to fight him, but the passion coming from him was making me weak, making me a slave to unfamiliar emotions. I had no idea how to fight sincerity when I'd spent most of my life surrounded by lies

197

and illusions, so I was comepletely sucked in by Tre and his overwhelming presence. His ripped the buttons off my shirt and and I barely got a chance to unhook my custom-made bra to avoid him destroying that as well as he laid me back on the bed and looked down at me, his eyes telling me I'd almost given him a heart attack by snatching away even one inch of everything his eyes were touching on my body. Just drinking in my body made him calm down a little and he lovingly slid my pants off of my body, letting his hands slowly slide over my soft, golden brown skin. He pulled off his own heavy t-shirt and jeans and dropped them on the side of the bed, less concerned with them, and crawled over me, staring down at my body and then down into my eyes. "A nigga cain't help the way he feel, Rio," he started, but I put a finger up to his lips. I knew where he was going and I didn't want shit to go that far. I didn't want to hear him say what was on his face. I didn't want to look that far into his heart, into his soul. Not when I knew what I knew. Instead I pulled him down to me, into my heat and that thunderstorm that happened everytime we touched each other. His tounge swirled around my neck and my collar bone, making me moan before he reached my breasts, my nipples standing stiff like two chocolate mountains, waitng for his warm tounge to bathe them. He did and I my whole body shivered. He tried to put both nipples in his mouth, but my breasts were large and firm, so he was having a hard time. Instead of breaking the mood, he smoothy took one into his mouth and played with the other one, pinching the tip of it as he bit the other, causing me to cry out. He knew I loved that.

"Tre, don't start that…" I pleaded.

"Don't start what?" he asked, pausing briefly. "You know as well as I do this shit got stared way before today and no matter what *you* talkin bout, it ain't stoppin no time soon," he added. Before I could protest, he'd slid a hot hand down over my stomach and inserted 2 warm fingers inside a hot sauna. I twitched violently as he bit my other nipple simultaneously, then pulled his coated fingers out and brought them to my mouth. "Taste how sweet you are," he told me, putting my own nectar in my mouth. I licked his fingers clean, knowing that drove him crazy. "See how good you taste?"

"Mmm,"I nodded, pushing his head further down. "I wanna taste myself on your tounge, baby," I told him, and he grinnned, knowing he'd got me. He bent my legs up, and told me to spread my lips for him. I did, and he slid his tongue deep inside me and expertly twirled it around, causing me to damn near sit up straight as he licked, sucked, bit on my clitoris as drank up every drop I let loose as Tre made my eyes roll in the back of my head. I was holding back my orgasm, but he could tell, and he was fighting me for it, like he was fighting me for my heart. I didn't want to fight, not tonight.

"Baby," I gasped, pulling his face from between my legs. I pulled him up to me and began kissing his face, licking my love from around his mouth. "I want to cum when you do... if we gonna do this... let's do this together, okay?"

"You so gatdamn sexy when you talk like that," he rasped, kissing me, his sweat dripping in my face. When Tre went to work on your pussy, the nigga went to *work*. If I was a different type of person, I'd rent his ass out. I pulled him up to me, prepared to return the favor, but he resisted. "I just wanna get inside you, ma. I just wanna fuck you so damn bad I don't even got time for no head. I wanna get in that pussy right the fuck now," he breathed, pulling me down and bending one of my legs back to my ear. I reached down, found his swollen fury and slid it in its throbbing home, knowing he loved it when I did it myself. I was so wet and so anxious that my pussy sucked him up with a slurping sound and my vaginal muscles put a vice grip hold on his dick as he grunted loudly and cursed. I slid himself in further by grabbing his ass and lifting my hips and stretched my walls, letting out a few hissed curses myself. Tre got himself together and slid an arm around my waist, gripped the headboard with the other hand, spread his knees a little. Then

WICKED BLUES Deszion Nasir

he proceeded to fuck the pure-d shit out of me, lifting me off the bed with every thrust, my sweat-drenched hair swinging back and forth against the rented sheets as I clung to him, riding like I was on an upside-down bull as I locked my legs around his waist and refused to let his passion override mine. Despite the situation, I wanted him to feel everything I felt for him through my actions, so I made sure I kicked it in overtime. I started bucking so hard Tre had to get on his back, and when he let me get on top of him, I made him lay with his head facing the bottom half of the bed.

"Why I gotta lay this way?" he got out.

"You'll see," I panted. I wiggled my hips to make sure I had a good connection, then I began a slow rise and fall. He moaned out his pleasure then I picked up the pace. I grabbed his hands and leaned back, bending my body back and started riding at such a severe pace he started yelling out "Shit, girl!" as he started sliding against the mattress. Eventually, Tre was the one hanging near the edge of the bed. He had to use his hands to keep himself up, but I was zoning out on him and we ended up on the floor, both of us yelling like we were fighitng, the sound of sweat and cum from both our bodies making a loud slurping sound as my pussy and ass slammed into him over and over. He finally wrestled me over and rushed to get his excited dick back inside me. There was already cum from both of us inside me and it squirted out in protest as his large dick forced its way back inside my still hungry pussy. Soon the sound of Tre's balls and the feel of them slapping me in the lovebox had me trembling as I felt the big orgasm I'd been waiting on creep up on me.

"Aw, shit, I feel that baby; I feel that coming," Tre grunted. "You feel mine coming baby?" he asked.

I managed to nod. His dick was swelling up to an enormous size inside of me, the pressure of an impending nut threatening to blow my lungs out of my back. Tre bent over me until he had me in a true doggy style, with his arms locked around my thighs, playing with my clit as he forefully showed his flexibility by pounding in and out of me bent over that

200

way. I felt the energy roll through me, roll through him and meet in the middle and we both yelled out as lightning struck at the same moment. Tre's dick thrashed around inside me furiously like a caged animal and he almost cut off my oxygen before he finally let me go and slumped to the plush carpet, gasping for air, drenched in sweat, his lower section comepletely glazed in my cum. I could feel his and mine dripping down both thighs and staining the soft fibers under me as I tried to breath normally. While I was recovering, Tre- with a large amount of difficulty-crawled over to me, grabbing the plush blanket off the bed, and pulled it over us, wrapping an arm around me, kissing me over and over on the shoulder and on the neck. We didn't speak for a minute.

"A nigga never came like that. Never," he admitted. "The last time I came even close... shit, I was with *you*,"

"I feel the same," I told him, my back to him so he couldn't see the tears streaming down my face. I managed to make it seem like I was snuggling the blanket so it'd catch my tears, and kept my voice low and even like I was exhausted.

"So you see why you cain't leave me, right?" Tre pressed. "We just... we gotta work this shit out, Rio... okay?" he was drifting off now.

I waited until he'd been snoring about 30 minutes before slipping out from under his warm embrace. I got dressed in a hurry, leaving my shoes off, and quickly got my stuff together. I opened the door to the room and glanced back one last time at Tre, sleep, looking so peaceful, the face of a little boy having a wonderful dream peering out from under the blanket. I sucked up anymore tears and walked out into the cold hallway, the chilled air reminding me that it was a representative of the real world. Everything in that warm room wasn't real. I couldn't let it be real. If I did, Tre'd end up dead. I could garauntee that. I'd rather have him hate me than have one more person I loved cooling on a slab because of me.

WICKED BLUES Deszion Nasir

JARI'S STORY 2 weeks later

When I woke up in the morning, for once, nobody was home. I wasn't complaining, but I was shocked. Since I was a kid, every morning there was usually some kind of disruption going on in my house 24 hours a day. Rio not being home wasn't really suprising, but at least my mother would be here to fuck with me. The only thing my mother loved doing more than trying to make my life as miserable as hers was getting money, so that meant some poor chump had fallen for her bullshit for more than one night. Don't get it twised: Moms was beautiful, but she was a cold-hearted bitch and she didn't have any trouble letting anyone feel the ice as soon as he made the mistake of letting her get her paws in his wallet. Whatever. As long as she wasn't here to bother me.

As soon as I swung my legs out of bed, I had an urge to look for a little baggie of mine I had in a drawer. Why not start the morning off right? I dug around for it and was holding the lighter under my scorched spoon when a sudden wave of nausea came over me and I fell to my knees. I watched in horror as my dinner hit the table and mixed with my heroin; together they slid onto the cheap carpet in my room. "Shit!" I screamed, damn near hysterical because I didn't have anymore drugs in the house. I couldn't call Gemini for anymore cuz he would only give it to me when I was working, and I didn't have a client till later on tonight. What the fuck was I supposed to do until tonight? I won't no fuckin junkie. I didn' have no dealer to go cop from… I closed my eyes and tried to keep from shaking. Lately I'd been shaking a little when I freaked out about my heroin, but if I just calmed down I could usually get it under control.

"Damn, this fuckin *baby*," I muttered to myself, annoyed as hell. I wanted to get it scraped out, but Gemini said I'd be out of commission for too long and it was about to be college weekend around here.

"You got like 3 more months to take care of that, just chill the fuck out," he'd told me. He'd been right about being able to charge more for pregnant pussy. My pussy'd never been so wet and juicy, but this morning sickness bullshit happened to me all day everyday and I was struggling not to hurl on my customers. The only good thing was that Tre wouldn't touch me, cuz I always complained that I was uncomfortable when he wanted to rub on me or whatever. I think he was a little hurt, but I was really feeling guilty about the whole thing. I think he was still tipping out sometimes, but I couldn't be sure, and if he was, who was I to be pissed about it? All I know was that he came home every night-I called his house phone- and gave me whatever I wanted, made sure I was comfortable and rubbed my feet, even though I wasn't even showing and my feet weren't swollen or anything yet. He knew how hard it was for me living at home again and just said he wanted me and the baby stress free.

I cleaned up my mess with shaking hands and decided to take a shower to get my mind off the wasted heroin. A warm shower usually helped… usually. It relaxed me and I put on a t-shirt and some boy shorts and was lotioning my legs when there was a heavy knock at he door.

Thinking maybe it was Tre, I sighed and went to the door, not bothering to put any clothes on. When I swung the door open and saw Gemini's blue eyes peering down at me, I frowned and tried to walk away. He reached out and grabbed my arm.

"Nigga, get off me," I snapped, jerking away from him so hard I tripped.

Gemini came in and closed the door. "What's the fuckin attitude about? It's 9:00 in the damn morning, Jari," he said, shaking his head at me.

"What's the attiude about? Nigga you didn't pay me at *all* for yesterday, that's what the fuckin attitude is about. You got me like, 6 g's short. I'm in here *broke*, nigga."

"First, off, it ain't my fuckin fault your ass don't got no money management skills. If you make over 20 grand a week and your ass is broke from missing one night of work, that's on you. Second, I didn't give you your money cuz you was too fucked up to see straight. You woulda lost it or got jacked before you got home."

I crossed my arms. "Whatever, nigga."

Gemini laughed like I was a child. "Jari, you think I need your lil money? Seriously? I'm tryna help *your* ass out. You think you doin *me* any favors by having to keep these cats from bringing in extra niggas or having to babysit your ass because everytime you drink too much you wannna let stray niggas fuck you in the ass for *free*? Jari your ass is reckless as *shit* and I call myself tryna look out for you and that kid you got coming and you wanna give *me* fucking grief?"

I crossed my arms and glared at him, but eventually I had to look away. He was right. I'd been living reckless lately. I don't know what was wrong with me. My hormones were out of control and I'd just be glad when this shit was over so I could have my wonderful, sane body back.

"C'mere," Gemini said to me, lowering his voice and leaning against the front door. He held his arms out and I sighed. I floated over to him and let him wrap his huge arms around me as I melted. Even though it was bullshit, I felt safe and wanted this with him sometimes, and those rare moments were the ones I craved. I *could* have had that with Tre but I'd fucked up and distanced myself from him because I'd wanted to keep my options open. I learned too late that I'd made a mistake and now I knew he didn't look at me the same. Maybe this baby would be redemption for us... but I was caught up in too much shit now and I didn't know how to undo what I'd done... so I was reaching out for affection where I could find it... or where I thought I could create it.

Gemini kissed me on the forehead, then on the lips. It'd been awhile since we'd been together and I wanted him so bad I was ready to subject myself to all he painful things he loved to do to me. But I caught a whiff of a sweet perfume around his neck that stole some of my mind's ignorantly

WICKED BLUES Deszion Nasir

naieve romance. Gemini shut it down anyway when he pulled back form me. "I ain't come over here for all that. Cool out."

Seeing the hurt and rejection in my eyes, he grinned. "Hey, c'mon, now, don't be like that. I bought you something. I gotta drop it off and bounce, that's all. Stop looking so pissed off."

I couldn't get that smell out of my head but I shoved in the back into a locker when I heard him say he had a present for me.

"What is it?" I demanded, breaking out in a huge smile.

Grinning, Gemini stepped back and opened the door. He led me out onto the airy breezeway and pointed down to the parkinglot. There, wrapped in a huge pink bow, was a brand-new hot pink Lexus with my name on the plates. I screamed and ran down the stairs so fast I almost fell. I heard Gemini laugh behind me as I ran over to it, not believing my eyes. I snatched the door open and slid into the new car smell, taking in the gray leather and pink"J"s embossed all over the car.

"You got me a *car*?!" I screamed.

"You don't want it?" Gemini yelled back, coming down the stairs.

"No, of course I do... I just... damn... I didn't expect this..."

Gemini shrugged. "You've had a rough month. This should put you in a better mood. You could probably get a car seat back there," he joked, grinning.

"What am I gonna tell Tre?" I asked outloud.

"Tell him the truth. It's a baby shower gift. He knows I do shit like this all the time," Gemini shrugged it off. I wasn't so sure, but Gemini had known Tre a lot longer than I had. Besides, I wasn't about to fuck up my good mood. After Gemini made me go back upstairs and put some clothes on, he showed me the papers for the car gave me the keys and I damn near ran him over. I opened the glove compartment to

206

shove the papers in and found my $6000. I smiled and busted a right at the light to get on I64 West. I was going shopping.

Two hours and several shopping bags later, I was strolling through the mall toting a bunch of bags and smiling at all the men who'd been flirting with me since I'd screeched up into my parking space. The women had been hating and the men had been jocking my every move. I hadn't felt this good in years. I was in Victoria's Secret, picking out things to wear to work tonight. I was determined to make enough money-save enough money-to do just what I'd originally planned-get rid of this kid and get the hell out of VA. I wanted to keep a good man like Tre, but it might be better to just cut all ties with this fucking state and start over somewhere. I don't know, though. After today, I was even thinking of bumping Miss Teasha out of the picture and taking my rightful place as head bitch under Gemini's ever-growing empire. I smiled to myself, fantasies swimming through my head. If this was his baby, this might be easier than I thought.

I was looking at a purple see-through bustier set when a sweet perfumed scent invaded my senses, stealing my fantasies and my mood like a dark cloud. The smell was familiar. It was familiar because I'd just smelt it on my future sponsor.

I turned to my left and sure enough, there was the little red-headed paper-blocker sniggling and giggling with one of her friends, squirting the seductive body sprays Victoria's Secret had for sale on each other and whispering.

Feeling like fucking with her, I held my head high and sauntered over to her, making sure my keychain was sparkling and visible under the mall's lights.

"Hello, Teashaunna," I said loudly, putting on my biggest smile. Instead of the usual sneer I got from her, Teasha grinned widely. "Hey, Jari. How's the baby?"

"Fine," I said shortly. "How's work at the burger palace?" I asked pointedly.

Teasha's smile tightened, and her friend's eyes swung from me to Teasha, and back to me again, obviously trying to figure out what the hell was going on.

"I don't work there anymore," Teasha said quietly.

"Oh, I'm *so* sorry," I said, not able to hide my smile. "The economy is getting to everyone, girl. Don't worry. You'll find something else soon."

Teasha's friend straightened up. "Girl, you want me to handle her?"

Teasha smiled. "Naw, Chelsea. You go ahead. I got this."

"You sure?" Chelsea asked, looking like she was itching to do something.

"Positive." Teasha smiled at her. Chelsea glared me up and down before walking off, shaking her head at me. "I think we need to have a chat, woman to woman," she said to me, switching her purse from one shoulder to the other.

"Yeah, you right," I nodded. "You wanna go outside?"

"Naw, right here is fine." Teasha said, moving her shiny hair over a shoulder and readjusting her sunglasses ontop of her head.

"Whatever. We can do this right here and get it over with then."

"Oh, you must be confused, boo boo. It's *already* over with," Teahsa told me, waving her hand in my face. That's when I saw it. I don't know how I missed it before, because it was damn near blinding me now. A huge, diamond engagement ring was damn near choking her whole hand. I tore my eyes away from her hand and looked into her eyes, looking for a lie, but all I saw was a silent look of "Yeah, bitch, *he* gave it to me." The smirk on her face damn near sent me into warp mode as I was forced to come to terms with the fact that Gemini wasn't going to give me anything anywhere *close* to what I was dreaming about. The car he'd just given me wasn't even worth a quarter of the ring Teasha had on her finger. That told me two things: 1) I'd played myself, and 2)

Gemini had to be balling *way* more than I'd imagined to just be dropping paper like he was.

"Now, I don't think me and you have anything else to talk about, so I'ma just get my honeymoon gear-" she lifted her shopping bags, "-and be on 'bout my business." She turned to leave, then paused for a second, pointing to my keys, clutched in my furious fist. "Cute keychain," she tossed back at me before strutting off, leaving me standing there, embarrassed and feeling sick.

I should've just let it go. I know that now. But I just couldn't. I couldn't accept the fact that this bitch was living the life I should be living. What was so special about her? I was consumed by the shit, and I found myself following behind her as she strolled toward the entrance of the mall, slipping her shades on her face and pulling out a cell phone. She made a quick call, ignoring the men trying to holla at her, and as soon as the sun hit her dark golden-brown skin and made her hair light up like it was on fire, a sleek, aerodynamic blood red Mercedes Benz with Gold rims and detailing, and dark tinted windows pulled up in front on the mall. I was behind the crowd of people gawking at the car, and read "Gemini's" clearly written on the plates with a sickening sense of loss in my stomach.

The icing on the cake was when Gemini got out of the car, came around the side and snatched Teasha up in a hug, a huge smile on his face. A few people were taking pictures as the happy couple kissed and Gemini tossed her bags in the trunk quickly.

"So you finally on lockdown status, huh?" an onlooker called out excitedly. I held my breath, hoping with my last hope Teasha'd been exaggerating. As if he could sense me, Gemini's eyes wandered over the crowd and settled on me. His gaze paused for a moment, but he smoothly broke our gaze and slid an arm around Teasha's waist.

"You cain't call it lockdown," he said to the crowd. "Look at my baby. Who'd gonna call marrying *her* a punishment? I'm still tryna figure out what *I* did that made

209

her think I was good enough for *her*," he laughed, which caused the crowd to roar in laughter. Blushing, Teasha pulled his face down to hers and kissed him, and he beamed a smile down on her like I'd never seen. That did it.

"Oh, so that's it?!" I yelled out, causing and immediate wave of attention. Teasha's smile was frozen on her face, but Gemini's eyes darkened instantly as he focused on me as everyone parted a path from me to him and Teasha. I knew I should be quiet while I still had a chance, but my damn hormones had control over me.

"You just gonna buy me a rinky dink ass car and give her the ring? I feel so *fucking* stupid-"

"That's because you *actin* stupid. Shut the fuck *up* Jari," Gemini said in a warning tone, not veiling the threat in his tone at all.

"Or *what*? Or you gonna tell your bitch-" I stopped when I blinked and Gemini was instantly in front of me like he'd teleported across the concrete.

"You say one more fuckin word and I'll *murder* your ass," he hissed through clenched teeth. "I *promise* you," he added while Teasha shoved through the crowd screaming " Nah, nah… Tell me *what*, Gemini? What the *fuck* do she have to tell me?"

Gemini glared at me, then I shoved Teasha out of my way and tried to walk away but she grabbed me by the hair and snatched me down to the ground. The back of my head hit the concrete and dazed me for a second. When my vision cleared, Teahsa was on top of me, her arms around my neck, choking the shit out of me. "Bitch, you fucking *my* man? You tryna tell me you fucking *my* nigga?!" she screamed, cutting my oxygen off quickly. People were trying to pull her off of me, but everytime someone touched her, Gemini tossed them in the air like frisbees.

Teahsa pulled her fist back and punched me in the face 3 good times before I finally shook my head, realizing I was assed out on this end of the fight. I'd been caught off guard and won't no wins for me here.

210

"What, *bitch*? I want you to say it louder in front of *all* these muthafuckin people so this bullshit can be *over* with. Have you *fucked* Gemini?" She let my throat go but snatched my hair up in her tiny fist so hard my eyes watered.

"No!" I screamed, blood spurting out of my mouth where Teasha's oversized engagement ring had cut my gums.

"That's what the fuck I *thought*," Teasha growled, letting my hair go as Gemini finally made it back over to us and snatched her off the ground. The crowd was going crazy as I turned on my side and vomited, unable to avoid the cameras snapping. I'd never felt so low in my life. I wiped my mouth and tried to get up, that's when I saw Gemini quietly fussing at Teasha about her temper and rubbing her stomach. Something in me broke at the sight of that universal sign.

"You know better than that," he was saying.

"She... she's pregnant?" I got out, now standing.

Gemini whirled on me. "Yeah she is. Everybody knows but you? Damn... Both of ya'll out here like you don't got no damn sense... Rico..." he motioned to one of his boys standing nearby. I looked away from him because he'd been a client of mine a time or two. "Put Teasha in her car and take her back to our house-" *Our*?? "I gotta take this one home. Drop Teasha off and come get me from them apartments around Hampton University. Don't be all day, either, nigga. *Hurry up*." Gemini commanded. He said some things to Teasha, who was glaring at me and asking why Rico couldn't take me, but he whispered something in her ear that startled her. Her eyes darted to me, then back to him, and she nodded, letting Rico lead her through the crowd and to her brand new car. As soon as Rico pulled off, Gemini looked at me, his jaw tight. He grabbed me by the arm, his anger obviously only controlled because of the audience. "C'mon."

All of a sudden, I was scared to go anywhere with Gemini and I wanted to ask anyone... even a stranger, to drive me home instead, but from the look on Gemini's face and the death grip he had on my arm, nothing was up for negotiation right now. He ripped my purse from my arms and snatched my keys out of my pocketbook. He opened the passenger door and damn near tossed me inside my new car. I think if all the people outside hadn't been out there still looking at us, he would have. Gemini kept his jaw clenched and didn't say a word until we were on the highway on the way back to my house.

The silence was choking me, so after taking out a baby wipe and cleaning the blood and vomit from my mouth, I sniffled and muttered "I'm sorry."

My response from him was an open-handed slap across the face. Then he brought it back across my face with the back of his hand. I screamed and covered my face, but he didn't even swerve on the road.

"What the fuck do I want with your 'sorry?'" Gemini yelled, changing lanes. "You think I give a fuck about you being sorry? You a sorry bitch, you *supposed* to be sorry. What you *not* supposed to be is stupid. That shit you just pulled was fucking stupid. Are you tryna fuck your own shit up? What the *fuck* you think is gonna happen when Tre find out you was whylin out on Teasha in public? You gonna fuck your shit up, but more importantly, you gonna fuck my *money* up."

"Oh, that's all you give a fuck about, huh? Your damn money?"

"You *gatdamn* right. Don't act like we met yesterday. I already told you I don't give a fuck about *you*, dat nigga Tre *or* that fuckin kid swimming around in you."

"Which might be yours-" I tossed in.

"Doubt it. But that one who just whooped your ass back there? I *know* that kid's mine… Can you say the same?"

I sighed and crossed my arms.

"And that's what the fuck *I* thought."

The rest of the ride was silent. When we got to my house, Gemini got out of the car and lit a Newport, instantly calling Rico on his cell phone to see how far away he was. He hung up, pissed, and leaned against my car, his back to me. I sat in the car for a few minutes, I guess in hopes he was gonna come out and talk to me, but he didn't. Feeling like I had nothing to lose, I got out of the car and walked around to face him. When I came into his line of vision a look of irritation came across his face quickly.

"Can I just ask you a question?" I prodded.

Gemini dropped his Newport, stepped on it and sighed like I was wearing on his nerves, but he didn't say no.

"If we had've met under different cirucmstances, do you think... you think I might have been the one with the ring on?" I asked. "I don't know why, but I have these strong feelings for you and... I don't know what to do with them... I feel... lost Gemini..." I crossed my arms and looked away from him, embarrassed. I heard dead silence behind me. I waited a minute, but he didn't say nothing. I finally turned around and saw him staring at me like he'd never seen me before. A wave of hope flashed through my ignorant mind a second before he burst out laughing.

"Hell *naw* I'd never give your ass no ring. Are you fuckin crazy? Let's skip over the fact that you one of the biggst hoes *I've* seen in a minute; your main problem is your're a bitch. You come from a long line of bitches, the *biggest* one being your fucking daddy. What the fuck *I* look like wifing a crazy, bitch-ass, crack-head whore? You ain't good for *shit* but what you been doing, so go for what you know and leave the lady-like shit to the *ladies*."

I was so mad I started shaking. "Are you *serious* right now?"

"Am *I*-are *you*?" Gemini laughed. "All that fake-ass shit about feelings and whatever. Jari, all you give a fuck about is some shopping money, getting your pussy licked and getting your next hit. It ain't your fault. That's the way you was brought up. But don't mistake emotions for jealousy. You see Teashunna with shit your ass'll never get fucking around with Tre and all of a sudden you got feelings for a nigga? What the *fuck* would make me trust you after you fucked with my nigga, fucked me in a hospital room and now you fucking all these other niggas?"

"You asked me to!"

"You ain't my bitch, neither. I'd *never* get my woman to do no shit like that, and I could never claim no woman as mine who'd do no shit like that, neither."

"So, you saying I ain't good for shit but making you some money?!" I snapped, stepping up to his face.

Gemini pushed me out of his face. "Bitch don't get ahead of yourself. You ain't making nowhere near enough scratch to be in my fuckin face, yo."

"Nigga, you ain't gonna do shit." I yelled, furiously foolish and in the fuck-it zone.

"Bitch, I'll put your ass on a corner *tonight*," Gemini threatened, taking a step toward me.

"I'm not doin that shit no more," I told him, rolling my neck. "Fuck you."

Something in Gemini's eyes clicked. "Fuck *me*?"

"Fuck *you*." I repeated, tears in my eyes.

Gemini nodded, his lips, curled under and his jaw clenched. He bent down, picked up the cigarette butt he'd stepped on, shoved it in his jeans pocket. Then he pulled on a pair of leather gloves from his coat pockets and stood up, grabbing my arm again and drug me upstairs to my apartment. "Open the door," he commanded. I tried to snatch away from him, but he slammed me against the door, clearly meaning he wasn't about to ask again. Hands shaking, I slid the silver key in the lock and opened the door to the apartment.

As soon as we got inside, he tossed me on the floor and closed the door, sliding on both locks. "Fuck *me*?" he repeated, taking his jacket off.

"Gemini-"

Whack! I was airborne and landed ontop of the coffee table. The wind was knocked out of me and I couldn't feel the left side of my face. Gemini hadn't slapped me, but he'd punched me like I was a man. When my vision

214

refocused, I felt blood trickling down my neck and felt heat in my nose.

"Fuck *me*?!" he screamed, the timbre in his voice shaking the walls of the apartment and probably sending the bugs running for their lives. "Bitch, do you realize who the *fuck* you're talking to? Do you know what I *do* to niggas who come out they mouth at me the way you just did?" he yelled, hysterical with rage. He grabbed me by the throat and tossed me back on the floor as I tried to scamper up and away from him. I landed on my back and the wind left my body again. I think I lost conciousness temporarily, because I only remember slivers of the next few minutes, but I saw Gemini moving around the living room. He squatted next to me and slapped me across the face. "Get up."

Gasping, I struggled and sat up, shaking. Gemini dropped some shit in my lap. I looked down, then looked up at him, surprised.

"You need to calm your ass down. Go ahead and fix yourself up," he told me.

I looked down at the spoon, lighter, and other things to make a a shot of heroin in my lap. My body was craving it, but a voice in the back of my mind was warning me to run.

"I don't want it," I shook my head.

Gemini pulled out a Colt Defender and placed it against my head. "Ain't nobody *ask* you what the fuck you wanted. I don't give a shit what you *want*. *You* don't even give a shit what you want. *You* only pay attention to what the fuck *I* want. And I want your fucking *head* right for tonight. So do this shit before Rico get here. Hurry yo ass up."

Shaking, I prepared the needle, while Gemini glared at me, non-blinking. When it was ready, I looked up at him.

"What the fuck you waitin on?" he snapped, glancing at his watch.

I found a vein and slid the needle in, pushing the liquid drug into my system while Gemini watched, his blue eyes piercing.

WICKED BLUES Deszion Nasir

Despite the situation, I cain't even lie and say I wasn't grateful for my familiar sensation flowing through my body. But it didn't last long. Suddenly, my heart started beating too fast and it felt like it was fighting to get out of my chest. I couldn't breathe and I turned to Gemini, who'd stopped pointing the gun at me and was just watching me like a show on TV. I took a step toward him and I stumbled. I crashed to the floor, landing on my right arm. I heard it snap, and pain shot up my arm, but I couldn't focus on it or on the pain that came from my chest because I couldn't move. The last thing I remebered was Gemini's phone ringing and him telling someone to "Come up and snatch this bitch; I gotta get back to my baby," before my eyes slid closed.

When my eyes opened again, I was laying on the backseat of a car. There were two men in the front seat and the smell of weed was choking me as I slid out of concoiusness again.

The next time I came to I was being tossed on what felt like a mattress. I heard loud music in a nearby room and a lot of males talking loudly. I moaned and one of the men in the room came over and looked down at me. "Ay, she waking up. Bring me that needle, man."

Another man brought it to him. "Yo, I ain't sure about this shit, man. This shit is *foul*, son."

"Man, *fuck* that shit. That nigga paying good money for this shit. You know how much them white boys are paying for this bitch?"

"I'on know, man... a rape party?"

"You know white boys be on that sick shit, yo. They paying that nigga 10 stacks a piece to fuck this hoe. There's like, 20 muthafuckas out there ready to tear her ass up. *We* getting 10 apiece. So either get the fuck out and I'll keep the *whole* 20 or shut that emotional shit up and stick *that* needle in this bitch arm so you can keep child support off your ass, nigga. You *know* you bout to go to jail behind that shit..."

The other man shook his head and walked over to me. I was too fucked up to shake my head at him, and I could only

216

plead with him with my eyes. He looked away from my face and stuck the needle in my arm. Within seconds, I could barely move. I wasn't asleep, but I was helpless. The two black men left, and 3 white men came into the room. They were all middle-aged and balding, and wasted no time taking their clothes off and snatching off mine. One of them walked up to me and slapped me across the face. All I could do was moan.

"He was right. She's *into* this shit," he said excitedly. Encouraged by what they thought was simply drunken willingness, those men, along with 17 others, took turns, beating me, fucking me, biting me and fucking me in all three holes until I was bleeding and sore from all of them. They called me slave, black bitch, all kinds of whores and whatever else they wanted to while I had to just lie there and take it. I can't describe the pain I felt or how many times I hoped one of the hits would just kill me as I was tossed around, beaten and abused for money, none of it'd I'd ever see. I'd heard of rape parties, but I'm sure the girls who participated knew they were gonna be a part of it. I was partially paralyzed and all I could do was lie there and feel everything. I couldn't even cry and I wanted to throw up from all the different mens' smells invading my nose, their combined drunken stink making it damn near impossible to breathe. It all eneded abruptly, when two men-one who was fucking me roughly in the ass despite the blood and the other was pulling my face up by the hair and slapping me in my bruised face as he tried to shove his erect little penis in my cum-covered mouth-realized I wasn't breathing anymore. At least, that's what I imagined happened. I don't remember shit but passing out during that and waking up in a bright white room.   My movement brought a nurse over to me.

"Hey, hon. How're you feeling?" she asked me softly.

Realizing I was in a hospital, my memory-and pain, started coming back. I glanced down at myself and saw my arm in a sling.

WICKED BLUES Deszion Nasir

"My… baby…" I managed to get out.

"They're okay. It's a miracle, but… they seem to be okay so far. We're still running tests…" the nurse squeezed my hand.

What? "What? They?"

The smile froze on the nurse's face. "Oh, no… you didn't know, did you?"

"They?" I repeated.

"I'll go get the doctor," she said quickly, hurrying out.

Seconds later, a doctor came in with a clipboard. "Well, good to have you back, Miss-"

"They?" I demanded again, as loud as I could despite feeling like a corpse.

The doctor cleared his throat. "Well, yes. You're pregnant with fraternal twins."

My head fell against my pillow in shock. *Two*? I was carrying-fucking up the lives of *two* babies??

"Do you remember what happened to you?" the doctor was asking me, breaking my train of thought.

"What?" I asked, distracted.

"There was an anonymous call to 911. You were found in a hotel room, severly beaten, raped, drugged and unconcious. The police said it looks like a gang rape. We had to repair a lot of… damage and… you'll probably have to give birth by way of a c-section so you'll heal properly." he said, looking slightly uncomfortable.

"Damage…?" I asked, feeling sick and hollow inside.

The doctor cleared his throat. "There was substancial tearing and abuse done to your vaginal and rectal area. We had to repair it surgically."

Stunned, I asked " How long have I been here?" I asked.

"You've been here 2 weeks."

"Oh my God," I moaned, placing a hand over my forehead.

"A 'Tremeil' has been here repeatedly, checking on you. He said he's your children's father... and a Rio Souza identified you. Her number was in your purse," the doctor went on. "The male has been here everyday... checking on you and the babies... very concerned... and angry... he first got here when the police were here, but you were in no shape to deal with them and he was almost arrested chasing them out... I had a nurse call him as soon as you woke up just now..."

Less than 5 minutes later, Tre damn near tore off the door of my room, shoving security out of his way.

"Jari... who the fuck did this shit?" he yelled, coming over to me. "Baby, who did this to you and my babies?"

My mouth opened, but no sound came out. Trembling, I started crying again. "I don't know who they were," I lied, knowing telling the truth would be sending Tre to his own funeral.

"Fuck!" he yelled, punching the wall. A nurse screamed, but the doctor was finally able to calm him down and convince him to be there for me and the twins right now. He calmed down, but the look in his eyes clearly said that it was only for show. As soon as the doctor stepped out of the room to give us some privacy, Tre closed the door, pulled his chair up close to the bed and sat down. His actions appeared calm for the nurses we knew were watching us from the window, but his tone-even though it was low-did nothing to hide his fury.

"Look, Jari," he growled. "Let's keep the bullshit to a minimum. I already know you were still shooting that shit in your arm, and if you wasn't carrying my life in your body, your ass'd be done for lying to me about that shit, but since you are, you get a pass. I just want you to get better and get your shit right. If you wanna be a junkie, do that shit on your own time. For the next 5 months, that body don't belong to you. It belongs to my seeds, so since they can't take care of themselves, it belongs to me. I'ma find out who did this shit whether you tell me or not, and them niggaz are done. You

219

hear me? So is *whoever* is giving you this bullshit you sticking in your arm. You fucking him?"

Stunned by this suddeen change in anger, I couldn't answer.

"This ain't the time to be *playing* with me and it *damn* sure ain't the time to be lying to me. You *fuckin* that nigga, Jari?" Tre was so mad he was spitting on me. I could look at him and see he was just waiting for me to nod my head. But I was still more scared of Gemini right now and what he could do to me and Tre, so I shook my head no.

"You ain't *never* fucked the nigga?" Tre demanded again.

"No... I met him when I was partying and I was stressed out about Rio and Momma... I guess he could tell and was on some 'Try this' type shit. I thought it was cocaine... I didn't even know what it was until..." I drifted off... realizing that although I was spinning a tale, it was party true. I was about to say "until I was already addicted," but I'd never admitted to it. I'd never admitted to anything negative about myself, even as a kid. For what? My mom never left admitting anything an option. Whatever she said I was, I was, or I was gonna be...

When I was 15 was the first time I was convinced my mother wanted me dead. She'd always called me all kinds of names, blamed me for my father leaving-even though he left cuz she was cheating on him-blamed me cuz Rio's father left her-even though she was cheating on him, too. I was her scapegoat for everything bad that happened in her life.

Once she'd come to terms with the fact that Rio wasn't coming back and neither was the money that came with her, my mother went back to what she knew: trickin'. That was a full-time job for her because she lived above her means and had no life skills to pay for her lifestyle. My mother never worried about me. As far as she was concerned, I could eat at school, and as far as clothes went, I could wear whatever I could steal, just like she did when she was younger.

220

"It's just us, now," she'd tell me. "I gotta make sure the rent stays paid and the light stays on in this bitch. The least you can do is feed yourself. The chink store on the corner got a dollar menu. If you cain't come up with enough money to live off of that, you ain't never gonna amount to shit noway." was her response to me asking her for anything. It was usually followed with a slap or a shove. But she always wanted me to help her glue in her tracks when she was too drunk to do them herself when she was about to go out-which she called working.

"I gotta get to work. Wake your black ass up," she'd slur, coming into my room and shoving me off my bed. It'd be almost 10 at night and she was getting ready to hit The Alley nightclub if she needed money bad. If she had a lil change saved she'd go across the water over to a club out Norfolk, and if she was going with her other scandelous friends on a bonna-fide trick mission, they'd be going to Virginia Beach where the money was. Either way, I'd have to help her with her hair, squeeze her into her clothes or-if she was already working overtime-shave her pussy for her because she was too drunk to do it and "Don't know nigga wanna see gray hairs on no bitch's pussy."

The first time she'd told me to do it I protested and she'd slapped me in the face. "Stupid bitch. I didn't ask you to *eat* it, I asked you to *shave* it. Now take this razor and stop being so fucking stupid." I was eleven.

I got over that as times got worse for my mother. When things were slow, she wasn't above bringing men and other women back to the house and having sex with them right in the living room on the same raggedy-ass couch as we have in there now. I'd seen my mother eat other women out and make me bring them towels, have sex with men and make me pick up used condoms while the drained men felt on my ass and my mother laughed, even made me roll blunts for them when they were already to fucked up to do it themselves. By 15 I was numb to all that bullshit, but I was tired of being broke. I was moving onto my own hustle by now.

My girl Saidia had put me onto a scam she had going out Portsmouth. As soon as my mother went out for the night, I called Saidia and told her to come get me. I didn't brush my hair or do anything special, but I made sure to put on a short skirt, no panties, and no bra. It was chilly outside so I knew my nipples would show through my thin t-shirt. I put on a pair of old raggedy heels my mom'd thrown out and I'd saved from the garbage pile. When Saidia pulled up, I hopped into her car, glad she had the heat on.

"Girl, you look terrible," Saidia said, pulling off with a screech.

"Thanks."

"You nervous?"

"Naw... I smoked a couple of blunts before you got here. I cain't be nervous if we gonna do this shit."

"Good. Everyone else punked out on me, but I'm *telling* you, this is easy money, girl."

"That's what the hell I need. I have to get out of that damn apartment before I kill somebody, for real."

We zoomed over to Portsmouth. Saidia pulled up to a gas station in the worst part of town and let me out, giving me directions and an address.

"You sure this is gonna work?" I asked her.

Saidia sucked through her teeth. "Bitch, I know what the fuck *I'm* doing. Just make sure you know what the fuck *you* doing." She slammed her car door as sped off, spinning gravel everywhere.

As she left me, my nerves began to show. I'd lied to her. I was ready to do what I had to do to get this money, but I'd left a detail out...

I shook my nerves out and started walking to the projects across the street. It was cold outside, so it made it easy to shiver and rub my arms like I was fiending for a hit. I felt people's eyes on me, but I made sure to stay focused till I ran up on the address Saidia had given me. I shuffled toward

222

WICKED BLUES Deszion Nasir

the steps and up to the men on the step, who stopped talking when I came up.

"I... I'm looking for Mann," I said, my eyes darting around.

"What? Who is you?" one man asked with scars on his face and a du-rag on his head. He had that prison build on him and wore a simple white T and jeans.

"Monquez sent me over here," I told him.

The men looked at each other. "Oh, he did, huh?" the man asked. "I'm Mann. Turn around," he commanded. I did, and tried not to jump as Mann lifted up my skirt, exposing my bare ass to all the men, who whistled.

"Aight, come on," Mann said, getting up. He handed his gun to a man on the porch. "Watch the door, nigga." He walked inside the house and I followed him.

"What the fuck?" I heard one guy ask.

"Ay, you know Mann love them babies. Monquez be sending them over for bags of work. You know he got all them young hoes working for him..."

His words trailed off as the screen door swung closed behind me. I followed Mann past the people getting high in the living room and back to a room. The only thing in the room was a mattress on a box spring with no sheets and a dresser. Mann shut the door, went to the dresser and pulled out a bag of dope. He tossed it on the counter and turned to me.

"How long you been working for Monquez?" he asked, unzipping his pants and pulling his dick out, stroking it.

"A few weeks," I said, like Saidia'd told me to.

"Yeah, I can tell. You still look... *kinda* fresh." he grabbed my arm and pushed me to the ground. Without a word he grabbed my head and tried to shove his now erect penis in my mouth. I gagged, unprepared.

"The fuck is wrong with you? Don't act like you don't know what time it is," Mann snapped.

223

"Sorry... I had a hair in my mouth." I pretended to get it out and took hold of Mann's dick.

What I'd neglected to tell Saidia was that I was a virgin. I'd never had sex, much less sucked a dick. But I'd watched it done enough times in my own home to get the gist of it. Mann obviously didn't have a problem, because he was moaning loud as all hell immediately and I felt precum dripping on my tongue after only a few minutes. He snatched himself out of my mouth, pulled me to my feet, and bent me over the dresser and crammed himself inside of me.

I squeezed my eyes shut and tried not to scream out in pain while he humped in and out furiously. When I opened my eyes again, I saw a red dot dancing across my left hand where I was gripping the dresser. Out of the corner of my eye, I saw a shadow against the streetlight near the window. A second later something went *Psst!* and Mann fell away from me, grabbing his arm from a bullet that'd come from a silenced gun. The window in the room slid up and a figure dressed in all black came in the room quickly.

"On the ground, bitch," was the order thrown at me. I hit the ground, but I could still see the figure moving around the room, the gun aimed at Mann. The figure snatched all the drawers out until one filled with cash and another filled with drugs tumbled onto the floor.

"Shiit," Mann groaned, pissed.

"Nigga shut the fuck up. You know what it is. Be a good bitch and nobody gets popped. You even cross your eyes at me and I put two in this bitch here," the gun gets pointed at me.

"Ay, ay... be cool, man. You can take her, too. She ain't mines."

I turned to Mann, hurt at how invaluable my life was to him. At 15, I guess I was still in a fairy tale about some things like human decency.

"Oh yeah? Was she any good?"

"Hell, yeah… she young, too," Mann said quickly, clutching his bleeding arm, his fluids of life leaking through his fingers.

Thinking, the masked gunman tossed a stack of money back at Mann. "C'mon, bitch. Got something for you to do. If you be a good bitch, you get to go home," The gunman reached down and grabbed me by the arm. I tried to fight , but that got me hit across the face with the gun. Stunned, I collapsed in the gunman's arms as I was drug with the bag through the window and took off down the street. I was thrown in a car parked in the alley and we were on the road before I knew it.

"Damn, nigga, did you have to hit me?" I snapped.

"Bitch *please*, you been hit harder," Saidia snapped, pulling her mask off, laughing. We tore back up I64 and through the tunnel until we got back to Hampton. We got back to Saidia's small 2 bedroom house on Fulton Street and quickly went inside. After a quick count, we both had around $4700 to split. To a 15 year old who barely ever had unch money, that made me rich.

In no time, me and Saidia were sticking up crack houses all over the 7 cities. The story changed a lot to keep us from being found out. Sometimes we had to case the houses for a week or so to get cats used to seeing me, but at the end of the day, while the man in charge was busy getting some head or fucking me, Saidia was robbing him. Sometimes it came face-to-face and I got smacked around a lil' bit, but in the end I always got away like I was just another crack head tryna trick off for a blast. It happened so often in stash houses nobody questioned it.

Then came the deliema. Me and Saidia's target was a spot out in a place called Lackey, Virginia. It was country as hell, but fiends were everywhere. Saidia knew that the cats who ran the spot had a thing for black chicks. Really, young, really dark girls. I had been coping from them for a week now, and the main men, Travis and Bruce, had been trying to approach me the last two times I was there. I'd resisted, but this time I made sure I looked a little more desperate when I walked up to the house.

"Hey, Twinkie," Travis said, standing up when he saw me.

"Hey," I said, looking around nervously. I knew Saidia was already positioning herself in the back of the house in the woods, waiting for my signal. This would be a little more tricky because there were two men I had to distract. "Um... can I talk to you?"

Travis looked at my short shorts and my tank top tied up in the back over my dirty sneakers. "Yeah, we can talk. Where you wanna do the talking at?" he asked.

It was hot outside and I was sweating, the heat making my shirt almost transparent. My young breasts were clearly visible from under my shirt and Bruce interrrupted quickly. "Hey, if ya'll gonna talk business I think I should be in on the conversation, too."

Travis looked from me to Bruce. "How you feel about that?"

I scratched my neck repeatedly. "Yeah, okay. I guess I can talk to both of ya'll about it... not out here, though."

"Naw, of course not," Travis said, grinning at Bruce and showing off a mouth with some lonely teeth missing their neighbors. "C'mon in the back."

I followed the two men in the back of the house towards the bedrooms. I glanced to the right and saw one of the white boys with his pants around his ankles, holding up the legs of a black female laying on a pool table, fucking her so hard one of her heels fell to the dirty ground. With every stroke she was screaming out and reaching for something to hold onto. I didn't get to see much more because Bruce was damn near dragging me into a room with a twin bed, dirty sheets and a window with a sheet nailed to the wall over it.

"So," Travis said, sitting in an old kitchen chair and facing me. "What you wanna talk about, Twinkie?"

"I need to hold something," I said sheepishly.

"Hold something? You not in the hood, girl. What you askin?"

"I need something, Bruce. I don't get paid until Friday, but I come here all the time. You know I'll be back."

Travis and Bruce glanced at each other. "This ain't a bank, girl. Even if it was, banks don't loan shit without making a profit. What profit we gonna get from 'lettin you hold something?'" Travis laughed mockingly.

I licked my lips. "What do you want?"

Bruce raised an eyebrow. "Well, now... sounds like she's willing to bargin. You willing to bargin with the *both* of us, Twinkie."

"If that's what I need to do..."

"It is," they said in unison.

I pretended like I was thinking. "Fuck it, let's do this, then." I pulled my top over my head and the two white boys eyes bugged out of their heads. Travis got undressed first only because Bruce tripped over his shoe and Travis grabbed me. He started kissing me on my neck and breasts roughly while Bruce watched on with a hard dick in his hands, waiting for his turn. The plan was to wait until one came and the other one was coming to signal Saidia, so I got right to the point and hopped up on Travis. Excited, he stumbled and yanked his dick out of his pants, holding me with one hand and sliding his penis inside me with the other.

"Fuck!" he yelled out as I wrapped my legs around him and started bouncing on him. He backed into the wall and held my arms up as he slammed in and out of me. I was actually almost enjoying it, as I'd learned not to focus on my surroundings when I was doing this but instead on the money I'd be making. That was enough to get me wet. The marks always thought it was them making me that way and I'd let them think whatever they wanted.

"C'mon, hurry up," Bruce called out, beating his dick faster, irritated.

"Damn, this is some of the best black pussy I done had in a long time," Travis panted, rubbing it in. "Come feel this bitch's tits."

Bruce had taken two steps toward me when the door to the room flew open. The man who'd been having sex on the pool table earlier stumbled into the room carrying the woman he'd been banging out. They fell on the bed like we weren't even there, drunk as all hell.

"Dammit, Ralph, this room is *fucking* occupied!" Travis yelled, not breaking his stride. I opened my eyes at the commotion and looked down at the woman in the room. My heart skipped.

"Momma?!" I yelled out. The woman turned and looked up at me, trying to focus on my face.

"Jari?!"

"Momma?!" Bruce yelled.

"Who?!" Travis hollered. He was so thrown off he tripped, and I reached out to stabilize myself and snatched the curtain off the window. Unfortunatley, that was Saidia's signal, and a second later, bullets came slicing through the window. The first one sank into Travis and he fell to the ground, still holding me. I screamed as I hit my head on the ground. Momma's fuck buddy shoved her off of him and snatched his gun out. Momma ran from the room, but her man didn't make it. Saidia's next bullet hit his temple. Bruce, however, shoved me out of the way and fired rapidly into the woods. I heard Saidia cry out and grow silent. By the time he whirled on me to shoot me, I had Travis's gun pointed at him and shot him in the right eye. He died with a shocked look on his face.

Horrified, I dropped the gun, then thought better of it, grabbed it, my shirt and all the money I could find in the house and ran outside and down the street to Saidia's car. My mother was nowhere to be found as I pulled away from the backwoods house, crying, covered in blood and brains, clutching a measly $2500.

WICKED BLUES Deszion Nasir

I drove back to Hampton but I didn't go home. I drove out to Buckroe Beach. It was dark and closed, but I snuck into the boardwalk's bathroom and cleaned myelf up, sobbing and crying the whole time. I was scared and shaking so bad I kept dropping things. I cleaned the gun and left it in the trash can in the men's room. Not knowing what else to do, I left Saidia's car at the beach and walked the long few miles back to my house.

When I got there, it was pitch black inside the house. I sighed a sigh of relief. I didn't have any idea what I was going to say to my mom when she came home, but I wasn't ready to deal with it yet. Clutching my bag to me, I opened the door and went inside, closing the door behind me. Before I could turn around and turn a light on, something came crashing down over my head. I crumbled to the floor and dropped my bag as I bent myself up into the fetal position. when I grabbed my head I felt blood and glass and I realized I'd been hit in the head with a bottle. A light flipped on and I looked up into the furiously insane red eyes of my mother.

"Momma! It's me, stop Momma!" I screamed.

"Bitch, I *know* it's you!" Momma screeched, bringing the now broken bottle down ad slashing my arm open. I rolled out of the way when she swung again and she crashed, head first, into the door. "You tried to kill my ass and I'm just returning the favor, bitch! I cain't believe you brung your stupid ass back around here-" she swung at me again.

"I didn't know you was there! How was I supposed to know you was way out in Lackey?!" I yelled, smacking the bottle out of her hands.

"*You* tell *me*?" she yelled. She swung at me wildly. Pissed, I ducked and shoved her in the back. She went flying over the couch with a loud grunt. I ran to grab my bag and she beat me to it.

"Gimmie my bag!" I yelled, but she slapped me across the face with it and I fell down. While I got up, she yanked the bag open.

229

Stunned, she snatched out the money. "Oh, *that's* what the fuck you was doing, huh?" she said, grinning. "I'm just gonna hold onto this since you got me all traumatized and shit-"

Oh *hell* no. "Get off my fuckin money!" I screamed, grabbing a lamp and hurling it at my mother. It struck her in the head and shocked the both of us when she fell over backwards. I ran over to her, snatched up my bag-Saidia's bag-and stood over her, my chest heaving in and out. "The next time and *every* time after that you put your fuckin hands on me, I'ma put *my* hands on *you*," I swore. Drunk and in pain, my mother laid on the ground, groaning and clutching her head. I ran in my room, locked the door and pushed my dresser up against it. I snatched my blanket off my bed, crawled into the furthest corner of my room and curled in a ball, clutching the bag full of money, and cried myself to sleep.

When I came out of my room the next day, the house was still a mess, but my mother was gone. She didn't come home for 3 weeks. It was a scary yet relaxing time for me. I didn't know if she was alive or dead because she'd never been gone that long, but she wasn't here to attack me anymore either. I started to worry after the first week, though. What if she never came back? I couldn't pay rent for long with $2500 dollars. I'd have to do something drastic and do it quick. I was only 15. I couldn't work. All I knew how to do was get attention. I'd have to find a guy to take care of me. I was tall for my age, so it wouldn't be a problem passing myself off as older. I was beautiful, dark, had long, thick black hair that was all growing out of my scalp, and I'd never had a pimple so my skin was smooth and clear. Getting a man wouldn't be no problem. I needed more than a man. I need a baller. And to get one, I needed to be where the ballers were.

Listening to the radio while I was washing clothes, I heard about a party being thrown at a local club. It was being hosted by the club's newest DJ, Gemini the Wicked. I'd never heard of him, but it was being called the Player's Ball of the year, so I instantly made that my endgame. If I was going to get on, that's where I needed to be.

I caught the bus to Coliseum Mall and went on a hunt for a dress no one else would be having on. I ended up buying a Coogi dress that hugged my hips and shoes that matched the colorful fabrics in Coogi's signature palate. I spent a good chunk of my money on that outfit. Next I went to a hair shop in the hood and got my long hair blown and blunt cut in a China Doll style to show off my high cheek bones. I went home, threw a scarf on and did the three S's : shit, shower and shave, before I went into my mother's room and used the high end eyeshadow and M.A.C. lipstick to make sure I looked like a runway model. I called a limo company to take my perpetrating to a whole 'nother level, but I didn' want to pay $500 for the limo driver to come over here, so I made reservations to come to them and just get transported to the party and home. I know I looked crazy getting off the bus at the limo station, but the owner kept his comments so he could keep my money. I showed him my best fake ID and me and my driver were off.

My heart was beating harder the closer we got to the club, because cars were parked several blocks away and there were a ton of security working V.I.P. that night, waving cars in and out. When one guard saw my limo he waved us right to the front.

I put on my game face as the driver got out to open the door for me. I saw everyone who was having to wait in line watching intently to see who was getting out. I almost threw up, but by the time I got out, I had my game face on. People were all whispering tryna figure out who I was, but I held my head high, paid the fee to get in cash like I had $200 to wipe my ass with, when in reality I was carrying my last $700 in my small clutch bag.

The atmosphere in the club was something my 15 yr. old mind couldn't concieve of. The club's speakers had been placed so that as soon as you entered, your whole body was pulsating. LL Cool J was shaking the room for the people who'd actually come to the party to dance nstead of show off.

As I looked around, I was aware that every female they were letting in was bad as hell in her own right. But I knew I was a fresh face and I was alone, so I'd stand out.

Sure enough, I was there less that 20 minutes before someone bought me a Long Island Iced Tea. I thanked the waitress who bought it to me and smiled at the man she pointed out, but I could see his fake gold watch from across the room, so I kept moving across the club. As the club grew fuller, I was approached more, and I turned down several offers. One thing I learned from my mother was you were more valuable the more untouchable you seemed. I was also secretly hoping my new sponsor wasn't old enough to be my damn father. My young mind wasn't thinking about the fact that most guys in my target zone-early 20's-weren't balling yet unless they were drug dealers, so after an hour or so I was frustrated and leaving the bar area, where I was getting propositioned left and right. I didn't want to be a rent-a-hoe; I was looking for a sugar daddy.

Thinking this was a bad idea, I was on my way to the bathroom to cry and reshuffle when a strong hand touched mine. I turned and looked up into a pair of dark eyes that seemed to look green when the flashing lights in the club played tricks with them. He had chocolate brown skin like me and neatly waved hair that was edged to perfection. He had on a button-up shirt, fresh slacks a white undershirt so crisp it looked like it'd cut him if he moved wrong. He looked good and he damn sure smelled good, and his baby face told me he wasn't that much older than me. I felt my panties dampening just looking at him.

"You're not leaving, are you?" he asked in a smooth voice, smiling and showing off a halogen set of white teeth. "I been trying to get over to you all night, but you see how crowded it is in here... and you keep moving around so much," he laughed.

WICKED BLUES Deszion Nasir

I felt my face flush with heat and I smiled back at him. "I *was*, but if you were working that hard, if I left now it'd be rude, wouldn't it?"

"A lil' bit... I'm Tre, and I was wondering if you had time to come hang out at my table and talk for a few minutes before you left...?" he trailed off, waiting for my name and a response.

"Jari," I blurted, caught up in Tre's smile. I held my hand out and floated close to him. He smiled and led me through the crowd over to the V.I.P. section. I felt like screaming in celebration because I had been seconds away from figuring out where I was going to have to live in a few days and here comes the man I was dreaming about. I saw all the other golddiggers glaring at me, on the same mission as me, so I knew I'd have to play my hand close and do whatever I needed to do to hold onto him. He was my only option at this point.

I felt important as he led me up the the V.I.P. section and even the DJ, a tall, light-skinned guy with a wild mess of black hair waved at him, yelling his name out on the microphone. Tre was obviously somebody important and I'd hit the jackpot.

"So, what're you doing in here by yourself?" Tre asked as we got comfortable on the plush couches and alternated between looking at each other and watching the other partygoers.

I shrugged. "I've been stressed. I just wanted to get out and be around a bunch of people I didn't know. You know, be away from the drama..."

"Be someone different for the night?" Tre guessed. He waved a waitress over and ordered him something called E&J and another Long Island for me.

I smiled at him. "You say that like you know me already," I told him, half-joking.

"I know your eyes," he told me, stretching his arms across the back of the seat. I had to look away from him

233

because Tre had always had a way of looking at people in the eye so he could see all the things they tried to keep hidden.

We talked and drank, Tre never leaving my side even once when people would come and try to call him away from his table to meet or see whoever. His response to all of them were "I'm good here." I finally looked around and realized Tre had this whole section to himself, and we were the only ones who'd entered and I felt important. I felt like a queen and like this was where I needed to be. I was finally getting a break in life. I was so happy and tipsy I slid closer to Tre.

"You know what, you're really sweet," I said in his ear.

He grinned at me, put his arm around my neck and pulled me close to his ear. "Are you sure?"

"Yes. I mean, you've been perfect all night. Why did you pick me out of all these women? You said you been watching me since I got here."

He nodded. "I have."

"So why me?"

Tre shrugged. "You're the most beautiful woman I've ever seen. Period. When you walked in here? It was like you were glowing. And I ain't saying that to get no ass, none of that. That ain't the type of nigga I've ever been. Ass is free and plentiful out here as long as you got something a chick *think* she wants. I brought *you* up here because something about you stood out from every other woman in here. I came at you as soon as I saw you because the thought of another man getting some of whatever...auroa you kicking out made me crazy. Short story? Saw you, had to have you for myself. Period."

He was saying all he right things, but I had to be sure..."You just met me... you talking like you wanna keep me," I told him, looking into his dark, forrest green eyes again.

"You were mine as soon as I touched you," he told me, leaning over and kissing me. I damn near blacked out. I'd never been touched out of love in my life, and the

234

WICKED BLUES Deszion Nasir

difference and Tre's open and forward emotions sent me into instant overload. When the kiss got broken by the waitress, he pulled away from me, his passion thrashing in his eyes so fiercely the waitress could only giggle and set our drinks down. As she blended back in with the crowd, Tre wiped his face with his hands to calm himself.

"Come here," he told me. Obediently, I scooted over to him and let him wrap his built arms around me. "I'm not gonna ask you nohing about your past, cuz that's not how I work. Nothing about you existed before today, okay? I know it's more to your story than what you giving me, but I'll learn that later. Right now I just wanna get in your head. So let's just focus on that right now... cool?"

"Okay..."

I relaxed into his arms and allowed myself to be pampered, fed and envied for awhile, finally living the life I'd seen on TV and videos, until someone came up to Tre and said "Nigga, you better report for duty in the morning."

"Fuck you, Newsome. I know what the hell I'm doing," Tre laughed.

Duty? Keeping my game face on, I smiled at Tre. "Does he work for you or something?"

"Work for me? Naw, that's my Superior Officer. He came out with us tonight because I gotta ship back out in a couple of days."

My heart dropped. "Oh, you're in the military?"

"Yeah. My mother passed, so I came home for a few days. They tryna cheer me up, so they got me this V.I.P. table..." Tre's voice trailed off as my heart sank. I wanted to scream. Tre wasn't a baller. He wasn't even rich. He made decent money, but he'd most likely only been in the military a couple of years, so he wasn't making anywhere *near* enough money to be able to afford me. He probably didn't even have a fuckin car. *Shit*.

"Hey... you okay?" he was shaking my arm gently, trying to break the traumatized trance I'd thrown myself into.

"Huh?" I asked, coming back into reality and already working out how to get out of here and land a real baller. Tre was everything I'd dreamed of, but nothing I needed right now... and right now I was on a survival mission, *not* a fantasy trip.

"I said, it's cool, I'll only be gone a few more months, then I'll be home for awhile. When I get back, my apartment should be ready. We could spend a lot of time getting to know each other the way we was talking about." Tre said, smiling at me.

I sighed. "I need to go to the bathroom,"

"Bathroom," he repeated, picking up on my sudden cool in attitude.

"Yeah. Stomach cramps."

Tre sat back. "You were fine a minute ago, though."

"You know how chicks be," I shrugged, picking up my purse and setting my glass down.

Tre sighed, took a sip of his drink. "Yeah... I guess I do."

I felt bad but I had to take care of myself right now. Not looking back, I got up and left the V.I.P. section. I already had my eye on an older man who'd been making eyes at me since I'd been up here. He had on a lot of jewelry and was flashing a lot of my favorite color: green. He saw me headed his way and licked his lips. He shooed a begging female from the stool next to him and suddenly I was staring at the hardwood floor, dazed and watching the cherry from someone's drink slide away from my body as a throbbing pain shot up the side of my head. I felt a sharp pain I my side as I was kicked over and found myself staring up into the clouded eyes of Mann, the first guy me and Saidia had robbed. And he was pissed.

"Surprise, surprise, *bitch*," he yelled, hocking up a mouthful of green phlem and launching it in the air. It seemed to fly in slow motion before it landed on my face and slid down my chin, leaving a slimy trail of disrespect in its path. I tried to get up and Mann pulled out a 9mm, making

WICKED BLUES Deszion Nasir

everyone jump back. "I guess you out here tryna make my money back, right?" he demanded.

Scared shitless, I opened my mouth but the words were too scared to leave my throat.

"Oh, speak up. You ain't have no trouble opening your mouth *or* your pussy when you was pulling your little bullshit robbery." He yanked the hammer back on his gun. "Bitch I'm about to-"

Suddenly, Mann vanished form my sight as someone screamed. His gun flew in the air and everyone ducked, ran and shoved each other out of the way, not trying to be in its path if it landed and went off. Like a circus monkey, the tall, lanky DJ-who'd been on break-jumped into the air and easily caught the gun. He was already taller than everyone so he had the best view of it. He caught it and dissapeared back in the crowd like a phantom. I scrambled to my feet, wiping my eyes to clear the filth out of them, and was amazed to see Tre beating the shit out of Mann like a man possessed.

Mann was trying to fight back and got in one good blow before Tre headbutted him. Mann fell back, the fight gone out of him, but Tre whooped his ass like he owed him money and I couldn't help thinking that was the beating I should have got. Even when Mann passed out, Tre was still going to work on that nigga, breaking his nose, his jaw... blood was everywhere. Tre's military buddies got to him before security could break through the crowd and drug him and me to the exit. Minutes later we were tearing up the side streets, his boys laughing and hollering, but the superior officer who'd spoken earlier looking very upset as he kept glancing in the back of his huge SUV at Tre.

"Are you crazy?" he said loudly. Everyone in the truck grew quiet. "Boy you could've *killed* that muthafucka. You almost did. What did we talk about?"

Silence.

"Answer me, Soldier!" he yelled, banging his hand on the steering wheel.

"I'm sorry." Tre said quietly.

237

"You gatdamn right you are. I want you in my office first thing in the morning. *First* thing, you hear me?"

"Yeah…"

"What?!"

"Yes, sir," Tre said, louder.

The rest of the ride back was silent, except Major Newsome asking where I lived and me responding. I couldn't look at Tre. I was embarrassed and caught up in a new emotion: awe. No one had ever stood up for me for anything in my life. And Tre barely knew me and had damn near killed someone over me.

When we pulled up to my apartment building, I got out. I turned to Tre and forced myself to look into his eyes. "Thank you," I said. My heart hurt when I saw the pain I'd caused him looking back at me. He didn't respond to me and one of his comrades reached over him and slammed the door closed. The truck took off and I sighed. I was turning the key in the lock when I heard the vehicle screech to a halt. The back door flew open and there was a lot of shouting and arguing, the Major's being the loudest. Tre got out of the truck, despite Major Newsome yelling his name repeatedly, and he stromed back to where I was. I tried to hurry up and go inside, thinking he was about to attack me. Tre walked up to me, snatched the keys out of my hand, threw them somewhere inside the dark house, and grabbed me to him and kissed me. I was so caught off guard I fell back against the screen door, breaking the screen when he fell with me. I heard the truck's car door slam hard and the sound and smell of burning rubber invaded our senses as we stumbled into the apartment. We crashed onto the floor and started snatching our clothes off, the cost of this Coogi dress forgotten. When we were naked, Tre sat up above me, the moonlight highlighting his chiseled body. "Let me clear some shit up with you, right?" he said, panting but firm. I nodded, silent. "I'm not with that bullshit you was tryna kick earlier, you hear me? I'm not no bitch-ass boy and I'm not no sucka-ass nigga like the ones you was looking for tonight. You don't

238

need a nigga like that. Whatever you was in there looking for, however you was tryna get it, you need a *real* muthafuckin man to give it to you. And that's what the fuck I am. But I'm *not* with the bullshit. You hear me, Jari?"

I nodded again.

"I don't even wanna know what the fuck that bitch-nigga was about to air you out for, but whatever it was, that shit is done. *Done.* You understand?"

"Yes," I nodded a third time.

"Good... good..." my responses seemed to calm him down and he simmered back down into the loving, attentive man I'd first met at the party. We never spoke of what he did to Mann again, even though I had nightmares about it for weeks.

I had it good back then, but I was too young and stupid to see it. I never saw Tre display his temper like he did in the club again, and although I heard whispers around town about him being crazy, the only side of Tre I ever saw was the warm, sweet, loving and over-attentive guy I'd met. That made me smell myself, and after awhile I started pushing, making him buy me things I knew he couldn't afford and send me shit from overseas. My mother had come home by now, so I didn't have to worry about rent. She kept her distance from me... mostly, and Tre just kept spoiling me. But when he was disccharged from the Army, things changed. Tre ended up having to get two jobs to keep up with the rent on his new place and keep me happy. It still wasn't enough money for me, so I started to distance myself. I'd gotten used to being spoiled, so when he couldn't do the things for me like he used to, I started looking for men who could.

Tre wasn't having any of it. I told him I think we needed to scale back. "We've been going so hard since we met, Tre. We got involved too deep the first night we met and I just don't wanna regret it later."

"What are you worried about regretting?" Tre demanded in his controlled voice. "Finding a nigga with more paper than me? Is that it?"

"Tre," I started, but he cut me off when he punched the wall beside my head in a sudden burst of fury. I screamed and froze as he snatched his fist out of the wall, drywall raining down around me.

"*All* the shit I've done for you... you *still* only in it for the money? I should've let that nigga blow your fucking *face* off at that party," he snarled, his eyes black orbs of fury. "You wanna *leave* me, Jari? You tryna leave me like everybody else did? After all the shit I did for you and every other muthafucka in my life, in my platoon, you wanna leave me like the rest of the fuckin world?!"

I shook my head. "No, no, Tre... that's not it," I lied. He was panting like a rabid animal, waiting for me to continue. "If we gonna be together forever, I just don't want us to wonder if we rushed this, you know... I don't want either of us regretting this later. I don't wanna break up, Tre, I swear..."

The madnes faded from Tre's eyes some. "So what is this shit? You wanna date other niggas but still fuck with me? What if I start fucking with other bitches?"

"Don't bring 'em home, nigga," I told him.

Tre stared at me a minute, then smirked. He sighed, then moved away from the wall. "Damn... got me fucking my walls up and shit..." he shook his hand and I started breathing again. "Look... I mean, you gonna do what the fuck you wanna do anyway. If you wanna carry shit like that... it's whatever... but don't *bullshit* me, Jari. Don't let me find shit out in the street somewhere. I *mean* that shit. And don't come crying to me later when you don't find whatever it is you *still* looking for and come back here to me when I get my paper back up."

I just nodded, happy he was calming down. I figured I could keep Tre around for the basic shit and find my new sponsor to finally get me back on top where I knew I needed to be...

Flash forward to the present, and we can all see that never happened. Tre was the one who came up and he was right, it was never like it was in the beginning again. I'd been young and stupid then and I was still paying for it now, laying up in this hospital bed. My life had come full circle. Once again, after dealing with the wrong muthafuckaz, Tre was at my side trying to make sure I was okay. My knight. And all I kept doing was shitting on him. I looked at him closer, past his concerned face, and saw something purple on his neck. It was barely visible, but I'd seen enough of them to recognize it. It was a hickey. A big one, too. I sighed loudly, realizing I'd probably lost the one man who gave a fuck about me. He was most likely still dealing with the same chick he was creeping around with. He was here now, but he'd obviously been with her very recently. I'd been so caught up in trying to get with Gemini I hadn't been paying attention to where Tre'd been. He was the last life line I had and I had to make sure I didn't lose him anymore than I already had. I finally realized what I had.

"I'm not fucking anybody, Tre. I'm sorry. I'm sorry for all the stupid shit I've taken you through since we've been together, but there's a lot of shit about me you don't know and I've been letting it affect our relationship. But this last incident... let me know the only thing important are these babies... I need you to help me get right for them, Tre. I cain't let them pay for the fucked up shit I done to myself."

Tre sat back, running his hand across his five-o-clock shadow and letting a frustrated breath out.

"Jari," he said finally. "We been doing this shit for a few years now. I'm tired. I'm not gonna keep going through this shit with you, baby. If you gonna be with me, you gonna have to let a man be a man and stop all these fucking games you playing. If you wanna keep dooing your own shit, you can... but you gonna wait until these babies drop. I get my kids, you get your body and take it wherever the hell you wanna take it."

"I wanna be with *you*, though."

"Heard that shit too many times. Every time your shit gets fucked up you wanna be with me. I'm *telling* you,

241

Jari. You gonna do shit my way this time or your ass is fired."

"Fired?" I repeated.

"Muthafucking *fired*," he snapped, bringing his face close to mines. I looked deep in his eye and decided my best-and safest-bet was to lie back, reshuffle my cards and come up with a better way to get myself out of another stupid-ass situation before I fucked around and got myself killed for real.

TREMEIL'S STORY

Overlooked. Slept on. Nobody knows *shit* about me. None of you bitches. All these mutherfuckas are busy running from Gemini's ass and worrying about finding gold-plated buckets to catch his shit. Nobody ever looks in the shadows to see what's watching them. But that shit's cool with me. I don't *want* you pussy-ass cats looking at shadows… cuz in the shadows is where I rest. It's where I rest, where I move, where I live.

I ain't who ya'll niggas think I am.

I left Jari at the hospital and drove across town to another appointment I had. When I walked into the doctor's office, I saw the receptionist smile at me, but I saw the fear in her eyes. I also saw the dent in the wall a repairman had tried to cover when I'd thrown a chair at the wall. Or so I'd been told.

I walked in Dr. Langley's office and saw him sitting with another person. Another guy.

"Who's this?" I asked, dropping my keys on the couch where I always sat.

"This is Melvin. He's here… for…"

"I know what he's here for," I interrupted, sitting down.

Dr. Langley suffled some papes on his desk in tens silence. "So, how've you been, Tremeil?"

I sat back. "Fine, I guess. More stressed than usual. Jari's pregnant."

Dr. Langley looked startled. "Jari?"

"Yeah."

"I wasn't aware you were still in contact with her. I thought you were involved with another young lady… Rio, wasn't it?"

"Yeah…"

"But… Jari's the one pregnant?"

"With twins."

243

"Twins? Do you think that was a good idea?"

"Do I think *what* was a good idea? Fucking her or getting her pregnant?" I asked, smirking.

Dr. Langley shook his head at me. "Let's be reasonable, Tremeil. We talked about this before and we decided it was in your best intrest to take strong percautions not to get anyone-"

"*You* decided," I cut him off, feeling heat rush over me.

"Tremeil, Tremeil, calm down; I just meant that we'd discussed it before, remember? Do you remember that?" the doctor said quickly, sliding his chair away from his desk. Melvin acted like he wanted to stand up, but Dr. Langley held a hand up. "Don't irritate them." he said quietly to Melvin.

"Why the fuck are you always worried about *them* when you're in here talking to *me*?" I demanded.

"I'm not, Tre. Please, calm down. You've made so much progress the last year or so-"

"Then what the fuck is *this* nigga doing in here?" I demanded, glaring at Melvin.

"Melvin step outside. Just *do* it," the doctor said firmly when Melvin frowned at him. Reluctantly, Melvin stood and left, and I felt my rage calm some. Dr. Langley could sense it and he calmed down, too. "I'm sorry... I should have spoken to you about him... my insurance company made me do this, you know I didn't want anyone else in here."

I took a few controled breaths and nodded. I relaxed my shoulders.

"Tell me about Jari, then," Dr. Langley said in a controlled voice.

Don't tell him shit. "I don't wanna talk about her right now," I said quickly, leaning forward and rubbing my head.

Noticing the change in my attitude, the Dr. stopped. "Why not?"

Cut his throat. I told you to slice his fuckin'neck the last time. You know they the same as the police. "I just don't." I stood up, stumbled, feeling light headed. "I need to use the bathroom right quick." I needed to get out before the room began to spin.

The Dr. jumped up and put a hand on my shoulder. He spun me around and looked deep into my eyes. "Who are you?" he demanded.

The next thing I remember, I was being thrown in the air and I hit the ground hard. I gasped for a breath and tried to remember where I was. My vision was blurred, but when it cleared I saw Dr. Langley being helped to his feet, his face red, purple marks around his neck and his nose bloodied. Melvin was helping him to his feet and glaring at me from across the room. I looked down at my hands and saw blood on them. I scrambled to my feet and backed against the wall, horrified at a familiar-yet unfamiliar sight.

"What happened?" I demanded.

"I'll call Eastern Med-" Melvin started out, but the doctor stopped him and told him to wait outside the door... with it open, of course.

"Tremeil... son... I *strongly* recommend that you check yourself in for evaluation."

"I'm sorry," I said, wiping my hands on my jeans, shaking.

"I know. It's not your fault."

"Who was it? Who attacked you?"

"I don't know. But whoever this one is, he's dangerous. Jamal metioned him in another session, but as soon as he tried to talk about him, I lost him. Jamal is terrified of him."

"Another session? Hold up. How long have you known about him?" I demanded.

"A few weeks," Dr. Langley admitted, then quickly added "-but I was trying to get more information about him so I'd know what to tell you-"

"How about telling me a crazy muthafucka was walking around in my fuckin head?" I yelled, standing and kicking over a chair. Melvin stepped back into the room and took a step toward me. Instantly, I swung out and caught him across his temple and laid him out. The violent outburst seemed to satisfy something in me and I calmed down like someone turning a gas stove down.

"Dr. Langley, I don't think this is working out," I told him. I snatched my jacket up.

"Tremeil, you need help," Dr. Langley pleaded.

"This is some white people shit. *I* don't need help. *They* need help." I yelled. "If other niggas are livin in *my* head, they need the gatdamn help, not me."

"You're losing control of them-"

"I'm not losing control of *shit*!" I boomed, picking up a paper weight and hurling it across the room. It crashed against the wall and exploded. I stared at it, shocked, then slid down the wall on the floor, banging my head with my hands, trying to pull myself together.

Dr. Langley slowly came over to me, placed a calming hand on my shoulder and helped me get to my feet.

"Son, you need to-"

I whirled on the doctor. "How the fuck do *you* know what I need?" I snatched the door open. "You don't even know who the *fuck* you're speaking to." I walked out and slammed the door so hard the glass cracked. The receptionist was behind the glass window of the office, peering at me in fear. I ignored her and stormed outside to my bike, got on and tore off down the street, vowing to never come back here again.

I drove down to Chesapeake Ave. by the water, pulled over in one of the observation spots and turned the bike off. I tugged my helmet off and stared at it.

"I'm in control of my *own* shit..." I told myself repeatedly until calmness came back over me. I felt something in my back pocket and reached down to pull it out.

246

WICKED BLUES Deszion Nasir

My cell phone. I felt my stress level rising immediately. I wanted to call her.

Let me speak to her. A voice demanded in a whisper.

"No..."

Let me speak to her.

I closed my eyes to shut the voice out, but all I did was see her eyes behind my eyelids. He wanted her, but he couldn't have her. He was gonna fuck my shit up. I knew who I wanted. Jamal knew who he wanted. I was having enough trouble dealing with the two of us. Now this new nigga was bringing the worse possible scenario into the situation. I tried to put the frantic whispering out of my head, but he kept on going, louder and louder, non-stop until I was sweating. I couldn't hear anything else going on around me and I didn't want him to take control, so I picked up my phone and dialed.

"Hello?" she answered on the 2nd ring.

"Hey," I said, trying to make my voice appear normal. As soon as she answered the phone the whispering stopped, soothed by the sound of her voice.

"Tre?"

"Yeah,"

"Okay..." I could here confused hesitation, yet politeness in her voice. "What's up?"

"Just... I don't know. I think I just needed to talk to someone."

"It's cool," Teasha said, her voice softening. "I've been there before... a lot's been going on, right?"

"Hell yeah," I admitted. "Been working a lot... then you know... dealing with being a daddy now and everything... dealing with Jari..."

"I bet..." Teasha said strangely, then the lightness came back to her voice. "How are the two of you doing?"

"Man, I don't even know."

"You don't know? How don't you know how you and your child's mother are doing?"

"T, me and Jari ain't on it like that. I know G told you that."

"Yeah, but people tell me a lot of shit. I hadn't heard it from *you*, so…"

"Well, you heard it from me. I *tried* to be that way with her, but… she wasn't tryna hear it, man."

"What? Why not?"

"Wanted to keep her options open, I guess."

"She's pregnant. She kept a lot more than her damn options open."

I laughed for the first time in days.

"I guess. I'm just tryna be there for my kids, you know?"

"Kids?"

"Yeah, she's having twins."

"Oh, *shit*." I coud almost see Teasha shaking her head.

"Yeah… It is what it is… I heard you got one on the way, too."

"Yeah… just found out."

Something in me lurched.

"Ya'll ready for that?"

"Does it matter?"

"I guess not…"

Teasha sighed and I picked up on it. "What?" I asked her, unable to keep from digging.

"Nothing, it's just that… between you and me?"

"Yeah, of course, ma…"

"I think this is all movin' too fast… I mean, I really wouldn't even be talking to you about it, but I don't have no family or nobdy else… and you know, you seemed cool when we were talking at Mama Rosa's those few minutes…"

"Yeah, I remember," I said, thinking that was because she was talking to someone else for a few minutes…

"But I mean… it's only been a few months, and now I'm pregnant and he wants to get married and everything…

it's just too much but I don't know how to tell him all that. He's all happy and determined."

Tell her the truth. Tell her... tell her who he is... "Not now-"

"What?"

"Nothing... I'm just saying... you should talk to him..." I said weakly.

Tell her... give her to me... fuck that nigga... that nigga's dead... you know he's dead... you give her to me... I'ma do him anyway... that nigga don't give a fuck about you or her... The whispering was getting louder quickly to the point I could barely hear Teasha.

"Look, T... I gotta go... but thanks for, you know, listening... sometimes we all need that person to just listen to us, you know?"

"Yeah, trust me, I know... " Teasha laughed her golden laugh. "You seem so different right now... you're usually so quiet, now you're like... open, I guess... you seem different..."

"I'm just real,T."

"Hmm..." Teasha sounded thoughtful. "That's what I'ma call you then."

"What?"

"'Real.'"

I smiled, finally glad to have a name. "That's a great idea."

I eneded up staying on the phone with Teasha almost an hour. That nigga Tre was tryna punk out on my ass so I figured I'd better step into the conversation before he fucked shit up for me. He didn't see what I saw in her. There was something else going on with that girl. There was something she was hiding. Something dark in her. I could see it in her eyes when I first met her and I damn sure saw it when she tried to stab that hoe Jari at the club. *That* bitch was nothing short of trifflin' but Jamal was hooked on that walking herpes sore. The nigga was soft, tryna wife that yamp. Now he done fucked around and knocked her up, but I didn't give a fuck

249

about her *or* those fuckin kids. Him and Tre could deal with them bastards if they wanted, but whatever dark spirit was hovering over Teasha's head, I was connected to that. Tre had a thing for that fine bitch Rio, but that's cuz she was high-maintenance like his ass. She had too much shit going with her for me. A nigga like me didn't have that kind of time. And as for Teasha belonging to G? I did't give a fuck about that nigga Gemini, neither. Shiit, I saw shit Jamal and Tre refused to see and it was only gonna be a matter of time before Gemini fucked that up anyway. And when he did, I was gonna be right there to clean his mess up.

I'd spent a lot of time watching what was going on lately, watching the moves Tre made. I didn't usually bother him unless he hesitated to do what the fuck needed to be done. I'd handle shit like a fuckin soldier's supposed to: instantly. Life didn't offer up a lot of time to be hesitating and shit. A nigga'd end up cooling on a table like that. Working with that nigga Gemini had allowed me to be more active in the last couple of years and now I wasn't content with just handling shit on occasion. So much more shit could get accomplished when it was done my way, so I was putting my plans into motion to make that happen. Let that bitch nigga Jamal cry over consequences…

I snapped to when I heard the operator telling me my call could not be comepleted as dialed. I looked down at the phone in my hand as the rapid signal came on the line, letting me know the phone had been of the hook for awhile. I clicked the phone up and dropped it on the floor.

"Shit," I muttered. How long had I been on the phone with Teasha? What the fuck had I said to her? I sat down on the couch and put my head in my hands. This blacking out shit was stressful as a bitch. And this new nigga was reckless as hell. He was gonna fuck around and get me tricked up.

The first time I remember hearing him was when I was real young, like 8 or 9. My pops had come in the house all drunk up and shit, and my mother was screaming on him

250

WICKED BLUES Deszion Nasir

to just shut the fuck up and go to sleep. That shit won't nothing new, but this night he decided to bring his drunk ass into my room and grab me by the feet and snatch me out of the bed. I banged my head on the floor while my mother ran in the room and screamed for him to leave me the fuck alone. My pops shoved her off of him. Whenever my pops got real fucked up, he would either fight me, her, or both of us. I'd just gotten in a fight at school earlier behind a bully trying to take my lunch again-I was smaller than most kids my age back then-and I was already pissed because I'd gotten detention for defending myself. I'd come home and gotten my ass whooped cuz my mom gotten a call on her job from the school-again-about me, so I was in a shitty mood from jump street. My pops coming in here, yanking me out of the bed and punching me in the face like I was grown sent a heatwave through my head and I struggled to turn over and kicked him in the face. Stunned, he fell back and I ran out of my room, damn near fell down the stairs. I heard my dad right behind me, telling me to bring my black ass back here, when he grabbed my foot. I fell forward and my head slammed into the bottom stair.

The next thing I remember, I heard screaming, felt heat and I was being held down by more than one person. When I gathered my senses I stopped fighing and looked around. The screaming was coming from me. The heat was the warm blood covering my face and body and I was being held by a couple of neighbors while my mother cowered in a corner, her lip busted, looking terrified. I looked to my right and saw my father lying motionless on the ground, his throat and face a hacksawed mess, multiple stab wound all over his torso. I looked to my left, to my hand... I was gripping a kitchen knife that still had blood and chunks of meat on it. I dropped the knife in shock and froze.

"Momma..." I started, but she jumped back like she was trying to blend into the wall.

"Get him the fuck away from me!" she screamed over and over while I stared, totally confused.

251

WICKED BLUES Deszion Nasir

"Momma… what happened?" I yelled over and over until the cops came and carried me out. I was taken to the juvinille psych ward until I was 15. I was diagnosed with MPD-Multiple Personality Disorder-but I was given a light sentence because of the abuse that had gone on in the home. The doctors assumed the alter had surfaced in response to my father attacking me one time too many. The violent alter never resurfaced the whole time I was there, and I never mentioned the fact that I'd begun hearing another voice-Jamal-because he was normally the one who tried to keep me calm when I got frustrated or angry. By the time I was 15 the doctors figured I was well enough to go home. I'd only stayed there so long because I'd killed my father. I had to serve *some* kind of sentence.

When I came home, my mother steered clear of me. She *stayed* gone. I knew she was still scared of me, but it was cool. It won't like she was the ideal mother before I'd gone away in the first place. She stayed out of my way, I stayed out of hers.

The next time the violent alter surfaced was the reason I was discharged from the Army for a Section 8-i.e. they think a nigga's crazy. We were in Turkey and a local got hostile and ran up on us when we were just in town at a bar. He called us all kinds of bullshit names… nothing we hadn't been called before. But when we got up to leave to avoid an incident the mutherfucker hit me in the back with a chair. The next thing a nigga know I'm on base strapped to a hospital bed being told I broke the sonofabitch's neck. Apparently, after his neck was snapped I kept breaking bones on his body until my fellow soldiers pulled me off of him. Said I wouldn't stop screaming. That was the end of my military career.

Once I came home, with that kind of record it was damn near impossible to get a fucking job. The more time I spent alone, the more frustrated I got. The more frustrated I got, the louder Jamal got. But once I ran into Gemini, and started fucking with him again… this other alter started

252

whispering. He'd never spoken to me before. He'd just shown up. But now, because of the nature of the violence Gemini had me involved in... he seemed to be... revved up more often, and now he was in my ear, too. With Jamal in one ear and now this nigga in the other, my life wasn't my own anymore. I managed to keep the peace most of the time by trying to please both of them, but lately? The shit was getting more difficult. Especially since this nigga seemed to be obsessed with Teasha. I don't know why, but that shit wasn't gonna end well for nobody involved. Who the fuck was I supposed to talk to about this shit? Niggas didn't have these kinds of problems. Where I was from, they always told us that was white people shit. If I didn't bend to this new nigga, I could wake up in prison. I couldn't let that shit happen. Regardless of which one of us got her pregnant, Jari was knocked up, so that meant all us were gonna be a father. I had to hold shit together for my babies. But how the fuck was I gonna hold them down when I couldn't even hold my mind together?

When I got back to my new apartment I threw my keys on the couch, mentally exhausted. I kicked my shoes off and sighed. It was quiet, and while I was grateful for that, I knew it was only temporary. Despite all the shit going on with me, the Earth was still spinning, business still had to go on, and I still had responsibilities. I wanted to drink that whole bottle of Gin I had in my cabinet, but being drunk won't a good idea in my condition, so I settled for a big bag of bright green weed. I was licking a blunt closed and was picking up my lighter to seal it when I noticed my hands were shaking. This life was making my nerves bitches. I had just gotten the blunt lit and was on my way to calming my mind and spirit when my phone rang.

I sighed again, then reached ove slowly and picked it up on the third ring.

"Yeah," I grunted, inhaling and filling my lungs as best I could.

"Got moves for you to make," Gemini said.

253

WICKED BLUES Deszion Nasir

I kept my irritation to myself. I didn't have no problems being a soldier on my team, but Gemini was using me like a fucking thug. I was already in the military once. I wasn't tryna be no hired killer no more. When Gemini and I had run into each other after I'd gotten discharged, the nigga had carried it like I was gonna be the 2nd in command to the big things he'd been doing. I was, for a minute. But as time went on, I eneded up doing all this covert operation bullshit. That was what all them other 804 Boyz were supposed to be for. Gemini won't the only smart nigga, but he was acting like he was doing me a favor and shit, giving me more and more of this bullshit to do until I barely ever had any major decisions to make. Gemini had another partner, from what I hear, but I'd never met him. I felt like I was being pushed aside, like he was setting my ass up. He knew I was in a fucked up position where I needed the money right now, so he was being an asshole. He was shitting on me like I'd never looked out for him when he'd stumbled into Lincoln Park that day back when we met…

"Nigga, can't you get Charger to do that shit?"

"No, because I need *you* to do it. I already put the payment in your account for it. I need these niggas done today, and I need that shit done right."

"Who is it?'

"Nigga from up top. He's in VA tryna do business and kickin dirt on us, saying we in his pockets out here. I'm like, *fuck* that nigga. If we cain't eat in *NY*, then his bitch ass cain't eat in *VA*. You know how we do it, son."

"No doubt."

"This could be our ticket in, man. If we take the top nigga down, the pawns will fall. Same way we did here. When word gets back how a nigga got smoked here just for poppin off at the mouth, niggas'll take us more serious." Gemini explained.

"Or try to kill us…" I added.

"If they try to kill us, they *definitely* taking us seriously,"Gemini insisted.

"Yeah… you know I got you, G… when we rolling?"

"Oh, you rollin' solo, son. This your time to shine, my nigga."

"Nigga, you buggin. Where your ass gon' be at?"

"Gotta business trip to make."

"This ain't business?"

"Different business. Got money matters to discuss with some white boys. Me and my business partner got the money end, you and me got the street end."

My fist tightened over the phone. "The dirty-nigga shit, right?"

"Nigga, stop cryin. Look, what do you know about overseas accounts? Investment banking? Stock market scams? My other partner deals with all that shit. I told you, we doin this shit big. But to do this shit big, I need my commanders to control their positions. You do what you do and let my other head do what they do. When the shit comes together cain't nobody touch us. This shit ain't just about money, Tre. We can have all the muthafuckin money in the world and never mean shit cuz we ain't got enough power. To get that power, we gotta get in good with them white boys. And you know that. So stop bitchin like you the last kid picked for dodge ball and dead them niggas." Gemini slammed the phone down, leaving my mind swirling as I had a meeting in my head about whether or not to follow through with my orders, kill Gemini, or both.

Less than 15 minutes later, there was a knock at my door and a brown envelope was leaning against my door when I opened it. Inside the envelope was simple an address and a picture. I was hesitant about moving like this, and I was getting a general bad feeling about the whole thing. Something wasn't right about the way Gemini'd been moving.

Nigga, fuck that shit. Handle your muthafuckin business. There's other shit to be done today.- hissed the new voice in my head

Look, man, you should look into this shit before you move. Find out who you movin on. What if this shit turn on you. Is Gemini as big as he's saying? What's to stop niggas from coming after you? Jamal asked logically.

Fuck that shit, yo. Stop being a bitch. Following orders got you where the fuck you are now. If niggas did retaliate, they'd come after G, not you. You're just a shooter.

Yeah... you're just a shooter... that's all the fuck he using you as... nigga's playing you...

The arguing continued until I had to shake my head like I was trying to shake one of them out of my head. Before I knew it I was headed to my safe and pulling out my 9mm. The whispers were shouts now, with Jamal pleading with me and the other voice demanding me to take action. Hand shaking, I stumbled into the bathroom to splash water on my face. When I turned the water on, I glanced up at the mirror and was startled by the face looking back at me. It looked like me... but my eyes... they looked damn near black. I dropped the gun in the sink. The loud sound made me jump and I snatched the gun up.

"Who are you?!" I yelled into the mirror. "Get the fuck out of my head!"

Right before I blacked out, I watched myself point the gun at the mirror and smile. "I'm Real, nigga. And trust me, you'll be gone long before I will."

BANG!

WICKED BLUES Deszion Nasir

REAL

I brushed the shattered mirror off of my clothes and glanced around the bathroom. I stepped over the broken glass and headed back to the safe. I opened it and took out two other guns-an assault rifle and a glock, some more ammo, and the keys to another motorcycle Tre didn't know about I had taped to the top of the safe and slammed the safe closed. I snatched up the address, memorized it and the photo and broke out of the back door. I jogged up the street behind a closed fishery, and went behind some equipment and snatched the covering off my Ducati motorcycle. I was tearing up the road in under a minute, headed for the Oceanfront.

Nobody had time to argue with those niggas. I had a job to do and I wanted that shit done quickly. I had another stop to make after this. Tre's ass was falling off. I wasn't used to having to run shit so much, but I had to do what the fuck I had to do to keep shit spinning. What I had to do was figure out how to get rid of that nigga Jamal. He was smellin his ass lately.

Let's clear some shit up first. I was here before Jamal. I've been here since we were fucking kids. I didn't need to say shit back then because me and Tre stayed on the same wavelength. I materialized to protect us from the niggas moms kept bringing around-including pops. You read all that shit already. Jamal showed up out of guilt. Guilt is a pussy emotion that don't have no place in my world. No one ever felt guilty about the shit they did to us, so fuck feeling guilty about another nigga.

This nigga Jamal had been getting vocal since he'd met that bitch Jari. I wasn't having it. The way to get rid of him was to get rid of her... but Tre wanted these fuckin kids... I'd work that shit out... trust me...

I was deep in thought all the way to Virginia Beach. The address on the package I'd gotten was for an oceanfront hotel called Playa de Carmen. It was midlevel. Made sense.

257

It had the luxury of being on the oceanfront, but not the notoriety, because a dirty cat from up top knew the Marriott or something would have much better security and staff that could recognize him. Virginia Beach was a huge tourist area and fucking with their reputation would make them come down on a nigga like the wrath of the Almighty.

I parked two blocks away and made sure all my guns were loaded. Then I walked to the back of the hotel, pulled out a gun, and fired on the boxes behind the hotel until I saw lights go off inside the hotel. Knowing I had a very small window, I ran inside the service entrance as sooon as someone ran outside to see what happened. I ran to the front desk and snatched out the assault rifle. I hit the girl at the front desk in the face with it and caught her before she hit the ground.

"Where is this man?" I yelled, shoving the picture of him in her face and giving his name.

She screamed, cried, pleaded and shook her head. I hit her again and put the gun against her head. "Where is this man?!" I yelled louder. "Last time!"

"Senor Harrington," she stammered, her Spanish accent heavy. Trembling, she pulled a book out and slid it to me. "He called-had a delivery to room 315-"

I pulled out another gun and put a single bullet in her head. All that took less than a minute and I was running up the stairs as the guests ran aound in confusion, trying to see in the pitch black hotel, the dim back-up lights barely offereing enough illumination to see your hand in front of your face.

When I got to the third floor, I saw gaurds rushing around near the end of the hallway and I made sure I had a gun in each hand before bursting into the hallway. Tre's military training smashed the half-ass wannabe thug behavior as I dropped three of the men within seconds. Hearing the commotion, more men ran in the hall, but I'd ducked into a doorway by then. I could hear shots and the men trying to figure out where I was and where I'd come from. I reached in my jacket, pulled out a smoke grenade and tossed it down the

258

hall. When it went off, there were more shots, screams, coughing and confusion. I held my breath and ran through the smoke, firing, blowing the heads off the shoulders and other random body parts off with my sawed-off I'd had tucked behind me until I kicked in the door to the hotel room.

I felt a bullet slide past my cheek, but I kept firing until 6 more bodies hit the carpet of the suite, either dead or on their way until I was face-to-face with the man in the picture, Evan Harrington. I had my shotgun aimed at him, he had a Desert Eagle pointed at me.

"Nigga, you got a death wish," he growled.

That made me laugh. "How can a man that ain't alive have a death wish?"

A look of confusion passed over Evan's face. "What the fuck do you want, man? The money? Who the fuck sent you?"

"The Devil," I responded before pulling the trigger. He pulled his, too, but he was already flying back into the wall. His bullet shattered the window as he slumped to the ground. I made a quick search of the room and found 3 bags full of money. I slung them over my shoulder and ran to the balcony. I was three stories up, and I could already hear the police coming. I hopped down one story to another blacony, then jumped to the ground on the grass behind the hotel. I came down rough on my right ankle, but it wasn't broken so I didn't feel the need to dwell on it. I took off top speed and ran to my motorcycle and was gone before the cops pulled up, held up by the traffic in the area.

I hauled ass through back streets until I got to Norfolk. I pulled into a gas station on Newtown Rd., grabbed my bags and went into the bathroom. I changed my clothes, dumped the old ones in the trash, flushed the keys to the bike and snatched another set of keys to a Dodge Ram I had taped to the inside of a toilet. Yeah, I had back-up plans every where. I knew what I was, and to be successful and what I did I had to think 20 steps ahead of myself. I glanced in the

259

bags I'd lifted from Evan. Two were full of 100 bills, the last was full of what looked like crystal meth.

I left the bathroom and swiftly walked around the corner to where the Dodge Ram was parked. When my hook-up at the gas station noticed the bike, he'd move it until closing, wipe it down, repaint it, change the plates, and put the bike and keys at another stash spot of mine.

With my job done, I decided to spin out and up to Williamsburg to my other appointment. An hour later I was walking into Second St. restaurant. I looked around until the sunlight pouring in the window bounced off a red-head's locks. She was sitting by herself in a corner and hadn't noticed me come in. I walked up to her and smiled. The shadow I threw over the table got her attention and she looked up at me, startled.

"Hey," I told her.

"Hi," she said uneasily.

I slid in the booth. "You look nervous."

"I am nervous…"

"Why?"

"Why? You dropped a lot of heavy shit on me the last time we talked, Tre."

"Oh, you can't call me Real no more?" I asked half-joking.

Teasha grinned and shook her head. "Ok, Real. Seriously. Where did all that come from?"

I shrugged. "I don't know, T. I told you… there's something about you I can't get away from… I keep thinking about you…"

Teasha shook her head and stood up. "This was a bad idea. I shouldn't have even come out here."

I reached out and grabbed her hand. A shock passed through me and into her. I know she felt it because she jumped and snatched her hand back. "Please, T… just… hear me out… just let me get this shit out and you don't never gotta speak to me again. When you leave here, this conversation won't ever have existed," I promised.

260

Rubbing her hand, Teasha looked like she was thinking hard, then finally sat down.

"Look, I know how fucked up this looks. You think this is some simple shit for me? Jari's pregnant, you pregnant by my best friend... if I was just playing games... do you think I'd risk all this fuckin drama to be funny Teasha? Seriously?"

Teasha took a deep breath. "But why, Real? Why now? Why didn't you just speak to me first when we met? What changed? You're so different..."

I leaned forward in my seat. "Inside everyone there's a dark side of them they don't want nobody to see. I can see yours T. What I can see in you... that's the real you... not this... this... Barbie doll Gemini got you dressed up as. Don't get me wrong. Not that you don't deserve to be treated like that... but I don't see the real you... the beauty inside of you is raw... like... pure energy someone's keeping in a jar... but for some reason, when you're around me, that jar's made of glass. I can see all that raw power inside of you and it's like a fuckin magnet, T. I'm... it's like I'm pulled to it because I got the same shit inside of me. I spend very *fucking* day trying to be what the rest of the world tells me I need to be... I don't feel like I gotta *do* that around you and it fucks with me to look in those eyes of yours and see the shit I see in mine when I look in the mirror."

Teasha stared at me, her eyes boring into mine to see if I was trying to play her or if I was being serious.

"Are you saying... are you telling me you feeling me because... you think I'm crazy?" she asked finally.

"Naw, never that... I'm tryna tell you I can *hear* whatever's in you trying to get out. It's calling me... I just wanna know who you really are..." I told her.

Teasha balled her fist up and banged it on the table so hard a few other tables looked at us. "I *can't* be her no more." She glanced around, calmed herself slightly and leaned forward. "I can't be who I used to be no more, Tre. I got a different life now."

"Your life is a lie," I insisted.

"But it's still mine," she said, grabbing her purse and standing up. I tried to grab her hand again, but she was quicker this time.

"T, don't leave yet."

"I think I better."

I sighed and sat back, watched her damn near run out of Second St. I tossed a $20 on the table for the salad she never ate and followed her out to her car. I grabbed her by the arm, spun her around and took hold of her by the face.

"Don't run from yourself, Teasha... who you really are is gonna come out one day, I *promise* you," I told her. Her eyes watered up and spilled over. I bent to kiss them away and she trembled for a minute before she shoved me away. She hopped in her car and sped off, leaving me staring after her.

By the time I made it home, I had 3 messages. All 3 were from her.

WICKED BLUES Deszion Nasir

RIO

Knock, Knock.

"You almost done?"

"Get away from the damn door." I called out crossly.

The hotel suite's bathroom swung open anyway and Gemini stared down at me, bending over the sink, putting on my rose-colored lip gloss. All I had on was a silk bra and thong set the same color as my lipstick. My hair was pulled back off my face and held back by yellow diamond clips on one side while the other side fell in waves over my left shoulder.

I straightened up and put my hands on my hips. "Out. Right now."

"Damn, Rio. You been teasing a nigga for years. When are you gonna give me a fuckin break and let me just sample some of that?" Gemini asked, walking in closer to me and admiring me in the mirror. He came up behind me and brushed his lips across my neck. "Damn, you always smell so fucking good, too," he muttered. A chill crosed my back when his tounge ran across my skin. I put my lipstick down and turned to face him.

"You're serious, aren't you?" I asked him.

"Do I look serious?" he asked, pointing to where his penis was trying to rip through his pants.

I crossed my arms and regarded him for a minute.

"Don't front like you won't never curious, Rio... and I know it's been a minute since you got some," he told me, grinning when he saw me hesitating.

I finally grinned back and he smiled triumphantly. I walked up to him, grabbed him by the collar, and pulled him down to my level. "You not worried about being late to this meeting?"

"We won't be," he said confidently.

"We'll see," I told him. I shoved him off of me and back into the bedroom area of the Waldorf Astoria room we were in. We were supposed to be meeting a high-profile bank

263

president in an hour or so, but Gemini's hormones were getting the best of him. I knew Teasha's pregnancy was fucking with his sex life and here was only so much stray pussy he could get and stay interested. He'd been coming after me for years, and I guess he figured since we were out of town together he'd go for it.

Gemini backed into the bed and grabbed me by the thighs. I fell forward with him falling backward and I ended up onto of him, straddling his large frame. I licked the side of his neck, and snatched his shirt up roughly. I heard him grunt in appreciation as I slid my hand down his body and latched onto his dick. I started rubbing it through his pants with one hand and unbuckling his belt roughly with the other as he grabbed one of my breasts through my bra and bit one roughly, making me cry out. I pushed him back and sat up, gazing down at him, his eyes full of lust.

"You been waiting on this, huh?" I asked, reaching behind me and unsnapping my bra.

"Fuck yeah," Gemini said, licking his lips at my full breasts swinging in his face and him staring like he was hypnotized.

I licked my hand and pulled his huge dick out, massaging the head of it. "You been waiting on this, too?" I whispered.

"Mmm-hmm," he moaned, dropping his head against the pillow and closing his eyes. I took my other hand, licked my palm, then raised it and slapped the shit out of him. He jumped up half a second after I did, a hand print on his face.

"Gatdammit!" he yelled, stumbling with his pants and trying to pull them up over a hard dick. "All I wanted was some fuckin pussy!"

"No, nigga, all you wanted was MY pussy," I corrected him. I snatched up my bra off the floor and put it back on. I stormed into the bathroom to get dressed and slammed and locked the door. Seconds later Gemini was banging on the door like the Feds.

"You think that shit is funny, Rio? Getting' a niggas dick all hard like that and then puttin your hands on me?"

"Gemini *fuck* you. You put your hands on someone for breakfast, lunch and dinner, nigga." I yelled back.

"Yeah, and you about the be the next one, bitch-"

In one smooth motion I had my gun in one hand and had snatched the door open with the other hand. I swung the handle of the gun at Gemini's head and he ducked. We eneded up on the ground, him on his back and me on top of him. He wrestled me over and snatched the gun from me, but I punched him in the face. He grabbed both of my hands and pinned them beside me and I head butted him, my hair flying out around my head. He let me go and fell back, cursing. I climbed to my feet, panting.

"I got your *bitch*, nigga..." I snapped, my chest heaving as I straightened my hair. "Now stop *fucking* around and let's go get this money."

"That shit is so fuckin' *sexy*," Gemini panted, getting to his feet. He grinned, slapped me on the ass and went into the other bathroom to get himself together. I sighed and leaned on the sink in exasperation.

Forty minutes later we were in an elevator going to the top floor of a plush Manhattan office, no trace of our earlier scuffle visible, unless you could count the tiny red spot of Gemini's forehead, but you'd have to get way closer than he'd let you to see it.

After a short wait in a front office, a secretary who made it her business to look me over throroughly escorted us into the office of Emerich Vestanutti. He was a tall man with regal, silver hair and a red carpet quality suit and tie.

His eyes swept over Gemini's hair, which was tamed and pulled back in a ponytail, making him look Latin, and his tailored suit, which made him look Latin *and* rich, then at me, who had on my fitted sapphire blue dress with a clinched waist that showed just enough leg and cleavage to cause a slight rise in Emerich's pants without him thinking I was trashy. Everything about me screamed classy and he could smell it. He knew I wasn't here as eye candy.

"Mr. Knight, charmed," he said, holding his hand out for Gemini to shake.

"And I as well," Gemini responded, grinning widely.

Emerich puled back and studied me, his eyes twinkling.

"This is-" Gemini started.

"Oh, I know who this is…" Emerich interrupted him. "This is Rio Souza. She looks just like her father. Just like him. My, my, dear… your name is making quite a buzz around the world…"

"Is it?" I asked sweetly, making sure I kept strong eye contact with him. "Positive or negative?"

"Who's to say? That determination would be based on the recipient of the information," Emerich said, his eyes laughing. "I respected your father deeply, Rio. I wouldn't be the man I am today without his guidance, but I must say I'm puzzled as to what you want from me." He gestured to some empty seats and we sat down before he took his seat behind his desk.

"Me and my partner are looking into international investments," Gemini said pointedly. "We're looking to grow and expand our overseas portfolios and make our money start working for us, instead of us working so much for it."

"That's the smart way to live," Emerich nodded. "How much are you trying to put to work?"

"200 million to *start* with," I said firmly.

Emerich's smile was frozen on his face. He blinked a few times, then looked into some files on his desk. "That's quite an investment, Mr. Knight. May I ask how you acquired such finances? Your personal businesses are quite lucrative, but not 200 million doallars worth…"

Gemini leaned forward. "My business partner has inherited a rather large sum of money when her father passed, as you know, and she's done quite a good job of handling *her*

266

money as well as *mine* up until now. But with new days come new responsibilities. It's time for us to spread our wings, so to speak... now, of course you know we don't have a problem compensating the one who assists us in learning how to fly..."

Emerich's thoughts were almost visible. "How much compensation?"

"10% of this deposit, and 10% everytime we double our money. So how much you make really depends on you, Emerich."

Emerich sat back, shocked.

I slid a cell phone across the desk to him. "Call your swiss bank account now. There should be a notification that a new account was opened this morning and a deposit of 20 million dollars was made. Deposits can only be made by us, withdrawls can only be made by you."

Emerich did as I asked, and after a few minutes, a look of amazement came across his face.

"How did you do this... get my information?"

"I can do a lot of things, how I do them is of no importance to you... but all we're interested in is making money. I'm going to be making some major moves in a few months, and I need all my finances delegated before it happens." Gemini told the stricken man.

"What if I refuse?" Emerich asked.

"Refuse 20 million dollars?" I asked. I smiled and reached out, laying my hand across his, stroking his ring finger. "Nobody refuses 20 million dollars, Emerich."

He looked at my hand, then at me and my face, which read nothing but friendship. He swallowed and nodded.

"I'll have to doctor the paperwork to fit your actual business to keep it under the IRS radar... but it can be done... how do you want the 200 million spread out?"

"However you see fit. My father trusted your judgement and so do I. But make sure to put some in the hands of the biggest crooks: politicians."

WICKED BLUES Deszion Nasir

When all was said and done, me and Gemini had successfully become a part of the business world. Within a month, Gemini's businesses were overflowing with new customers and new money. His strip club was renovated and now catered to more upscale clients-i.e. white executives and regular ballers who wanted to step their game up. On the weekends, though, the hood still ran the spot, and money flowed in like wine. Gemini hired more barbers and stylists to cater to Caucasian clients as well as Black and Latino ones and eventually opened three 24-hour salon/barber shops besides the four he already owned. He stopped working at the radio and bought stock in Clear Channel, but every week he'd throw a huge party at different clubs around Hampton and Newport News, all hosted by 103 Jamz. Within three months Gemini'd gone from local money maker to business tycoon. His name was everywhere, his money was everywhere, and the 804 Boyz were gaining ground in Richmond, North Carolina and Georgia.

2 months later Gemini bought a closed down club in New York City. He had it gutted and totally renovated. It was the next step to him breaking into New York.

I now had everything I wanted: Money, power and respect. I owned a home by the water in Sandbridge, an exclusive area in Virginia Beach where most of the homes were so expensive they were only affordable by way of timeshares, and another in Hawaii, cars, jewels and clothes that cost more than some people's homes. But I lived there by myself. What had been the point of all this bullshit?

I'd been battling with the decision of what to do about my situations with Jari and Tre. The decision was taken out of my hands when Jari went into labor a week later.

JARI

I was curled up in the shower shivering when I went into labor. I'd woken up that morning already in a horrible mood because the last few months had been nothing but misery and heartache for me. Tre'd been coming around more often as my belly'd swollen up, but it wasn't like it was. Something was going on with him. It was like he wasn't even here most of the time. You know, like, the lights are on but nobody's home? That kind of shit. I thought we were trying to work shit out, but sometimes I had to damn near snap my fingers infront of his face to get his attention. His job had bags under his eyes and sometimes when I looked at him, his eyes looked dark... like he was disgusted when he saw me.

I got so depressed today I dug through my stuff and pulled out the last dose of heroin I'd been hiding. I'd been clean since the hospital, but today I was so stressed I actually had the belt around my arm when I felt one of the babies kick me so hard I dropped the needle. It fell on the hard tile and broke. I dropped to my knees, horrified, looking at my reserve supply now ruined, and that's when I started shivering. I'd already been through withdrawl, but just being that close to that shit had my body betraying me again as I curled up in a ball and held myself. I felt my teeth chatter and suddenly a monster cramp took hold of me, strangling me so hard I lost my breath. While I laid there in the tub, trying to recover, another one hit me. I'd been having Braxton-Hicks contractions, but they didn't feel anything like what I was experiencing now. Scared to death, I managed to reach the sink where I had the house cordless and dialed Tre's cell phone.

"Tre-" I gasped as soon as he picked up.

"Jari, not now. I'm at-"

"I know where the fuck you are. But I'm in labor."

"What? Labor? You sure? It's too early-"

"I know... I know... Tre, please..." another wave of cramps hit me and I dropped the phone, screaming. I heard

269

Tre call my name twice before he hung up. 20 minutes later he was bursting into the house, taking off his suit jacket.

"Oh, shit, baby…" he tried to help me up and we both stopped when we saw liquid running from between my legs. Tre snatched the phone off the floor and call 911. Minutes later I was being rushed to the hospital and screaming my ass off.

By the time the doctor had me in a gown and stirrups, one of the babies were already crowning, ripping me open and destroying what the mega rape had already damaged. There was no time for any pain medication and Tre was right there, holding my hand as I screamed, pushed, cried and pushed. The first baby came out screaming at the top of its lungs, waving its tiny arms like it was ready to fight.

"It's a girl!" the doctor called out before the nurses came to get her. Tre wanted to cut the cord but I wouldn't let his hand go. The other baby was on the way out. The second one was a boy, and he barely made a sound at all in comparison with his sister.

I fell back in exhaustion, ready to collapse.

"Lemme see my babies," I called weakly.

The nurses and doctors were gathered around the babies, whispering to each other, occasionally glancing at me and Tre.

"What's wrong?" Tre demanded. "I know they're early. Are they too small?"

"Uh… well… as far as preemies go… they're normal, but-" the doctor stammered.

"Well 'what,' nigga? Give us our kids." he demanded. The doctor nodded at the nurses, who hesitantly brought the babies over to me. I struggled to sit up so I could hold both of them. They both had a head full of ebony black hair that already covered their eyes and almost touched their shoulders. Then they opened their eyes.

Their big, blue eyes.

Scared to death, I looked up at Tre as the nurses stood huddled in a corner, watching and waiting. The look in his

WICKED BLUES Deszion Nasir

eyes was so terrifying the nurses came and scooped the babies up. Their instinct was on point, because the second the babies were out of my arms, Tre had his arms around my neck and was trying to squeeze the life out of me. The nurses with the babies rushed out of the room and the doctor yelled for security to come assist him. They pulled Tre off of me just before I passed out. I gasped for sweet air before the tears came. Tre was thrown out of the hospital screaming like he'd been mortally wounded and I lay in the bed crying, sobbing and wondering why the hospital staff hadn't just let Tre kill me.

GEMINI

"Come on, Mr Knight, one more."

I grinned and turned to the right, hugging Teasha against me snugly. We were posing for pictures at our wedding reception. We'd gotten married outside at the Botanical Gardens in Norfolk like Teasha'd wanted. That was fine with me. It was still warm here in the fall. The press could get all the pictures they wanted without the drama of them sneaking into an inside wedding. We were now at a friend's private beach on the water in Buckroe. Teasha was smiling and sparkling for Essence, Ebony and some other big name black media outlets. There were a couple of mainstream media there too, and that was even better. Neither me or Teasha had any family, so the whole guest list had been made up of friends and business associates, including Emerich and his wife. Once the money started flowing in, he wanted to be my best friend. I knew how that shit went, though. As long as I was rich, he was rich, so I was his favorite nigga... or mutt... or whatever the fuck I was.

We'd just posed for what seemed like our 50 thousandth shot when the rumble of a motorcycle engine got everyone's attention. We all turned to see Tre zooming past the parking attendants, over the grass and out onto the sand toward us. People started screaming and jumping out of the way.

"Gemini what-?" Teasha screamed, but I shoved her into the arms of one of the photographers just as Tre jumped off the bike. He snatched his helmet off and hurled it in the sand before he tackled me in my tux. We crashed into the sand and Tre punched me in the mouth. I tasted blood and retruned the favor. Seeing I was a lot bigger than him, though, he flew off of me and landed on his back. Before I could get to my feet, he had a .45 pointed at me. I froze and Teasha screamed.

"Tre what the *fuck* are you doing?!" Teasha screamed, struggling against the photographer. She

272

eventually elbowed him in the balls and he screamed and fell to the ground.

"He stole my kids," Tre yelled.

"Stole your... stole your what?" Teasha demanded.

"My babies!" Tre yelled, cocking the gun. "Jari just had the twins. Guess what color their eyes were?"

There was dead silence on the beach. I knew the answer to that question as soon as he asked it. It took Teasha a second later to catch on.

"Gemini... please tell me... oh my God... those babies..." Teasha started shaking and clutching her own slightly swollen stomach.

"*Bitch* ass nigga," Tre yelled, then fired at me. I rolled out of the way and scrambled to my feet. I was in a fucked up situation. The press was out here so I couldn't respond the way I wanted.

"Tre," I said calmy, while inside I wanted to pop his head off his shoulders. He pointed the gun to fire at me again, but I lost sight of him when Teasha came flying out of nowhere in her wedding dress and attacked me. I barely caught sight of something glinting in the sun's setting light before it sank into my upper shoulder. I yelled out and fell to the side, crashing into the vegetable table. All the catered dishes fell on me and all over the sand. I reached up and grasped a handle. I pulled out a steak knife Teasha'd grabbed off of a table and watched my blood drip from it as Teashaunna stood over me, crazed and crying.

"You *fucked* that bitch?! You *lied* to me, nigga?! You fucked that bitch for *real*?! You stuck *your* dick in that dirty crack-head bitch and then stuck it in me? Ain't that what you told me? She was a dirty crack-head bitch? Nasty muthafucka-" She snatched another knife up and hurled it and me. I moved and it still sliced my neck under my ear."I told you not to *fuckin* play with me, didn't I?" she screamed, snatching the gun from Tre's shocked hands and fired at me. I felt a bullet sink into my leg before someone tackled her, the gun flying into the water. Tre sprang into action and shoved the guy off of her.

"She's pregnant, bitch!" he yelled, slapping the guy away like a fly. He pulled her to her feet but she shoved him away. She snatched her ring off and hurled it into the roaring ocean. Then she kicked off her shoes and ran back to the house. She talked someone into giving her a ride and she was gone.

"Nigga, your ass is *done*," Tre panted, glowering down at me before storming away. My first instict was to blow a hole in his back. But with all the people watching, all I could do was watch my next target storm off across the sand. I know he was pissed, but no matter how mad he was, when the dust settled, please believe *I* wasn't gonna be the nigga in the box.

TEASHA

It been 24 hours since the fake-ass wedding and I was still holed up in a hotel room in Norfolk. I'd paid for it in cash so no one could trace one of Gemini's credit cards. After leaving the beach, I'd had the lady who'd given me a ride drop me off at a gas station in my wedding dress. She kept asking me if I was alright, but my mind was on auto-pilot. Make-up running and mixing with my tears and staining my wedding dress, I walked into an Arab-owned corner store, went to an ATM and used the black card of Gemini's he'd given me and kept withdrawing $400 until the bag I asked the bugged out attendant for was full. Then I bought a cheap t-shirt, sweat pants, bookbag and hat and changed in the bathroom. I balled the $25,000 wedding dress up and left it in the trash, used a payphone to call a cab, then came out here to Newtown Rd. If he traced the card all he'd come up with would be this gas station. While I was waiting I hit the ATM up outside a few more times until I couldn't fit anymore money anywhere in the bag so I'd be straight until I figured out what I was going to do.

I couldn't even cry anymore now. I'd been crying all night and all morning. I wasn't answering my cell phone and no one knew where I was, so I was alone with my thoughts... my terrible thoughts... and the new life growing inside me. My first thought was to get rid of the baby. It was too late for an abortion, but I could give it up. I couldn't keep a baby with Gemini. I knew what he was about and I now I knew what he was. But that was fear talking. It was my choice to put myself in a situation to get pregnant by a man that I knew was doing foul shit. It wasn't the baby's fault. Then came the horrifying fact that I'd be raising a baby alone when I didn't have shit but some cheap clothes from the gas station, no skills and a bookbag full of money. I didn't even have anywhere to live.

My phone started ringing agan, but it wasn't Gemini's ringtone. I looked over at my phone on the

275

nightstand and scooped it up. Mixed emotions raced through me as I saw Real's number illuminated on the screen. I swallowed, then picked up the phone. I answered the call, but didn't say anything.

"Teashaunna,"

My eyes watered back up against my will as soon as I heard his voice.

"I know, ma... I know... let me come see you..."

"No..." I shook my head and sobbed.

"T, please... I know your head is fucked up right now... but can you even imagine the shit *I'm* tryna deal with right now? I mean... to go through *all* this shit with that nigga and that *bitch*... then to *sit* there and watch them kids slide out with those blue eyes? Do you know what that shit... *man*..." Real sounded damn near hysterical.

I was silent, thinking. I needed someone in my corner right now, and the only person who'd been totally honest with me was suffering as bad as I was. "Where's..." I trailed off, not wanting to even say his name.

"Fuck would I know? I left right after you did so I wouldn't kill his ass. He was busy tryna play shit off with the press. I had to get the fuck up outta there before One Time showed up... Look... I just need to see you... can I just *see* you? I know you need somebody right now... and I don't got nobody else in the fuckin *world* right now... I lost my best friend, my girl *and* my kids all at the same time, T..."

My heart breaking for him, I relented. I told him where I was and hung up. I drug myself out of bed and took a shower. I had to put the same clothes back on, but at least I smelled better. I used the hotel toiletries and some tap water and managed to pull my hair back in a ponytail. It'd been growing and thickening like wildfire since the pregnancy, and the simple struggle to get it into a ponytail almost had me in tears. After the 2nd rubberband broke, I gave up, tears sreaming down my face again, but I sucked it up, determined not to let a fucking rubberband be the last straw that made me break.

I was sitting on the bed, staring at the mess of my hair when there was a knock at the door. I jumped, forced myself to calm my nerves, then stood and looked out of the peep hole. Sighing, I stood back and pulled the door open. Real was standing there, his eyes red from either crying, smoking or liquor, maybe a combination, and all he had on was a t-shirt that looked like he'd been sleeping in it and some jeans and sneakers. He had a bookbag slung over one shoulder, and his helmet in the other.

We stared at each other for a minute, both of us taken aback at each other's disheveled appearance as we confirmed we were the two idiots. Real was so emotional he was damn near shaking, and it must've been the lights blinking in the hallway or something, but it looked like his eyes were changing colors.

"Hey," I said to him, brushing a heavy lock of red out of my face. Real just watched me for a minute, watched the hair stubbornly fall back in my eyes. He finally reached out slowly and raked my hair back off of my face. When his hand reached the nape of my neck, it cradled the side of my face. Just feeling his hand on my face broke me down again and I burst into tears. Real pulled me to him and just hugged me while I let the river flow. He backed into the room, closed and locked the door, putting the Do Not Disturb sign outside, then stretched out on the rented bed, pulling me into his arms and just stroked my head until my eyes were worn out. He still hadn't said anything.

"I'm sorry," I said finally.

"For what?" Real asked finally.

"For bringing you over here and crying and shit…"

"Come on, ma. I called you, remember? Where else would I go? Where else would I be right now? I was already here, anyway…"

"What do you mean?" I asked, sitting up.

"I was already in the city when I called you. I told you, T. Something in you is connected to me. I didn't know exactly where you was, but I could feel you. When you called I was like, 5 blocks away. I just rode around for awhile to give you some time."

"Why even tell me that then?"

"Because I'm keeping shit real, T. You don't think we've been lied to enough?" Real demanded.

I sighed and relaxed against him again. "I can't believe this shit… what am I supposed to do now? I *married* this nigga and… this baby…"

"*Fuck* that nigga. Get that shit annuled. Keep the baby, it's a part of you."

"It's a part of him, too."

Real snickered in disgust. "I'm not tryna hurt your feelings, but trust me, if G was worrying about that baby he wouldn't have been fucking Jari raw and fucking you raw, too."

I shivered at the thought. "Were you fucking her raw?" I was bold enough to ask.

"I haven't touched her since she got pregnant, but when all this shit went down about her doing drugs and shit while she was pregnant I went and got rapid-response tested for HIV and everything else. Everything came back good, but I'ma keep getting tested for awhile, you know some shit takes awhile to show up."

"That's scary as hell to think about," I shook my head.

"But it's real. Shit, *you* should be more worried than me."

Startled, I looked up at Real, green eyes to green eyes. "What?"

"Come on, T. If G was already fucking Jari, who else do you think he was fucking? You don't think he knocked down every chick in the the strip club at least 10 times already?"

"What strip club?!" I screeched.

Real sighed. "Did you even *talk* to the nigga before you got married?"

"I mean… *I* talked…"

"Naw… did he ever tell you *shit* about himsef? I mean anything important?" Real pressed.

I thought hard, but couldn't come up with anything significant other than the fact that he didn't know his parnets. I shook my head, feeling young and stupid.

For the next hour, I listened in horror to Real break down everything from how he met Gemini to how he'd taken over the strip club, to how he'd come to run the 804 Boyz and now he was a big player in white collar America thanks to his mysterious partner. I figured Gemini did something… extra, but… the magnitude of what he was keeping from me made me so sick my baby got upset and started kicking me.

Seeing the distressed look on my face, Real stopped. "You know more about me and we've only had a handful of conversations," he said, haking his head.

"I feel so… I don't know what I'm gonna do now… I quit my job… I gave up my apartment…"

Real hugged me tighter. "I got you, T. If you don't know nothing else, you should kow that by now."

"No. I already fell for that once. No disrespect or nothing, but I have to get my own shit. I been doing it on my own my whole life, and the second I stop, I end up in this situation. Now I got a baby in this mess… I have to do this myself."

"Well, what're you gonna do, then?" Real demanded, obviously a lil pissed.

"I don't know yet," I snapped. I tried to shove him off of me, but he wouldn't let me go. I kept shoving him, but he kept holding onto me until the shoves weakened and I relaxed against him.

"You just gonna let this shit go and move on with your life?" Real asked finally.

I pulled back and looked at Real in the eyes. "Oh, *hell* naw. That nigga's *done*. I don't care how rich or how big he is… the muthafucka comes *down*."

Something in Real's eye flashed and he grinned. "You serious?"

279

WICKED BLUES Deszion Nasir

"Dead *ass serious*. He's gonna be the last nigga to pull grimy on me. Trust and believe."

Real's eyes, narrowed as he searched my face, seemingly wondering if I was ready for what he was going to say. He leaned forward on his elbows and stared into my eyes intently, trying to glimpse inside of me, trying to reach that dark part of me I'd been trying to deny for so long. "You wanna lay that nigga down… or do you wanna make him crawl in the box himself?"

The dark side of me, the hurt part of me, the vengeful part of me responded. "I want him to crawl."

"Then you gonna have to trust me. You gon have to do shit you don't like and become a woman you said you didn't wanna be. You can only do this if you stop bullshitting and be who the fuck you really are."

I nodded. "I can. Being someone else got me here in this fucked up position now."

"And you know what? I believe you," Real said. He leaned over and pulled me to him. I kissed him before he kissed me, kind of like a show of my pent up assertiveness. The same shock that hit me when Real first touched me shot through me again. He responded like he'd been starving for any kind of affection for years. I tugged his shirt over his head and shoved him back on the bed, straddling him.

"Look," Real said, panting, running his hands up and down my body. "You already know I got feelings for your ass. I'm not the type of nigga that's gonna take it well if you just fuck with a nigga to get back at Gemini. We can do the get-back shit because he fucked my life up, but if you *fuck* with me, you *stuck* with me…" he said seriously.

I stared down at him. "I know what I'm doing." I assured him, pulling his belt smooth out of his pants. He grabbed my hands as I unbuttoned his jeans.

"Do you?" he asked. "Don't fuck with a niggas emotions, girl. I can hate as hard as I can love," he said, almost sounding like he was threatening me.

"So can I," I promised, leaning down and smothering the skepic look on his face with my full lips. I sucked his tounge into my mouth as I yanked his pants down. He lifted me up as he slid out of them, his swollen rage now resting under me. He slid his hands up my cheap shirt and took hold of my swollen breasts, bigger than their normal size. He undressed me while I sat ontop of him, then pulled me down to him, his fingers like lines of electricity all over my skin. He kept kneading my skin, kissing my skin, sliding the power all over me until I felt myself twitching and I realized I was having an orgasm without any penetration. I moaned out that sweet song in surprise and while I was still trying to let the vibrations die down, Real lifted me slightly and eased me onto his lightning rod. My vagina was pulsating so hard I know he could feel it radiating. I looked down to watch him slide in and out of me and after the first thrust his dick was totally coated in my sweet elixir, making a loud gushing noise. Real cursed loudly and gripped me firmly, dropping his head against the pillow.

This wasn't just about sex for me. Real was trying to have something with me nobody else seemed to give a shit about: a deeper mental connection. So I wanted to make sure I gave him a deep physical connection to complete that circle. I threw my head back, closed my eyes, isolated my hips and ground my hips around, against, and up and down on Real's dick like I was dancing. The bed started to swirl, and between both our moans, the bed, and the constant slurping sounds my pussy was making as it greedily slurped on Real's dick, the noise in the room was like a pornographic opera. But... it was so weird... it was raw, it was nasty, but it was so beautiful at the same time. I can't lie and say I wasn't thinking about what was going to happen next. I can't say I wasn't scared about it. But what I can say is that I was determined to go through with it. As the lightning storm growing between me and Real swirled towards a climax, my thoughts were pulled back to him. When we were done, I fell into the most restful sleep I'd had in months, cradled in Real's arms.

I woke up hours later, the cheap clock reading about 3 in the morning. I carefully slipped out of Real's arms, took a quick shower, tiptoed through getting dressed, and picked up my bag full of money. I stared down at Real's peaceful face, wanted to kiss him, but decided not to wake him up, then eased out of the room. I quickly walked to the 7-Eleven on the corner, called a cab, and went back to my husband.

WICKED BLUES Deszion Nasir

TRE

I rubbed out the Newport butt I had in my hand and picked up the pack next to me. When I realized it was empty, I grabbed my jacket and whipped out another pack, damn near ripped the top off of it, and lit another cigarrette. I was halfway through it before I went from the balcony back into the hotel room I woke up in. I stared down at the fucked up bed and the stained sheets. I didn't remember shit after I saw the twins being born. Waking up this morning in Norfolk in a strange hotel room was my next clear thought. It didn't take a rocket scientist to figure out that I'd fucked somebody. My dick was sticky and satisfied, I was tired as hell... I mean, come on. The fact that I didn't know who the fuck I'd stuck my dick in had me fucked up, though. I searched the whole room top to bottom and couldn't find a rubber nowhere. *That* fucked a nigga's head up even more. As I was putting my clothes on to get the fuck out of there, I saw something glinting in the zipper of my jeans as I picked them up. I held them up closer to my face and froze.

A long, orange-red hair.

Shiit.

I've only seen that shade of hair on one female. I don't wanna think about what the fuck has probably gone down, but I don't have a choice. A nigga ain't in control of myself and if what I think happened done really happened, shit is about to get real on a nigga. I gotta get my head together while I'm still in control of it. I snatched up my helmet and left out one of the back doors of the hotel. It took me 15 minutes to find my bike, and I jumped on the highway when I finally found it, pissed off and anxious at the same time. I rode near the triple digit mark without really knowing where I was going. By the time I got off the highway and looked around, I realized where I was and followed the roads to the place I told myself I'd never go. As I turned my bike off, my cell phone was vibrating. I pulled it out of my pocket and saw Gemini's number showing up. Somethng balled up

283

inside of me and I turned the phone off instead of throwing it through the window of the car sitting in the driveway. The whispering that'd begun in my ear was silenced temporarily as I slid the phone in my pocket and I closed my eyes for a moment. I waited until the only voice I could hear was mine as I got off my bike and walked up to the door I knocked on the heavy door.

At first I didn't think anyone was home, then, the door swung open and I was looking into the golden eyes of Rio. Her hair was pulled back off of her face in and you could see how beautiful she really was without make up. It was also easy to see how surprised she was to see me standing on her doorstep.

"Tre?" she asked, a question on her soft lips.

"Hey, ma-"

"How did-how did you know where I lived?"

I paused, then shrugged. "I don't know."

Rio regarded me for a long, uncomfortable second, then licked her lips and crossed her arms. "What's wrong?"

The whispering started back up, but shit had gone to far for me to try to handle shit on my own. "I think somebody's gonna try to kill Gemini…"

"What?! *Kill* him? Do you know who? Do you know how hard it'd be to kill that nigga? Who's gonna kill him? And why are you coming to me with it?"

"I'm coming to you because you might be the only person who can stop it, Rio."

"*Me*?!" An uncomfortable look crossed Rio's face I took note of. "Tre, you not making any sense. Who do you think is gonna try and kill Gemini?"

I rubbed my eyes, tired. "Me."

Nearly 2 hours and 2 packs of cigarettes later, I sat back on Rio's poolside couch, out of words. I'd told her everything about me, Jamal and this new, dangerous side of me. I told her about the twins, I told her about waking up in a hotel room and the red hair. "If this other cat in my head is willing to fuck with Gemini's pregnant wife, he's gotta be

284

willing to go head up with the nigga. Whether G gives a fuck about T or not, you best believe he's coming after the nigga that banged his wife, man. The shit is out of control and I mean, I ain't wanna believe the shit, but what the fuck am I supposed to do, Rio? I ain't wanna bring this shit to you, but I really don't got nobody else."

I could see the wheels turning in Rio's head as the sun's rays played tricks with her light eyes. "Who else have you told any of this to?"

"Nobody."

"You haven't told Teasha or nobody any of this?"

"No."

"What about... the other dude?"

"I don't know what he's done. I haven't spoken to Teasha. When he's with her I'm not... it's like I black out."

Rio looked thoughtful. "You need to find out what she knows."

"Hold up... you don't think I'm crazy?" I asked her.

Rio sighed. "Tre... Multiple Personality Disorder is just that... a disorder. It doesn't mean you're crazy... you're just sharing one brain with three people. Usually your alters develop from traumatic experiences. The strongest one forms from the deepest experiences to protect you from something, and it protects you by blocking you from it. What's happened is that this has been going on so long your brain is probably being overloaded and this alter is getting stronger behind it."

"*This* shit is crazy," I muttered, picking up Rio's glass of Vodka and pomegranate juice and downing it. I grabbed the bottle of vodka from beside the couch and guzzled it. She took the bottle from me and sat it on the ground.

"Tre, listen to me," Rio told me. "The only way to deal with an alter is to intergrate it and figure out what it's sticking around for. What is it blocking? You said he's blocking shit with Teasha. What is it about her?"

"I don't know. But whenever I get around her or think about her he goes crazy."

"I mean, you said he's dangerous... most niggas like that-the really crazy ones-are drawn to the same kind of personalitites."

"Teasha don't come off as crazy."

"Maybe not. But you gonna have to figure out what the fuck's going on with her before he gets you both killed." Rio pointed out.

I looked away, at the pool, the house, the peaceful property before looking back at Rio. "Why are you helping me? This shit could get you killed too, couldn't it?"

Rio snickered. "I'm not worried about Gemini killing me, trust me. And maybe I'm helping you because... no matter what I do, you keep popping back into my head. I've tried to forget about you, to leave you alone, ignore you... it's not working."

I grinned, scooted closer to Rio. "Cain't stop thinking about a nigga, huh?"

Rio rolled her eyes at me, but a smile escaped and danced around her face.

Something was still bothering me, though. I wanted to let it go, but- "Seriously, though. What do you do for G?"

The grin faded and for a minute I wished I hadn't asked, but shit was too serious for me not to know what the fuck was going on.

Rio looked away from me to the sparkling water, then back at me. "Tre, I don't *work* for Gemini. I'm his partner. I fronted him all the money to shoot his business to where it was."

"What? You're the partner?" I asked in disbelief.

Rio nodded.

I glanced around at the house, took in everything I knew. "Who are you exactly?"

She grinned, almost amused. "You have no idea, do you?"

"Naw, not really," I said, feeling stupid.

"Tre, my whole name is Rio Souza. I'm the daughter of Antonio Souza."

286

The name echoed in my head while my mind's Rolodex flipped. It stopped on the page that held Antonio Souza's info: famous Brazillian drug cartel whose reach stretched across the globe. He'd been killed in a all-out brawl with the FEDs, but he'd taken a ton of them down. There was a rumor that he'd had one heir to his legendary millions, but the child was never found-

"Fuck," I groaned. "You're-"

Rio grinned sadly.

I stood up. "I can't drag you into this shit,"

Rio stood up and grabbed my hand. "Tre, I've lived a life you can't even begin to imagine. But one of the things I've learned was that nobody can ever make me do shit I don't want to do. I don't need Gemini for shit. When I came to America I used him for something and he used me for something. Yeah, we make money together, but don't ever get it twisted and think I need his ass. I make my own decisions. And despite all your damn drama," she grinned. "I make the decision to be with you. But we gotta get all these knots in your life untangled before they strangle you. Don't you worry about shit you can't change. " She reached into my pocket and handed me my cell phone. "Call her."

I stared at the phone, the pressed it back on. I started to dial Teasha's number, but all of a sudden the whispering went to full fledged shouting and I couldn't see the numbers on the phone.

"Tre?" Rio called, concerned, but it sounded like she was far away. I dropped the phone as the whispers turned to screams and covered my ears to drown the sound out.

REAL-

I scooped the phone up and threw it against the side of the house. I turned to Rio's shocked face and took a step toward her. "Bitch, you *must* be crazy. I ain't goin' *no* muthafuckin where. And if you call my baby and fuck up what we got you gonna fuck around and end up floating on top of that water," I snarled at her.

Rio looked horrified for a minute, then she looked into my eyes. "Who are you?" she demanded.

"I'm Real, that's who the *fuck* I am; and *trust* me, you don't wanna know no more than that."

Rio stepped away from me, but she kept a determined face on. "Look, Real, I'm not the enemy... I'm just tryna help Tre out-"

"Help him do what?" I yelled. "Get *rid* of me?" Rio swallowed, didn't shrink away, but she didn't answer me, neither. "Bitch, please. I'm not going *no*-fuckin-where. You *need* to stay out of grown folks' business before you fuck up some shit you don't got no business in in the first place." I told her.

"But Tre thinks-"

"You cain't tell me what the *fuck* that man thinks! You ain't in here! I'm here every fucking day, 24-7. You just some uptight bitch looking for some Mandingo dick to keep her busy. You're probably fucking Gemini, too."

"I've never fucked Gemini," Rio protested.

"Whatever. I don't really *give* a fuck, for real. But you can tell that nigga Tre he better stay the fuck away from T. He don't run shit. And if you wanna *really* see a nigga show his ass, *keep* fuckin with me," I shoved her out of my face. She shoved me back, her face changing.

"Nigga, you got *me* twisted. You put your gatdayum hands on me again and you gonna *see* somebody showin their ass, I *promise* you," she snapped.

"I'm not Tre, little girl," I told her, but before I could get closer to her she struck out and slapped me hard across the

288

face. I slapped her back and sent her to the wet ground, scraping her knees and the palms of her hands up. Rio looked down at her hands bleeding, let out a growl, and when I closed my eyes to blink, I opened them surrounded by water. Rio'd sprung at me like a fucking tiger and knocked both of us in the pool. I struggled to get her off of me but she had her legs wrapped around me like an octopus and her arms were around my neck tight, cutting off my air supply. I was trying to get above water to breathe, since I was caught off guard and swallowed a mouth full of water instead of air so I was already in trouble. Rio was tightning her grip around my throat. I managed to break the surface of the water for a second and gulp in some air as she screamed "I *got* your little girl, nigga!" before we went under water again. I felt myself losing conciousness, so I went street on her ass and rammed the back of my head into her face. The impact caused her to let me go and I saw a crimsom trail of thick blood swirling in front of me as I shot to the sweet air above the water.

As I gulped the air in I turned and saw Rio's still figure floating under the surface of the pool. A cold wave of dread shot through me as I coughed, gaping for air. Before I let the fact that I was in a pool register I shot back out into the water and grabbed Rio. I drug her out and laid her on the concrete next to the pool in the warm sun. The water had washed blood away from her face and I could see where her nose had been busted open. I checked for a pulse, then performed CPR on her until she coughed up blood and water all over herself. When she opened her eyes and saw me hovering over her, she screamed, swung out and punched me in the mouth. I fell back and she attacked me, crying, screaming and coughing until I grabbed her hands and pinned her down. "Rio!" I yelled. "Rio, it's me, chill the fuck out! What happened?!" I yelled over and over until she stopped swinging at me. Panting and shivering, she peered into my shocked eyes, then snatched away from me and backed away on her bottom until her back was against the back of her house.

WICKED BLUES Deszion Nasir

"Baby, what the fuck, yo?" I yelled. "Why are we wet?"

"Tre?" Rio asked.

"Yeah, it's me... what the fuck just happened?" I demanded. I took in the look on her face and the bruises and blood and answered my own question. "Oh, shit," I walked over to her and squatted down next to her. "Baby, I'm sorry... I'm so fuckin sorry..." I reached out to pull her up. She hesitated for a minute, but she let me pull her up and I looked her over with a heavy heart.

"What did he do?" I asked, brushing her soaked locks out of her face.

"He's not gonna let you anywhere *near* Teasha," Rio told me, still shaking. "He came out when we were talking about calling her and the nigga snapped, talking about we were gonna fuck something up he got going on with her."

My gut told me shit was already going too far... "Did he say what it was?"

Rio shook her head. "Naw, he didn't say nothing about it, but he said he wasn't going nowhere, and he put his fucking hands on me and we eneded up in the pool. He head-butted me when I tried to choke his ass out... then, next thing I know, you were giving me CPR."

I sighed and hugged her to me. "Anything else he said I need to know?"

Rio nodded. "He said his name was Real and Teasha was his 'baby'. He definitely got something going on with her."

This whole thing was over my head. I couldn't talk to Teasha and I couldn't talk to Gemini. I wasn't in control of shit. At that moment, I was seriously thinking about taking a gun and blowing my fucking head off just to stop the drama and the fucking whispering. As I held Rio's shivering body to mine, I tried to come up with a way to gain control and handle shit without getting the only person I gave a fuck about murdered.

WICKED BLUES Deszion Nasir

JARI

Someone was tapping my shoulder again. I forced my eyelids to open and saw the same nurse looking at me with the same pitiful-ass face.

"It's time to try and nurse again," she said. I looked behind her and saw the two bassinettes on wheels with the twins in them.

"I already told you I'm not doing that shit," I grumbled. I turned away.

"I know, honey, but I was hoping you'd try-"

"No." I said flatly.

"Well, can you at least hold them?" the nurse asked.

I sighed. I honestly didn't want anything to do with them, but she wasn't going to leave me alone until I did, so I nodded. She propped both babies up in my arms and stood back like a proud grandparent. I forced myself to look down at the perfect sleeping faces in my arms. As much as I wanted to hate them, I couldn't. They were so beautiful. They looked identical, from their tiny noses to their caramel skin and long, thick, ebony hair that rested across their eyes and shoulders, spilling out from under their hospital-issued caps. I'd named the girl Jasmine and the boy Scorpion, since they were both Scorpios and Jasmine was my favorite flower. Scorpion had a scowl on his sleeping face and he wiggled in my arms like he had gas, but Jasmine was the one who pooted. I couldn't help but smile.

"They're gorgeous," the nurse told me. "No matter what, their yours and they need you," she told me, patting me on the shoulder before leaving the room.

I sat there for awhile, staring at them, thinking about the miracles I was holding, until Jasmine opened her eyes, and I looked down into those blue eyes. The twins' eyes were actually a darker shade of blue than Gemini's icy blue ones, but they had the same glint in them. Scorpion opened his soon after, and he immediately began fussing and squirming. The nurse came rushing back in as the fussing turned to

292

screams. Rattled, I watched her expertly calm both babies and lay them back in their beds.

"It's alright, honey, you'll get the hang of it," she promised before leaving again. As I stared at the two swaddled bundles, I felt an overwhelming sense of failure. What the hell could I do for these kids? I couldn't take them to my mother's house. I didn't have anywhere to stay, now. To be truthful, when I got out of the hospital, I was probably gonna go get drunk and get high as a fucking kite. I didn't know any other way to live anymore. I had to make the one sensible decision I knew to make. I hurriedly got my clothes on, taking the IV out of my arm. Tears running down my face, I bent over my sleeping babies, kissed them on the cheeks, then ripped the hospital bands off my arms, left them in the cribs, then snuck out of the hospital. The best thing I could ever do for those kids was never be a part of their lives. I was as sure of that as I was sure that the next best thing I could do was hope their father never ruined their lives like he did everyone else's. I don't give a fuck about right or wrong no more. I wish death on his life, because he damn sure attached it to mine.

WICKED BLUES Deszion Nasir

GEMINI

I was in my gym wearing out another punching bag when my security alert let me know someone was walking up to my house. I stopped working out, panting, and snatched the remote up off of a weight bench and aimed it at a row of television screens. When they clicked on, I saw Teashaunna siding her key in the front door. She looked like shit and she didn't have anything with her but a bookbag, even though I hadn't been able to find her since the wedding. I dropped the remote on the floor, grabbed a towel and headed up from the basement gym to meet her.

After Teasha disappeared I couldn't find her or Tre. The press had a fucking field day with the whole story, but my publicist made good use of her paycheck and spun the situation as a jealous ex-boyfriend trying to get his 15 minutes of fame. Since neither Teasha or Tre was around to dispute nothing, the story stuck and the buzz had been low, but I was pissed all the same. The shit was embarrassing and bad for business. A lot of my public image was centered around Teasha and I had to keep that shit squeaky clean. That nigga Tre was a dead man for overstepping like that over a piece of ass, and I'd handle that nigga when I ran up on him. He must've gone insane or something to come at me like that. *Fuck* that nigga. He bled like every other nigga on Earth. In the back of my mind it stung because he was the only family a nigga had, but that's how shit went. I had too much going for me now. This shit was bigger than just me and Tre. If the nigga closest to me was allowed to come at me fucked up like that in public, it was only a matter of time before every crab-ass muthafucka under me or around me would try the same shit. Tre'd brought this shit on himself. It'd hurt, but the shit had to be done. I couldn't have no weak links on my chain.

Even deeper in the back of my mind, I was having mixed feelings about Teasha. Yeah, I was dead-wrong, but where the fuck had she been for the last few days? She was carrying my seed around, and if she was on some get back bullshit like most females were, I might have to do the dirty thang to her ass, too, wife or no wife. Call it a double standard if you want to, I don't give a fuck. It's just some shit bitches ain't supposed to do, gatdammit.

As I stormed to the door, I was ready to cut into her ass, but when she swung the door open and stood in the doorway, I took a good, long look at her. Her eyes were red, swollen and dry like she'd been crying since I'd seen her last; her hair looked like she'd been fighting, her skin was dry and she looked at me with the emptiest glare in her eyes that stopped me in my tracks. I could see all the pain I'd caused her staring me back in my face, crystal clear, and it fucked with a nigga's head, on some real shit. We just stood there, staring at each other for a long ass time until she closed the door the echo making the house seem larger. She dropped her keys on the floor, then her bookbag. She started to walk past me like I wasn't there.

"Where you goin?" I demanded.

She paused, but didn't turn around. "To take a bath. Then to sleep." she responded in a daze, then kept walking.

"Where you been?" I called after her, a lot harder than I meant to.

At the foot of the stairs, Teasha turned to me with the same cold, blank stare. "Nigga, you're not allowed to ask *me* shit. *Ever.*" she emphasized, and kept climbing.

"Hold the *fuck* up. I know you mad right now, but you not gonna come in *my* shit disrespecting me. I asked you a muthafucking –"

"*Your* shit?" Teasha glared down at me. She waved her wedding ring in my face. I could've sworn she'd thrown it in the water, though. "*Our* shit, Gemini. Remember? Or did you forget between fucking stray bitches and knocking up your best friend's fiancee? Maybe it slipped your mind when you stuck your tounge in one of those radioactive pussy hoes? When you get your fucking *memory* back, flip through the pages and pull up your definition of 'disrespect,' nigga.

When it comes to you, I'll be in the tub," she shoved my hand off her arm and kept walking up the stairs. "Instead of worrying where the fuck I *been*," she called, "you *should* be on your muthafuckin knees thanking God I even *came* back," was the last thing I heard before a door slammed hard and I heard water running a minute later.

Knowing she was right but still being angry, I needed an outlet for the anger building up in me. I'd been doing a good job of suppressing it lately, but it'd been growing. White collar America didn't look to favorably on powerful non-White men as it was, but non-White men with anger problems became targets for bullshit form the media and corporate snitches. Luckily, I had underground America to take shit out on. I stormed to my master suite and looked at the suit I had laid out to go to the Friday meeting I had scheduled to have my top generals bring in my money. I looked at Teasha's separate bathroom and thought I heard her crying behind the door. I was about to go in there and apologize for being an asshole when my phone rang. I sighed, snatched it up.

"Yeah."

"Yo," Came Charger's gritty voice.

"What's good?"

"Shit. Heard from your nigga Tre?"

"I told you, that nigga's done. I got stacks on his head."

"Yeah, well, you might wanna chill on that shit."

"The fuck yo talkin' bout?"

"Look, man… the nigga been all over your spots, yo, puttin all your business out there, tellin heads how he came at you at the wedding and how you ain't do shit cuz you a pussy-ass nigga and some ol' sucka shit, man. He tryna bait you, my nigga. You do some ill shit to him One Time'll be all ove your ass."

My blood was bubbling, but I held the shit down so I could focus. "Who he been talking to?"

"Man, everybody. Wood, Snook, Mel, Zone," Charger rattled off all the names of my generals I had under him.

"I bet all them niggas thought that shit was funny, huh?"

"Man, I 'on know. Somebody hit me up and told me about all of it just now, my nigga."

"But not none of Zone and them?"

"Naw…"

"Cuz them niggaz think the shit is funny. See, niggaz think a muthafucka done went soft just because he tryna make bigger moves and he wearing a few suits and shit, right?"

"Man, you know I ain't on that bullshit, G."

"Naw, not you, man…" I glanced over my shoulder at the suit on the bed. "You know what? I think it's time for an employee performance review. You down to hand out a few pink slips, my nigga?"

I could hear Charger grinning. "As long as you sign 'em in lead."

I smirked over the phone. "You know that's the only type of ink I use, nigga."

30 minutes later I was heading out the door. Teasha was still in the bathroom, and the suit was still laying on the bed. I had on a pair of dark jeans, a bullet-proof vest, and some semis, Desert Eagles, and other assorted job management materials. When I went outside Charger was already waiting in a black on black Benz racing car. It was fast enough for the track but nimble enough to navigate the streets I needed to travel.

We traveled to Downtown Newport News first, where Wood was. He was in an apartment in a building called The Towers, that overlooked the water and gave the false impression of waterfront property. When me and Charger got out and strolled up, all the young cats standing around outside did a double take. When they realized who I was, and saw how I was dressed, they didn't even try to give me dap or offer any hellos. They quickly and quietly got the hell out of

297

the way. The fat, ignorant-ass security guard saw us coming, even saw me screwing on a silencer, and still stood up like his punk ass was gonna do something with that radio around his neck. I raised my gun, put one through his right eye. The bullet exited his skull and hit the security pad, causing it to malfunction. Charger pulled the filthy glass door open and we walked inside, heading for the elevator.

"Take the stairs," I commanded.

"They gon know we coming," Charger protested.

"And? You scared or something, nigga?" I gave Charger a disapproving frown.

"Naw, never that." Charger shut up and followed me. By the time we reached the 4th floor, people were ducking out of the hallway and grabbing their kids. I strolled down the hall to Wood's door and was surprised that no one was outside guarding it, seeing as his monkey ass was holding around 100 grand of my money in this shitty ass apartment. Charger raised his gun to blow the lock off the door but I held my hand up, signaling that I was listening to something. I leaned in, careful not to touch the sticky door, and I could hear grunts and moaning.

"This nigga in here fucking when he 'posed to getting my shit together," I shook my head. I reached into my pocket and pulled out a set of keys.

"How you get a set of keys to Wood's spot?" Charger laughed.

"I got a set of keys to your house, too, nigga."

The laughter stopped.

I shook my head and opened the door silently. The first thing hat hit me was the smell of weed and pussy. Wood been in here for awhile. I spotted my dough scattered all over the floor, and I saw a pair of plum-colored toenails on ashy feet moving back and forth ontop of my fucking money straddled around a pair of jeans around a man's ankles. Charger shook his head as we came farther into the room and saw Wood fucking his girl doggystyle, stinking up my money like it was all good and shit. He had her by the hair and by

298

the looks of how he was sweating, he was on his last round. Right before he shot his load I grabbed him by the dreds and snatched him off of her. He shot his load all over his stereo and television as he was thrown on his back on the coffee table. The girl screamed and Charger jumped out of the way damn near killing himself to avoid being splattered by Wood's nut sprinkler.

"Nigga what the fuck is you doing?!" Wood yelled out before he saw me standing over him.

"Nigga, what the fuck is *you* doing?!" I yelled, my voice making the room shake.

"Oh, shit, Gemini-" Wood went pale, glancing around at the mess he was making of my money.

"I know you won't about to bring me that dirty-ass money, was you?" I demanded.

"Naw, man... I was just-"

"Nigga shut up-" I slapped Wood in the face with the gun. His girl screamed, but Charger pulled his gun on her, freezing her in place, ass up, hair falling in her face.

"I heard that nigga Tre was 'round here talking shit about a nigga and you let that shit ride," I asked Wood.

"Naw, man-"

"Where is he?"

"He-he ain't say-"

"Oh, so he *was* around here?"

"No-yes... Gemini-"

"Naw, son... I ain't tryna hear that shit. You let that nigga carry me like a bitch?"

Trembling, Wood wiped his bloody mouth. My eyes drifted to his girl, still frozen in place. "Speaking of bitches... that one yours?"

Wood didn't answer. Charger lifted the girl's hair off of her face, revealing the pretty, but terrified face of Wood's woman. "Yeah, that's her." he confirmed.

I shook my head. "See, since you work for me, and you didn't do shit to me *personally*, I ain't gonna do shit to you *personally*... but I think you know more than you tellin' me, Wood. I ain't gonna put the beats on you, though… but I do apologize. I don't think ya girl was finished getting the beats put on her."

Wood's eyes widened, but I walked over and shoved my gun in his mouth and the nigga froze.

"Charger, show that bitch how a real nigga get down, man." I told him.

Charger looked from the firghtened girl to me. "You serious?"

"Hell yeah, I'm serious. Pull yo shit out and knock the bottom out that pussy, man. I bet if you bang her hard enough, this nigga's memory'll come back."

The girl snapped and took a swing at Charger with a little knife that was laying on the floor. Charger easily kicked it away, but now he was pissed. "Dumb bitch," he snapped, slapping her down on the floor. He flipped her over on her stomach and held her down with one hand as he unzipped his pants.

"Wood!" the girl screamed and cried, but Wood was being stubborn. Charger snatched the girl's legs up and rammed into her, causing her to scream out.

"Bitch, shut the fuck up!" Charger yelled, slapping her in the mouth with his gun. He fucked the girl viciously while she fought, but Wood just closed his eyes, tears in them.

"Yo, think he likes that shit," I said over the girl's cries.

"Yeah?" I bet he won't like this shit," Charger said, pulling out and shoving his entire dick in the girl's unprepared asshole. She screamed like she was dying, yelling for Wood to please just tell us what we wanted to know as Charger beat her and fucked her ass until she was twitching like an epileptic from the pain and shock. When she started bleeding, I pulled the hammer back and told Wood to open his eyes. When he saw the condition his girl was in, he finally nodded. Charger pulled out of the girl and she lay on

WICKED BLUES Deszion Nasir

the floor, paralyzed in pain and terror, tears staining the money she was laying on.

"That nigga... he didn't say where he was going, but he said what you took from him he'd take from you... I ain't know what the fuck he was talking about... he was on some other shit, man... saying his name was 'Real' or some shit... the nigga done lost it... I ain't wanna get in the middle of that shit man..."

I used the gun to slap him on the ground like he was one of my whores. "Bitch-nigga you *in* the middle of it!" I yelled, motioning at the floor where his girl was still trembling.

"That's a waste of a good pussy, man," Charger said, shaking his head and zipping his pants up. "You want me to waste this clown?"

I thought for a minute, then shook my head. I squatted down next to the girl. "Hey... hey Miss Lady, get up for a minute..." I took her by the arm and helped her get into a sitting position. She wouldn't look at me, but I turned her face up to me and I shook my head. "You see what kind of nigga you got? You see what he let that man do to you for that lil' bit of information? I bet you been with him a long time, too. I bet you been through a lot of bullshit with that nigga... you know he be down at my club fucking all them hoes I got working for me, right? You *got* to know... but I bet you put up with it cuz you love the nigga... think about how your ass feels right now... you think that nigga loves you?" The girl's eyes left my face and settled on Wood's, narrowing. I grinned at Charger, then pressed my gun from my gloved hand into her shaking one.

"Hold on-hold up-baby-" Wood backed away against the wall as me and Charger turned to leave. By the time we were heading into the stairwell we heard the scream, one shot, then silence.

Melvin Carson was a low-key killer that lived in Buckroe. Buckroe was pretty quiet and filled mostly with white, lower-income families with a splash of color here and there, but back in the day you could leave your doors unlocked at night. Mel didn't do his dirt there, but it was where he rested his head at night with his girl and his kids. His girl had no idea what he did, but she never asked. She also had no idea that his kids' mother died from a cocaine overdose at a strip club 2 weeks after giving birth. Mel wanted her back making money and the pressure of having a newborn, a 1 yr. old and Mel beating on her was too much for her. Mel tossed her body in the dumpster of a Papa John' Pizza restaurant and went on about his business. His new girl Trina was content to stay home, clean, cook, and look after his two girls while Mel went out and slang birds and bitches. She met him when she was coming out of Wal-mart with his daughters and seeing him with his kids fooled her into thinking he was simply a single father trying to do the right thing. So you can imagine what was running through her head when she came home this day with the girls and saw me and Charger waiting for her in the dark. She jumped, dropped her keys, but she didn' scream. She held the hands of the oldest girl, 2, tighter, clutched the 7-month old to her and swallowed.

"Ya'll can have everything we got, the jewels and money are in the back room, but just let us go... I ain't even gonna say I seen nobody... I can just say I came home and the house was already robbed," she said, turning her eyes away from our faces.

I smirked. "Be easy, love. We ain't here to rob you..."

"I'm still not gonna look in your faces," Trina swore.

Charger shook his head. "You seem like a smart chick... but most smart chicks make stupid ass mistakes in relationships."

Trina finally looked up with confused eyes. "This is about Mel?"

"No question."

"What's going on?" Trina asked, looking from me to Charger.

"Where's your man at?"

"He… he supposed to be on his way home… he normally gets off work about this time… I took he girls out to the park so they'd be tired, you know, so they'd sleep and me and him could relax tonight…"

"Damn shame," Charger said, leaning against the dining room table.

"What is?"

"You know what happened to them girls momma?" I asked her, reaching in my coat pocket. Trina flinched, then looked fearful, but curious as I pulled out a stack of pictures.

"She left him… didn't she?"

"You could say that." I tossed the pictures at Trina. She let the 2 yr. old's hand go and scooped the pictures up, gasping at the sight of the girl's mother dead at the strip club, cocaine all over her face, half-naked, Mel's name tattooed on her neck and Mel posing over her body, drunk and laughing. Trina dropped the pictures and backed away from them like they were on fire.

"Oh, my God," she moaned, covering her mouth. "Did he do that to her?"

"May as well have. He gave her the drugs. He also dumped her body in a trash can… he picked you up as a replacement."

"Why… what… what are you tellin' me this for? Why are you in my house?"

"*Technically*, this is my house. My money paid for it. Mel works for me… and his ass is about to be fired. Now, you got a choice. You can either take these kids and get the fuck out of here before he gets here… or you can *leave* the kids and get the fuck out of here… or you can *stay* and roll with him… it's on you, ma…" I said while Charger walked over, grabbed Trina's purse and took her wallet and ID out. He looked it over and slid it in his pocket. Just then, a set of headlights pulled up in the driveway. Panicked, Trina looked out the window and saw Mel's car.

"What's it gonna be, love?" I asked. Tears in her eyes, Trina grabbed up her coat, glanced at the babies, who were looking at her curiously, and fled out of the back door, leaving it wide open. Her footsteps had just faded when the front door swung open.

"Trina! Guess what I brought you baby...!" Mel came into the room all smiles, until he saw me and Charger standing in the living room. He froze, then saw his daughters. "Where's Trina?"

"Oh, she hauled ass after we showed her them pictures you took at the club when Lichelle died," I laughed, nodding at the pics. Mel glnaced down at the pics and the color drained from his face.

"What you doin' here, G?" he asked, calm but obviously nervous.

"A little bird told me a snake came slithering through here... you didn't think I needed to know that critical piece of info?" I asked.

Mel's breathing sped up but he managed to get out "My kids, man..."

I nodded at Charger, who walked over to the girls. He turned the infant car seat around so she couldn't see and sat the 2 yr. old in an overstuffed chair. He pulled a Blowpop out of his pocket and gave it to her, turning her chair around as well. She was totally engrossed in the candy and not paying us any attention.

"This shit is foul, G." Mel said, a tear in his eye.

"Just shut the fuck up so you don't scare your kids, man. This house is full of bitches..."

Charger handed me a gun, but I shoved his hand away and pulled a machete out. "Fuck a bullet, son. He kept his mouth shut when he should have spoke up, so it seems to me he ain't making the best use of that loud-ass voice of his. If he cain't use it right, he don't need it-" Mel panicked at the last minute and tried to swing, but I was damn near a foot taller than him and his blow didn't do no damage. I grabbed him by the face and stuck the knife in his neck, blood squiring

304

everywhere. He kicked and fought, but he couldn't stop me as I proceeded to saw out his voicebox. Only when I was done did I let his body drop and he grabbed at his throat.

Charger actually looked sick. I shook my head at him. Tre might be an enemy now, but he damn sure had a lot more heart than this nigga here. "C'mon," I said to him as the 2 yr. old climbed out of the chair and froze at the sight of her daddy writhing in his own blood on the floor. Mel tried to wave her away, but she climbed on his legs anyway, calling him over and over.

"You just gonna leave the kids like that?" Charger asked.

"Naw, Trina left em like that. Her prints are all over this house, on the pictures..." I bent down and picked up her purse, left in her hurry to get out of the house,and smiled.. "And in her purse." I walked out of the house, and closed the door on the sound of the little girl crying for her bitch-ass daddy.

Zone and Snook would prove to be more difficult to get to. They were always together, and they were always in Phoebus. A nigga couldn't just roll up in Phoebus on no bullshit. It was like that section of the city could smell shit coming. Sure enough, as soon as Charger's truck turned off Woodland Rd. onto Chamberland Ave., I saw a teenager take off like a track star behind a group of townhomes that belonged to the section of town called North Phoebus.

"Get ya shit right," I warned, reaching under the seat instantly. Seconds later, as I passed Scotland Rd., I realized everyone outside had vanished.

"What the fuck-?" was all Charger got out before the gunshots exploded all around us. Charger swerved, but kept the car on the road as I hung the automatic out of the window and started firing. The rapid hail of gunfire from me and Charger sent the attack retreating quickly back into the windows of the townhouses as bodies fell from the windows and people began screaming. Charger stopped the truck and I jumped out, still firing. I was in font of Zone and Snook's spot and had to duck as gunfire peppered Charger's truck.

"Man, fuck this shit," I snapped. I went into the back of the truck and pulled out a grenade launcher. Within seconds I fired it into the front door and the downstairs of the partment exploded. Screams and debris flew everywhere as the backdoor flew open and people came runing out of the house, some on fire, some injured. From the upstairs window, I saw Zone and Snook coughing and smoking as they basically fell to the ground below, the guns they were clutching sliding away into bushes and the driveway.

I stormed over to them and kicked Zone in the mouth. "Nigga are you crazy?"

"G, we already know what's up. We got the call about Mel and Wood, and we knew you was on your way here… you know how cats out here do… you ain't just gonna run up in Phoebus and pop shit off, nigga…"

"Oh, but your bitch ass was popping shit off wit' that nigga Tre, though?" Charger spat.

Snook looked up at Charger like he was stupid and laughed through blood-covered lips. "Is that what he told you? You think this shit is all about *Tre*? Youz 'bout a *stupid* nigga, yo…" he coughed and spit out a tooth, cursing under his breath.

Charger paused, then looked at me. "What the fuck is this bitch talkin 'bout, G?"

"Oh, he ain't tell you? Yeah, we was hollerin at that nigga Tre about that snake-shit G pulled, but you really think G would off all his captians behind a bitch? Dumb muthafucka… Blue about to link the 804 Boyz with them Harlem 5 niggaz from uptop. He gets into NY, they get in down South. He was originally gonna off the top nigga from the Harlem 5, but right before G's bitch Rio cut the nigga's head off she made a deal with him…the deal is, for him to get in good with them, they want their people to run some shit down here…5 top positions, no bloodshed between the two…guess who's getting demoted?"

Charger's face was blank. He looked from Snook to me.

"And your *stupid* ass helped him, didn't you? Clown-ass nigga..." Snook laughed, groaned and choked on his blood at the same time, rolling on the ground.

"G, is that shit true, man?" Charger demanded, turning to me, betrayal staining his face purple with rage.

I shrugged. "Consider this your 2-second notice, my nigga." I raised Charger's gun and put 2 in his temple. He fell ontop of Zone, and I put another in him and stood over Snook, who was grinning up at me.

"You awful chipper, my nigga."

"Cuz I know I'ma see you again in a tick or two, bitch."

"Behind who, Tre's bitch ass?"

"Naw, bruh... behind Real. *That* nigga's coming fo' that ass."

"Same nigga. He can call himself whatever he wants, he'll die the same death."

"Yeah, aight... don't get pissed when you get to hell and see your reservation instead of his, nigga," Snook said like he knew something I didn't. "Your ass is *dead*, G-"

I ended my irritation and shot Snook through the heart before climbing back in Charger's truck and taking off. I knew 5-0'd take their time getting out to this neighborhood even though they were five minutes away. As I drove what Snook said was weighing heavy on my mind. This was the second time I heard the name Real in refernce to Tre. Something was going on with that nigga. Whoever the fuck he was, he wasn't about to catch me in an off-moment. Both of them niggas could get a hot one.

I wasn't done yet. I dumped Charger's car and caught a taxi to one of my used car lots, then made a trip out to Chesapeake. I rolled up to Rio's door and banged on it. As soon as she swung the door open I swung on her. I hit her so hard in the mouth she flew over a table she had in the foyer and knocked it over. The table and Rio slid backwards on the huge marble tile. Quick as lightning, Rio grabbed for the overturned table. I wasn't fast enough and had to jump out of the way as she snatched a throwing knife out of the drawer. She missed my right eye by a hair as the blade sliced off a piece of my hair and sank into her front door.

"I done had just about enough of ya'll niggas rolling up in here puttin your hands on me today," Rio screamed, springing to her feet and jumping on me. The force of her weight and mine sent us flying against the wall and I banged my head against the door. She snatched me up like a nigga but wrapped her legs around my arms as we crashed to the ground and she punched me in the face, cutting my cheek up with her ring before I freed my arms and tossed her off of me.

"What nigga? Where's your bitch-ass boyfriend?" I yelled, pulling a gun out. She swung her long leg up, kicked the gun out of my hand and caught it with her left hand.

"Nigga, are you *high*? I'm *talking* about Tre. That nigga came in here and straight *snapped* on my ass earlier. Did you tell him where I lived?" Rio demanded. "What the fuck is up with you?"

I let the rage simmer some and took a good look at Rio. The side of her face was swollen and she had a bruise on her leg.

"What did he say?" I demanded.

"What did you *hit* me for?!" Rio screamed.

"What did he call himself?" I yelled back.

"Somebody named Real-"

I turned and snatched Rio'd front door open and walked out.

"Oh, you think you just gonna come fuck *my* shit up and bounce? You think I'm one of your bitches? Well let me ask you about your *head* bitch," Rio yelled after me. I kept walking. "Where was Teasha last night, Gemini?"

I stopped, then turned around slowly. I looked into Rio's furious eyes, then walked back up to her, still clutching my gun, finger on the trigger.

"Do you know where Teasha was?" I demanded slowly, nose-to-nose with her.

"No... but you should ask her... better yet... ask Real. He knows where she was... shit, he even knows what her pussy smells like... hope your baby don't pop out with a dent in his head," Rio said smugly. Her smile vanished and blood shot out of her mouth and onto my face as a reaction from the knife I'd stabbed her in the back of her brainstem and out of her throat. Rio fell against me, but slid to the ground as I pulled the knife out. I kicked her body off my feet and shook my head at her, still beautiful even in death. "Should've just given me some pussy."

TEASHA

I was stepping out of the shower when I heard the roaring engine of a powerful motorcycle outside the huge house. I wrapped a towel around myself and my swollen belly. I was such an emotional wreck that the baby was agitated, but I rubbed my stomach through the fluffy towel until the kicking stopped, then made my way downstairs. I headed for the front door, but I heard the back door sliding open. I nearly slipped on the trail of water my hair was leaving on the floor as I backpedaled to the rear of the house just in time to see dark green eyes peering at me from a flawless chocolate-skinned face.

"Hey, baby," I said, reaching up to wrap my arms around him, but he pulled back.

"What's wrong?" I frowned, growing anxious.

"Teashaunna, I gotta talk to you before he come back,"

I waved him off. "Gemini won't be back for a long time," I told him. I undid my towel and watched his eyes slide over my body, still sexy even with the pregnancy. My breasts were fuller and perfectly round, my skin was glowing and my hair was driping in a river down to my freshly manicured pussy.

He licked his lips and I stepped to him, wrapping my arms around his neck. I took his arms and put them around me, letting them rest on the silky skin of my ass. He squeezed it briefly before letting me go and backing away from me like he was being tormented.

"T, I'm not talking about G... I'm talking about Real..."

I blinked.

"Look, I know this shit sounds crazy," he went on, setting his helmet on the floor,"but you gotta believe everything I'm telling you, T. I'm Tre. The nigga you dealing with, Real...he's not a real person. He's an alter ego. I got Multiple Personality Disorder."

I let out a breath and turned away.

"Listen, I know, I know... but I'm dead-ass serious, ma. That nigga Real is crazy, he's a killer, and he's gonna get you and everyone around you killed. I been trying to get to you to warn you for a minute now, but he keeps blocking me from you. I been struggling with this shit to gain control, and I been able to squash this nigga for a little bit of time, so I was like... I gotta warn you before he comes back. I can't control him and I don't know what happens when he takes over-"

"This is some get back bullshit because of what he did to you about that bitch Jari and the twins, ain't it?" I demanded. "Get me thinking you give a fuck about me, then come up with this bullshit to get out of it once I fall in love with you and shit-"

"Wait, hold the fuck up-you in love with Real?"

I threw my hands up. "Are you fucking *serious*? Oh, that's right... you don't remember... *what* the fuck ever... nigga, tricks are for kids..."

"Naw, naw, T... I ain't tryna make it seem like you don't matter... this nigga is playing with you... this shit is all a game to him... but it don't have to be... he ain't real, baby..."

I paced the floor. "Are you sure?"

Tre paused. "What the fuck you mean, am I sure?"

"I'm saying... if *you're* the one blacking out and not remembering shit... you say he's in control and you only shows up when he lets you, are you sure *you're* not the alter?"

Tre looked striken. I shook my head and walked away from him. He called after me and follwed me.

"Don't follow me, Tre," I called out, storming towards the gym.

"I need to know, though, T. What makes you say shit like that? What the fuck that nigga tellin you?"

"Does it matter?" I snapped, flipping on the light and making sure to stay out of Tre's reach.

"T… you have no *idea* how much the shit matters. He tried to kill Rio-"

"Rio?"

"Gemini's business partner. Me and her-" Tre broke off suddenly.

I turned to face him. "You and her what, Tre?"

Tre sighed, realizing he'd let too much out in his frustraion.

"You fucking this girl? So that's what's going on? When you're Tre you fuck Rio and when you're Real you fuck me? That's the sick game you playing?"

Tre grabbed his head in frustration and turned to punch the wall. Him putting his fist into the wall was sound number one. Sound number two was the crack of one of Gemini's bats against the back of his head. The third was the sound of Tre hitting the floor.

An hour later, Gemini burst into the house like he'd been tossed through the door by a hurricane. I was still naked, sitting in the middle of the living room, 9mm beside me, smoking a blunt. I didn't move other than to dump the blunt's ashes when he stormed up to me. He looked like he was about to choke the shit out of me until he took in my being naked and the gun, which he knew was loaded.

"Where the fuck were you the last two nights?" he raged, his hands balled in fists the size of bricks.

"There you go with the questions," I said calmly, taking a long drag and blowing it up in his face. He reached out to smack it out of my hands but froze when I stuck a gun in his face.

"Nigga, I wish you *would*," I said, serious as a heart attack. Gemini didn't look scared, but he wasn't stupid, neither.

"Was you with Tre… or Real… or what the fuck ever he calling himself."

I nodded. "Yeah."

Gemini curled his lip under. "Did you fuck him?"

I laughed. "Only once. How many times did you fuck Jari?"

Gemini's eyes took on an insane glint, and he was so angry he was damn near vibrating. "You know I'ma kill you, right?"

"Doubt it. Back up," I waved the gun at him. He took a step back and I stood up. "C'mon," I told him, motioning toward the gym. He hesitated. I pulled the hammer back. "Nigga, I'm not playing with you. If I wanted to kill you-like you say you wanna kill me-I'da pulled the trigger on your cheating ass as soon as you walked in the door. I'm tryna *fix* this shit, but I don't need you doing no stupid shit right now..."

"Bitch, you cain't fix this shit."

I shook my head at him. "You keep underestimating me. I fixed shit on the boat, didn't I? You keep looking at me like I'm just some piece of eye candy, Gemini. But you have no idea what you got, because you never took the time out to look below the surface and learn anything about me other than how far back I can bend my legs," I said, swinging the door to the gym open. Gemini peered past me at the pool of blood, then stepped into the room and saw Tre's body sretched out on the floor.

"What the fuck did you do?" Gemini demanded.

"I *handled* shit," I repeated. "His bitch done caused us enough trouble, so he tried to play on my emotions cuz he knew I was hurting behind that trifflin' shit *you* did. Infidelity can be dealt with, but that nigga is tryna bring your business-*our* business, *our* life, *our* reputation, ... everything we built together down behind a junkie bitch. So I had to dead his ass." I looked at Gemini's shocked face. "And we got this one here to think about," I said, grabbing his hand and putting it where the baby was kicking. After a long minute, I turned to him and held his face in my hands, pulled him down to me and kissed him. "So you gonna help me dump this body or what?"

313

Gemini stared into my eyes searchingly before shaking his head and taking the blunt from me. "Go put some fucking clothes on."

I grinned and ran upstairs. I threw on some sweats and one of Gemini's workout t-shirts and a pair of old sneakers I used to walk the dogs. When I came back downstairs I was pulling my hair up in a ponytail. Gemini had tossed his jacket to the side and was dragging the cover from one of the pool tables to the gym.

"I got it," he told me. "You can't be dragging shit."

"You seriously gonna keep telling me what the fuck I *can't* do?" I demanded.

Gemini glared at me, then almost smiled. "Grab this bitch's feet, then."

I bent down and took hold of Tre's feet. We got him in the cover and drug him out the back of the house. Gemini's suggestion was to get rid of the body on our property, since we had so much of it. Shit was too hot right now and Gemini was too famous to try to carry a body anywhere and get rid of it. He grabbed a couple of shovels and a hand saw and we piled everything in the back of the little golf cart we used to get around the grounds.

As we were zooming along , Gemini glanced at me.

"What?" I asked, moving my ponytail from whipping in my face.

Gemini sighed.

"I'm sorry, T. I fucked up, yo. I been fucking up my whole life and I never knew why. I been told I was the fucking devil my whole life. How you expect a muthafucka to act when you hear that shit day in and day out?"

"*Demonic*." came a gutteral voice from behind us. We both tried to turn around but all I could see was metal, then an exposion of blood as Gemini's back opened up. He lost control of the cart and I screamed as it tipped over. I flew from it and somehow managed to turn my body so that I landed on my back and not my side. When I was able to look up I saw Gemini on his back, flaps of flesh hanging open and

314

blood pouring from his body from being sliced open with a huge machete. Climbing to his feet behind him was –

"Tre-" Gemini spat.

"Naw, it's Real, bitch. That nigga Tre died back at the house. There ain't room for both of us." Real growled as I climbed to my feet.

"Nigga, think about what you doin'… you ain't in your right mind…" Gemini tried to reason with him.

"Bitch nigga, I never been more in control of my mind than I am *right now*," Real yelled.

Gemini's eyes went to me. "Teasha-"

"Oh, I *got* her," Real said, taking me by the arm.

Betrayal flashed across Gemini's eyes. "Bitch, you set me up? Ya'll set all this shit up?"

"Nigga please, you cheated on me," I spat. "I told you… you don't know shit about who I really am… nigga *you* fucked up."

Gemini laughed. "Ya'll niggaz is dead."

I raised my 9mm. "Doubt it." I fired and left a bullet in Gemini's head. I stared at his unmoving body, in a trance before Real shook me.

"Hey… baby… did you get those safe codes?"

I nodded.

"C'mon… we gotta get the fuck outta here."

We ran the mile back to the house, went through every safe and stash spot and snatched up every dollar, jewel and piece of info before Real torched the house. We fled the house and left the hell in Virginia behind.

315

WICKED BLUES Deszion Nasir

EPILOGUE
6 MONTHS LATER

We ended up in Ecquador. It was there we watched on CNN about how mogul Gemini Knight's estate was totally destroyed. It was believed that Gemini and his wife were murdered in the fire, being that their DNA was found in the house, but no bodies were ever found. I felt bad for the shit I had to do to Tre, but I had to do what the hell I had to do for me and Real.

I gave birth to a 8 lbs. 11 oz. baby boy Real named Terrence. He had some of Gemini's features, but he was colored like me, with dark red hair and bright green eyes. We stayed in South America for two years peacefully before we decided to travel. Real was making money down here as a mechanic for some underground bosses. He'd been working at a local repair shop when he was recommended around, and now he worked exclusively for big money cats. It afforded us the opportunity to live well and still be annonymous.

Terrence loved to go to work with his father. He learned to speak fluent Spanish by two and life was peaceful. I never regretted my decision to give up my life in America to live a dream. Whether Real originated as an alter or not, he was in comeplete control now and he was the man I'd fallen in love with. He took care of me and I could be free to be who I really was. Like today: I was bringing Real and Terrence some Empanadas and yellow rice for lunch on a job he was on. I waved at the locals, who always tried to flirt with me and compliment my skin, whick was a deep brown color now, due to all the sun I got down here in this beautiful country. When I reached the grounds where Real was tightening something on a car, Terrence ran up to me and wrapped his arms around my legs. At 2, he was as tall as a 4 yr. old. He would be as tall as Gemini.

I kissed him on the head and walked up to Real. "Hey, baby," I told him. He looked frusrated.

WICKED BLUES Deszion Nasir

"Hey, love," he grunted, tossing a wrench on the ground.

"Whoa, what's the problem?" I asked.

"I been working on this muthafucka all day and I cain't figure out why it won't start."

"Well, what the client say was wrong with it?" I asked, sitting the food on the top of the car.

"He don't know. It was a gift from an associate for a deal, but when he tried to drive it, the shit wouldn't start. They're in the house bullshittin' now…" Real shook his head.

"Nice guy?" I asked.

"Ma, you know I don't know. I just work, I don't meet and greet."

"Well, come *eat*." I told him, bending down to pick up the wrench. When I did, something caught my eye. A tiny flashing green light was coming from under the car. I bent down further to look under the car and saw wires-

"Real!" I screamed. "Bomb!"

Real didn't hesitate. He grabbed Terrence in one arm and my hand in the other and took off running. As we got to the bottom of the driveway I glanced back up at the house where the upstairs balcony doors were open. I stared into a pair of ice blue eyes a second before the car exploded and my world went black.

WICKED BLUES Deszion Nasir

GEMINI

I raised my glass at Teasha when our eyes met as the present I'd delivered to Emelio exploded. I turned away from the window as everyone near the car-the workers and lawn care people-screamed, running around and collapsing as they succumed to the fire that was killing them.

The wind blew my unbuttoned shirt up, exposing the huge scar on my back. My hair was braided to cover the scar from where I had a metal plate in my head from a point-blank gunshot. I couldn't use my left hand like I used to, but I was working on that.

Emelio ran into the room, screaming. "What the fuck did you do, you crazy muthafucka? I invited you down to my home to discuss business and you try to kill me?"

I drank more rest of my healthy dose of Dominican rum. "I wasn't trying to kill you."

"You fucking lunatic! I'll have your whole family murdered-!"

He was cut off when I pulled a Glock out and shot him in the head. His body dropped at my feet and I tossed the drink on his body. I stepped over him and calmly walked out of the house while everyone left alive ran around in confusion, trying to figure out what happened and who was still alive. I didn't need Emelio or his petty-ass connections in this slum-ass town. I checked my watch. I had a plane to catch to New York.

WICKED BLUES Deszion Nasir

DO YOU EVER REALLY STOP HAVING NIGHMARES ABOUT THE EVIL YOU DO? PEER INTO THE EYES OF AN *UNCOMMON DEVIL*... EVIL NEVER DIES...

Gemini watched from behind the two-way glass as X stumbled back to his friends. A pretty light-skinned girl with short hair hugged him, then looked concerned as she noticed he seemed disoriented. Gemini, however wasn't focused on them. His eyes were on the girl standing up on the edge of the VIP, waving a glass around, and attracting the attention of most of the people in the club. She was tall, beautiful, and had the attention of almost everyone within her line of vision. Even the bouncers were standing alongside Gemini and commenting about her while he sat back and watched her. After a long minute, he picks up a glass of bourbon and walks over to the security cameras.

"Zoom in on her and the kid with her," he commanded, taking a sip from the glass. When the security guard obliged him and zoomed in on the tall, red-haired, green-eyed male with the wild-haired Amazon, he dropped his glass. It shattered loudly on the floor and scared the shit out of everyone in the room, who'd never seen their boss lose his cool, ever.

"Damn, G, you know that kid?" the head of security managed to get out, breaking the tense silence.

"Think so," Gemini said, after he found his voice.

"Who is it?"

Gemini glanced at the screen again. "My blood."

TJ

It was damn near sunrise by the time we made it back to the hotel. Everyone in the truck was white-boy wasted. I'd drunk as much as everyone else, but since I was bigger than

319

everyone else, the liquor was taking longer to get to me. I was drunk, but I wasn't *fucked up*, you know?

Shawn and Joi were in the other car with X and Yaya. Joi had already passed out from drinking too much, which- from what a nigga like me could see- was becoming a pattern with her. X had disappeared for awhile, then came back shook like a bitch, but he wouldn't tell nobody nothing. He drank damn near half a bottle of Patron but all of a sudden he didn't want to smoke nothing with us no more. Some weird shit was going on with him, and this trip to New York wasn't as fun as I'd planned. I mean, not for my *friends*, but at least Jasmine was having fun. I'd sold everything in that suitcase in the attic, and gotten a shit load of cash for it, so I was able to take Jas shopping and do all the high-maintenance shit she'd wanted to do. In the back of my head, though, I knew the money was gonna run out, so I hoped she'd see what a good nigga I was before that happened... or at least give me some ass before then.

Jasmine was so drunk she was falling all out of the car. She'd been kissing all over me all the way back from the club. It had taken everything in a nigga not to pull over and bend her over the back seat, but I was still trying to show Jas that I wasn't just a fuck-ass nigga like these other guys she was always complaining about. Jas didn't open up to a lot of guys, so I'm thinking the *least* I could do was get her back to the room. She wasn't making it easy, though...

First of all, Jasmine was 6 feet tall. 6 feet of hair, titties, ass, thighs, drunkenness and wandering hands was a lot to get into a hotel, a lot to drag through a lobby, and damn near *impossible* to get into an elevator without almost carrying her. As the doors slid closed behind us, she pushed me up against the wall and snatched my shirt open, the buttons bouncing on the floor of the elevator. She stepped close to me and ran her tongue up and down my neck while she slid her hands under my t-shirt, over my abs and chest and pinched my nipples.

WICKED BLUES Deszion Nasir

"Baby, chill," I said, trying to take her hands off my hot spots. I was two seconds from screaming like Tarzan, ripping her clothes off-she won't wearing much-and hitting "stop" on the elevator.

"Do you know how long it's been since I got some dick?" Jasmine whispered in my ear, the heavy scent of lust and intoxication sneaking its way up my nostrils.

"How long?" I heard myself asking. She took one hand and forced me to stare down into her clear blue eyes.

"Awhile. Why do you think I act like a bitch all the time?" she asked.

"Damn."

"Damn indeed. You gonna help me adjust my attitude?" Jas licked her lips and got on her tiptoes. She brought her lips right up to mine and licked my bottom lip before sucking it into her mouth just as the elevator doors opened.

"Gatdayum right I am, shiit," I growled, grabbling Jas by the arm and dragging her down the hall to the room. I heard her giggling behind me as I tried to reach around a hard dick in my pocket and pull the room key out. I got the door open and tossed her towards the bed, kicking my shoes off in the process. As I snatched off my pants and ripped shirt, Jas stood up on the King-sized bed and unzipped her dress. By the time she finished all I had on were my boxer briefs and I was about to bust out of those. Jas threw her dress towards the door and stood there in her turquoise lace bra and thong set, raking her hair off her face and down her back. I stared at all the curves and legs and breasts, stunned for a minute, before I took a step toward her. She squatted down on the bed, her eyes on me, and leaned back on the bed, scooting back against the pillows, a hungry vibe radiating off her body. I climbed on the bed and reached for her and then she goes "You gotta condom?"

And of course I don't. Cuz you know when I nigga's dick is as hard as a damn brick, he never has a fuckin rubber. So, tripping, cursing, and trying to snatch a pair of jeans over

321

a boulder-hard dick, I run my stupid ass down four flights of stairs, too anxious to wait for the elevator, and go to the café shop. It's closed. I have to run two blocks down the damn street with *no* shoes on into a corner store to buy a box of Magnums and let the Arabs laugh behind the glass at me and haul *ass* back to the hotel. I run back up the stairs-four flights-and when I get back down my hall, I see someone banging on my door. Of *all* the people I'm *not* tryna see right now, it's-

"*MOM*?!"

My mom spins around and glares at me. She looks like a crazy woman. Her hair looks wild and she's wearing shit she usually wears to clean up the house in. I stop running and she stops banging on the door. I stare at her clothes and she stares at the box of Magnums in my hand, which I was so pressed about I didn't wait for the Arabs to bag.

"What the fuck are you doing here?" I asked her.

"What the fuck am *I* doing here?" my mother screeched. "What the fuck are *you* doing here? Where did you get the money to come here from? Who'd you come up here with? Who's in that room with you? Oh, *shit*, you about to fuck somebody, my baby is about to go *fuck* somebody..." My mom grabbed her bushy hair and paced the hall.

"Mom, go home," I hissed, not wanting Jasmine to hear her.

"Oh my God, look at your penis! Get away from me with that. Oh my God, this shit isn't happening..." my mom shoved me.

It damn sure wasn't. All it took was my mom mentioning my "penis" and it was deflating. I had to squash this shit quick. "Look. I know I shoulda probably told you I was leaving or whatever, but you know it's been real stressful at the house, so I figured I'd come out here wit' my folks, chill out, let you and dad get reacquainted and whatnot..." I trailed off.

My mom takes some deep breaths, tries to calm down, then looks at the condoms in my hand again, frowns and says "Who're those for, Terrence?"

"*Me.*"

"You know what I mean. Who are you gonna use them on?"

"*Ma.* That's none of your business, damn."

"Is it Jasmine?" she demanded, shaking again.

"*What* is your damn issue with her?"

"Is it JASMINE?" my mom screamed.

"Yes!" I yelled back.

"No! *No...*" my mother smacked the box out of my hands.

"You think that's gonna keep me from doing what I want to do?" I laughed.

"Get your shit and come home. *Now.*" my mom commanded.

"What?! I'm not going *no*-fuckin-where right now. You gotta stop over reacting."

"I'm not leaving until you pack your stuff up and leave this hotel." Moms crossed her arms and stood like "Move me, nigga."

I pulled out my room key. "Then I suggest you get a room with a view, cuz there's only one bed in here," I told her, going to open my door. I picked her up and sat her down on the other side of the hall gently, out of my way.

My mom burst out: "You're so *fucking* stubborn, just like Gem-" then she froze.

I paused, then whirled around with the key still in my hand. "What did you just say?"

Moms had her hand on her mouth, a busted, horrified look on her face. "Nothing."

"Naw, fuck *that.* I'm just like who?" I took a step toward her and she backed up. I'd never hit her, and had no plans on it and she knew it, but she was hiding something from me and she knew I was about to get it out of her and she was panicking.

"Terrence, just get your shit, *please*," she pleaded.

I crossed my arms.

"Aight, I'll make a deal with you: I'll go in here, pack my shit, leave with you and never speak to Jasmine for the rest of my life if you tell me why the *fuck* you just said I'm just like Gemini."

My mom turned pale.

"That's who you meant, right? The whole time I been here, I been hearing people whisper that name all around the fucking city. What the *fuck* ain't you tellin me, ma?"

My mom swallowed. She looked like she was about to fall apart at the seams, but she made a decision. She closed her eyes, and said in a shaky voice, "Terrence, please... just trust me and come home with me... now..."

Wrong answer. "*Hell* naw. You tell me to trust you and you been lying to me? I heard you and pops on the phone. I read one of his letters. Ya'll lied to me about why he got locked up, you cain't come up with a good reason why you don't like my girl, and now you up here acting all crazy tryna make me come home like I'm a fuckin runaway. I'm a *grown-ass man*, ma. If you cain't *tell* me the fuckin truth I'ma find out on my own. And if you won't tell me what the fuck is going on I *might* not come the fuck home at *all*." I reached out and snatched my condoms off the floor. "Now move out my way so I can go fuck the taste out my woman's mouth." I pushed past my mom, shook her arm off me in a last attempt to stop me and opened my door. She tried to get me to come back out of the room by banging on the door, but I heard hotel security come and tell her she had to leave or get arrested. The banging stopped and I heard her being escorted out of the hotel.

Sighing, I banged my head against the door a few times and took a moment to get my head together before leaving the foyer and going back to the bedroom...

Author's Comments:
You mad at me yet? Good. If not, WAIT. It gets worse.

Quick facts:

1)Every one of my characters in every story I write is based off of somebody I know in real life. Yes, that IS frightening.

2)Yes, one of the characters is based off me. I'll never tell which one.

3)Yes, some of the events in some of the stories are based on fact. I'll never reveal which of those are real, either, to protect the people in my life involved.

4)Untrust is based in 2012, Wicked Blues in 1994, and Uncommon Devil about 2008. There's a reason for that I can't reveal yet...

Feel free to ask any questions at deszionnasir@yahoo.com

WICKED BLUES Deszion Nasir

DEDICATION:

Sits back and sighs It's done... Destani, Zion, Shamar and Amani, thank you for giving up so much of mommy while she got this done. I know it wasn't easy. Everything is for you. Mom... I have no words for what you do. And you know that. You're the ONLY Leo I can tolerate. That says a lot. -_-. Little/big bro James... I only have one brother because I couldn't have a better one.

Daddy... I miss you and know that you'll always be the coolest dude in the world. And I make sure everyone knows that.

Danny. You get your own line. Just because.

Real Women Vs. Real Men. You all need to be committed. Thank you. (Cami make me a couch).

Taniya & Dre, Deanna... you get a line for watching the minis when I needed to sleep/work/WHATEVER was required to get this done. You stepped it up. Love ya'll for that.

Dat's It! SEE YOU NEXT NIGHTMARE!

BE ON THE LOOK OUT FOR THE NEXT BOOK FROM DESZION NASIR:

A paranormal urban tale!

WICKED BLUES Deszion Nasir